The Brightwood Stillness

The Brightwood Stillness

a novel

Mark Pomeroy

Oregon State University Press
Corvallis

The paper in this book meets the guidelines for permanence and durability of the Committee on Production Guidelines for Book Longevity of the Council on Library Resources and the minimum requirements of the American National Standard for Permanence of Paper for Printed Library Materials Z39.48-1984.

Library of Congress Cataloging-in-Publication Data

Pomeroy, Mark, 1969-
  The Brightwood stillness : a novel / Mark Pomeroy.
     pages cm
   ISBN 978-0-87071-750-5 (pbk. : alk. paper) — ISBN 978-0-87071-751-2 (e-book)
   1. High school teachers—Fiction. 2. High school students—Fiction. 3. Sexual abuse victims—Fiction. 4. Portland (Ore.)—Fiction. I. Title.
   PS3616.O5475B75 2014
   813'.6—dc23

                          2014023868

Oregon State University Press
121 The Valley Library
Corvallis OR 97331-4501
541-737-3166 • fax 541-737-3170
www.osupress.oregonstate.edu

for Brooke

Pardon me, if when I want
to tell the story of my life
it's the land I talk about.
This is the land.
It grows in your blood
and you grow.
If it dies in your blood
you die out.

—Pablo Neruda
(translated by William O'Daly)

Portland Police Department
Portland, Oregon
Special Report

Report Type: SPECIAL   Case Status: Pending   Classification:

Incident Type: SEX CRIME   Subject of Report: INTERVIEW OF VICTIMS

Original Report: 11-6-96   This Report: 11-8-96

Location: 2236 N. Hargrove Street

       Port., OR 97203

Name: DET. SGT. DON WALLACE   DOB: Sex: Race:

Address: PORTLAND POLICE DEPT.   Phone: 823-2120

Employment: Position: Phone:

Subject: NGUYEN, HIEU TRAN   DOB: 08-08-55   Sex: M   Race: A

Address: 2959 N.E. LOFTON CT. PORT., OR. 97212   Phone: 269-8894

DETAILS:

MENTIONED:

Hieu T. NGUYEN, suspect, see above. Wilson Green High School
Teacher.

Malisha JONES, victim, DOB: 03-02-80, 103 N. Mallson Apt. #31,
Port., OR   97201. Junior at Wilson Green High School. Lives
with aunt, Cherise LOGAN.

Sasha ANDERSON, victim, DOB: 02-20-80, 300 N. Phillips, Port.,
OR   97201. Junior at Wilson Green High School. Mother's name is
Marguerite ANDERSON.

Desmond BARNES, mentioned, DOB: 06-01-80, 273 N. Adams Apt. #4,
Port., OR   97201. Junior at Wilson Green High School. Mother's
name is Tammy HOLMES.

Desiree THOMPSON, mentioned, DOB: 11-15-54, Health Teacher –
Wilson Green High School. 2100 N. Ulrich Rd., Port., OR   97201.

Sgt. Don Wallace/7181   Approved_____

Portland Police Department
Portland, Oregon
Special Report

Peter WINCHILL, reporting person, DOB: 12-10-42, Wilson Green
High School Principal. 2100 N. Ulrich Rd., Port., OR   97201.

Carson SANDOVAL, mentioned, DOB: 05-01-80, 387 N. Phillips,
Port., OR   97201. Junior at Wilson Green High School. Father's
name is Juan SANDOVAL.

Nate DAVIS, mentioned, DOB: 10-30-58, Humanities Teacher -
Wilson Green High School. 2100 N. Ulrich Rd., Port., OR 97201.

ACTION TAKEN:

Friday, 11-8-96, 10:00 a.m. I made contact with Mr. WINCHILL
at Wilson Green High School to continue this investigation.
WINCHILL told me that 31 students participated in a walk-
out on Thursday (11-7-96) at 10:45 a.m. in protest against Mr.
NGUYEN. All 31 were suspended from school for the remainder of
Thursday and today for their participation in the walk-out.
WINCHILL reported that prior to the rally, Carson SANDOVAL
came to the main office and said that he had witnessed NGUYEN
sexually touch both Malisha JONES and Sasha ANDERSON on
Tuesday (11-5-96) during fifth period general science class.

I immediately requested interviews with both victims. In
WINCHILL'S office, my discussion with Sasha ANDERSON began at
10:12. I started by reminding ANDERSON that our conversation
would be tape recorded and that this was a criminal investigation. I then asked her to recount the sequence of events in Mr.
NGUYEN's fifth period class on Tuesday (11-5-96).

ANDERSON said that she had spilled some hydrochloric acid onto
her lab notebook and that NGUYEN reprimanded her when he saw
the accident from across the room, saying, "In my office now."
ANDERSON followed NGUYEN into his office, which adjoins the
classroom. I asked her if he closed the door and she couldn't
remember.

ANDERSON claimed that NGUYEN began waving a finger in her
face, then suddenly he grabbed both of her breasts and said,
"Be more careful," giving each breast a squeeze. At that point,
ANDERSON pushed NGUYEN away and ran out of the office and

Portland Police Department
Portland, Oregon
Special Report

back to her table. She said that Desmond BARNES saw her tears
and asked what had happened. ANDERSON told BARNES, "I can't
believe he grabbed me. I hate him so much." At this point in the
interview, ANDERSON began crying. I asked her if this was the
first incident of touching she had encountered with NGUYEN.
After composing herself, she replied yes, but that her friend
Malisha JONES had experienced NGUYEN'S harassment earlier in
the year. ANDERSON said NGUYEN had slapped JONES on the buttocks and massaged her shoulders "sometime back in September."
(JONES apparently reported this to ANDERSON one day after
school; ANDERSON did not witness the alleged touching.) When
I asked why JONES hadn't reported the incident, ANDERSON
shrugged, then said, "She probably thought nobody would believe
her." I wondered why ANDERSON thought that; she shrugged
again, giving no reply. When I inquired about whether she could
name any other possible witnesses in either instance of harassment, ANDERSON said that Carson SANDOVAL "might have seen
into the office." She wasn't certain about possible witnesses in
JONES'S case.

Finally, I asked ANDERSON what she thinks about NGUYEN as a
teacher. She replied that he is "way too strict" and grades too
hard. I pressed for details. ANDERSON lowered her head and
said, "I just hate him so much. I don't understand why he did
it." I told her that I would conduct a follow-up interview soon.

Part One

—⁓—

Ice-coated Keyhole

Invasion

When the door opened, Hieu Nguyen remained seated in the plastic class-room chair beside the head secretary's desk, talking pro basketball with Monty, the albino custodian. He'd been summoned to the main office a few minutes before by Peter Winchill's hoarse voice over the school's intercom. They happened often, the calls that had once seemed so omi-nous, what with Winchill's penchant for detailed conversations about anything that made him feel more authoritative as principal of a school widely regarded as one of the city's toughest. Hieu, though, like most of the other veteran teachers, had grown used to them, normally managing to swallow the hollow meetings as part of his duty. But this time there was no forced grin on Winchill's face when he emerged from his office, no *There he is* with the extended chubby-fingered hand.

Monty cut off his rant on the various mental illnesses of most big-time NBA stars he could name and reached to the front counter for his work order clipboard, eyeing Douglas Falsworth and Maggie Bailey from the district office who were seated before Winchill's desk. Lips puckered, brow raised, Monty glanced back down at Hieu and cocked his chin toward the seldom-seen visitors, and as he turned to leave said, "Cheers, bro."

In the office, Winchill clicked the door shut behind Hieu and offered up a chair without making eye contact. Falsworth and Bailey both gave tight-smiled hellos and immediately looked back at Winchill. A heaviness spread over Hieu's chest, and his mouth felt dry. District functionaries like the two sitting on either side of him came across town to Wilson Green High School for two reasons only: irresistible PR opportunities (or "ghetto hype," according to Terrell Martin, the band teacher) and sticky personnel issues.

In their rare, brief encounters at the central office and from all the spirit- and butt-numbing motivational speeches at the start of each year,

Falsworth had always struck Hieu as a tentative man, prone to spells of rubbing about his face and neck. As for Bailey, she seemed to be a soul lost even further in bureaucracy's labyrinth, her caffeine-activated eyes housed in a face ravaged by a hundred hungry details eating away at her.

Now fully attuned to the tension, Hieu steadied his breathing and searched the faces, the flexing jaws and still-averted eyes.

"Good news?" he said, watching Winchill roll a pencil between a thumb and index finger. Another pause hit before Falsworth turned and lifted a notepad and a pencil from the breast pocket of his coat.

"Please excuse my bluntness, Mr. Nguyen, but I need to be absolutely clear on this." Falsworth let out a small sigh, one that Hieu had trouble interpreting. "You've been charged with sexually touching two students. Sasha Anderson and Malisha Jones. The police have already been contacted, we just wanted to tell you first, get your side of the story."

Falsworth spoke with considerable poise, even a hint of bravado, Hieu initially noticed; while the man surely valued restraint and objectivity, the rush of scandal had begun to flood through him.

Hieu nodded occasionally and pretended to listen to the remainder of the speech, a thumb pressed to one side of his angular jaw, eyes steady in spite of the panic. He had heard Falsworth say *You've been charged with sexually touching two students,* then mostly blanked out. When the office went silent again, Falsworth done with his spiel on district policy, Hieu lowered his hands to the tops of his thighs, took a deep breath, and let out the only word he could think of: "Shit."

It was then that Winchill came around from behind the desk and knelt before him on the office's cement-grey carpet.

"You've worked in this building thirteen years," the principal said, "and your file shows nothing but good from you. Now you just need to tell us what happened fifth period, okay? Nice and easy."

While Hieu had always strained for, and usually achieved, patience with people who used a condescending tone or spoke too slowly or loudly, sometimes shouting, in order to make themselves clear to a person with a Vietnamese accent, something about Winchill's beef-witted ways had always managed to prick at his heart. Yet another unconscious insult on top of the horror he had just been handed made the world seem like it was leaving him. The stinging in his stomach intensified.

"Incredible," he said, noticing his pulse in his throat. "I will not tell any-thing without a lawyer." He stared into Winchill's widened eyes. "Those girls are awful."

Winchill nodded twice, the tip of his tongue massaging his upper lip, and after a time said, "Well, that's fine." He looked over at Falsworth, at Maggie Bailey, back at Hieu. "But I need to tell you you're being placed on administrative leave. You won't be allowed back into the building till the case is closed, and that is, of course, assuming everything's cleared up." He stood and bent over to brush off his tight-packed khakis, paying too much attention to the knee that hadn't touched the carpet. "A Detec-tive Sergeant Wallace will be here in ten minutes or so to take you to the North Precinct over on Hargrove for some questioning. You can grab anything you need from your room, contact whomever you'd like."

As if aware of trying too hard to seem concerned, Winchill righted himself and paused again.

"Suppose this is good-bye for awhile." He extended a hand, then re-turned to his chair when Hieu didn't shake it. "I'm sorry about the shock. I do look forward to hearing your side."

At this, Maggie Bailey scooted forward, her first noticeable movement since the beginning of the meeting. She turned toward Hieu and smiled, her teeth bleached to an alarming gleam. In a moment, the smile fell away and she said, "As I'm sure you can imagine, your testimony will be crucial, Mr. Nguyen. The detective needs to know *exactly* what happened. He'll be interviewing a number of your students, too."

Whether it was third-rate plastic surgery, eyeliner and rouge applied while battling a hangover, or simply his own torched mind, it appeared to Hieu that Maggie Bailey's face barely hung on her skull. He was relieved when she gathered up her black leatherbound notebook and matching purse, consulted her gold watch, rose stiffly and approached Winchill's desk for a low-volume exchange. Why he was so affected by her pres-ence at such a poignant moment of his life was odd, but then again, the surreality of the previous few minutes could surely explain the strangest of feelings.

In his classroom, in the quiet of after school, he didn't know where to begin. He walked twice around the room, weaving numbly around the lab tables, and decided to gather up the framed photographs that had long-been on his desk. His wife, Anh, standing in a mist before Haystack Rock on the Oregon coast, a haze of blowing sand nearly covering her from the knees down: would she believe his version of events? His seventy-one-year-old mother, Hoa, stern-faced beside a small sculpture of a beaver in the downtown transit mall: would she understand why her son suddenly wasn't allowed to work? His three children probably wouldn't be any easier to reach. Then of course there was his best friend in the room right across the hallway.

Hieu wrapped the photos in some old copies of lab instructions on proper dissection techniques and stopped to take in the room's stillness. He liked to think that he could sense the lingering energy from the daily battles: curious minds grappling malnourished bodies and spirits, instincts to understand fighting back hordes of fears. His classroom, he had always believed, was a place where powerful things happened.

From his office doorway, he scanned the wall posters, aware of his gut churning over the imminent arrival of Sergeant Wallace, and his eyes finally settled on the eight-by-ten black and white photograph next to the multicolor periodic table above the lab counter across the room. He walked over and leaned in closer. It was a scene of a partially bombed paddy, a print he had found down in San Francisco at an outdoor market. In the foreground, a young woman wearing a conical hat had interrupted her harvest, stretching her neck to look up at the photographer, an expression of surprise blended with annoyance. In the background: elephant grass, a water buffalo's glistening flank, a perimeter of stumps and shredded limbs, and in the far distance, the edge of a hamlet. The woman hadn't been asked permission for the shot, Hieu had always suspected; the ancient rhythm of wet hands pulling rice had been broken by yet another kind of invasion. For a good minute more he studied the woman's face, gradually admitting that he understood her expression more clearly than he had ever wanted to.

Push

In the room across the hallway, as he began reading the second paper in a four-inch stack of persuasive essays on human overpopulation, Nate Davis heard Sergeant Wallace's unfamiliar voice and rose with a wince. From his doorway, he looked over at Hieu's room and heard Wallace say something about the importance of giving a detailed account of events, then the officer and Hieu stepped into the hall and set off toward the main office, Hieu's eyes lowered.

Nate told himself to stay calm. But before he knew it, he was trailing them.

"What's up?" he said, coming alongside the men. While he was about the same compact height and weight as Hieu, similar in lean build, his movements normally weren't as fluid or poised.

Almost to the office, Hieu finally stopped.

"Please call Anh and tell her I will be home in an hour." He still avoided Nate's eyes. "There was … a problem with a couple of students. If you could grab my plants on your way out, the little cactus in my office, too." With that, he nodded once and continued ahead.

When Sergeant Wallace glanced over a shoulder and said that Winchill would apprise the entire staff of the situation, it appeared to Nate that the officer was exhausted, the spindly frame slouched a bit, eyes bagged; laughter looked like it came hard to the man, maybe only when he was alone in front of a television at that. Yet his voice was crisp.

The urge to pursue struck again, but this time Nate honored his friend's privacy, the boundaries of which had been made clear years ago. He watched Hieu wave to someone in the office window, then disappear with Wallace around the corner.

His side throbbing, he went back up the hallway and peeked into the health teacher's office, just off the room next to Hieu's, to see if she'd heard anything. The tiny windowless space—minus Desiree Thompson—looked, as usual, as though it had been ransacked by a troop of lemurs, papers and books and various confiscations (half a dozen pagers, a pack of corn nuts, a rubberbanded stack of five condoms) strewn over the desk and floor. The air smelled of potpourri deodorant spray. Though Desiree had remained one of his two closest friends on staff for nearly a decade, Nate had long since made a point of staying clear of her office if at all possible.

The other rooms in the north wing of the main floor were empty as well. Mitch Vance, the calculus phenom, a kind but somewhat aloof third-year man who'd had a leg amputated during the Gulf War, had left his stereo playing, Coltrane's "Blue Train" floating out into the hallway.

It wasn't until he turned back toward the main office that Nate guessed he had missed the call to assemble for an impromptu meeting. He could hear Winchill's husky raised voice now, so he cut through the copy room just beyond the office, then through one of the graffiti-plastered detention cubicles, before rounding the corner of the lounge and stopping next to the juice and soda machine. The entire Wilson Green faculty turned to look.

Winchill, after a terse "Welcome," continued.

"The sergeant will be interviewing Hieu's students and some of you. I do ask that you keep rumor control at the forefront of your minds, please. This could get out of hand fast, as I'm sure you're all very aware. We just want to get this done quickly and professionally. I need to ask, also, that you not call or visit Hieu while the case is pending."

When it appeared that Winchill ("Chilly" behind his back) was finished, or at least pausing to enhance the gravity, Clyde Jackson, the twenty-two-year veteran humanities chairman, pushed himself up off the edge of the Formica table in the center of the lounge. He was a large man, tall and wide around the middle, cheeks pockmarked.

"I think it's important for us to understand that any person here could be in the exact same situation," he said. "We owe it to Hieu to stand behind him. Just plain impossible for me to believe that a guy of his character could go around fiddlin' with kids."

Approving nods began bobbing all around, someone in the crowd saying, "No doubt."

But then Uli Wegman, Hieu's science department partner, spoke on cue, as most everyone had been dreading. His ongoing quarrel with Hieu over everything from instruction styles to allocation of grant monies to matters of classroom decor had begun soon after Hieu's arrival at Wilson Green in the fall of 1984.

"On the other hand," Uli said, "every one of us knows it's about keeping signals clear. I can honestly see how his style could provoke this. When a teacher persists in—"

"*Save it,*" Clyde said, and Winchill clapped his hands.

"Folks, we need to maintain professionalism here. Gossip, squabbling won't help us get through this …" Winchill hesitated and seemed surprised that everyone was riveted on him. "Beginning Monday I'll have a roving sub for those of you who're summoned to answer some questions in my office. Please have your plans on your desk."

The meeting broke and Chilly fled to his office.

After getting a rundown from Desiree, Nate sat at one of the long tables to ease the ache in his side and half-listened to the banter about the accusing girls. Incensed colleagues surrounded him, yet all he could now focus on was a fragment of a conversation with Hieu at the North Side Racquet Club just over a year before. It had been a disconcerting moment, instantly imprinted in him, a standout exchange among the many funny, genuine, sometimes healing post-workout talks he'd shared with his friend over the years.

The usual Thursday evening routine at the club had always been simple: shower after the matches, dress at a leisurely pace, grab a lobby table for beers and a bowl of pretzel sticks, catch up and sometimes dabble at philosophizing for an hour or two. But the day before Halloween last year, Nate had made an off-hand, quintessentially shallow locker room remark about how many of the girls like to show off their blossoming bodies with tight clothes, driving the poor boys wild. He and Hieu had been talking about a freshman they each had, Yolanda Moreland, and how developed she was in so many ways for her age. While it had been a thoughtless remark, not particularly worthy of a response, Hieu sat down naked and dripping on the bench in front of his locker and said, "I know. They are sexy and curious." It had made Nate turn away and pretend to have lost his deodorant stick. The way it was said more than anything.

Nate replayed the exchange, the chatter around him starting to subside. Across the table, Uli Wegman sat alone, sipping at a can of apple juice, eyes fixed upon a napkin dispenser. Clyde Jackson had once mentioned that Uli's face—the thin dark lips, the pinched nostrils on the off-center nose—coupled with his small head sometimes made him think of a cubist painting.

"So you think his style provokes things?" Nate said.

Uli took a final swig of juice and ran a hand over his widow's peak.

"If you had the chance to observe him, Nate, you'd understand. The little touches on kids' shoulders, those long, overly personal pep talk notes written in those journals he requires. Little pokes on the sternum during discipline sessions …" Uli pushed his chair back and stood, shaking his head. "I still, for the life of me, don't understand why most of you cling to your image of Hieu as the epitome of decorum. I really don't."

With that, Uli walked off toward the office, clearly disdaining the thought of any response. Nate had learned from both his and most everyone else's experiences with Uli to try and let it go. The poor guy was off in his own world, having engineered his austere professorial life, immune even to the gestures of forgiveness some of the more patient faculty members had made over the years to bridge the gap he'd so skillfully dug. After surviving a concerted campaign to get him fired in the spring of '92 over some thinly veiled racist remarks during a staff meeting, Uli had managed to hang tough and remain perfectly crusty to everyone at Wilson Green save Monty, whose six-foot-seven-inch, muscle-packed frame and well-practiced bluntness commanded universal respect, no exceptions.

Stitches itching, Nate made his way back to his room to fetch his raincoat and satchel. Only a few steps before his door, though, he heard a metallic clattering from behind and turned to find Monty jogging toward him, keys bouncing against one hip, a black iron dustpan waving at the end of a pumping arm. A distressing spectacle.

"Nate-o." Monty wasn't out of breath when he came to a stop. "Wanted to let you know some of us are planning to get together, give the detective our opinion of things even if we don't get called in."

Nate gripped his classroom doorknob.

"Count me in."

"You know the girls?" Monty gave the dustpan a twirl.

"I have Sasha first period. Wouldn't have pegged her as someone who'd lie about something like that, but—"

"Man, all I know is Hieu didn't do shit. Guy's got way too much integrity." Monty banged the dustpan onto the lip of the metal garbage can beside Nate's door, veins in his milk-white hand bulging. "Anyway, I thought you should know. You take it slow out there, bro."

After signing out and hanging up his room key and photo ID security badge in the main office cabinet, Nate rolled up the latest batch of union notices, staff bulletins, state content standards amendments, workshop advertisements, and magazine offers he found crammed into his mailbox, stuffed what he could into his coat pockets and the rest into the recycling bin, then made his way through the lounge toward the parking lot. Clyde Jackson was still talking with Desiree over by the coffee makers.

"You doin' all right?" Desiree held a hand out in front of her, eyeing Nate as he passed. "It hurting still?"

"Not bad, no worries."

"I'm serious now, you need to take more time. One week and you're back goin' around like it never happened. Don't be a ding-a-ling on me, sweetie. You sure you don't want anyone to walk you out?"

Nate gave a half-smile. "You'll hear screaming if there's any problem."

Out in the parking lot, the newly installed security lights cast a piss-colored spray over the asphalt and brick, enhancing his dread about the walk to his pickup. A rain shower had just passed, the air moist and chill, the scent of dead leaves mixing with the sweetness of damp cement. Exactly one week ago, two days before Halloween, he had made the same trip to his truck a few minutes past six, keys dangling in hand, satchel flung over a shoulder, mind chewing a chunk of minutiae. But that evening, as he was about to finish up another frenzied high school day, the usual routine had been shattered in five seconds' time.

Fuck you, Davis.

The bare, wet, startlingly powerful arm clamped around his neck. Words spitting into his right ear. A hot ripping in his right side, between the two lowest ribs.

Round one, you dumb-ass bitch.

Aaron Harrington. It had to be, the deep adolescent voice too familiar. The smell of alcohol and bubblegum. The small blade yanked out after a hard, quick twist, then the fading blur of white shoes tearing across the soccer field.

Visions of the attack rocketing through him, Nate locked the door and started his truck. Nausea, on cue. While the Wilson Green faculty had offered its support in the form of cards and baked goods, nobody except for Hieu and Desiree seemed to recognize that the aftereffects hadn't come close to wearing off. Nate believed he still had most everyone fooled into thinking that he was coping fine, putting the incident behind him like any gritty veteran would; after two days back on the job, he realized that he was more than adept at going through the daily motions with a pleasant enough manner. It was what you did at schools like Wilson Green. To fret over the possibility of violence was to be paralyzed.

There had been other events in other years, of course, namely a few instances of students punching teachers, the handful of prank bomb threats, but never much of anything worse. So with the stabbing and the accusations against Hieu, in spite of the willed amnesia required to carry on, it had been a memorable week at Wilson Green, one that prompted Monty to remark at the conclusion of Chilly's briefing, "What the *hell* is going on around here anyway?" It was a week Nate would end up looking back on as maybe the most important of his life, one that had given him a final push into a long-feared journey.

His truck finally warmed up, he backed out and turned on the headlights. Glanced at the soccer field and the commons and forced himself to think again of the girls' charges against Hieu, the whirlwind afternoon: stoic police officer, staff meeting, Monty banging his dustpan on the garbage can. Drained to the point of blank staring by the time he pulled away from the school, Nate turned up the radio and tried to lose himself in a Tommy Flanagan tune.

Empathy

The monkey tree in front of the Nguyen's house had lost a quarter of its limbs in a windstorm the year before. Nate, in a tipsy state after leaving one of Hieu and Anh's typically superb dinner parties one night five years prior, had named the tree Bing for no particular reason other than it made him even more cheerful.

Standing under one of Bing's tail-like limbs the rainy morning after everyone had been informed of the accusations, Nate jammed the last of a toasted onion bagel into his mouth and rehearsed what he might say when the front door opened. Shapeless grey clouds still raced in from the southwest, wind swaying Bing's crown and the two Japanese maples in the upper yard.

The Nguyen's place was always a somewhat odd experience, but he loved it nonetheless. Its light, welcome feel had always put him at ease. From outside, the old two-story house looked like many others in the neighborhood: long wide porch, steep roof, a stone wall dividing the upper and lower lawns. But every time he passed through the front door, he entered a new world, a tenderly crafted amalgam. While there were staples of many North American households (sofa and love seat, easy chair, stereo system and TV), the shrines in both the family room and Grandma Hoa's bedroom, the wall of sexy Vietnamese calendar cut-outs in Vo's room, and the dozen or so black and white photographs of Vietnamese people on the wall surrounding the family room shrine and throughout the front room signaled the precarious straddling. Inside: a blend of Vietnam and modern USA, the generational tug-of-war. Outside: the hurricane-paced land of the Golden Mountain Dream.

Hieu had spoken of the Dream only a couple of times, and only when he'd already put away a drink or two. It was a Chinese term adopted by some Vietnamese meaning the chance at material wealth in the United

States—the mountains of gold awaiting the opportunistic, hard worker. Especially during the latter stages of the American War, and immediately after the fall, the Dream caught firm hold, enticing many among those who risked their lives to escape. Though freedom was the primary goal, the Dream helped fuel the belief that an escape attempt was worth the substantial risk. Hieu had remained a believer even after arriving in the land of abundance in the spring of 1975 to the sight of drab processing camp barracks at Fort Chaffee, Arkansas. He'd remained a believer after finally landing in cool, stormy Portland. And while he'd often considered the Dream's contours—the extent of its promise, even its dark underbelly—it still meant liberty and opportunity. Having heard so many refugee accounts of the communist regime's brand of living back home, freedom made him love his new land like family.

On the rain-splattered porch, Nate pulled his jacket sleeve down over his hand and wiped crumbs from his lips. His hair still shower-wet in spots, dark brown curls coiled at the nape of his neck like little slugs, a reddish brown stubble coating his cheeks and chin, the practice of daily shaving long since abandoned. He knew his knock might set his friends scrambling as it was only ten after seven, but not dropping by wasn't an option. The porch light was on, drapes shut, the morning *Oregonian* leaning against the screen door. Chewing the last of his bagel, he tapped the door twice with two fingertips, and after only a moment Anh peeked through the white lace curtain.

He saw that the news had hit hard, Anh's normally robust greeting reduced to a whispered *hi,* her eyes moist and swollen, nose purplish at the tip. Her grey-black hair tied back in a loose bun, one of Hieu's old cardigans over her shoulders. She offered to take Nate's jacket and he extended his hands toward hers.

"It'll be all right," he said, stepping out of his shoes. There was a squeezing in his stomach, the usual sensation whenever he tried to play cheerleader.

Anh nodded and smiled, then gave his hands a shake and motioned for him to remove his jacket.

"He's in the kitchen. Could I make you some breakfast? Eggs and toast, yes?"

"I already ate, but thank you."

The house was normally bustling what with six occupants going about their lives, but it was quiet and cold that morning, even though it was a school day. Nate noticed the absence of the usual early smell, *pho*. At the stove he poured himself a cup of Darjeeling, then rounded the corner into the nook and found Hieu sitting at the pine table in shadow.

"Thought I'd bring your plants by," he said. "They're out in the truck."

From what he could see, Hieu's face remained stern, back rigid, the blue oxford shirt the same as the day before.

"You can turn on the light."

Nate flipped the switch, sat and began picking at a mound of cashews from a saucer at the center of the table. Best to act casual. Keep it simple. On the wall behind Hieu's chair, a newly framed finger-painting of a rickety-looking plank bridge crossing a palm tree-lined river hung next to the photograph of a teenage girl leaning against a bicycle in front of a crowded Saigon food stall. The light outside the kitchen windows remained low.

"I told them," Hieu said. "It went how I thought it would." He finished off his tea with a quick tilt and began rubbing his forehead with a thumb and index finger. "They are all in shock I think. My mother has been locked in her room for the past nine hours. Anh and the kids will stay home today."

Nate made himself maintain eye contact.

"Must have been something."

Hieu stood for more tea.

The house's silence continued to seep through Nate's skin; it had never been the case that music, a debate of some sort, or at least laughter hadn't greeted him within five minutes of his arrival, no matter the time of day. Whether it was Grandma Hoa giggling at the television even though she had no idea what was being said, Anh barking at Vo to turn down his tunes, Dat zooming up and down the stairs with his latest model airplane, or Le Phuong practicing the cello, the house had always been full of life.

When Hieu returned to the table, he pushed the cashew dish closer to Nate.

"Eat," he said.

"Need to get over to school in a few. Just wanted to tell you to hang tough. Everyone's behind you."

Hieu leaned forward and propped his elbows on the table, his puffed eyelids making his gaze even more severe. Whenever the man leaned forward and clasped his hands, Nate knew, he was about to cut to it.

"I thought if I worked hard, you know, everything would be okay." Hieu rubbed his forehead again, set his hands back onto the table. "Those girls are liars, Nate." He sat back and raised his chin to the ceiling, stretching his already taut neck. "You become a teacher to light fires in students' hearts. Then the day comes you are called down and told you must pack up. Not allowed inside the school. 'Sorry, but you need to get out now.'" He drew a breath, puffed his cheeks and blew it out. "I do not know how to handle all of this."

Mind storming, Nate nodded and sat there awhile. Reached for another cashew. "Let me go get the plants, be right back."

In the living room, Anh was curled up on the sofa, slippers still on, a silk pillow with lavish embroidery between her knees. She was already asleep it appeared.

It took two hushed trips to bring all the plants inside. When Nate set the little cactus onto the dining room table, Hieu came to the doorway leading to the kitchen.

"I was lost when I asked that favor."

"Can you tell me what happened with the sergeant?" Nate kept his voice as low as his friend's.

Arms crossed, Hieu leaned against the door jamb.

"He took a statement, you know. He needs to do a lot of interviews."

"So what next?" Nate's sudden awareness that he didn't know what to do with his hands made his face flush; he slipped one into a jacket pocket, the other down next to his warm wallet in the butt of his khakis, and decided to leave them be.

"I try not to go crazy," Hieu said. "Wait and pray. The interviews will take time. Three or four weeks, or longer maybe, he is not sure. Then who knows? I just try to avoid going crazy."

After the silent good-bye (the usual arm wrestling grip and two hard shakes), Nate flung his hood over his head and descended through the downpour to his truck. The grey sky had barely brightened, and one of Bing's low branches swept over his windshield as he pulled away from the house. He saw the porch light go off and pictured Hieu in the kitchen nook shadow, Anh on the sofa, the kids and Grandma Hoa dreaming uneasily.

When a few minutes later he turned onto Ainsworth Street, though, he envisioned the parking lot, the scene he would come upon soon. Tapped yet again into those moments with Aaron Harrington, gut tightening, he found himself guessing that Hieu's shock was at least a bit similar. He pulled over, cracked his door and vomited part of his bagel onto the asphalt. Wilson Green now in view up ahead through the thinning bigleaf maples, he tried to comfort himself with the idea that maybe such a touch of empathy could help him overlook his suspicions.

Portland Police Department
Portland, Oregon
Special Report

At 10:30 a.m. my interview with Carson SANDOVAL began. I explained that our conversation would be tape recorded and reminded SANDOVAL he had approached Mr. WINCHILL the day before
and reported that he'd witnessed the alleged touching incident
in Mr. NGUYEN'S office. SANDOVAL said that he stood off of his
stool and peered into the office after NGUYEN followed Sasha
ANDERSON in. The door had been left open.

SANDOVAL proceeded to recount the following: NGUYEN began
waving a finger in ANDERSON'S face, scolding her for spilling the hydrochloric acid, then "he pressed up against her and
grabbed her tits." When I asked SANDOVAL again if he'd seen
NGUYEN touch ANDERSON'S breasts, he nodded the affirmative,
then said yes when I pointed to the tape recorder. ANDERSON
ran out of the office and back to her desk, crying. SANDOVAL
sat down when NGUYEN reentered the classroom; he spoke with
ANDERSON after class. I asked why, in his opinion, ANDERSON
had remained in class instead of fleeing the room. SANDOVAL
replied, "She didn't have a hall pass, I guess." I asked if he
thought being sexually touched by a teacher was excuse enough
for leaving class to report the incident; he said yes, but added,
"Maybe she thought it would be best to wait before she told."
When I asked why, SANDOVAL shrugged and said he didn't know.

I asked SANDOVAL what he thinks of Mr. NGUYEN as a teacher.
He answered that NGUYEN is mean, he "pushes kids too hard."
At that point, I reminded SANDOVAL that he told Mr. WINCHILL
he'd also witnessed NGUYEN touch Malisha JONES in a sexual
manner during the same class period the alleged touching of
ANDERSON occurred. SANDOVAL said yes, that NGUYEN had come up
behind JONES and "snapped her bra strap and slapped her butt."
This apparently occurred after the ANDERSON incident, during journal time, a 10-minute quiet period at the end of class
to reflect upon the day's lab. SANDOVAL stated that NGUYEN
approached JONES because she was trying to get ANDERSON'S
attention. The bra snapping and buttocks slapping followed. I
asked whether or not anyone else in the classroom might have
witnessed this and SANDOVAL said, "I don't know. Nobody said

Portland Police Department
Portland, Oregon
Special Report

nothing after class except me. Out in the hall I went up
and told Sasha (ANDERSON) and Malisha (JONES) that I seen
everything."

I told SANDOVAL that I would most likely have some questions
for him at a later date, then concluded the interview.

At 10:47, Desmond BARNES arrived and began recounting what
he witnessed during NGUYEN'S fifth period science class on
Tuesday (11-5-96), this after I explained the seriousness of this
investigation. BARNES said that he had seen neither instance
of alleged touching, but that Carson SANDOVAL had said it was
all true. I reminded BARNES to recount only what he'd actually seen. He reported that Sasha ANDERSON came running out
of NGUYEN'S office crying, and that she said, "I hate him so
much" when she returned to her stool. BARNES asked ANDERSON
what had happened in the office and she replied, "He grabbed
me." BARNES wanted to know where NGUYEN had touched her and
ANDERSON pointed to her breasts. I then inquired about whether
or not BARNES had witnessed any activity from Malisha JONES
before or after she'd reportedly been slapped on the buttocks.
BARNES said that the class was "totally quiet" during journal
time; he saw or heard nothing unusual.

BARNES described NGUYEN as "okay, but strict." I asked BARNES
if he'd ever had any problems with NGUYEN and he replied, "I
once got a referral for calling someone a fag during a lab,
but that's it." Finally, I requested that BARNES sketch out a
plan of NGUYEN'S room, label the key positions, the location
of NGUYEN'S office, etc. At 11:06, after BARNES explained his
sketch, I ended the interview.

Safety

Seconds after his students poured into the hallway at the three o'clock bell, Nate got a call over the intercom: telephone, line nine. In Max Walker's Student Management office three doors down, he shut the door on the clamor, lifted the receiver on the outside line phone, turned to look out the rain-streaked windows and heard the person he'd just been thinking about. The office, as usual, smelled of cologne and pastries.

"How are you?" he said, pulling up Max's high-backed swivel chair.

"I heard about Hieu." Lang's voice was a notch lower than her hello.

Nate checked his excitement, lowered himself into the chair. It had been three days since he'd spoken with his girlfriend. He peeked into the doughnut box next to the phone and fought the temptation of a single remaining bear claw.

"I was over there this morning," he said. "Place sort of scared the bejesus out of me."

Lang sighed, her breath like rattling notebook paper through the receiver. "Anh called. It sounds like everyone's pretty bad. I guess my mother came out of her room once to use the toilet, then just locked herself up again. How did Hieu seem?"

"Like he hadn't slept. Blasted nerves."

There was an extended silence.

"About our talk …" Lang said. "I apologize. I just hate you acting trapped."

"Could you explain that a little more?"

"Look, I was just trying to say, it's not like you to live in the backseat of your life. You know? Your soul speaks, you listen. You've always had courage that way, at least since we've known each other … I guess I snapped because all you've been talking about lately is taking some kind of leap and—I don't know, maybe I'm scared."

"Of?"

"Don't know." Her volume dropped further, as if someone else might hear. "Maybe that whatever leap you take will mean we're done. Then I get scared you *won't* take it."

"So what I hear you—"

"I can't do this right now, I have a draft due by five. Let's get together later, though. I just wanted to hear about my brother. I'm worried."

"I am too."

"I'm stopping by there after work, see if I can get mother to unlock herself. I'll come over after, okay?"

When she hung up, Nate set down the phone gently. Took the bear claw and crammed it into his mouth. He leaned back in Max's chair and stared at the poster before him of a stern-faced kayaker negotiating a narrow section of rapids, the anonymous quote beneath: *Winners never quit, quitters never win.* Veins at his temples protruding with each chew, he let the phrase float through him, around the lingering images of Lang, the lovely woman he hadn't slept with in over two weeks. Pictures soon spinning: Lang naked in candlelight, reaching out to him; then the pile of essays still to be graded on his desk; Hieu at his kitchen table, steam from his tea rising around his hard-set face. The dim parking lot, Aaron Harrington's mouth almost against his ear. *Fuck you, Davis.*

When Max Walker shoved the door open, in an obvious hurry, the swivel chair jerked, wheels shooting forward, and Nate fell back on the linoleum floor.

Max dropped his pile of student progress reports beside Nate's head and stooped over.

"No worries." Nate rolled out of the chair, grunting.

Max picked up the pile and set his chair upright with only one of his meaty hands. "Just had my interview with the sarge."

Ignoring the rising lump at the back of his head, Nate stood there. Max was the first staff interviewee he'd heard about.

"How'd it go?"

"Oh, you know. He just asked if I've seen anything weird is all. Have I ever heard Hieu talk nasty about girls or seen him touch kids. Only lasted about ten minutes. The guy was a pro. Smooth, real organized."

Max snatched his Army green poncho from the coat rack between his desk and four file cabinets overstuffed with discipline records. He smiled down at Nate, who was nearly a full foot shorter. "I'm outta here," he said. "My kid's got soccer practice at four-thirty. You gotta make a call?"

Nate followed Max out, wanting to ask more, respecting the man's priorities. Though they got along fine and all, they'd maintained a certain distance over the three years since Max's arrival at Wilson Green. A pleasant-enough, strictly professional relationship. Not that Max Walker had done anything in particular to make him cautious; it was simply a case, most likely, where a seemingly instinctual arm's length reaction toward others had bested him once again.

Another parking lot flash: the bare, wet arm and the voice.

Nate drove away from Wilson Green slower than usual. Teaching, he considered for the umpteenth time that week, was undoubtedly losing its allure, not to mention the fact that it was turning into a serious gamble in many parts of town. The soul-stirring discussions, the moments he seemed to be sparking kids' minds, were occurring less often, it was true. In years past, the hours of planning lessons, grading papers, calling parents, and meeting with various committees had been parts of a noble whole, all necessary aspects of a vocation in which he could genuinely help people. But now it really was different.

Just that morning, he'd meandered the aisles of his classroom while reading aloud Langston Hughes's "Thank You, Ma'am" and nearly choked during the opening paragraph he'd always loved about the large old woman, Mrs. Luella Bates Washington Jones, who kicked an adolescent mugger's ass, literally. She "put a half nelson" about the kid's neck, dragged him along the street to her apartment, made him go to the sink and wash his face, then served up a supper of lima beans, ham, cocoa, and ten-cent cake. He adored the story, had taught it most every year in his remedial freshman class. But the words made him pause now. Clear his throat. The students' eyes on him. How many of them knew Aaron Harrington? How many knew the odds of another attack? The eyes watching him read.

Then in the halls before and after school, more uncertainty. Kids brushing past him, a pencil prick on his forearm. The frequent, sincere-seeming comments ("Glad you're okay, Mr. Davis, we missed you") sprinkled with the wisecracks ("You should take a longer vacation, Mr. Davis, you ain't lookin' right"). And the pockets of silence, entire huddles of kids stopping to look at him pass by. How many could see through the smile and purposeful stride, the business-as-usual approach? How many could tell that his invincibility had been snapped in half?

Even during the Tuesday and Thursday after-school tutoring sessions in his classroom—the hour-long periods he'd always offered to any interested students—he wondered if the dozen or so regulars detected his fear. They didn't seem quite as loose. Less banter before digging into their assignments. Less eye contact, too. Benjamin Greene, for example. Gangly Benny Greene, as polite and earnest as they come despite a childhood clobbered by divorce and evictions, a bespectacled kid with huge front teeth who'd busted his ass to bring up his grades the past two years, yet who still read at a sixth-grade level—even Benny seemed different. He'd shown up unusually late the Tuesday after the stabbing, books pressed to his side, and instantly begun jabbering about what he'd seen on MTV the night before, this show where "college ladies were getting drunk on big ol' slushy drinks" in Hawaii. One of the girls had pulled off her bikini top and her titties were all blurred over.

Nate held a forefinger to his lips, but Benny wouldn't stop talking; the boy refused to look at Nate's face. The other kids, their desks arranged in a circle in the middle of the room, largely ignored Benny, most of them focused on their work.

"So tell me what you brought today," Nate said, voice hushed. "You still doing that nutrition project in health class?"

Benny Greene's brow flexed, but his smile remained. Still no eye contact. "Huh?"

"That project in Ms. Thompson's class you were worried about last week."

"Oh … oh, naw … naw, that's all done. Yeah, my auntie helped me on that. It's all good."

"Way to go, man. Told you it would be okay."

Benny shuffled back and forth, shifted his books to the other hand.

"Yeah … Well, I guess I don't got nothin' I need help with. I'm just used to coming by, you know?" Then his voice dropped to a mumble. "Wanted to, you know, see how you was doin' and everything."

Nate said he was doing well, he appreciated the concern, sat down in one of the student desks in the circle and nodded. Looked up at the side of the boy's face and nodded some more.

"All right then." Benny moved away, running his free hand along the backs of the other kids' chairs. "Maybe see you Thursday, I might have some work by then." He paused at the door, surveying the other students again, and swept his eyes over Nate's face before putting his head down. "See ya, Mr. D. All right." And then he walked out.

Nate scanned the scenes through the chop of windshield wipers, turned on the jazz station to loosen up. Instead of taking the usual left on Knott, he continued down Martin Luther King Jr. Boulevard toward the city center. He wanted to keep driving for some reason, even though driving was basement low on the list of things he enjoyed, especially with the growing traffic problems; the decision amused him since it was still rush hour, cars and trucks with tight-jawed drivers lurching from light to light. Two scowling boys in a low-riding Lincoln were right behind him, their stereo's bass rattling his windows.

The wipers' rhythm soon lulling.

He had to get clear, arrive at a better understanding of what exactly was making him drink so much wine, eat so much ice cream, watch so much TV; over the past week, long strings of eighties' sitcoms had become more and more irresistible. Always the nervous feeling. Almost always now.

At a bus stop, a swarm of kids in baggy pants and dark hooded sweatshirts, faces hidden, hands in pockets. In front of a corner grocery, under the awning, two Hispanic men laughing, an elaborate handshake, secret code. At another red light, the boys in the lowrider again, this time pulled up alongside. The driver bent forward, a lighter's burst. Nate tried to concentrate on the jazz.

On the wet steel grating of the Broadway Bridge, the truck slid, jarring him. He steadied the wheel, rolled down his window and heard the shrill starlings on the bridge's girders. Only a few downtown lights visible through the clouds. A cold rain had been falling for two days straight.

As a kid, he'd loved rain. The walks through Laurelhurst Park with his young mother, Acacia, and their three-legged greyhound, Tripod, were never complete without feeding the ducks along the edges of the rain-rippled lake, or sloshing through big curbside puddles. There had been the occasional years when the rains were light, when puddles weren't as fun, and he had longed for a storm to bring back the moist, comfortable feeling to life. But he'd never had to wait long. The smells of mosses, wet leaves and soil, the sound of water channeling through the house's gutters, and the calming grey skies had combined to make the world seem more predictable—safer than the wide-open, burning days of summer. The idea of a life without steady rain had seemed threatening. The soggy people who lamented another showery day just didn't get it.

Nate headed down Broadway over the neon-streaked pavement and recalled his love of rain, concluding again that he'd been an odd child. The grey days were simply too depressing to love. Inevitable: the blues set in after seventy-two hours of incessant drizzle.

At a stoplight next to Pioneer Square, he watched a teenage couple—a boy and girl clad in all black wearing thick-heeled boots and miffed expressions—swagger in front of his truck, the girl's trench coat raised for shelter, and more thoughts of his lover came: Lang's intense eyes and fit body, her smile, her sweet mysterious self. Though she made him insane at times, and though their relationship so often seemed to bring out the most infantile responses in both of them, she was still his companion. His ally. Whether it was their Friday night routine of takeout and a video or Lang's fondness of surprising him with new clothes once or twice every month in spite of his insistence that he could dress himself, the relationship had so often anchored him, especially after particularly agitating days at the high school.

They'd met at Hieu's eldest son's twelfth birthday party at Old Town Pizza four years earlier, where Lang had embarrassed her nephew by singing a Vietnamese folk song in front of all those assembled in the upstairs room. It was while she was singing to Vo with teasing smiles that something had sparked in Nate, not only a groin-tingling attraction, but gratitude at having had his lust piqued after a long dry spell. Up to that point, there had been a few too many relationships with women every bit as neurotic as himself.

It was at the birthday party, also, that Lang's mother, Hoa, had watched Nate's reverent expression from across the table and seethed. For Hoa, even the faintest prospect of her daughter striking up with a white man was literally sickening; to let Lang date and possibly marry outside the Vietnamese community would be to endure another blow not only to her family, but, of course, to the very foundation of Vietnamese tradition. Hoa had raised this point nearly every time Lang came to visit during the four years since Nate had become a more conspicuous adjunct to the Nguyen family, and while Lang tried to argue back at first, straining to be understood, after awhile she grew resigned to nodding and looking away, showing the required respect.

The trip to America, into the heart of the Golden Mountain Dream, certainly hadn't been Hoa's idea. It was her younger son, Hieu, who had insisted most passionately that she come, he who finally made her believe that they might be hurt or killed if they didn't. Something in her boy's eyes had convinced her it was true, though she still had no satisfyingly firm idea as to why they would have been a target. It was Hieu's eyes, she often remembered, that had made the difference. Especially after everything that had already happened to the family—the bombings, the long separations—it would have been impossible to go on resisting his demand.

On the freeway, on the top deck of the Marquam Bridge, Nate pictured Grandma Hoa, the deep-wrinkled brow accentuating her eyes. While he understood the old woman's bitterness on an analytical level, the fact that she gave Lang such a hard time still made his palms sweaty now and then.

Swept into the rush, he changed lanes and glanced left at the downtown skyline, the lights more visible from directly across the Willamette, and felt just how excited he was over the imminent meet-up with his girlfriend. He even wanted to see Hoa sometime soon. Something about smiling at the old gal—the boiling the gesture seemed to bring on—usually brought a taste of victory. (Sophomoric, but still.) After all, Hoa couldn't end her daughter's relationships. Lang was too strong-willed, modern.

A half hour after leaving Wilson Green, he pulled up to his apartment believing that the impromptu city tour had brought a little perspective.

While Portland was no longer the distinctive place of his boyhood where a floral parade marked the cultural event of the year, it still had pockets of charm. The teeming Saturday Market under the Burnside Bridge where you could gobble a huckleberry shake while bypassing various hemp products. The dozens of city parks where stubborn natives walked dogs through downpours. The overall landscape, however, continued to change drastically. In fact there were days that he felt like a refugee in his own hometown—a knowledge that he'd lost something. Mostly a reaction against the blocks of characterless new buildings, the poisoned rivers, traffic snarls in once-calm neighborhoods. (Was it progress when cities all began to look the same?) Or maybe it was his admittedly pessimistic belief that the incredible human talent for short-term thinking would keep killing off the remaining natural beauty. Whatever the main reason, the sensation of loss had begun to jab. Especially over the past week. He hated to admit it, even Lang couldn't help him feel safe anymore. At home.

He stepped toward the apartment building's front door, focusing on the darkness behind the rhododendrons and photinia, his key ready. He strained to picture Lang's candlelit body, the exquisite curves of hips and back, but the image came only in flickers, the scene refusing to hold still. He needed to make amends with her, somehow work it out, despite the shadow-lurking hunch that he would, in fact, end up taking the leap they were both so scared of.

Hard and Tough

The sound of Le Phuong's cello from upstairs made Lang's neck muscles relax. She sat in the same kitchen chair across from Hieu in which Nate had squirmed early that morning and sipped at her second cup of chamomile, eyes closed. Her younger nephew, Dat, stood gaping into the refrigerator; the boy had slept all day after being awake most of the previous night as the typically brief family meeting had stretched into nearly four hours of debate and lament. When the music stopped, Lang opened her eyes, emerging from the concentrated calm, and noticed that her brother was staring at her.

"Her playing keeps improving," she said. They had been alternating between English and Vietnamese that evening, since Hoa still refused to come out of her room. "You're proud of her progress, yeah?"

With a quick nod, Hieu turned to Dat, who remained fixed before the refrigerator, holding onto the door handle as if it were keeping him from collapsing.

"Find something to eat or close it."

His head lowered, pillow-fresh hair spiked on one side, matted on the other, Dat shut the door. He glanced over at his father and aunt and began tucking his green turtleneck into his purple pajama bottoms. "Oh, hi auntie. I didn't even see you."

"Eat what's left in the oven and on the back burner," Lang said. "We finished a little while ago."

She watched Dat scoop some rice into a bowl. Though flighty, he was a good boy—respectful, enamored of both *pho* and mustard-slathered hot dogs, usually able to absorb his father's lightning-strike mood shifts.

From across the table, Hieu observed Dat straining on tiptoe to reach the countertop and he sensed himself relaxing finally. The boy seemed to be managing all right, steadily building himself a meal, until Vo sauntered into the kitchen, his face composed into a cocky glare, and wasted no time in poking his little brother on the butt while making a farting noise with his stuck-out tongue. Vo laughed when Dat jumped and flung his spoon into the air, launching a shower of rice. With the ferocity of a cornered mongoose, Dat began swinging his arms, face contorted. Vo took a few punches to his abdomen before casting a mock-forlorn look toward his aunt and father, then picked up Dat, flipped him upside-down and held him by the ankles.

Hieu whipped around the table.

"Enough!" He bent to set Dat upright, then shot up and smacked Vo with an open hand on the side of the neck, the swiftness making everyone hold their breath. "Not time for playing. You do not understand that?"

Vo turned to his reflection in the window above the sink, and Hieu laid a hand on the back of Dat's neck.

"You will be okay," Hieu said, conscious yet again of his difficulty with contractions. As hard as he had tried in conversation over all these years, as polished as his English had become, he could never, for some reason, get the hang of contractions. The fact that Lang sounded more fluent, regardless of the situation, didn't help matters. "Someday you will be big and cool like your brother. You both clean this up and get your dinner." He saw that Vo's hands had become fists.

After pouring himself another tea, gradually mastering his adrenaline, Hieu returned to the table and searched his sister's face. He knew that she would have handled the situation differently. It had come up before, his approach with the kids, most recently when he'd forbidden Vo to play bongos in the Grant High School talent show with a band called Spastic Gorilla, an unexplained move that had added more than a few layers to Vo's animosity. Lang, Hieu anticipated, would soon be compelled to voice once again that he was treating the children too roughly, like their own father had treated them. While he waited for her to muster the strength, or perhaps the calm, he pictured their father and their village, images revisited daily, despite his half-hearted attempts to block them out.

The hamlet had been nestled against the edge of a forest in the province of Tay Ninh, an area along the Vam Co River near the Vietnam-Cambodia border that eventually ended up suffering heavy American bombing because of its National Liberation Front sanctuaries. Both Hieu and Lang could remember the setting clearly: the village enclosed by banyan trees, bamboo, and elephant grass; water buffaloes in the paddies; golden eels and white catfish in the stream and pond.

During monsoon season, the paddies always flooded, but sweet potato, hot pepper, and Indian mustard crops provided plenty of other chores. In the dry season, most of the men hunted wild chickens while the women and children dug for medicinal roots and picked tea leaves, bananas, and jackfruit.

But while life in the hamlet was cyclic and routine for the most part, it had been more difficult than it needed to be because of their father's personality. Seeing life as a struggle only, the man made sure that his children would grow up, as he always put it, "hard and tough to deal with the hard, tough world." He had ordered both Hieu and Lang and their older brother Minh to tend the rice daily, weeding a constant chore, and to pick the tea leaves and fruit, maintain the garden, and sometimes go on special errands to stinky old Trac's house down beside the Vam Co. It hadn't always been rigorous work, but the fact that their father spent most of his hours on his sleeping mat, lost in an opium otherworld, outlined the incongruities between word and action. As early as either Hieu or Lang could remember, it was their mother who toiled, leading by example, their reclining father who took care of the preaching.

There were also the times—often while they were in front of their hut playing with friends—when their father had called them inside, given each a few slaps on the arms and neck and face, then shouted at them to get busy. All part of a careful strategy.

It was all that Hieu and Lang had known, and with the devotion to family that surrounded them, it would have been unthinkable not to obey. Because the ancestral tombs were just meters away at one edge of the village, the reminder was always present, a message permeating, in a whisper, all village activities: *Family is everything. You are part of a whole.* It was understood that spirits watched over the living, spirits sure to intervene in some way if you strayed from a life of prayer and virtuous action. Life was meant to be lived with gratitude, with humility.

But then in early 1968, the B-52 raids began.

When the first planes appeared high above, the villagers, many of whom had never even made the trip to Saigon, thought the spirits had sent flying messengers. Yet what kind of news they carried wasn't clear.

Hamlet meetings were called, theories professed and debated, then word finally came from a small band of pajama-clad guerrillas that the Americans were planning to destroy the entire area. They had appeared out of the evening mist before, the soldiers who descended the hills to speak of a struggle to oust yet another group of arrogant foreigners; but they had never been so adamant. Despite the guerrillas' zeal, though, only a few of the villagers seemed to understand what was happening, what the intensifying war was all about, Hieu and Lang's father not among the aware. Hieu would often recall the dreamy-eyed man saying, "The flying messengers will bring news from the afterworld, you will see."

Four days later, the first raid leveled most of the tombs. Because everyone wished to live and eventually die near the sacred site, the attack brought a double dose of terror. Some villagers fled crazed into the forest, some into ditches they had dug in their yards. But many just froze, curled up on the earthen floors of their huts. Hieu, twelve at the time, could still call up the utterly amazing scene: explosions that more than once made him defecate, the shaking ground, ripping and crashing trees, his sobbing mother. Only his father had seemed composed.

It was in the second raid, only three days after the first, that the remainder of the hamlet had been destroyed, most every hut and animal pen blown apart, every garden demolished. It was during the second raid, also, that Hieu's father refused to crawl down into the family's fresh-dug tunnel, which began just outside the hut's door. When the planes finally passed and the family re-emerged, it was Hieu who first found the chunks of pig and buffalo and human flesh strewn across their former compound. He knew that he needn't keep looking, but something pushed him on through the smoke and debris.

On a patch of scorched elephant grass ten yards beyond where their closest neighbor's hut had once stood, Hieu found the upper half of his father's body, the spinal cord protruding like a tail. The blue-glazed eyes had widened, his father having finally realized that the spirits were angry. The arthritic hands twisted into knobs. Chin and mouth blasted off. The smell of burnt hair and flesh and nearby fire. It was a scene Hieu would be able to summon instantly from then on, as if it were pinned to the inside of his skull and he had only to flash an inner light upon it. It was a scene he had tried and failed to describe to his older brother and several other members of the National Liberation Front who arrived a day later to survey the damage. Minh only remained silent, head bowed, as he sat on the ground amongst the few blank-faced survivors, his arms trying to steady his still-trembling mother.

When Lang shifted in her chair, Hieu caught himself harvesting the past again. He looked at his sister's bowed head and arrived at his usual semi-troubling conclusion about his own children: he was doing his best to help them grow up right—to be hard and tough in a hard, tough world.

During the lull in conversation as the boys cleaned up the spilled rice, Lang had initially groped for something tactful to say, then decided to let silence carry her message.

"I know what you're thinking," Hieu said in Vietnamese, "and they'll be fine. Vo still hasn't learned there's a time and place."

Lang saw that her brother was avoiding her gaze again, just as he had an hour before when she'd probed about the police investigation. Hieu had told her he didn't want to get into it, saying only, "The girls lie." But she saw an opening now.

"You're afraid," she said, briefly catching her reflection in the window behind Hieu. It looked confident.

Hieu sat back with a smirk.

"You don't want to talk about something, brother. I can tell by your eyes."

Vo and Dat had finished wiping the floor and counter and stood spellbound. Hieu flung looks at both of them.

"You are planning to *eat,* yes?"

The boys hurried their bowls and plates into the dining room, returning briefly for their glasses of tea. When the kitchen was quiet, Hieu leaned forward and let the silence squeeze.

"My eyes show nothing," he said just above a whisper.

"You see? Defensive. You're holding something in. You—"

Hieu slammed his hands onto the table, then immediately pressed his palms together and sat back. He drew a long breath and let it out slowly, his lips a tight O, and after a time said, "Forgive me."

In the doorway leading to the dining room, Anh appeared, holding the handle of her empty mug in a childlike fist. She had been upstairs helping Le Phuong practice a Tchaikovsky piece when she heard the noise. She avoided Hieu's eyes as she stepped into the kitchen.

"You look spooked," she said, coming up behind Lang. She set down her mug and laid her hands on her sister-in-law's shoulders. "What was that sound?"

"I'm fine," Lang said. "Just our man letting off steam."

At *our man*, Hieu popped from his chair. He brushed past his wife, set his mug in the sink and left the kitchen.

In his wake, the two women remained still.

"More rattled than I expected," Lang said, when the only sound she could hear was the boys' smacking from the dining room. Her posture remained stiff, neck muscles clenched again. "He's going to be all right?"

Anh kept her hands on Lang's shoulders, gentle swirls. "You know his strength."

"What about you and the kids?"

"Only Le Phuong seems to see the severity of it. She acts composed, but she's shaken. Dat's too young to really understand. I think Vo is secretly happy to see him suffer."

Anh gave Lang's shoulders a pat before stepping around and taking Hieu's usual seat.

"This does scare me," she said, pressing along her cheekbones in a long outward sweep. "Last night he kept saying how racist the girls are, how they're targeting him. He doesn't understand how to make the detective see that."

"What about other students? They still make fun of his accent?"

"He doesn't talk about school very much these days." Anh looked down at the dish of cashews in the middle of the table. "I'm wondering if it's more, though. I think maybe what's upset him most is that after everything we've been through, you know … He thinks the spirits are displeased with him. They're making him pay for some sin."

"Did he say what it is?" Lang tried to catch Anh's eye, but couldn't.

"He's not sure. At least he won't talk about it if he does know. Of course your mother insists this has happened because we abandoned the home-land. A long time coming she says."

Lang focused on her half-empty mug, nodding. Pictured her mother locked away upstairs, back rigid, sitting cross-legged on her sleeping mat before her shrine. Hoa had a way of latching onto her first impressions, her initial explanations of events, that had always baffled Lang; her mother's obstinate self-righteousness riled her even back in Vietnam, during the days right after their hamlet had been leveled.

When the B-52 raids continued, bombs scouring the already devastated forests along the Vam Co, Hoa had at first refused to leave for Saigon. But Minh, as eldest son, insisted that she flee. He tried to make her understand that he would look after the remnants of the tombs, and then send for everyone when things were less dangerous. But Hoa stayed firm longer than anyone suspected she would, even after her best friend, Rieng, died in a mid-morning raid that rocked the remaining underground shelters. The hastily dug cavern in which Rieng had been hiding with her two young sons collapsed, suffocating them all.

It had taken over a week of arguing, along with another close call during an early morning raid, before Hoa finally assented. But the spectacle was wrenching. Lang sometimes revisited the numbing blend of sorrow and disgust she'd felt watching her mother wail and carry on over the course of the two days they prepared to leave. Over and over Hoa said that she would never see the village again; the spirits had been visiting in her dreams, telling her to say good-bye.

After a boatman from a neighboring hamlet offered to take them down the Vam Co as far as Ben Luc, and after she made her farewells to the tombs and few remaining friends, Hoa became strangely quiet. Minh's explanation of the impending journey was met only with a faint nod. And when Minh said that he needed Hieu to stay behind to help with the cleanup effort in some nearby villages, that he would send his young brother on to Saigon as soon as he could, Hoa merely closed her eyes and bowed her head. Lang tried to hold her mother's hand as the boat pushed off, as they watched Minh and Hieu waving from the bank, but Hoa pulled away and clutched her fingers to her chest, lips moving with silent words.

"Well, my mother will think how she needs to," Lang said. "She always has." She noticed that Anh's brow was pressed from her own meditation. "What matters is that Hieu stands up for himself and he's honest."

Anh's face didn't loosen until Vo loped in with his empty bowl rattling against his tea glass, Dat following him. The boys rinsed their bowls and approached the table.

Dat peeked up at Vo and got an approving flick of the chin.

"Is Dad gonna be okay?"

"Yes," Anh said. "Everything will be all right." She opened her arms and Dat went to her.

Vo leaned against the counter and slipped his hands into the front pockets of his black jeans. "I'm serious. He messes with me again, I'm defending myself."

"You take it easy," Anh said over Dat's shoulder.

"Tell him that. He's the one always freakin' out."

"I'm sure you understand he's dealing with a lot right now. He was trying to be up-front with us last night."

Vo turned to his reflection above the sink, and Anh gave Dat another kiss before announcing that it was study time. The boys would fetch Le Phuong from her cello session, then they would all sit together at the table in a corner of the master bedroom, Anh helping each of them, making sure they were putting solid effort into their work.

After washing the dishes and calling Nate to say she'd be over shortly, Lang refilled the tea kettle, wiped down the kitchen and dining room tables, and then jotted a note on the refrigerator's magnetic chalk board: *Have faith in truth.* What with Hoa and Hieu competing for the role of chief brooder in the family, she'd often felt compelled to be the optimist, though it came hard.

In the living room, Hieu was in his easy chair, flipping through an old Wilson Green yearbook, the hollows of his face accentuated by the floor lamp's lowest setting. His eyes were nearly closed. She jingled her keys, but still he didn't look up. Instead of trying to reach him, though, like she had so often over the twenty-one years since their arrival in the States, Lang turned away and called another good-bye up the stairs. Pulled on her coat and let herself out into the pouring night.

A Better Man

Nate noticed the tapping of rain and hailstones against his front room windows and held his uncle's second Indonesia postcard up close, examining the faded Denpasar, Bali postmark in the room's low light. His third glass of six-dollar chardonnay on the coffee table before him, a Freedy Johnston CD playing at a volume that the upstairs neighbor had already thumped her disapproval over, his fiery girlfriend on the way. Despite the oddly refreshing after-work drive through the wet city, however, he sensed the wine nudging him toward the brink of another funk. Thoughts of Lang and Hieu, and of his ghost uncle—the connections in his life to a far-off country he'd never seen—made him want to keep drinking.

Up until he met Hieu at Wilson Green, it had been a mysterious, distressing word: Vietnam. When he was a boy, when his uncle went off to fight, to help keep dominoes from falling in a land of steamy dark jungles, it was a word he hated. Exactly why his best buddy needed to go had never been adequately answered—the more his mother or his grandparents or the men on TV tried to explain, the more confusing things got.

In April of '68, when Sammy left for Vietnam, Nate was six months away from his tenth birthday. For the first few weeks after the goodbye, he would sit for hours on the front porch steps of his grandparents' house and mope (as his mother put it) like a wet cat. Predictably, the other adults in his life tried to pick up where Sammy left off, spending bits of time here and there playing whiffleball or Hot Wheels or Watch Stuffed Animals Fly, trying to mimic Sammy's energy. But they figured out early on that Nate wasn't quite convinced. None of them could match Sammy's whimsy, the way he would start clucking, mooing, or growling, then chasing Nate around the dining room table or up and down the stairs to the bedrooms. There had been many times, when they'd all been sitting around the table listening to another of Grandpa Davis's Bad Sinner prayers, that Nate peeked through his lashes to find Sammy looking back cross-eyed with his mouth dropped open, revealing whatever they were about to eat in a chewed-up blob.

Since Nate's father had vanished seven months before Nate was born, and since Acacia had given birth to her only child two and a half weeks ahead of her sixteenth birthday, her brother Sammy was a strong presence from the start. Before he left for Vietnam, they'd all lived in the big grey house on Lincoln Street with swallow nests in the eaves, a raccoon family usually camped out in the backyard laurel hedge. Grandpa worked long hours for Portland General Electric, Grandma volunteered part-time as a secretary at the Lutheran church four blocks away, Acacia took care of her son and shelved books at the downtown library four afternoons a week. Sammy, Nate later learned, divided his time between reading Russian novels and Romantic poetry, putting in a few hours a day at a used bookstore over on Hawthorne Boulevard, lifting weights, getting laid, and helping raise his young nephew.

Nate still kept an old photo clipped to the last page of his journal, one of Sammy on all fours, teeth bared, shaggy brown hair dangling around his tanned face. Nate was straddling Sammy's back, grinning, a black and red cowboy hat tilted forward on his white-blond head. And there was another shot as well, one that he kept in Acacia's care at the old house because he couldn't bear to lose it. It was of himself at three sitting with his young uncle on the front steps of the family's mossy-roofed cabin up in Brightwood at the western base of Mt. Hood. Sam was shirtless on the step just behind Nate, his already muscle-streaked arms folded across his nephew's tiny chest, his smile wide and white, a thin line of black between his upper and lower teeth as if he were about to crack a joke.

Now, thirty-five years later, especially in the soft hours when sleep wouldn't come, Nate often visited the increasingly vague impressions of his uncle—the unrestrained laugh, the gleaming-eyed intensity, the bushy hair—and, as ever, they combined to remind him that for all intents and purposes, despite the murky distance between them, Sammy was his dad.

When he was six, during a nasty bout of chicken pox, Sammy had read him *Little House on the Prairie*, given simplified yet vivid summaries of his favorite Tolstoy novels, and drawn exaggerated crayon pictures of ducks, wacky-eyed fish, and Grandpa Davis. Nate had always savored the memory of waking up fevered and itchy and finding his uncle asleep in the chair next to the bed, a book splayed across his lap. And it wasn't just during the chicken pox episode: whenever Nate fell ill, Sammy made sure his buddy knew that he wasn't alone, either by bringing in a cold washcloth and a 7-Up or simply sitting by the bed. While Acacia had done more than her share (the hugs after bee stings, the hundreds of high chair feedings, long walks to marvel at leaves and puddles and neighborhood pets), Nate had slowly come to intuit over the years that she was still a kid herself: caring but preoccupied, present but wistful. Acacia, only eighteen when he tore into his terrible twos like a weasel through a henhouse, had always tried to mask her anger over having allowed herself to get pregnant so young, but Nate picked up on it from the beginning. Sammy's infectious passion, his inspiring immersion into whatever game or task was before him, made Acacia's mindset more obvious.

So when his wild soldier uncle finally returned from Vietnam in the summer of '70, after inexplicably extending his service another 395 days beyond his initial tour, Nate had been ready for a whopping father-son-like reunion, in spite of the fact that they'd received only two postcards over all that time, both saying the exact same thing: *See you soon. Love, Sam.*

There had, of course, been a major change, but not an easily labeled one. Both the smile and the charm were still there, even a couple of the old barnyard animal sounds; yet something had happened in that distant place that made Sammy seem, as Acacia always put it, *distracted*—a word none of them had ever before come close to using when describing him.

But distracted was what he was, even during the reunion itself, despite the amiable front. It happened so suddenly. One hot late July evening, Sammy just tramped through the front door with his duffel bag slung over a shoulder and said, "Smells good." Nate, who had been organizing baseball cards on the sofa, would never forget the ape-like guttural noise his grandmother made in the kitchen when she heard her son's voice, then her hobbling charge to the front room, where she fainted. He could still picture his grandfather barging up from the basement workshop, a dust-caked apron tied around his portly midriff, how the old man had given Sammy one hard slap on the back and immediately turned to fetch a cold towel for his wife. Then there was Acacia's entrance from the backyard, where she'd been barbecuing chicken below the open kitchen window: more hugs, tears, stilted sentences. The reunion was pleasing enough, actually, the rush of reacquaintance bringing on a giddiness, especially in Grandma after she recovered and had a few bites of food. To Nate, the chicken and homemade coleslaw tasted better than ever. Soon, though, when surprise finally loosened its hold, everyone began to notice the depth of Sammy's transformation.

Within three days, Acacia called a basement summit at Grandpa's drafting table. They'd begun to fret over their soldier's new habit of taking 3:00 a.m. walks, and over how he seemed to now enjoy spending hour after hour alone in his room. Nate eventually learned that Acacia had been chosen to confront her brother, to voice the family's worry as gently as she could, try to open him up about what had happened. While Grandpa offered his services, both Acacia and Grandma knew that sitting father and son down for such a talk would only make things worse. The battles, especially during Sammy's teenage years, had sometimes spilled outside, on one occasion prompting the Henson brothers, the jowly bachelors next door, to telephone the police. In that particular instance, a rainy Labor Day evening, Grandpa had resorted to flinging rocks at Sammy with his slingshot from the front yard garden. Across the street, shirtless, stoned, and bellowing, Sammy hugged a telephone pole, daring his father to hit him.

But as it happened, Acacia's approach didn't go over very well. On the rare occasions when his mother brought up the story, Nate could understand why, seeing how her abrasive, lay-it-out-there style had vexed him time and again. Sammy, it turned out, was in no mood for a confrontation that scorching July afternoon in the backyard.

He was lying on one of the plastic lawn recliners when Acacia brought out two bottles of beer and a chopped up frozen Baby Ruth bar. The discussion began well enough, Sammy's affection for both beer and sweets temporarily overcoming his suspicion. When Acacia reached over and turned off the transistor, which was playing "Proud Mary," Sammy pulled off his mirrored shades and rested them on his baby-oiled washboard stomach.

"So what's the word, good-lookin'?" He gnawed a hunk of nougat.

Acacia wiped away lines of sweat droplets from her triceps, then held her beer to her forehead.

"Just wanted to talk. See how you're doing and everything."

Sammy smiled, put his sunglasses back on, raised his palms to the bright cloudless sky. "Soakin' up a day."

At that point Acacia figured she'd made the requisite small talk.

"We're confused, Sam … The late walks and everything."

"My walks? Jesus, the folks still that uptight? Just some jet lag."

Acacia shook her head. "You stay up in your room, you don't talk as much—God, *half* as much—as you used to."

Sammy sat up, grabbed his *Hang Loose Hawaii* tank top from the close-cut grass, and swiveled to face her. The state trooper shades and buzz cut made him seem even more unknowable.

"Listen. I'm just wrapped up in some thoughts is all. Trying to get steady."

"Get *steady?* What does that *mean?* Why can't you tell us what *happened?*"

Sammy reached down to turn the radio back on, but Acacia snatched it by the volume knob and chucked it toward the laurel hedge. With a closed-mouth smile, he heaved himself up, collected his beer and the Baby Ruth wrapper, and walked into the house without a word.

Ten hours later, in the cool of early morning, after another neighborhood stroll, after repacking his duffel and putting a handwritten note on the kitchen counter, Sammy left again, this time for good. He had only played with Nate a couple of times, absently whinnying, then bucking much earlier than in times past. He'd only winked when Nate peeked through his lashes during Grandpa's tired dinnertime prayers. Nate had tried hard to think that his uncle was just tired or down, that he would come around sooner or later.

When Grandpa found the note on his way out to work, he woke everyone, hollering *"Damn it!"* and shattering a juice glass against the fridge. In a daze, Nate slogged downstairs in his pajamas and asked what happened. Acacia dabbed her face with a wet paper towel, picked up the note, led her boy to the living room sofa and read aloud.

7/26/70

Dear Davis Clan,

What can I say?

I don't know where I'm headed, but I'll be thinking good thoughts for all of you. (Even you Dad.)

Sis, get on with your life. Keep watching out for weaselly men.

Ma, you're a great one. I'm sorry.

Please tell Nate that I love him and please trust that I'm at peace with this decision.

I'll miss the smells in this kitchen.

Love, Sam

And that was it.

While hearing the letter had made his hands clench, Nate always liked that he'd been included at such a major moment in the life of the family; he appreciated the chance to feel more grown up. But then being treated more like an adult, he soon found, only seemed to worsen the pain.

Weeks passed to months without word. As absurd as it initially seemed, they began to consider that they might never see Sammy again. An amazing thought. The old house remained a sorrow-drenched place that Acacia escaped as much as she could, sometimes taking Nate and Tripod to Laurelhurst Park or up around the Mt. Tabor reservoirs for long walks when she wasn't working at the library or studying for her GED tests. Under the grey sky, out in the elements, perspective usually came easier.

As Nate stretched further toward the promised land of adulthood, he kept trying to understand that it wasn't his fault that his uncle had left, but there were nights when he went to bed with thoughts of Sammy crowding out all others. I could have made him stay, he told himself. If only I'd shown him how much I needed him. *Did I do something wrong?* But by the end of his thirteenth year, when walks with his mom and Tripod were too nerdy, he'd begun referring to his long-gone uncle as "The Prick," though Acacia and Grandpa would have none of it.

Acacia had grown fond of defending her brother, repeatedly concluding that Sam had "some issues" he needed to sort out before he could be good to anyone; he needed to "get his shit together" before he could come back home. But for Grandpa, the stiff-upper-lip approach was the only conceivable response, as it was to every other source of sorrow in his life, Guadalcanal having taught him well. When his wife of thirty-three years died of a brain aneurysm in October 1975, his feelings toward everything, even his grandson, were blocked to the point of seeming gone. The man found it grueling to show any emotion other than anger, perhaps because he secretly believed his crazy hippie son had somehow brought on his companion's death.

When the first postcard arrived in early '78, with the cherry-red cursive *Indonesia* below the scene of a pristine palm-lined beach, Grandpa Davis checked his rage for three long seconds, then blurted, "Who does that dickhead think he is?" Acacia and Nate were at the Lincoln Street house for the usual Saturday bologna sandwich, corn chips, and ginger ale lunch when the card arrived, tucked in between a water bill and a glossy porcelain doll magazine addressed to Grandma. The silence was savage during that lunch, Nate always remembered.

The picture on the second postcard, five years and two months later, was identical to the first—same tropical paradise with the cursive *Indonesia* beneath—but the postmark was legible that time: Denpasar, Bali. Acacia wrote Nate (who had been away on one of his own walkabouts in Europe) that she and Grandpa considered trying to track Sammy down, but had ultimately decided to settle for continuing their prayers and getting on with their lives. It had been, Nate always knew, a turning point. They'd gained a measure of power.

Nevertheless, the message on that second postcard made the choice an especially tough one. The handwriting, always so firm and tidy, was nearly illegible, the words rambling about becoming an apprentice woodcarver, living in a bungalow at the base of an active volcano. Sammy also mentioned that he hadn't been feeling well, not bothering to specify. When Acacia found the card stuck under a fridge magnet one afternoon after she'd moved back home to help out her declining, flu-wracked father, her first impulse had been to telephone the American embassy in Jakarta. But she waited, stilled by warring thoughts. After running the idea past Grandpa and getting no response, she opted finally for not calling, giving in again to her belief that it would be wise to leave her troubled brother alone. Though a part of her certainly wanted Sammy home safe, she remained spooked over his aura of distraction. And though she knew that Nate still secretly worshiped his uncle, she clung to her conviction that Sammy's decision to leave was really best for everyone. Some buried part of her was ashamed about not phoning the embassy, not tracking down the man they all still adored, but she'd been abandoned before and, if anything, Acacia knew she could never allow herself to feel that desperate again.

Nate told himself it would be best to keep things as light as possible tonight when Lang arrived—no argument, no analysis of their lives or The Relationship, no posturing. Just some companionship to beat back the week's stress, maybe some lovemaking to jump-start the senses, reconnect.

How he would be able to adequately communicate his impulse to up and leave on a solo trip still confounded him. He knew that Lang expected a direct approach, yet only three days earlier they'd shouted at each other about freedom, then loyalty and commitment, when the subject had been broached. But within himself, too, there was a muscular fear of the unknown that always seemed to awaken whenever he was on the verge of something big, like the time last year he'd been tripped up by the decision about whether to propose to Lang.

Down at Rockaway on the coast over spring break, the desire had filled him as they walked beside the waves one evening, cold wind on their faces. For some time, he'd been able to imagine a life together. But in the end he buckled, reining himself in from such dangerous impulsivity, leaving her wondering if anything was wrong. They ended up arguing over something petty, something he couldn't even remember, because she misinterpreted his looks at the sand and the sea.

Biting the inside of his cheek now, Nate got up from the sofa to pour himself a fourth glass of the chardonnay.

A few minutes before eleven, Lang let herself in through the kitchen door and hung her coat on the oven handle, raindrops dribbling onto the black-and-white checkered tiles. Nate remained asleep on the sofa, his empty glass and a drained bottle on the coffee table beside him, his mouth open. In the fireplace, ashes flickered from the fire he'd lit a few hours earlier; in the background a Chopin nocturne soared.

From the doorway to the dining room, she watched him awhile, eyeing the form of his thighs through the khakis, his whiskered face, the gold toes of his black socks. Then she turned down the music (which brought him out of his nap) and dropped into the love seat adjoining the sofa and crossed her legs, sleek black slacks unwrinkled.

"Sorry I'm so late," she said. "I needed to drive."

Nate sat up, reached for his glass and saw it was empty. He blinked hard.

"I was just meditating."

"The gaping mouth position?"

"The Sumerians developed it. Smashing."

Lang rose, settled onto the sofa and pressed herself against him.

"I think you're smashing." She tasted her lips after the kiss. "And sauced."

Nate kissed her again. "I took a little spin myself, after work. Did it help any?"

"Not much."

Lang yawned, and Nate realized how nervous he was. She still had the power to make him feel like a little kid at certain times, it was nuts.

"So how was Hieu's? Has your mom come out yet?"

Lang pushed herself from the sofa and turned down the music further, muttering that it was still too loud.

"She'll stay locked up another day or two. I tried to get her to open up, but she wouldn't have any of it."

Nate stood, rubbed his cheeks. "Drink?"

In the kitchen, Lang leaned against the doorjamb, hands clasped behind her. Nate, as he uncorked another bottle, threw occasional looks at her, the outlines of her nipples in the silk blouse. What if he just walked over and undressed her, made love to her in one of the kitchen chairs? The cork took too much concentration.

She looked on for a few moments, holding back a smile. "Sorry to cut through the romance, but I'm exhausted and I need to ask you something. I want to hear what you deeply feel about this, okay?"

Nate tried to hide his swallow. He nodded for her to continue, the faint crackling of hailstones against the front room windows starting up again.

"Do you think he touched those girls?"

Like that, in his mind, the locker room exchange. Hieu's wistful tone.

"Not sure what to say to that."

"I need to know what you think. I think maybe he did. Or at least something happened he's not proud of, I can tell."

The words died out, and there was a squeezing in Nate's stomach. He saw now that the evening might actually take the course he dreaded, but made himself show calm. He handed Lang her glass, lifted his own, and led them back to the front room.

"You know," he said, back on the sofa, "I don't have an opinion right now. I need more info."

"But his *eyes*. He kept looking away. You know that's not him. When I asked what happened, he just cut me off, said the girls are liars."

Nate took a drink.

"He's only fuming. I don't blame him. I probably wouldn't want to talk too much about it, at least at first. Like I don't feel much like talking about getting knifed. I respect his way of dealing with it."

"I get that, I do. But I know when he's scared. I just wondered if you noticed anything. You're his closest friend."

Nate made to take another sip, then stopped.

"We're friends, but hey …"

He saw the answer didn't satisfy, and it was then, his ears filled with a low thudding, that his decision on the leave of absence began barging through him. He took another drink. He would open up. Now? Why not now? He'd do it. Okay. Let the impulse flow, try to trust it this time. Whether or not the relationship could sustain the separation remained to be seen, but the time had come. So much for a mellow evening. The Bali postcard on the coffee table was his only physical guide.

"Hey …" Streaks of burgundy spread across Nate's cheeks. "I'm sorry I don't have any answers, but I don't really know what else to say."

Lang didn't respond, her eyes settled dreamily on the coffee table before her: a small hand-painted vase Nate had bought years ago in New Mexico.

"But listen," he said. "There's something I've decided."

She sat up straighter, breasts filling in the blouse. Nate forced himself to dig in. It had to be the right time.

"You've heard a lot about my uncle, too much probably …" When he gauged her, she nodded. "Hear me out, all right? I'm going to try to find him. That's why I need some time away."

Lang's face was calm save her mouth. Muscles had tightened, pushing the lips forward slightly. She didn't reply.

"It's something I've needed to do for a long time and, I don't know, but this is the time. I'm not sure how long it'll take, but I have to try. It's completely insane, I know."

Nate got up and raised one of the window blinds, golden light from the closest street lamp streaming into the room. The rain had lessened some, yet still slapped against the photinia just beyond the window.

"This is what I was trying to talk about," he said, looking out over Fifteenth Avenue. "I know it's awful timing, and I'm sorry." He turned and looked down at her. Peered out again at the rain. "This might sound messed up, but maybe the stabbing was what I needed. I just have this feeling that if I ignore this, I'll be in bad shape down the road. Sammy's been popping into my head so much this past week, more than usual. I guess maybe with the stabbing—and yeah, it was relatively minor—but it was sort of a wake-up call, you know? I mean, what if he'd had a gun?" He paused for a few beats. "It's this feeling that before you die, you have to do certain things, get a handle on certain things … This is something I need to do, Lang, even if the odds seem long. I have to find him. Or at least find out what happened."

He was unaware of rubbing his hands together until he turned and glanced down at her again. Surprise seemed to play on her face now, her eyes wider than normal.

He stepped over and pushed aside an *Utne Reader* on the coffee table directly in front of her and sat. "I have to know what happened."

Lang only nodded.

"Please don't shut me out here." He saw that she wasn't listening. "Don't be like your brother."

On the next beat, her hand flashed from her lap and smacked his face. He thought she might start crying, though she had only let him see her cry once, right after she'd been fired from *The Oregonian* five months earlier for being, as her editor said, "too timid for a reporter." Lang stood and moved toward the dining room. At the threshold she turned and faced him, her arms crossed.

"Listen," he said. "I'm taking a *leave of absence*. I'm not quitting, my job or us. This is—"

"We make this work or we let it go," she said, enunciating each word. "There is *no way* I can let four years of work on this ... whatever this relationship even *is* ... get put on a shelf while you take off for God knows how long, searching for a guy who *clearly* does not want to be found."

The hail had started again, rapping against the windows as Lang paused. Then she shook her head.

"Seems to me you need to be a better man here, Nate."

The words made his teeth gnash. But instead of countering, he focused on the thought that had just hit: it was Sammy who'd given him the best model of manhood. Not that Grandpa Davis hadn't done his part, but the poor guy had always been so closed off. Grandpa, Grandma, Acacia, while supportive and all, hadn't been able to make him feel grounded in the world to the degree his uncle could. Weak as it probably sounded for a grown man to admit, there it was. All these years, this unfinished business. Something so far from settled. Far from addressed.

And then there was another, more familiar response: he needed some space in order to clear his head before reconsidering a journey into the wilderness of marriage. In the hospital right after the stabbing, the same idea filled him, the need to step back, air things out for a bit.

"I think the time apart could be healthy," he said. "Finding him could end up helping you and me."

Lang flashed a tight smile. "*Sick.*" She turned for the kitchen.

"I'm sorry to hear that," Nate said, forcing himself not to follow. "Don't you see I have to do this? If I don't do it now—"

"*Sick man!*"

He heard her shake her coat out, mumbling something in Vietnamese, then the back door opened and slammed shut.

The wine-buzz still thick, he lowered himself onto the edge of the coffee table and closed his eyes. Listened to the hail and the soft piano, the rumble of Lang's SUV fading.

Page 1   Case# 96-0081A2

Portland Police Department
Portland, Oregon
Special Report

Report Type: SPECIAL   Case Status: Pending   Classification:

Incident Type: SEX CRIME   Subject of Report: SUSPECT
INTERVIEW

Original Report: 11-6-96   This Report: 11-12-96

Location: Portland Public Safety Facility

2236 N. Hargrove, Port., OR 97203

Name: DET. SGT. DON WALLACE   DOB: Sex: Race:

Address: PORTLAND POLICE DEPT.   Phone: 823-2120

Employment: Position: Phone:

Subject: NGUYEN, HIEU TRAN   DOB: 08-08-55 Sex: M   Race: A

Address: 2959 N.E. LOFTON CT. PORT., OR 97212 Phone: 269-8894

MENTIONED:

Hieu T. NGUYEN, suspect, see above. Wilson Green High School
Teacher.

Malisha JONES, victim, DOB: 03-02-80, 103 N. Mallson Apt. #31,
Port., OR 97201. Junior at Wilson Green High School. Lives
with Aunt, Cherise LOGAN.

Sasha ANDERSON, victim, DOB: 02-20-80, 300 N. Phillips, Port.,
OR 97201. Junior at Wilson Green High School. Mother's name is
Marguerite ANDERSON.

Carson SANDOVAL, mentioned, DOB: 05-01-80, 387 N. Phillips,
Port., OR 97201. Junior at Wilson Green High School. Father's
name is Juan SANDOVAL.

Peter WINCHILL, mentioned, DOB: 12-10-42, Wilson Green High
School Principal. 2100 N. Ulrich Rd., Port., OR 97201.

Nate DAVIS, mentioned, DOB: 10-30-58, Humanities Teacher -
Wilson Green High School. 2100 N. Ulrich Rd., Port., OR 97201.

Sgt. Don Wallace/7181   Approved_____

Portland Police Department
Portland, Oregon
Special Report

Clyde JACKSON, mentioned, DOB: 10-06-53, Humanities Teacher –
Wilson Green High School. 2100 N. Ulrich Rd., Port., OR   97201.

Desiree THOMPSON, mentioned, DOB: 11-15-54, Health Teacher –
Wilson Green High School. 2100 N. Ulrich Rd., Port., OR   97201.

ACTION TAKEN:

On Tuesday 11-12-96 at 9:00 a.m., Mr. Hieu NGUYEN and his attorney, Mr. Blake SAYLOR, met with Det. Sgt. Bob HAMMOND and
myself here at North Precinct. The meeting was for the purpose
of re-interviewing Mr. NGUYEN regarding the Sex Abuse allegations brought against him by two female students. The events
allegedly occurred on Tuesday, 11-5-96, at the school.

The interview was tape recorded with Mr. NGUYEN'S and Mr.
SAYLOR'S consent.

Mr. NGUYEN was again advised of the charges brought against
him by Malisha JONES and Sasha ANDERSON. He denied each.
NGUYEN said that he occasionally touched students inciden-
tally, or for emphasis during conversations, but never in a
sexual manner. (Refer to transcript.)

Investigation to continue.

Case# 96-0081A2 – Sex Abuse

Transcribed Tape – 11/12/96

Wallace: (Unintelligible) Detective Sergeant Don Wallace. This
is November 12th, 1996. Tuesday. It's 9:05 a.m. We're in the interview room, Portland Public Safety Facility, 2236 N. Hargrove,
Portland, Oregon. Okay, Mr., uh, Nguyen, you're aware that this
conversation is being recorded?

Nguyen: Yes.

Wallace: Due to an audio malfunction during last Tuesday's
initial interview with the suspect, we're having to go over the
same information. The case number is 96-0081A2. There will be no
arrest made today, the results of the investigation being nowhere near complete. More interviews have to occur. Mr. Nguyen,

Portland Police Department
Portland, Oregon
Special Report

you're aware of the charges of Sex Abuse by two of your
students, Sasha Anderson and Malisha Jones?

Nguyen: I am aware of the charges.

Wallace: When this investigation is complete, the results will
be submitted to the District Attorney's office. Mr. Nguyen,
please clearly explain your take on the events that took place
during your fifth period science class on Tuesday, November
fifth of this year.

Nguyen: First I would like to say that I deny all of the
charges.

Wallace: Yes. Please just slowly recount the events as best you
can.

Nguyen: Some girls at one of the lab tables were playing
around, Sasha Anderson was among them. Some hydrochloric acid
spilled. From across the room, I was helping another student,
I saw that Sasha was laughing about something, and then the
accident happened. I asked her to meet me in my office. I made
sure that the other students at her table were cleaning the
spill properly, then I met Sasha in my office.

Wallace: Was the office door open or closed when you began your
meeting with her?

Nguyen: Open. It was open. I told her that she was receiving
a warning for being off-task and the next time she neglected
her safety responsibilities she would receive a detention. She
said that she was sorry and she understood, then we reentered
the classroom. I - uh, yes okay - I returned to the student I
had been helping before the spill. When I looked up to check
on Sasha's group, some other students had gathered around her.
She was upset, crying, you know, but the group got back on task
when they saw me watching them. The evil eye.

Wallace: And was there any kind of incident with Malisha Jones
the same period?

Nguyen: Toward the end of the period, during journal time, I
had to approach Malisha because she was trying to get Sasha's

Portland Police Department
Portland, Oregon
Special Report

attention by waving her arms and mouthing something from
across the room. I began to walk toward Malisha and she turned
around and continued her writing. I think I leaned over her
shoulder and said, "Good choice," or something like that. It is
very hard sometimes to remember everything exactly of course.
I am involved with so many things at one time, my mind jumps
from one thing to the next, it is difficult to recall something
exactly. But I know I did not harass or sexually touch those
two students. There have been times when I have touched a student's shoulder, for emphasis during a conversation, or maybe
I patted someone on the back when they did something good, but
never in a sexual way.

Wallace: Have you ever touched students while you were disciplining them?

Nguyen: No.

Wallace: Have you –

Nguyen: Well, I am sorry. Occasionally, thumping them lightly
on the chest with a finger or two, but no sexual contact.
Nothing other than that, the thumping.

Wallace: Did you touch Sasha Anderson as you disciplined her
in your office last Tuesday?

Nguyen: I might have thumped her on the chest, right here
(points to area approximately three inches below base of
throat) as I spoke with her, but, to be very honest, I cannot
remember clearly. I might have done that, however.

Wallace: Another of your students, Carson Sandoval, claims to
have witnessed both incidents. From his seat, could this student see clearly both into the office and Malisha Jones's seat?

Nguyen: Carson could see into the office because he sits across
from it, but I think he would have to move a little bit to get
a clear view of Malisha.

Wallace: Are you aware of any kind of relationship between
Sandoval and the two girls?

Portland Police Department
Portland, Oregon
Special Report

Nguyen: They are all friends, but I am not sure how close. I see them talking in the halls sometimes.

Wallace: Is there anything you'd like to add? Of course, if something occurs to you later, we'll conduct a follow-up.

Nguyen: I guess I am surprised still over all of this. When Peter (Winchill) called me in last Tuesday, I had no idea what was about to happen. I hope that my colleagues will paint a different picture of me. People like Nate Davis or Clyde Jackson. Desiree Thompson. I am concerned about my reputation when this gets cleared up. My character has been damaged I think. I still want to teach in this community. I love teaching.

Wallace: Be assured we're trying to get to the bottom of this as quickly as we can, Mr. Nguyen.

Each Dying Moment

There had been a number of staff lounge blow-ups before, mostly over this or that school-related crisis or the latest district controversy, but Nate couldn't recall one ever coming as close to a brawl as when Uli Wegman and Clyde Jackson squared off over Hieu's case.

It happened Friday of the week the charges were leveled, the two men having already tangled during Winchill's initial briefing. Of course, the feud had been ripening for years, ever since Uli arrived in November of '81 as a long-term sub and managed to annoy most of the staff at only the second meeting he attended by saying he wanted to "forget about how many idiots walk the earth" during a presentation on how to combat Wilson Green's low parental involvement and community support. His brand of elitism brought out the worst in Clyde, a man who intimately knew the hardships with which most of his students were dealing and who took pride in having learned himself out of poverty.

So when Uli finished his cup of yogurt and announced to everyone at the main lounge table that he had "simply told the sergeant the truth" about Hieu, Clyde sat up straight, lowered his salami and cheddar sandwich onto his paper sack, and raised a finger.

"Get that outta here." Clyde took a quick look behind him, pushed his chair back and leaned out over the table. Both Desiree Thompson and Nate stood up on either side of him and tried to calm, but there was no doing. Everyone stopped eating.

"I swear, you mess with his reputation in any way, shape, or form with your jealous bullshit, I'll make it so you *can't* teach here. Understand me?"

"Easy," Desiree said, holding onto Clyde's arm. "Not worth it. Never has been."

"This is different."

Seemingly unmoved, Uli pushed his own chair back, crossed his legs and brushed a few crumbs from his slacks. When Clyde finally sat back down, Uli took a sip of his apple juice and shook his head.

"I just told the sergeant some things I've seen during Hieu's labs is all. No one here has actually *watched* him teach, correct?" He raised his eyebrows and glanced up and down the table. "I drop by a fair amount to discuss this or that. Now, I've never seen anything of a *sexual* nature, but he does touch students, Clyde. Signals do get mixed." Uli smiled when Clyde wouldn't look at him. "So please, save your anger. Maybe for someone at home."

Like it had been choreographed, Nate, Desiree, and Max Walker shot up to seize Clyde before he could fully extend himself across the table. Napkin dispenser jabbing into his chest, Clyde spewed something about tearing Uli a new mouth, but then pushed himself up. By the time Teresa Blanchard, the perpetually disheveled vice principal, rushed in, he had sat down again and was chewing on his sandwich, watching Uli's eyes.

"What happened?" Blanchard said, her tinny voice puncturing the silence. "I thought I heard someone yelling." She looked, as usual, as if she'd just spent fifteen hours as a hostage in a bank heist, her eyes red and glassy, purplish semicircles beneath them.

No one spoke. In the pause, Uli gathered his juice can, sandwich container, and yogurt cup into his lunch box, pushed in his chair and left through the doorway to the office.

Teresa Blanchard muttered that she must have been hearing things, it had been quite a day already. She followed Uli and a hush fell in the lounge. Someone called Uli "a sad pecker" and people chuckled.

When the first bell for sixth period rang, Clyde, Nate, and Desiree remained at the table after the mouth-wiping, mint-popping exodus.

"I cannot apologize for hating that guy," Clyde said after the room had gone still. The muted hallway cacophony framed the quiet.

"One frustrated dude," Nate said.

"Hey, you know, I don't care a lick if the man's frustrated. We're all frustrated here. Frustrated's part of the deal. But he has no right to fling that bullshit around. I'm serious, I won't take it anymore, and if Chilly won't take a stand, I will."

Desiree rose with a smirk and crumpled her lunch sack.

"Now what does that mean? You gonna go beat his bony ass? Show him what time it is? Please."

Clyde looked up at her. A staredown. After several tense beats, his brow softened and he grinned.

"Touché."

—⁓—

The afternoon seemed to be stretching out long to Nate as he circulated amongst student groups struggling with a poetry project. Each group, he had instructed during a mini-lesson at the beginning of the period, was to come up with an effective strategy for presenting a poem by a twentieth-century Central or South American poet, then deliver a five-minute lesson to the whole class the next day. It was a simple activity he'd orchestrated for a few years now, with generally positive results; but there was no denying it had lost some of its appeal, too many lessons seeming a bit stale.

After a time he knelt beside one of the groups and asked how things were progressing and immediately fell to thinking of last night, how he'd been unable to keep Lang from leaving angry. Her face when she said the word *sick*. Then Laura Pelican, a raisin-eyed, flat-nosed girl who'd been reporting her group's status, asked, "So, like, what do you think, Mr. D?"

Nate had no clue as to what the fruity-breathed girl was talking about, and didn't want to admit it since he had just reminded everyone of the need for effective listening.

"Sounds good," he said. "What does everyone else think?"

All five students voiced their agreement and began scooting away from each other.

"Whoa." Nate stood, unconsciously puffing out his chest. "We still have twenty minutes."

"You said we didn't have to be a group since we can't agree on nothing," Laura said.

"Must have misheard you, I'm sorry. Not an option. You guys have time to work something out."

Charles Caldwell, a boy in overalls about four sizes too large, mumbled, "Man, this *sucks*." Nate motioned for him to return his desk to the circle, squatted down and asked softly about his thoughts on an after-school conference or a phone call home. And at that moment, watching the kid's face, he could hear Aaron Harrington.

Fuck you, Davis. Round one, you dumb-ass bitch.

The quick twist of the blade. Smells of October evening, alcohol and bubblegum. Did Charles Caldwell know any secrets?

When the boy scooted, still glowering, back toward the group, Nate slipped away. By the time he leaned against his desk at the front of the room, his legs covering the poster of John Cleese in the midst of a ham-string-popping silly walk, he'd already blocked out Aaron's voice by working himself back into thoughts of the previous night.

From the edge of the coffee table, he'd opened his eyes and watched Lang drive away up Fifteenth Avenue. The hail had been falling hard, wind shaking the gold-tinted shrubs. He'd come close to chasing her down out in the driveway, telling her to trust him, the Asia journey would prove to be just another stage of their relationship. But it wouldn't have helped, he told himself once more as he gazed over the chattering class; Lang would've cursed him out at the least. Chasing her would have only made it seem that he was doubting his decision.

But what if he was? Finding Sammy could well prove impossible. Then again, he'd often wanted to see parts of Asia, ever since the vagabond days of his early twenties, backpacking around Europe and taking Greyhound and Green Tortoise cross-country in search of what he had dubbed "raw life." He'd heard stories about the mystical East from some of the more hard-core fellow travelers. Sunrise on the Ganges. Sunset at Borobudur.

When a student approached, he caught himself and checked his watch.

"All right," he said. How often in a school day he prefaced instructions with those two words. "Let's get the desks back."

The student standing next to him, Tammy Campbell, one of his main-streamed Special Ed kids, an affectionate girl with Down syndrome who enjoyed giving unsolicited hugs to students and teachers alike, tapped Nate's shoulder when he finished his announcement.

"Mr. Davis?" A glob of hazel snot crept its way toward Tammy's upper lip. "Mr. Davis, are you all right? I was watching you and you looked funny."

Nate scanned the room again before turning to her.

"Did I?" He looked into the girl's eyes. "You know, I'm trying to think about too many things at once probably. But I'm okay, thank you for asking, Tammy."

"Your face looked funny, Mr. Davis. You looked *worried* about something." The girl's tongue flicked out like a lizard's, twice, lapping at the snot stream.

"Well I guess that happens sometimes. I'm sort of a nut." He wanted to look away when he heard a desk still clattering, but instead focused on the girl. One of his daily goals: pause long enough to at least look at each kid. "How'd your group do?"

Tammy ran her sweatshirt sleeve across her nose and gave two thumbs up. When she started to break into one of her wiggly dances, Nate told her to grab a Kleenex from his desk, and then reviewed the homework assignment with the entire class before the bell: a one-page account of a day in ancient Athens from the perspective of a famous Greek philosopher they had discussed, another page from a slave's point of view.

Students grumbled, pressed the Velcro on their graffiti-plastered binders and filed out, Tammy turning to give her usual wave and grin, and Nate noticed a flicker of the old passion, the guarded satisfaction over enlarging a few kids' worlds. But while he believed his work was still crucial, the feeling was simply fading too quickly lately.

At the computer table next to his desk he readied the word processor and surveyed the wall opposite him: the posters of Pelé, Mia Hamm, Bob Marley, Georgia O' Keefe, one of Michelangelo's *Unfinished Prisoners*, and Chief Joseph interspersed with quotations from the likes of Cicero ("A thankful heart is not only the greatest virtue, but the parent of all other virtues") and Mark Twain ("A man cannot be comfortable without his own approval"). Nate looked at the collection, image and word soon blending. It was good to sit in the after-class silence. Did all of it—his desire to find Sammy, his dissatisfaction with teaching—amount to a lack of gratitude? Did he genuinely approve of himself? Good lord. The questions began their demented dance.

8 November 1996

Peter,

    This is to let you know that I'm taking a half-year leave. You were right: I would like a little time to recuperate. I hate to leave the kids mid-year, but I've realized that I was being stubborn in wanting to return so soon. (Stubborn is putting it mildly. How does pigheaded sound?)

    Thanks for your support over the years, especially lately. I'll deal with the paperwork from my end and leave a framework of plans for the sub. As of now, I'm planning to return next fall. Please see that the necessary forms get in reasonably soon as I'd like to have everything in order before winter break.

                    Yours,

                    Nate Davis

P.S. Desiree has offered to take on the Tuesday/Thursday tutoring program.

Though he worried that any remaining desire to return to Wilson Green in the fall might completely fade, there was no reason to hurry the decision. Better to let go, see where things led. Yet doing so would prove challenging, as ever.

It was something Hieu had spoken of a few times during their beery post-workout talks, this idea of learning to live confidently in the midst of life's greyness, the tendency in most Western cultures toward impatient, ambiguity-fearing, either/or thinking. On a couple of occasions, he'd also relayed his mother's belief in the constant intersection of the spirit and material worlds, the intermingling of dimensions many people choose to ignore.

While they mostly puzzled Nate, these talks of spirits and mortality and of dealing with uncertainty, Hieu's words had always gotten under his skin, made him aware that each moment was dying, his life was sprinting onward, days never coming back. But then it was these same realizations that had invariably pushed him to set about grading papers, paying bills, or watching Monday Night Football, music videos, or sitcoms. The thought of living with a bold acceptance of uncertainty and

of death had always seemed too awesome to consider more than occasionally, only at those times when some nebulous voice demanded that
he dig deeper, stop charging around so blindly, pull out his journal and
grab some impressions. Even Hieu had confessed to having difficulty
embracing mortality; it was merely something he often suspected might
point him down a path that made him feel more alive.

For Hieu, however, there had always been a bigger obstacle to such a
state of being than Nate ever realized, namely the daily imaginings of his
father's blue-glazed eyes, his bombed village, and the young point man
he'd blown apart in the name of liberty. Death, for Hieu, wasn't something
to meditate upon, let alone embrace. Not after what had happened in the
forests of Tay Ninh.

A Taste of Killing

After the riverbank wave good-bye to Hoa and Lang—watching them drift off on the bamboo raft under a heavy midday sun—Minh had guided Hieu back to the camouflaged National Liberation Front camp outside the nearby village of Tam Loc.

For Hieu, the separation from his mother and sister was easier than he had expected, at least for the first few days; being closer than he'd ever been to his world-wise older brother seemed to adequately fill the void. But when the time came to follow Minh's orders to join the struggle and to address him by the code name *Ba Cham,* Hieu began to miss Hoa and Lang as sharply as he missed his father. It had been only two weeks since he'd found the upper half of his father's body lying near their obliterated compound, two weeks of enduring the B-52 raids through which it seemed the Americans were trying to erase the entire region. The guerrillas, though, Hieu now among them, had managed to hide and survive, except for a few groups of men.

When the shock of having his life cracked open by the bombs began to abate somewhat, Hieu finally accepted that he'd become part of the storied Viet Cong. His older brother, now angrier than ever, had recently been promoted as assistant to one of the NLF's Central Committee members.

Whenever Minh had visited during the previous four years, he tried to explain to his skeptical parents that the Americans were yet another group in a long line—the Chinese, the Mongols, Khmers, French, Japanese—bent upon eradicating Vietnamese cultures and that he'd chosen a path he hoped they could learn to be proud of. But Hoa and her husband remained convinced that the spirits would eventually take care of the foreign devils; they had no idea what the enemy even looked like, so it wasn't worth the energy to become riled up or scared. Yet Minh had persisted in warning the other villagers about what was to come. For four years leading up to the first bombs, he spoke to his people of such abstract things as Vietnamese pride and liberation, of flying metal beasts and more foreign domination. To Hieu, the words themselves had sounded important enough, but it was his brother's passion that always held his attention.

So when it came time for Hieu to leave on his first mission, he asked Minh, or *Ba Cham*, to pray for him so that he'd have the passion needed to survive the long, violent struggle.

"You must *focus* upon what you're doing," Minh said. His already lean face had become more severe, cheekbones jutting out, the corners of his large-lipped mouth bent downward. "You're helping save your homeland. That will give you the fire. Think, also, of what they did to our village."

The pep talk worked, at least for a short while; it helped keep Hieu from dwelling upon how much he missed his mother and sister. After rolling up the pant legs on his black pajamas and slipping on his new "Ho Chi Minh sandals" made of old jeep tires, he obediently filled his pack with the prescribed essentials: another pair of pajamas, two pairs of underpants, mosquito netting, a few square meters of light nylon (for a raincoat or a roof), his twenty-kilogram ration of rice, a hunk of salt, a piece of monosodium glutamate, a few strips of dried beef, and his "elephant's intestines"—the common term for the long tubes of rolled cotton that could be filled with rice and slung across the back.

When everything seemed to be in order, he made sure his Chinese-made AK-47 was clean, stuffed ammo into the side pouches on his pack, and met one last time with Minh before joining his group at midnight at the edge of the village. His brother was waiting for him in the shadow of a banyan tree.

"You will live like a hunted animal the next month of your life," Minh said, skewering his attention. "You are young, but very strong. You must be constantly alert or you will die. Do you understand this?" He waited for Hieu to nod before he went on. "Malaria is a problem as always, be careful. There are many vipers where you are going, too. Keep your mind *active* at all times."

It was a last-minute crash course, even after the exacting two weeks of training. Minh's eyes pierced the remnants of Hieu's denial, the stealth and brutality of the ordeal ahead sinking in further.

"Remember." Minh grabbed Hieu's skinny arms just above the elbows. "You will *collapse* mentally if you don't constantly remind yourself that you're fighting for your homeland. You will see many bad things, so you must remain in control of your feelings. You are understanding this?"

Tears coated Minh's eyes.

"You're scaring me," Hieu said.

"You need the fear to stay focused. Keep telling yourself that we're fighting with one aim: Remove the Americans. Simple. Don't let yourself get swayed by any ideological rantings you hear. We are fighting to free our people. It's what they want."

"Yes," Hieu said, wincing from Minh's grip.

"I know this is happening too fast, but we need you."

Hieu's team called for him. For an instant, the brothers regarded each other. Then Minh leaned in close and whispered the last words Hieu would hear him speak: "Don't forget what they did to father. Family is everything. Now go."

After completing only a few nighttime missions, Hieu learned to recall Minh's words clearly. While he cooked over a carefully built smokeless fire or treated his insect bites, he would replay his brother's command over and over in attempts to brace his understanding of why he was in the midst of such bloody situations.

There was the convoy of American and South Vietnamese trucks they had blown up, then the American platoon they ambushed their fourth night out. It was during these astonishing episodes that Minh's words sounded most crisp. Hieu would hear the cries for medic and mama, for people with strange names like Suzanne or Clarise, and he'd summon his brother's directive in order to focus, to recall the simple reason for it all.

It had slowly become easier, though, especially after reports of a mass killing in An Giang Province, a hamlet called Vong-The: the Americans had shot nearly a hundred villagers. And of course there was the Thuan Yen massacre on March 16, of which details were still spreading through the villages: over five hundred Vietnamese civilians dead. With the reports also circulated what would become an oft-quoted phrase from one American major, after he ordered another hamlet bombed to bits: "We had to destroy it to save it."

Much later, those words would sometimes seep through Hieu, now and then while he was teaching, often accompanying images of his father, or of Minh, or the rubble that was once his village. Three years after arriving in Portland, after learning passable English, he'd come upon yet another quote, this one in a popular news magazine, an admission from a returned American soldier: "We usually couldn't tell who or where the enemy was. We just shot first, asked questions later." The amazing words, images, the melee of feelings. Hieu would never become immune.

When the guerrillas slipped like ghosts into VC-friendly hamlets and discussed with more informed villagers how the Tet Offensive had clearly shaken many American citizens' support for the war even harder, Hieu's spirits picked up further, despite the cold fact that many VC had perished during the campaign. He grew more and more convinced that he just might have fallen into something worthy of his sacrifice, something his father would have been proud of had he been able to understand the nuances of the fight.

But then, not far into the spring, his swelling ardor for the long, violent struggle was abruptly snuffed out.

He had been huddled on a thicketed hillside at the high end of dusk, awaiting an American patrol, twelve men total, that crept along an established two-foot-wide path, weapons at ready. Bitterns, lorikeets, and finches flitted about in the understory, songs carrying through the stillness. Cicadas chirred. The air had just begun to cool, the usual steamy *green* scent tinged with smoke from a distant fire. The lead soldier, a husky black man of no more than twenty, appeared confident establishing a perimeter, a cigarette dangling from his lower lip. And then it happened, one of the few moments in Hieu's life that he sensed was predetermined: the point man stepped directly onto the hidden grenade and mine.

From his concealed perch, he'd made a fist as the soldiers approached the magic spot, and was initially proud when the black man hit the target. But when the smoke and the debris began to clear, when the spray of bullets ceased, when he saw that the soldier's legs had ripped from the torso and landed on the red clay ground meters away, the burning in his stomach began. He would later think that if it hadn't been for his stomach, he just might have considered the scene a dream.

He ducked low as the Americans fired their rounds into the forest, some of them screaming, then peeked up again when the shooting stopped. The dying man made high-pitched whimpers. Blood sprayed over the other men's pants and boots, and nobody bothered to pull out a compress. Hieu envisioned his father's body—the eyes and the missing legs—and he understood, there in his concealed hillside perch, that he had lost the heart to kill in the name of anything. Even in the midst of what felt like shock, it had been that simple.

When the *whop-whop-whop* of the copter receded, the dead man's legs gathered up and slipped into a black bag and loaded in a small nearby clearing, the birds returned and resumed their evening calls. Then, after one yellow-haired boy took off his helmet and knelt and laid a pack of cigarettes on the spot where the black man blew apart, the Americans retreated. Hieu, though, remained frozen. It seemed more humid now. His pajamas soaked. At length he heard the two distinct wood-on-wood clicking noises that meant it was time to rejoin his team, but still he couldn't move. The black man had burst into the air, his body twisting in a shaft of soft forest light. Staggering how fast the other men had reacted, their bullets tearing up the surrounding shrubs, fierce voices making them seem so invincible.

Incredible, too, how perfectly the mine had worked. It was the first he had ever hidden, though he'd watched the technique at least a hundred times on pathway after pathway: the grenade with its pin removed weighed down by the mine set on top, soil and brush and dead leaves covering everything. If the mine was detected and defused, the grenade would still trigger. But the black man hadn't carried a sweeper, hadn't even looked down. The Standard Operating Procedure had been abandoned. Or perhaps it was simply a lapse. Regardless, it had all worked too well. Been too easy.

It wasn't until the end of twilight, when one of the others finally thought it safe to come fetch him, that he was able to stand. They returned to the nearest village two valleys away, Hieu absently listening to his partner's recounting of the day's activities, the listing of other deeds, while he continued to replay the moment of the explosion.

That night, in the temporary safety of a village hut, amid the banter that usually marked mealtime, he refused the catfish supper. He curled up on a sleeping mat. The guerrillas, he'd learned immediately after joining, were experts at joking around, performing for each other, and singing in order to combat the stress, just as the Americans were adept at their own forms of release. But not even the reassurance of his companions eased the burning in his stomach that night. Another defining moment of his life had come so hard and fast, so quickly on the heels of the last. The spirits had spoken. While he believed in the promise of freedom, believed in his hatred of the men who had destroyed his village, he wasn't made for the struggle's requirements. A taste of killing was enough. The time had come to give in fully to missing his mother and sister, his father, his people.

Knees drawn up, Hieu turned toward one of the hut's bamboo walls, the desire to run away cutting through the heart of his wish to live up to Minh's brave example.

Ice-coated Keyhole

The investigation dragged on longer than anyone, including Sergeant Wallace, had expected. Some conflicting student testimonies required follow-up meetings, transcripts were misplaced in the cluttered North Precinct office, and the two-week winter break made it harder to track people down.

By the time classes resumed in early January, though, forty-four students and nearly three-quarters of the staff had been interviewed, Hieu had given three testimonies, and Wallace finally began to see some openings in the case. But when Nate was called in, a week before semester's end, the detective was forced to incorporate a new element into the story of what had happened in Hieu's fifth-period science class.

It was an exceptional day for Nate, even before the interview, what with an in-class fistfight and an early dismissal due to freezing rain. The fight erupted second period between two freshmen who'd broken up the evening before. The girl, as it happened, took offense to a certain obscenity mouthed by her ex and saw fit to burst from her seat, charge across the room as Nate was introducing a short story assignment, and tag the boy across the face. Shoving, tackling, rapid-fire slapping ensued, the boy's desk flipped over, arms and legs flung wildly to the delight of everyone except Nate, who, finally realizing it was his job to do something, began shouting *Whoa* in his best Sylvester Stallone, extracted the screeching girl from the maroon-faced boy and escorted her to Max Walker's office.

So the day had started off with a rush of passion. Something he secretly enjoyed given the sense of release brought about by his primal roaring, his funk seeming to fade a bit more with each full-throated *whoa*. He was down mainly because he'd spoken with Lang only a handful of times since she had fled his apartment. The Sunday after their wine-fueled late-night clash, he'd called to ask if they could meet again.

"I can maybe explain better," he said.

When no reply came, but no hang-up either, he tried to keep her on the line.

"Lang, this doesn't mean we're over. Like you say sometimes, it's good to air out the soul."

But that was as far as he'd gotten. She hung up without a good-bye, leaving him alone in the kitchen in his bathrobe looking out at the bald vine maples in the backyard.

When he returned to the classroom after depositing the flailing girl in Max's office, Nate found that his other students had commenced social hour. Kids leaning against windowsills, sitting on desktops, Jamila Watkins up on the whirring and clicking heater practicing X-rated dance moves, Bryan Jaspers and Mario Ramirez drawing oversize sex organs on the blackboards. Instead of shouting, however, he opted for stepping back into the hallway. He waited for nearly a minute, listening to the whispers, threats, and shufflings, Mario telling someone to "sit the hell down or I'll beat your mama's boy ass," then reentered and strolled to the front of the room, letting his eyes speak. Everyone was seated.

In front of the blackboard, he stopped and examined a googly-eyed ape with large droopy breasts and an even larger erect penis, testicles the size of pineapples. "Lovely," he said.

Most everyone turned to look at Bryan and Mario, but no one spoke. Jamila Watkins put her hands over her face. Mario, mouth quivering, clearly on the brink of watering himself. But Nate let the silence stand awhile longer, until the dismissal bell rang and a few students began gathering their notebooks.

"Hold on," he said, stepping back toward the door. "One thing before you go. A nugget of advice I received once in a coal-blackened village outside Istanbul … It was this skinny old man, had a long white beard, food all caught up in it. Some peas, carrot shavings as I recall. Anyway, he told me something important." His face was perfectly stern, the room stone-quiet again. *"Don't drink out of any strange toilets."*

Nate opened the door and students began filing out, some smiling, a few with pronounced confusion on their faces. Jamila Watkins, as she entered the hallway with one eyebrow raised, said, "That man crazy."

He let out a laugh. Best, he'd come to believe, to throw curve balls every now and then. Keep the little wieners guessing.

Then toward the end of sixth period, the intercom clicked on and Winchill announced there would be an early dismissal. Emergency bus routes were read off, warnings about fallen power lines given, and Nate decided to flow along with the frenzy by raising the shades and inviting everyone to come look.

"Lights, please?" he said to Milton Valenzuela, a rotund, withdrawn student on the other side of the room.

In the dimness, kids huddled close and listened to the rain crackle. The asphalt near the commons had already taken on a milky sheen.

"Man, most teachers won't let us go to the windows," someone in the crowd said.

Milton, who had just joined the group, stood next to Nate and mumbled, "Uh-huh."

Amid his students, Nate raised an index finger to his lips and waited for everyone to catch on. First only a few kids saw, then more heads turned and soon the room was silent save for a few laughs. Thirty-seven sophomores and Nate, in the low grey light, gazing out at the freezing rain. For almost a minute the quiet held, and he observed the teenagers around him. How many had already been hardened to the point of not stopping to watch and listen? How many came from homes where such a pause would be looked upon as wasteful or downright weird? From reading their poems and short stories, though, he knew most of their souls were still open, even if just barely in some cases.

He turned to Milton—the chubby brown face, eyes transfixed on the nearest window, for a few moments free from the teasing and the strain— and sensed it again, the power of teaching. The ability to create a space where kids could step away from the hurry and the drama long enough to just notice things: it could still give him goose bumps.

Then someone farted and everyone scattered like pieces of shattering ice.

After reminding about the power lines, he gave his customary dismissal nod, watched the rumbling exit, and turned to fetch his coat from his closet. Abdi Ahmed leaned back through the doorway and said, "That was cool, Mr. D," but shot back into the hallway before Nate could respond.

Satchel crammed with story drafts, reading journals, and his planning book, he returned to the windows. He liked that his hometown had fairly distinct seasons. The snow and ice storms during his boyhood had never failed to bring some happiness, even after Sammy left. Granted, there had abruptly been no one to chase him around the backyard like a deranged yeti, but Acacia and Grandpa tried to pick up some of the slack with respectable snowball fights.

Nate kept watching the crowded commons from his solitary spot, forcing himself not to glance at his truck over in the parking lot, and shortly the intercom came on again, this time Sergeant Wallace's voice.

"Mr. Davis, I realize you need to get home before the roads get bad, but I'd like to fit in one more interview. Shouldn't take long."

Nate said he'd be right down. Breaths coming shallower, he told himself what he'd practiced: it would go fine, everything would be all right. It had usually calmed him to dwell on such a simple phrase during stressful times, though he had never, in any instance over the course of his adult life, believed it deep down. *It'll be all right.* The words used to work, but their strange magic had vanished.

At the doorway, he looked across at Hieu's empty room before turning to survey his own. The narrow aisles, wall posters in shadow, his heaped desk. The quiet struck him, such a contrast to the morning's bustle. It seemed that he could sense the students' energy flowing by, out the door and into the hall, like Hieu had occasionally talked about.

When he turned around again, full of a peculiar sadness, Monty was walking straight toward him with two bulky rolls of brown paper towels.

"You outta here, bro?"

"My turn with the sarge, I just got the call."

Monty came to a stop, now palming the top of each roll.

"Did you hear?" he said, voice lowered even though no one else was close by.

Nate cocked his head.

"Chilly got a leave of absence request from Hieu today. Surprised you didn't hear already."

"Jesus."

"Probably just needs time to rebound. Get his head in shape before coming back to this friggin' madhouse."

"Yeah ... If everything gets cleared up."

Monty shook his head, half-smiling.

"Show a little faith, bro." He propped one of the rolls against his chest and slapped Nate's satchel. "Need to finish up. You be safe out there."

In Winchill's office, in front of the mahogany desk, Wallace sat with his hands locked behind his head, a small black tape recorder and a near-empty mug of black coffee on the lamp table beside him. Winchill was still out front seeing buses off. Though the door was wide open, Nate rapped his knuckles under the nameplate.

"Mr. Davis." Wallace rose and extended a hand. "Thanks for obliging on short notice. I'm worried the weather'll keep school closed awhile."

Nate lowered his satchel beside the chair facing Wallace and sat. Why hadn't Hieu mentioned the leave of absence? Pretty major decision—why the secret? They'd gone out for a few beers only two nights before.

But he couldn't distract himself long. The tape recorder made the interview set-up even more intimidating than he expected. Whenever he'd asked other staff members about the discussions, nobody mentioned anything about a tape recorder, though of course he should have known. Desiree said that her interviews had actually been "good experiences," that it had been "sort of fun" talking about Hieu's professionalism.

Wallace excused himself, warmed his coffee in the lounge, then closed the door behind him.

"You're aware that this conversation will be recorded?" he said. Nate nodded, hands clasped. "All right, then let me just get this ... Okay, this is Detective Sergeant Wallace at Wilson Green High School. It's Wednesday, January 22, 1997 ... 3:04 p.m. I'm with Nate Davis, a humanities and creative writing teacher here. Mr. Davis, let me start by asking how you would describe Mr. Nguyen as a teacher."

Nate focused on the tape recorder's wheels.

"Committed, intense ... caring and firm." Just like he'd rehearsed.

"Have you ever witnessed any instances where Mr. Nguyen acted inappropriately toward students?"

"None at all." Something within him now—what he'd stashed in a far-off chamber—already beginning to emerge. Pitiful.

"How, in your opinion, do Mr. Nguyen's students view him?" Wallace's eyes remained steady on Nate's eyes.

"They respect him, definitely … I do think some kids might be a little nervous around him because, like I said, he's firm. He has very high expectations."

"But on the whole they respect him?"

"No doubt about it."

Wallace took a slow drink of coffee, his eyes not leaving Nate's face. Right then Winchill burst in and fetched his briefcase, saying he hoped everyone got home safely, the streets were awful, then shut the door again, a trail of cold air in his wake. Wallace's expression remained unchanged.

"I'll be more direct, Mr. Davis. Have you ever seen Mr. Nguyen make any sexual advances toward students, or even touch them in a way that might possibly be misunderstood?"

The locker room conversation still in Nate's mind. "Pardon?"

Wallace repeated the question and Nate glanced down at the tape recorder.

"I've never witnessed Hieu touch a student in a sexual way, no. I have seen him put a hand on kids' shoulders, or maybe tap their chests out in the hall to emphasize a point he was trying to make. I seriously doubt those were ever consciously sexual gestures, though."

Wallace lowered his mug to the lamp table and leaned forward, elbows on the ends of the armrests, fingers interlocked.

"Has Mr. Nguyen shared with you that he doesn't consciously harass his students?"

Nate shook his head, then said no when Wallace pointed to the recorder.

"Please just answer from your own perspective. Mr. Nguyen's intentions don't need to be guessed at here." Wallace pulled a notepad from a pocket of his navy blazer and jotted something. He looked no less formidable out of uniform. "So, just a couple more questions. It's come to my attention that you and Mr. Nguyen are friends outside of school."

"Yes." Mindful of every movement, Nate set his arms onto the armrests and made himself keep them there.

"I'm curious if you've ever heard him make any comments of a sexual nature regarding minors."

It felt, he would later think, as if the words had been lifted out. Like some part of him wanted to pin Hieu down, make him account, finally, for his enigmatic way. Take the leave of absence decision. God damn. It was that teasing effect, the classic male curse. Over beers on a normal day, you had a best friend you could talk to about things; when life hit hard and drinks couldn't come anywhere close to helping, you had guesswork and distance, unwittingly cold posturing that beat you down even more. Hieu just kept so much hidden so much of the time.

Nate concentrated on the recorder's wheels.

"About a year ago was the only time I've ever heard anything at all like that come out of him. He mentioned something about girls here being sexy and curious, or something like that. We'd just finished some racquetball. It was a dumb remark, nothing I took seriously."

"This was out of the blue? Or had you been discussing young girls?"

"Oh jeez … I made some stupid comment about how some of the girls here like to wear tight clothing to show off and Hieu just agreed, said they were curious or something. I can't recall his exact words."

"Of course," Wallace said. "Are there any other exchanges you remember? Other comments?"

Nate forced a cough. What in hell was going on? It was like he was some rattled, confused teen, the idea of withholding the truth terrifying and tempting at once.

"He sometimes says how full of life his students are, they glow with vitality or whatever. But I've never considered it odd or anything. He just really cares about kids. Has three great ones of his own."

"Yes …" Wallace took another slow drink of coffee. "Well, I think that's fine for today. I may need to speak with you again later."

Nate heard Winchill outside the door say something about tire chains.

"So you know," he said, "I'm here three more days. I'll be taking a leave of absence second semester."

"I'll make a note of that, thanks. I was sorry to hear about that incident in the parking lot. Not that that's necessarily related to your leave."

"It is."

When Wallace shut off the recorder, Nate settled into his chair and noticed his undershirt sticking to his back. The voices beyond the door gone now.

Wallace gathered his notepads, let out a pronounced sigh and reached down to unplug the recorder.

"Better get a move on," he said, giving Nate his most sympathetic look, which amounted to a slight raising of the brow. "I probably won't need to conduct a follow up, just a habit of mine to say it on tape. If I have any questions, I'll call tomorrow."

Nate nodded. He sat forward when Wallace stood.

"I'd like to say something off the record."

"Mr. Davis, I'm not a reporter. This is a criminal investigation."

"Those were private thoughts of his. I don't think he touched those girls. He loves his work too much."

"Thanks for the input, but he communicated those thoughts and that affects this case."

"Look … I had no right to even bring it up. That conversation took place over a year ago, the details are pretty foggy."

"Mr. Davis. I asked you a fair question and you answered it. Thank you for your input."

Wallace stepped out, his mug left behind.

Rain bounced off the office window, meshing with the steady buzz of the overhead lights, and right outside a twig cracked and fell onto the icy grass. Still on the edge of his chair, Nate listened. Closed his eyes and shook his head slowly.

In the parking lot, he took baby steps toward his truck, the only vehicle left except for Monty's grey El Camino. The soccer field completely frozen over now, the stinging rain falling harder. When he extended his key to the lock, he saw that ice had coated the keyhole; he turned and leaned against the slick door, pulled his coat collar higher.

After checking the passenger door, Nate headed back to the building. Apart from the rain and his crunching footsteps, he heard nothing— none of the usual traffic, no voices or distant industrial hum. But as he began climbing the stairs to the staff lounge, Monty broke the peace by yanking the door open.

"Bet those locks are *caked*." Monty stomped his big brown boots onto the ice and tilted up his face, stuck out his tongue and let the rain pelt him. "Saw you from Desiree's room, bro. Let's have a look."

By the time Nate caught up, Monty had already melted the ice on the lock with a tiny metal rod that heated up when extended, a device normally dangling from the rainbow *Visit Reno* key chain clipped to his work belt.

"Got this little sucker from my wife. Sweet stocking stuffer." He reached for Nate's keys, inserted the correct one on the first try, and thumped away the ice along the door's edges. "So how'd the interview go?" He passed the keys back and opened the door.

"Not bad."

"You set the guy straight?"

"Did my best."

Ice beads coated Monty's hair.

"Well Christ, Nate-o, cheer up. You look like you just got knocked in the nuts."

Monty chuckled and patted Nate's shoulders before shuffling back to the building, and when the parking lot was still again, Nate got in and turned up the heater. The sky showed no signs of clearing and the rain beat loud against the hood and roof.

He crept along Martin Luther King Jr. Boulevard toward his apartment trying to purge the old images, Aaron Harrington's voice still detectable over the whirling Javon Jackson sax on the radio.

Fuck you, Davis.

Round one.

A few blocks from his apartment, sliding along at ten miles per hour, he started yelling curses. Hit the steering wheel with one hand, steadied it with the other. Fuck it. He needed out. Fly away. Leave behind the inexplicable habit of wrecking everything he thought he held dear. *Scared of happiness,* he wrote on the first line of the first page of his new journal that evening after five glasses of merlot.

Scared of *happiness?* He picked up the Bali postcard and read it again.

Page 6   Case# 96-0081A2

                        Portland Police Department
                             Portland, Oregon
                             Special Report

At 11:16 a.m., I called Malisha JONES into the office and reminded her that our conversation would be tape recorded and
that her testimony would be crucial to this criminal investigation. I then asked her to recount the events during Mr.
NGUYEN'S fifth period science class on Tuesday (11-5-96).

JONES stated that she didn't see NGUYEN touch Sasha ANDERSON
in his office, but ANDERSON had sworn that sexual contact
occurred. When I asked JONES to clarify, she reported that
ANDERSON said NGUYEN grabbed her breasts and pushed his body
up against hers. I asked JONES again if she had personally
seen this happen and she said no. JONES then said that NGUYEN
had often touched both herself and ANDERSON in sexual ways,
grabbing their bra straps or brushing up against them. When I
asked why none of these previous incidents had been reported,
JONES replied, "No one would have believed us." I wondered why
she thought that and she said, "Because the teacher is always
right at this damn school."

I asked JONES again to recount what had happened to her during last Tuesday's lab. NGUYEN, she said, came up from behind
and snapped her bra strap, then slapped the upper part of her
buttocks. She had been trying to get ANDERSON'S attention
because she thought ANDERSON looked upset. She needed to "give
a smile or something." JONES reported that NGUYEN whispered
"Good choice" after slapping her buttocks. JONES then turned
around and resumed writing in her science journal. I asked if
any other students had witnessed NGUYEN'S actions toward her
and JONES said, "I don't know, Carson SANDOVAL might have seen
something."

I pressed, saying I found it strange that nobody else immediately around her would have noticed such an aggressive incident involving a teacher. I pulled out Desmond BARNES'S sketch
of NGUYEN'S classroom. Before I could point out the layout of
the room, however, the proximity of her neighbors' seats and so
forth, JONES started crying. She said, "I knew you'd be against
us." I told her that her rights are as important as anyone's,
just as Mr. NGUYEN'S rights are important. JONES called NGUYEN

Portland Police Department
Portland, Oregon
Special Report

"a pervert." I waited for her to calm down and reminded her
that I was interviewing many students, but that her honest
testimony was most crucial for the investigation. JONES stood
and shouted, "I knew y'all wouldn't believe us!" then ran out of
the office. After a meeting with Principal WINCHILL and myself
a short time later, she was sent home. I'll conduct a follow-up
with her aunt (Cherise LOGAN) present.

Part Two

—⁓—

Sweet Paradise

To be a traveler on this earth
you must know how to die
and come to life again.

— Goethe

Bridge of Dust

A gecko scoped for insects above him. A muggy breeze brought whiffs of incense from the compound's Hindu shrine, burning garbage across the alley, and the orchids and bougainvillea. On the covered rooftop patio of the Suji Bungalows, Nate swigged at an orange soda and watched the gecko's black eyes, the motionless pale green body, and remembered how Iggy, the Kiwi front desk worker, had told him just that morning that if you hear *gek-oh* seven times in the night it's supposed to be good luck. He turned to look out over the maze-like neighborhood: other guesthouse patios, palm trees, satellite dishes in a hodgepodge of dwellings. He had to believe that he would come upon some good luck.

The day before, he'd made the twenty-three-hour trip from Portland to Denpasar with stops in LA, Honolulu, and Biak, near-constant thoughts of Lang, Hieu, and Sammy not quite making him forget how much he loathed air travel. Warped gamelan music over the plane's PA system, a shapely stewardess with aquamarine eyes and other half-conscious impressions: the extended, orange sherbet-like sunset after leaving LA, the sunrise's slow explosion over the island of Biak; magazine articles on quaint old Malacca, body language, and Danny DeVito. Then the slam of Kuta Beach. Hawkers, scabby dogs, surfer dudes and tourist bars.

He finished his soda and scooped a final forkful of nasi goreng. His soul would eventually catch up to him, he told himself. Things would begin to seem less surreal. While he'd envisioned tranquil umbrella-dotted beaches, rejection-steeled artists in straw hats displaying watercolors and batik sarongs, he reminded himself that he hadn't yet seen the "real" Bali. The *Lonely Planet* had listed warnings about Kuta, but he'd simply underestimated them. No worries, as Iggy would say. No worries.

For the next two days he inquired about wood carving at every museum and art shop he could find. Where a Westerner might go to learn the craft. The curators and dealers—and workers in various Kuta travel agencies—said that most any village would be fine, it would just be a matter of finding a master sympathetic (and poor) enough to take on such an apprentice. But Sammy had mentioned living next to an active volcano. And so Mount Batur was the best option, a number of locals concurring that an artisan who spoke decent English lived up there. Last they had heard, the old man still occasionally tolerated a casual drop-in student.

———

On the bus inland, he tried to ingest the scenes. Marlboro posters on roadside snack stands, paddies shimmering through rows of bamboo. Dogs nosing through trash. The driver, a teenage boy with heavy eyelids and puffy orange headphones, appeared at ease with the high speed, certain he would steer his latest batch of tourists safely over the head-jerking potholes.

It seemed to Nate that the Balinese probably thought most tourists were crazy. When he overheard a group of young backpackers seated behind him, college kids trying to impress each other with lists of remote places they'd been, he considered the refreshing perspective he'd encountered in the few Balinese he'd met so far: an aura of acceptance, graceful pride, rootedness. Romantic drivel? Maybe. But as the bus rattled onward toward the mountain, the air through the windows soon cooling, he reflected again that Sammy's choice of destination might not have been haphazard.

Road-stoned, ravenous, he made it to Penelokan, a village on Mount Batur's outer crater rim. Smoke and thin clouds swooped over the inner crater and down the brushy southern slope, and another gust brought good smells from a nearby food stall. The pack of college kids trudged off toward a pathway going down, a big-boned girl with a pink bandana on her head leading the charge, guidebook in hand. At the stall, Nate gobbled a solo lunch and watched a starling weave around a dainty cow that was lumbering up the road. A short while later ended up passing the same cow on foot just before coming upon a roadside market.

Large bell-like baskets, jittery roosters locked underneath, were tucked behind stands piled with durians and papayas, men hunched beside the baskets on wooden stools, whispering to each other as he passed through. His unshaven white face gleaming in the beams of hard sunlight through the fast-moving clouds. His backpack bobbing. Scents of jasmine, begonias, and raw meat mixed with exhaust from passing trucks. One ruddy-faced old woman was selling bags of industrial-waste-orange tortilla chips, *Happy-Tos*. And then another woman, much younger but with many wrinkles about the eyes and mouth, asked if he needed a place to stay. When he smiled and said yes, the woman, Agang, led him farther up the road to the lip of the outer crater and a cluster of cement-block-and-mortar dwellings with corrugated iron roofs. Road Mode, he thought, that what-the-hell attitude he'd sometimes tapped into on his Europe and USA trips. It was good to let go again, even if just slightly. In certain moments, Portland already felt like it was on a different planet; in others he was aware that his troubles had come right along with him, hidden passengers that couldn't care less where they went.

On his porch overlooking the volcano, a sliver of the emerald Bali Sea visible to the east, he let out a tension-purging yawp, and Agang's eight-year-old son, Katut, who was weeding a flower bed along the cliff's edge, screamed too. The boy picked up his trowel and resumed fluffing the earth, turned and smiled uneasily, much like he'd done a few minutes earlier. During check-in, when Nate explained that he was looking for his uncle, Agang had shooed the boy out to the flower beds before recommending the tourist information office. She knew of only one master carver in the entire Mount Batur area, but he had died a couple of years before.

That afternoon, after asking at the tourist office, a restaurant, and some souvenir stands, he hiked to the farthest edge of Penelokan along the slow-curving outer crater and came upon another shop, this one with an adjoining cafe. A sandwich board at the shop entrance: *Far From the Midding Crawd—Coffee, Tea, Carvings*.

When *Carvings* came into focus, Nate stopped. He turned, the cliff right next to him, and looked out at the different view of the volcano, cirrus clouds ribboning the sky. A rush of blood to his head, ears ringing.

Incredible that Sammy could be only a few steps away. Almost too easy, even with the head-spinning letdown of hearing the old master had died.

The years of wondering—holding the Indonesia card up close, examining the words, the Denpasar postmark—ramming into the scene before him. There was too much to ask. Tell. He turned back to the sandwich board, saw that the handwriting didn't look familiar, and resumed his approach.

Inside, a strong smell of lavender and fresh-stained wood made him swallow, then breathe through his mouth. Hundreds of wood carvings rested on five long fold-out tables and on shelves lining the room, some incense sticks burned in a cactus-shaped holder next to the unoccupied cash register, and a faint squeaking came from a wicker basket off in a corner, a paper plate sign above it: FREE. He went over and found three chinchillas, one of them yawning, and it was then that through the adjacent doorway raining down thick blue beads he heard a man call out a hello.

As he moved toward the voice, more carved faces watching him pass, Nate believed he had found his uncle. It had happened, like that. This was actually it. *Unbelievable.* While he didn't recognize the voice, part of him hadn't expected to, the years having surely altered Sammy in many ways. Whether it was the potent smells or something else, he wasn't sure, but his eyes watered when he pulled back the beads and entered the patronless cafe. Immediately to his left, a brown-bearded man in a multicolored vest with gold embroidered pheasants on the pockets slouched on a stool next to an early model espresso machine, a chalkboard reading *Out-of-this-world brownies!* propped behind him, an *International Herald Tribune* splayed across his lap.

Nate froze. Studied the man's face. Though the beard and the shoulder-length hair made him pause for a moment, he saw that it wasn't Sammy. The eyes too large, nose too feminine.

"How's life?" the man said.

A sensation like crawling spiders spread over Nate's neck.

"I'm looking for someone."

The man folded the newspaper, stood and adjusted his blue jeans, and pointed to the nearest table, a silver bracelet dotted with garnets ringing the scrawny wrist of his outstretched arm.

On one wall, three-by-five photographs were plastered from knee-level to ceiling, on the others hung various Bali tourism posters of beaches and temples, two bright-costumed women striking exotic dance poses. On the counter, a plastic-covered cake, untouched. Peter Gabriel's "In Your Eyes" played softly.

When they were both seated, Nate reached to the inside pocket of his windbreaker and pulled out the photo of Sammy giving the horseback ride.

"My uncle," he said. "He fought in Vietnam."

The guy's face slow-bloomed into a smile.

"You gotta be shittin' me, man."

By the time Nolan brought him a second espresso, the story had, for the most part, been filled in. Sammy and Nolan had worked with a master carver for six and a half years in a two-room bungalow in Tirta, a village beside the small lake at the mountain's base. They'd met at a Kuta party in January of '83 and had been looking to get into the same sort of "authentic gig," so agreed to team up and hitchhiked to Mount Batur with the intention of "living with a different sense of time." An elderly artisan named Nyoman took them in after they explained they would pay not only rent, but for all of the food and raw materials as well. They learned the craft slowly, taking only a few local vacations over all that time, and dug as deeply as they could into village life. But finally Sam grew restless, talked about moving on.

"Something wasn't settled," Nolan said. "But he didn't ever talk about it."

One July morning in '89, Nolan and Nyoman woke to find Sammy vanished, no note. Of his roughly 350 carvings, he took only one of the little figurines he'd practiced on at the very beginning. It was a man on his knees, hands reaching toward the sky, head cocked back, mouth wide open. He had loved that one. Used to say it was how he felt a lot of the time.

Throughout the story, Nate only nodded and asked a few questions, but when Nolan came to the part where he'd heard a rumor about where Sammy had gone, the caffeine kicked in.

"Some of the villagers said he went up to Thailand, this island southeast of Phuket called Ko Lanta," Nolan said, brownie crumbs at the corners of his mouth and on the napkin before him. He'd begun to blink often. "This one night, after a few bong hits, I guess he slipped his secret to one of the village girls right before falling asleep in her lap."

At this point Nolan started speculating on Mount Batur's imminent eruption and complaining about ill-mannered tourists, the type who don't ask locals permission for up-close photos. He then saw fit to share that he was settled in Penelokan for good probably, that Nyoman had died of pneumonia two years ago and that one of the old man's last wishes was for him to open up a shop and sell off all the carvings. The cafe was his girlfriend Bernice's idea. She was away on a trip to Komodo with some friends visiting from New York. And so on.

When Nate tucked the picture of Sammy and himself back into his windbreaker and rose to leave, Nolan seemed to awaken and pointed to the wall of three-by-fives.

"Check this out before you go, it's the only one I have of him."

Nate approached the wall, and the photo came into focus above Nolan's finger.

"This was during the second year." Nolan peeled it off, handed it over. "Nyoman's eighty-first birthday."

Nate held it up close. Standing next to a bald old man with glistening eyes, Sammy held a big can of Foster's, his face strong, mouth calm, no smile, the eyebrows still thick brown. The eyes looked different, though, as if he were searching the camera lens for some critical clue. The hair, too, had changed: thinner, slicker, the old bushiness gone, the sides pulled back, most likely in a ponytail. But it was him, locked in a moment twelve years earlier, when Nate was twenty-six, a so-called man already.

After a long look, he passed back the photo and said he should be getting on. Needed to think things out, make a plan. (Had he heard a gecko call out seven times in the night? The dreaming part of him?) Whether Nolan's tip could be trusted remained to be seen, but he believed what he saw in the man's eyes when the picture of Sammy and Nyoman was back on the wall.

"If you do find the dog," Nolan said, "tell him I miss the hell out of him."

On the way back through the shop, Nolan gestured at some of Sammy's carvings. A glossy-eyed coiled snake. A village woman's smiling face, the "perfectly replicated" gaps between her teeth. And then a larger piece, a triptych of three squatting children with hand puppets. Nate bent in close, numbly searched the details.

Outside, they shook hands and he found himself asking why the sandwich board read *Far From the Midding Crawd*. It was Nyoman who had coined the phrase when Sammy remarked one afternoon as they were working that he was amazed he could be so far from the madding crowd and still have such a crowded mind. Nyoman had lowered his awl and said in his distinctive English, "But in a midding crawd, better chance meeting foxy chick who smooth your mind."

—〜〜—

On his room's porch, he gazed out over the volcano and the lake, Tirta village barely visible down on the near shore. Far sounds of dogs and water buffalo bells on the cool breeze, a tinge of sulfur mingled with smoke from village fires. Agang and Katut had retreated to their room by the office and no other guests seemed to be around. As he'd bought a pack of cigarettes after a chicken and rice dinner, he presently lit his fifth of the evening, though normally he didn't smoke, only a cigar now and then, sometimes with Hieu.

He pulled up another plastic chair for his feet, arranged his journal and Walkman and turned up the Freedy Johnston tape he'd packed, then clipped the photo of Sammy and himself to the page opposite the one he planned to write on and closed his eyes, trying to pin down the feeling that had been ricocheting through him all afternoon. Soon, though, wind rattled the windows right behind him; startled, he gave up trying to catch a perfect phrase.

> —On the rim of a Balinese volcano. I worry that I'm building a
> bridge of dust to Sammy. I'll start to cross and a gust will come.

He dwelt on the entry awhile, a satisfying insight still out of reach. He'd thought, of course, that by resituating himself thousands of miles from Lang and Hieu and Wilson Green High School he would begin to get clear. But it was still too early, and he was being a fool. Couldn't give in to such lazy thinking. He snuffed the cigarette and recalled Lang telling him how impatient he was, how it was probably all the hours plopped in front of the TV, especially in the years right after Sammy left.

A gibbous moon had risen and the chill made him shut his journal and fold his arms across his chest. A song about beauty and despair in New York City played in his ears as he watched the clouds speed over the mountain.

His leaving on this journey: No matter how much he tried to explain, reassure, Lang saw it as a selfish act, especially with Hieu's case hanging. Still incredible to consider that his friend might have touched the girls. But then he really didn't know anyone that well at all. Too often, life did seem like a rehearsal. Had he ever taken any significant amount of time, in the great bustle, to know a person? Someone's most cherished stories? How had he let himself get so damn used to filling up moments with minutiae? The daily drowning in details.

The leave of absence: beyond the stabbing and the resolutions it brought on, it also had something to do with trying too hard to be good. Nice. Good teacher, friend, lover. Always "there" for people. After years of focusing on others—his endlessly needy, wonderful students especially— time now to follow this path, finally, inconvenient as it was. (Would it ever be convenient? You could wait your entire life.) Could she maybe just trust him?

Hieu's emotionless face flickered in his mind. Another onslaught of shame over what he'd admitted to Wallace.

He wanted way too many experiences back, it was true. A chance to relive even a few of the hundreds of times he could have been a better man. But then this was where life had led him. Here. Right here. He stared out at the volcano.

Over the blurry Wilson Green years, he'd somehow given a bit too much.

A Measure of Comfort

Nearly two months had passed since Hieu had worked. Though the shock had finally finished its long bite, a lingering ache remained in the house—a quivering tension that made everyone all too aware that yet another argument might erupt any moment, for any conceivable reason.

He had given in often to his temper, shouting at Vo or Dat, even at Le Phuong a few times, over trivial matters concerning the kids' schoolwork or house chores. It was Anh, however, who'd seen the brunt of the anger what with her refusal to give in to her husband's mood swings. Almost daily, she would counter Hieu's attacks with all the force she could muster, knowing full well what was really happening. Only when guests were over did the house's energy change, like when Clyde Jackson and Desiree Thompson had rung the doorbell two days before Christmas. Anh had hurried into the kitchen and demanded that Hieu pull himself together.

"Say I'm sick," Hieu said, a week's grey-black stubble coating his face. But Anh only scowled right back, shook her head, and rushed out to the front door.

When Desiree and Clyde stepped into the kitchen, carrying a gift basket and poinsettia respectively, Hieu remained seated, his usual mug of Darjeeling in front of him. It was the same position in which they'd found him during their after-school visit three weeks earlier.

"Happy holiday," Hieu said, smiling. To do so felt like fighting his way up out of a slick hole.

Both Clyde and Desiree accepted Anh's offer of spice tea and cookies, then Clyde pushed the poinsettia to the middle of the table and asked Hieu how things were going.

"No change. Still crazy."

Desiree set the gift basket onto the table and turned it so Hieu could see the full display of jams, cheeses, and crackers.

"I think ol' Wallace is finally getting wise," she said. "When he re-interviewed me he seemed to be aiming toward breaking the girls' story open. More questions about them, you know. Motives and all that."

The house was quiet save the distant upstairs sound of Le Phuong's cello.

"So ..." Clyde tapped his fingers along the sides of his mug. "We just wanted to make sure you know everyone's still pulling for you. I'm betting it'll all be over soon."

Hieu summoned another smile and glanced over at Anh, who sat at the other end of the table now, watching him. He tried to listen to the news from Wilson Green—something about the pain of aligning various curricula with the new state standards—but the words filling the kitchen sounded garbled. He asked generic questions and tried to maintain an interested visage, but could think only about how glorious it is sometimes to be angry and alone. How a curious sense of power comes from convincing yourself that you don't need anyone. Despite the look in his wife's eyes, he enjoyed giving in to the notion.

On New Year's Day, on the Wildwood Trail in Forest Park, he hiked by himself through groves of spruce, hemlock, and beech. It was a sunny and cold afternoon, an east wind swerving down the Columbia River Gorge, spreading another wave of winter over the city.

The night before, he had declined a number of faculty members' offers of a ride to Terrell Martin's party, opting instead for a whiskey sour on the armrest of his favorite chair, some Beethoven in the background, *Dick Clark's New Year's Rockin' Eve* muted on the TV. Anh and the kids had gone with Lang to a late showing of *It's a Wonderful Life* at the Roseway Theater, leaving him in peace. As for Hoa, she'd been locked up in her room again, rattled over having heard Le Phuong dreaming aloud in English the day before when they'd been napping together; the sound of the foreign words flying from her granddaughter's mouth had been too much, yet another sign from the spirits that Vietnamese ways were dying all around her. After struggling to explain to his mother that Le Phuong would never lose her sense of tradition, Hieu had left her sitting cross-legged on the floor mat before the shrine in her room, knowing again that it was no use.

In a grassy clearing, he stopped and felt the sun's shallow warmth on the back of his head and pictured his mother alone in her room.

Lately it had occurred to him that Hoa was merely waiting to die, that she had been ever since leaving Vietnam. Yet the old woman, comfortable with bitterness as she was, remained for everyone in the house both eccentric, morose crank and unspoken leader.

Hieu held onto the image of her, wanting to remember their story again—his amazing past with her—in order to get a better handle on his sadness, the sensation of slow drowning. At the base of a purple beech, he sat down and listened to the wind bending the branches and soon fixed on the reunion with his mother and sister in Saigon. Twelve years old, he had slipped away from his team after a late-night mission, two days after watching the black soldier blow apart.

The guerrillas had spent the afternoon filling abandoned tunnels with scorpions and spiders of various sizes to further chill any inquisitive Americans. In a nearby hamlet that night, when his comrades finally fell asleep after the long meal, Hieu simply snatched up his pack, said a quiet prayer for safety, and crept away into the forest. When he moved into the shadows, Minh's words started up, as he'd suspected they would, but they had indeed lost their power to keep him focused upon such abstract things as national pride. He needed to see his mother. Get away from the killing. Somehow rid his head of the bad pictures.

For three and a half days he walked, finding villages for food and rest, scoping hard for tigers, snakes, and Americans. In one hamlet, everyone talked about the large soldiers who had come through two weeks before, questioning and frightening everyone, how the Americans shot the hamlet's best buffalo for no apparent reason. The villagers also mentioned how the men—some with cream-colored faces, some with coffee-colored—had taken off their boots, the skin on their feet peeling, and rubbed strange white paste onto their toes.

Hieu listened as he watched some of the elders pass an opium pipe, occasionally imagining his father curled up on his mat preaching nonsense.

There was another night on the way to Saigon, though, when he found himself nowhere near a village, when he slept under a pile of palm leaves and was awakened by a rustling. Suspecting the Americans, or perhaps another team of VC, he scrambled up a mulberry tree and sprawled across two close branches. But the rustling wasn't human. A twenty-foot horse snake emerged from the undergrowth and slid through his bed. He had seen only one of the dreaded monsters before, from a distance, on an outskirt of the hamlet when he was little, but never one so close. The brown skin glistening under the flecks of moonlight, pulsating directly below him, slithered off into the night, leaving him sick to his stomach and trembling.

By the following afternoon he made the edge of Saigon, the heat like drinking tea under all the hamlet's blankets, the intense greens of the paddies vibrating. Some of it was dehydration, some of it his fear of being detected and captured, but the city in the distance seemed dreamlike as it undulated under the humongous white sun.

When an American jeep pulled up behind him on an empty road through an outlying shantytown, Hieu checked his impulse to run and duck into an alley. But the questioning turned out to be surprisingly light. Through their leery-eyed ARVN interpreter, the thick-necked white men asked where he was going and from where he came. Hieu answered, in the deepest voice he could muster, that he was from a nearby village; his father had demanded at knifepoint that he go into Saigon and join the ARVN in order to prove his love for his country. Even though he hadn't yet been drafted, he knew what he had to do. He loved the Americans for their efforts. He would fight for liberty. With steady composure despite his worsening nausea, he told the soldiers that while he was terrified of fighting, he would honor his father and join up. Would they be kind enough to point him to the correct offices so he could do his duty?

Since he had managed to trade away his black pajamas for some grey pants and a baggy V-neck T-shirt, and since he'd buried his pack at the camp where he saw the horse snake, the soldiers squinted at each other a moment, told the skinny boy to jump in, then drove him into town, no further questions.

After the Americans delivered him to the ARVN Headquarters, where a South Vietnamese lieutenant flicked a hand toward a row of vacant ladderback chairs along a busy hallway, Hieu asked to go to the bathroom, then slipped away undetected in the jumble of offices and frowning uniformed men back out onto the even more chaotic boulevard.

On the sun-blasted steps of the building, the sounds of passing trucks, cars, and motorcycles merged into a soul-rattling clangor. Two cyclos lumbered past, one carrying a five-foot-high bundle of scrapwood, the other with live ducks tied upside-down to the handlebars and to the ends of two bamboo poles set across the passenger seat. He'd never before visited Saigon, but he had heard so many stories. Minh had traveled to the great capital a couple of times and told of a place where vehicles jostled for any remaining bits of street, where hundreds of women sold themselves, where money made people do all kinds of strange things. But instead of frightening Hieu, as they had Hoa and her husband, Minh's stories always made him long to see the distant city, breathe in its smells.

He remembered that Minh had spoken of district two, where their uncle and aunt lived, and where Hoa and Lang were staying; after asking a cyclo driver for directions and insisting for nearly a minute that he had no money for a ride, Hieu began walking along the garbage-strewn street. The city, as he experienced it that first afternoon, didn't come close to matching his dreams. Scraggly old women with poles across their shoulders hauled baskets of fruit and eggs. Grimy-faced children lugged pails of water, lank arms quaking. Bus horns blared. On almost every block, sidewalk eateries with wooden stools spilling to the edges of the street were packed with men, steaming *pho* and bottles of fish sauce and wraps of sticky rice taunting him. Though the energy was unmistakable, the outrageous racket, the stomach-flipping fumes of trash, hot tar, exhaust, and shit, the rude looks and foul words, the odd faces and dialects made Hieu step faster toward a measure of comfort.

When he finally found the correct apartment building in district two, he spotted his frail-looking mother and smiling sister sitting around a dim-lit table with his Aunt Mai and cousin Dat, his Uncle Phat waiting at one side of the doorway. He couldn't help bowing his head. To feel his mother holding him, to hear her sobbed words that close in his ear, to smell her—for the longest time he couldn't stop crying.

That evening, Aunt Mai cooked a chicken and set out a bottle of plum wine, and after Hoa stopped fawning over her son, Lang pulled Hieu aside to say that their mother seemed to be going mad; she had begun chewing on her forearms and fingers, sometimes rocking back and forth when she thought no one was looking. Lang was certain that Saigon was making Hoa's condition worse. They needed to find a more peaceful place to wait out the war, no discussion. She had heard about an island down in the delta where a monk named Ong Dao Dua was sheltering those who wanted out of the frenzy; it seemed the government, the Americans, and the ARVN were letting the monk quietly help the growing number of refugees and vagabonds. They could be at least temporarily free.

And so it went. Just three days after Hieu's arrival, after they had finished making arrangements and packed their few belongings into a single rucksack, Hoa, Lang, and Hieu said good-bye to the only family members they knew were alive and taxied to a northwestern outskirt of the city to meet another ride south. Planes and helicopters thundered in and out of Tan Son Nhut, the din making all of them quiver, especially Hoa. The staggering sounds.

It was then, as they waited in front of a bicycle shop for their connecting ride, that it first occurred to Hieu that his life would probably never resume its peaceful village way. He wasn't sure how he knew, but he'd left something back in the forest, where the terrified men stalked each other. He would come to understand later, in moments of surprising tenderness, that most surviving Americans felt the same way.

The winter afternoon had begun to die, high branches of the purple beech clacking in the wind. He noticed the cold air on his cheeks and decided to get going. Sixty yards down the trail, he entered a grove of sequoias and paused to smell the leaves that had blown in from a nearby cluster of maples. No other hikers seemed to be around, just the trees and the hard earth, the sound of his own breathing. He was thankful for the trees and the good air. He had always loved the land of his new home, despite its differences from that of his boyhood; the rain, sun, wind all felt different, but he'd loved it from the very beginning, ever since arriving in the green wonder of spring, 1975.

Hieu breathed deeply, letting the quiet work its power. The sourness in his gut that had been with him since hearing of the allegations had faded some. He closed his eyes for a moment and listened, worries about the investigation sent off to a comfortably distant edge of his mind.

Portland Police Department
Portland, Oregon
Special Report

Wednesday, December 11th, 1996. Principal WINCHILL arranged
for another roving substitute. At 9:15 a.m. Desiree THOMPSON,
a health teacher at Wilson Green High School, came in for a
follow-up.

I began by asking Ms. THOMPSON to clarify the remark she made
last week about NGUYEN "doing whatever it takes to get kids
in line." She said that she meant NGUYEN has a "no excuses"
policy with his students. He believes everyone will choose to
succeed if shown the consequences for late work, misbehavior,
etc. I asked THOMPSON again if she had ever seen NGUYEN touch
a student. (Last Friday during our brief conversation she said
that she couldn't remember.) THOMPSON reported that she had
witnessed NGUYEN "thump" a male student on the chest last year
in the cafeteria over some disciplinary matter, and that the
student had corrected the misbehavior. "It seemed perfectly
fine, considering the boy," she said.

When I brought up the specific charges against NGUYEN again,
THOMPSON began shaking her head and said that there was
"absolutely no way" NGUYEN would have done it, that he's "too
professional, too clean of character." I then asked whether or
not thumping a female student on the chest might be miscon-
strued as a sexual advance and THOMPSON said no. "There's a big
difference between emphasizing a point with a little thump and
grabbing a girl's breasts," she said. The interview ended at 9:25.

At 9:30, Max WALKER, Wilson Green's Student Management
Specialist, arrived for a second interview. I focused mainly
upon his experiences with Sasha ANDERSON and Malisha JONES
this time. WALKER reported that JONES has been suspended three
times over the course of her two and a half years at Wilson
Green. All of the suspensions have been related to severe classroom disruption, two for swearing at and threatening teachers. ANDERSON has never been suspended, but has received five
referrals during the past two years (she transferred to Wilson
Green during her freshman year). Three were related to classroom disruption and insubordination. I asked WALKER if any of

Portland Police Department
Portland, Oregon
Special Report

the suspensions or referrals had been a result of the girls' actions in NGUYEN'S class. WALKER replied, "They would never try
that stuff with Hieu (NGUYEN)."

I wanted clarification and WALKER said, "Hieu's style is such
that students understand quickly they're in his class to learn,
not play. He gives out a few detentions, or maybe a referral
or two, at the beginning of each semester to establish a tone,
let them know he'll follow through if he needs to, then he
never seems to have very many behavior issues. From all I've
seen, he's very firm, but fair." I then asked WALKER if he had
ever witnessed NGUYEN touch students while disciplining them
and he said that he'd seen NGUYEN jab students on the shoulder
or chest "to make sure they were getting what he was saying."
WALKER added that NGUYEN didn't do it too hard; the action,
while "risky," was in the bounds of propriety. "Teachers get so
loaded down and distracted, and NGUYEN is pretty high-energy.
He occasionally jabs kids to make a point, but he's strict
because he cares. He wants these people to make it. He won't just
let them slide on by without giving them everything he's got,"
WALKER said. At 9:40, I concluded the interview and awaited Mr.
Uli WEGMAN, NGUYEN'S science department colleague.

Sweet Paradise

In the Ubung terminal, north Denpasar, Nate squatted on an oil-stained curb and waited for his bus to Yogyakarta. Around him, a pandemonium of air horns, shouting men, barking dogs. Every few minutes, someone approached and asked if he already had a ticket, where he was headed, if he had a place to stay, or whether or not he wanted to buy a T-shirt, watch, knit bracelet, or soda. The late afternoon was steamy and drizzly, wet little boys with umbrellas for sale accosting tourists who were just arriving. Credence Clearwater Revival's "Have You Ever Seen the Rain" came over the station's PA system.

On the bus down from Mount Batur, he had deliberated about Lang. Before reconsidering a marriage proposal, he needed to understand why it felt like something was in the way, blocking the leap. Yet he missed her—the companionship, the faithfulness and integrity, even the ugly green curtains in her kitchen and her singing along to Bruce Springsteen, tone deafness no deterrent. Did the times he'd pulled away simply amount to his own fears?

He'd also, on the drive down, replayed the previous night's dream about finding his uncle on a coconut palm beach. He had dreamt of finding Sammy sipping at a gin and tonic under a rainbow umbrella, a lithe Thai girl rubbing oil over his feet. When he approached, Sammy raised his head, eyes hidden by wraparound shades, and said, "Who are you?"

At dawn he had awoken to the sound of Agang and Katut singing a happy-sounding Balinese song out in the cliff-side garden. Flipped open his journal on the nightstand.

—Don't come away from this misty-eyed, wearing silk boxers, glancing through *Actualized Man Quarterly*. It's good to live the questions and all, embrace uncertainty like a pro, but there's one catch: I'd like a few answers first.

Last night, after smoking six cigarettes on the porch overlooking the volcano, he had decided to bus to Jakarta via Yogya, then fly to Kuala Lumpur and catch another bus into southern Thailand. He felt a sense of urgency about finding Sammy, yet he didn't want to hurry to the point of exhaustion. He'd learned this during his first solo Europe trip, when he tried to see as many places as possible on a one-month Eurail pass and after three and a half weeks of rushing from city to city, ended up spending the last six days of the month in a Lucerne guesthouse bed, retching into a slop bucket.

When the call for the Yogya bus came, Nate rose from the curb and joined the mob of Java-bound passengers vying for a seat, his backpack squashed between two men who used it as a brace to propel themselves forward. By the time the engine started, he was the second to last to board, the only seats remaining in the very front, across from the driver. Because the luggage compartment was already full, and the nearby overhead bins, he stuffed his backpack between his knees, one leg pressed to the wall, the other against a surprisingly strong-calved elderly woman who'd climbed aboard right after him. The driver, another in his mid- to late teens, sat high on a pillow, his hands minuscule on the steering wheel, and announced in both Bahasa and English that the bus would board a ferry in an hour's time for the passage to Java. The trip would take another twelve or thirteen hours beyond that. Since Nate hadn't consulted the timetable, forcing himself (in the name of Road Mode) to let go, not worry about such matters, he lowered his head and smiled.

—⁓—

Sprawled in bed. The night before already a blur. He hadn't explored Yogya yet, and he was hungry, but being horizontal felt too good, the lull of the slow ceiling fan too powerful. On the edge of another nap, he fell to thinking of the people in his world, all of them struggling in their various ways. Lang carrying on in a place that still made her nervous. Sammy wandering Asia. Acacia and Grandpa Davis pushing ahead with

firm-set jaws, resigned to grinding out a hard existence. And Hieu leading an honorable life after fighting his way into the formidable society
of a new land, then having everything flipped over by some addicted-to-
anger schoolgirls.

He skipped to a thought of Hieu battling Hoa on Lang's behalf for her
relationship with a white man, lobbying to his mother's deaf ears, trying
to claw his way through her fears. How earnestly the man had argued
that love transcended all boundaries. *But then was it really love with
Lang?* Christ. The question made him scramble for some other thought.
Anything. Monty's picks for the NBA conference finals, Sharon Stone's
breasts in *Basic Instinct.* He pushed up off the bed, showered, then went
to inquire about another bus ticket.

—⁓—

After another cramped night ride, having seen all he wanted of con-
gested Yogya in one day, Nate found a restaurant adjacent to Jakarta's main
station and sat alone. The only other customers—a German-speaking
couple, the young man sporting shoulder-length dreads—were slumped
at a corner table eyeing their bowls of muesli, a fair-sized cockroach skit-
tered across the floor in front of the kitchen door, and the scene out the
windows reminded him of the overpopulation discussions he'd led over
the years. If only his students could see this. The packed-solid traffic, drivers pounding their horns anyway. Men on scooters using the sidewalks as
shortcuts, rivers of stone-faced pedestrians parting, then merging again.
A crane across the avenue hoisting beams for another new building.

At length he began flipping through his journal, scanning entries
mostly from various weekend trips, words carrying him to the hemlocks, cedars, and rhododendrons surrounding the Brightwood cabin.
The heavy surf, wind, and rocks down at the coast. Mt. Tabor Park in the
middle of Portland, under the Douglas firs. In the near-empty restaurant, looking out at the street, he found himself pining for that familiar
moist air. He wanted to be in Brightwood. Head down to the confluence
of Boulder Creek and the Salmon River, smell the water and last year's
leaves along the shore. Sit on a mossy rock and listen. He pictured the
exact spot, just upstream from the confluence, below the old fishing
hole he and Sammy used to frequent. He wanted to hike up Wildcat

Mountain, take in the clearcut, climb onto one of the big stumps and check out the view.

It surprised him to experience such a longing. A sensation he'd come to believe was pretty much gone. So often he'd felt far from settled when he was home. It seemed he lived merely on the land, not in it.

When the morose young couple left in a cloud of low conversation, Nate refocused and consulted the *Lonely Planet* he'd buried in his pack. Circled some travel agents and guesthouses, the little arrow pointing northwest to Soekarno-Hatta International Airport on the city map, then settled his bill. On a pedestrian overpass a few blocks from the restaurant, he paused to survey the spectacle—the gleaming office buildings, slums spreading up a hillside in the distance, fast-food joints and two shopping malls on either side of the gridlocked avenue—and as he gazed over the metallic river, it began to mist, the midday sun flickering off droplets, two rainbows blooming between grey towers a mile ahead. He stood there awhile, occasionally wiping his face, watching. The more he saw of the world, the more various and complex things seemed to get. The more he experienced, the more it occurred to him that he would probably never come to deeply understand that much at all.

That afternoon, having spent the greater part of the day sleeping, then talking about southern Thailand with a middle-aged South African couple in the Lubbly Jubbly Travel Inn's dining area, he set out for a nearby travel company to check for mail. Though he hadn't been sure of his itinerary beyond Bali, he'd given Hieu, Lang, and Acacia the address listed in his guidebook anyway, fairly certain that letters would get to Jakarta safely. He'd kept telling himself not to expect anything, but slipped into a slight funk nevertheless when he found nothing from either Lang or Hieu, only a short note from Acacia saying it had been raining a lot and that Grandpa Davis had gone to the hospital for a minor intestinal issue.

He walked on, arranged a flight to Kuala Lumpur for the following evening, then returned through the still-clogged streets to the Lubbly Jubbly. Brooding some, trying not to. He hadn't bothered to contact either Lang or Hieu; why the double standard? Wrong as well, probably, to still be so damn sheepish about getting an e-mail account.

In his room, an ancient window fan vibrating violently, he sat on his bed and chewed a not-quite-ripe banana. Chased it with cold tea.

—◆—

From what little he saw before he got sick, KL seemed to be just another city bent on getting bigger and flashier. More overcrowding, even taller skyscrapers. Construction projects on every other block, some from the minds of architects and moneymen who'd watched too much "Star Trek." But then he hadn't given the place a real chance since the diarrhea and vomiting started even before he landed. It had to have been the shrimp kebabs in the Jakarta airport; while the dirty-fingered cashier had given him pause, Road Mode daring won out.

He wanted to make the next afternoon's bus up to Penang—where he could find another ride into Thailand—but his stomach still felt like it had been inhabited by boll weevils. While the fever seemed to be dropping, shuttle runs to the closet-like bathroom continued well into the night.

By the following morning, he felt cleared-out enough to sip chicken broth from the guesthouse kitchen, but the fatigue and the shakiness in his legs kept him in bed another fifteen hours. Traveling a bit too hard, again. He would definitely ease up, spend some time on Ko Lanta, even if Sammy had fled from that place also.

But to think that the guy may have taken a similar path to Thailand, even this path … To follow in his footsteps like this: it was a powerful thing. He believed, wanted to believe, that he felt himself being guided onward. Sammy could be guiding him along, and right now there was no other way to see it. He had to follow. Trust where the path led. No matter where.

—◆—

When two days later he arrived in the Thai town of Krabi, the mainland port nearest his destination, Nate immediately began asking around. After a couple of misses at a dockside cafe and a chamber-of-commerce-like building with some of the most unhelpful clerks he'd ever encountered, he came upon a sporting goods store along the marina, a brawny six-foot blond Australian woman behind the counter. He handed over the photograph of Sammy and himself, cut to the part about Nolan's Ko Lanta tip, and the woman said that if any person on the island could possibly point him to someone who might know anything at all, it would be a well-connected fellow with local roots named Sterling who ran one of the beach-front hotels, the Happy Sea Bungalows. She pointed out the windows to where he could catch a longboat.

Not having a clue as to a better option, he went ahead and boarded a boat with twenty other tourists, most of whom appeared to be in the Honk If You're a Brand New Buddhist set, pilgrims with designer back-packs. A choppy half-hour ride. Antacid-saturated stomach. The Ko Lanta dock teeming with black-haired boys, each carrying armfuls of brochures and booklets on various resorts.

The instant the fresh batch of tourists touched land, the boys swarmed, some tugging at his clothes, pinching his arms and legs, all yelling prices, lists of amenities. Bombarded from all sides under the hard sun, he began swinging his pack back and forth to clear a little space. He was a bit lightheaded—the dock, the dozens of parked pickups, the wall of forest all beginning to shimmy—and before he was fully conscious of it he was shouting "Sterling!" As he let loose, a brief out-of-body flash: his pale-faced, backpack-toting self on a tropical island, surrounded by vicious pubescent salesmen, screaming as if he were being eaten by a shark. But despite the absurdity and dizziness, he kept yelling until a smiling buck-toothed boy wriggled through the riot clutching a three-ring binder with *Happy Sea Bungalows* in neon orange across the cover.

Within five minutes, some other trusting souls rounded up, the kid was tearing down a dirt road in a Toyota pickup while Nate gripped the door handle. AC/DC's "Hell's Bells" rocked from the stereo, two Finnish couples bounced and laughed in the back like they were on a Disneyland ride, the forest ripping past. But by the time he had tipped the driver, bought a cold can of Coke from the machine beside the Happy Sea's front door, and walked into Sterling's plush ocean-view office, things actually seemed all right to him. No worries. That is until Sterling looked up from a newspaper spread over his desk and said with a chuckle that he'd never heard of Sammy. Too many tourists to keep track, be serious man.

After seeing the horseback ride photo, however, and offering Nate some rum for his Coke and downing a shot himself, Sterling went on to say that another hotel proprietor, a British expat named Mick Lassiter, usually had anywhere between twenty to thirty "Pacific Rot" Westerners hanging out or working at his beachfront place at any one time, the hippies and pseudo-hippies so named by some of the locals because of their more or less rotting appearances and views of life. Lassiter had been running "quite a show" the past nine years, ever since his arrival on Ko Lanta.

Sterling dabbed his jowls with a folded handkerchief, offered more rum, and asked why Nate was trying to find his uncle. Nate accepted another shot and gave a brief rundown of his situation.

Sterling—loose-tongued and not giving a rip—revealed that the locals had started referring to Lassiter as Fat Man early on due to both his physical bearing and his immense pride at being the undisputed king of Ko Lanta's drug and sex scene. An ex-banker who up and left his wife and three teenage sons one spring evening in '86, Lassiter sold his Jaguar, withdrew his savings, and bought a one-way to Bangkok to follow his dream of (as Sterling succinctly put it) "finding sweet paradise in a land with a low cost of living and pussy that doesn't speak too much English." So Ko Lanta it was, a just-developing, still-forested island that was making contractors drool, and word of the newest, hippest, cheapest scene in Thailand spread through the backpacker circuit like a head cold in a classroom.

Sterling insisted that they each have another shot before he got back to work. Teary-eyed, flushed, he summoned the same bucktoothed boy who'd rescued Nate from the dockside frenzy, and then stood in the Happy Sea's front doorway dabbing his forehead and neck.

"Be careful down there," he said with a wave when the truck started. "Don' lose yourself!"

Holding the door handle again, Nate called out a thank you as the kid cranked the AC/DC, and in seconds they were hurtling farther down the road toward Lassiter's. To counter his sick-again stomach, he shut his eyes and tried to focus on the image in his mind: Sammy on the beach, sipping a drink under the rainbow umbrella, the Thai girl oiling his feet. It would be a powerful reunion rather than confusion and stilted speech. Reconciliation over cold grey distance.

—⁓⁓—

Alone at a table in the Sun God Bungalows' open-air restaurant, having already barfed into a wastebasket within seconds of checking into a single, Nate slouched with a can of 7-Up in his hands, squinting out over the beach. Sea kayaks on gravelly sand. Young palm trees. Immense rocks shooting up at each end of the three-hundred-yard private stretch. A topless woman reclined on her elbows, her linebacker companion rubbing lotion over her, and some local children lounged under the volleyball net, waiting for the next game, ready to bet a few baht against stoned tourists. Nearby, in the restaurant, people speaking Thai and German, then hard laughter, one woman's chortling sounding like an injured hog.

After a time he opened his journal.

> —9 February 1997, Ko Lanta
>
> Where am I?
>
> I haven't been able to meet Mick Lassiter, so here I sit dealing with a hard-on. The gorgeous English woman at the front desk tells me there are "quite large" snakes and spiders in the surrounding forest. (Quite large? Is that so, love?) I asked if she knew Sammy and she just shook her head and smiled. I should speak with Mr. Lassiter, she said, even though she doesn't know when he'll return from a business trip. It's not in the guidebook, but this seems like a nice enough place, even with the handful of people who appear to be orbiting Uranus. Major case of Circushead right now. Take it easy.

The red sun sinking into the ocean, Nate cupped the soda can, fighting fatigue. Truly a monster day. He returned to his room and passed out as the final flicker of direct light left that part of the world.

Of the dreams he traveled through that night, he would only be able to recall one of himself hiking alone on a fogged-in mountain trail, a great forest quiet surrounding him. A common-enough setting, he would think. A quick dance with an archetype. Still, the dream stayed with him, sticking like pitch. The path had been visible only a few feet ahead, but he pressed forward, urged on by an extreme desire, the destination that might have placed him unreached by dream's end.

So it Goes

2959 N.E. Lofton Ct.
Portland, OR 97212
U.S.A.

January 31, 1997

Mr. Nate Davis
c/o Pacto Ltd. Travel Services
Jalan Surabaya No. 8 POB 2569
Jakarta, INDONESIA 10330

Dear Nate,

I hope this finds you refreshed. I'm still confused about how you plan to receive your mail, but I trust you have it worked out. When you get free time, let us know how you are doing and what you have seen.

Things here are the same for the most part. The sergeant has begun calling more people in for follow-up discussions. What he is doing I don't know, but Clyde and Desiree stopped by again the other evening and said that everyone at school thinks that the girls' stories are beginning to crumble. But no one knows this for certain, of course. At my interview last week, the sergeant and I went over everything again for the third time. This continues to take my breath away. So it goes.

I'm sorry about this complaining. I have realized this past week how angry I am. I'm very sad that Anh and the kids have to be around me. To be frank, Nate, I have been wondering if it would be wise to get away for perspective, like you. Do you think it would be possible to use your family's cabin for a few days? Mountain air would help greatly, I believe. Please let me know.

We all send our best to you. Anh says to be sure you know that we already miss you. As for Lang, we have only seen her once since you left. She dropped off an article of hers that had been published recently, but she stayed only a couple of minutes. She did not seem herself. What are your thoughts? I'm interested, as always.

Travel well,

Hieu

Portland Police Department
Portland, Oregon
Special Report

10:05 a.m. Uli WEGMAN arrived. Since I'd already learned that
he and NGUYEN sometimes collaborate on science department
projects, I began by asking whether or not he has seen NGUYEN
teach on a regular basis. WEGMAN replied that he enters
NGUYEN'S classroom at least once a month to either consult
on a project or drop off materials. He said that NGUYEN
"runs a tight ship" and that his students produce excellent
work. I then asked if he'd ever seen NGUYEN touch students
inappropriately and he said, "Most people on staff wouldn't
consider jabbing a student on the chest or patting his or her
shoulder inappropriate, but I certainly do. I've seen Hieu
(NGUYEN) touch students in those ways regularly." I wondered
if WEGMAN, as the science department chairman, had ever approached NGUYEN about touching students. He replied that he
had, eight years ago, but NGUYEN defended his tactics, saying
something about needing to get students' attention in certain
situations.

I asked WEGMAN to rate NGUYEN'S performance as a teacher and
he began by stating that he has "never worked with anyone so
committed and focused." He continued, however, saying that he
and NGUYEN routinely disagree on a variety of matters, but
that the relationship is "professional." WEGMAN then reiterated his concern about NGUYEN'S habit of touching students,
"sending the wrong signals to kids." After explaining the
charges against NGUYEN, I concluded by again asking WEGMAN
if he had ever witnessed NGUYEN touch students in a sexual
manner. He answered immediately, "Never."

Note on Staff Interviews: I've met with half of the Wilson
Green faculty. Based upon further testimony from Sasha
ANDERSON and Malisha JONES, or any major inconsistencies
that surface, follow-ups may still occur.

Note on Student Interviews: My third discussion with Malisha
JONES will occur this Friday (12-13-96), again at the home of
Cherise LOGAN, JONES'S aunt. Transcripts from the first and
second interviews with JONES reveal possible fabrication of
parts of her story. Transcripts of last week's second interview
with Sasha ANDERSON also show slight discrepancies.

Greyness

Another storm followed close behind the gentler one preceding it, bringing nearly horizontal rain, obscuring Twin Rocks just offshore, and the already large waves pounded even harder against the land. Up in the dunes, tucked into a hole he had dug with his bare hands, Hieu leaned against the soaked sand and held his poncho around his body. Though the rocks were shrouded, the beach was still visible from his perch, no other persons sitting or walking. He pulled his knees up until they almost touched his chest and squinted down at the white lines of surf.

He'd come alone, this time for three days. Since he hadn't heard anything in a couple of weeks from Nate about using the Brightwood cabin, he decided to head for the ocean, to an old Highway 101 motel—The Fanta Sea—where he'd stayed with Anh many years before. And while at first he was uncomfortable about checking into a motel alone after so many family trips, the solitude soon began to calm him. In the safety of his sandy hole, the rain beating against his poncho, he thought again that being by himself was exactly what he needed.

It was something—solitude—that remained a largely foreign concept. Loyalty to his family and its struggles, and to his toughened colleagues, had always meant proximity to others, situations where seclusion would most likely be taken as haughtiness or a sign of some personality disorder. As far back as he could remember, he'd always been surrounded by people; there was no concept of personal space. It had been especially true during his teens on Phoenix Island, the years just before the fall.

The Phoenix Island monk, Ong Dao Dua, had been called Ong Hai, or older brother, by the residents of his colony, and The Coconut Monk by the Americans, who had chosen to look the other way even when rumors began to spread that Ong had taken in a number of VC deserters. Life in the colony was peaceful for the most part, the various nationalities and religions united in their hatred of the war, Ong Hai making sure that tolerance and kindness remained at the forefront of everyone's mind. Even Hoa, who had initially balked at the idea of living with so many strange people, began to relax.

By early April 1975, though, when it became clear that Vietnam would soon enter an even more uncertain period, word shot through the community that many southerners were arranging escapes. Clouds of panic gathering. After numerous discussions with other nervous members of the commune, debates over the substantial risks, it was Lang who brought up the previously unbroached topic of emigration.

"They could come after us when they learn about Minh and you," she said to Hieu one night before bed. "Minh spoke out against the northerners' rigidity many times. You know I'm right, brother."

But as they had worried, explaining the situation to Hoa proved to be grueling. Their mother, despite her belief that the spirits were telling her to move on, still clung to the notion that there was a chance she might eventually be able to return to Tay Ninh Province, someday die near the ancestral tombs. Getting her to flee the homeland began to seem, after nearly a week of tearful talks, utterly impossible. But oddly, it was an American conscientious objector—a tall, pale-skinned, twenty-four-year-old boy from Missoula, Montana—who managed to convey to Hoa (in his hacked Vietnamese) that the communists might indeed find it necessary to punish her family, in what manner nobody knew.

So by the middle of that April, after nearly three and a half years of living and working on the lush green island alongside the friendly Montana boy—harvesting sugar cane and bananas and *long nhan,* telling stories, giving and receiving language lessons, praying for guidance—the news of the imminent communist victory and the advice to flee as quickly as possible coming from Toby's mouth brought the sting of truth. Hieu and Lang knew that Hoa must, if necessary, be kidnapped out of the country. There would be no consideration of leaving her behind.

As for Minh, the man of the family, they hadn't heard from him in almost four years, his last letter having reached them just after Tet, a short note saying that the resistance remained strong, but that he'd been forced to cut back his duties because of malarial attacks and other unspecified health problems. For all of them, Minh remained heroic, in spite of their fear that he'd been drawn too far into the struggle. Out beyond the pull of family. Of identity.

In Saigon, Uncle Phat and Aunt Mai managed to arrange precious spots on an American military plane for Hoa, Lang, Hieu, their only child Dat, and themselves. Through one of Phat's diplomatic connections—what turned out to be a critical perk of being a political science teacher at one of the city's colleges—and through payment in gold from the sale of their apartment, the okay from the American embassy finally came after four weeks of letter writing and phone calls.

On April 26, Hieu and Lang helped their shuddering mother into the monstrous cargo jet amid a melee of yelling soldiers, droning engines, and well-connected Vietnamese bracing for their first trip into the sky. It was another scene Hieu would always be able to summon: the smells of fuel blending with smoke from nearby dung and garbage fires, sounds building to a nearly intolerable crescendo, excitement and remorse fighting for attention in his taut body. By then, he'd learned to forget his weeks with the VC to a point just short of amnesia, but stepping into the flying metal beast his mouth went dry. While he knew the chance of being pegged was remote, it still worsened the nausea.

During the entire flight to Wake Island, his mother opened her eyes only a couple of times, looks that made him put his head down and pray. The specifics of the war still remained unclear to Hoa, the games of men so distant from her desire to live where she felt close to life.

Lang's face had been drawn that day too, but she would later admit to feeling a quickly suppressed rush of glee when the plane finally lifted off. The singular breathtaking sensation of leaving the ground made her and Hieu simultaneously reach for each other's calloused hands, their stomachs tightening. By the time they arrived on Wake Island, however, any remaining thrill had returned to pure worry, the madness of the airfield snapping them back much faster and harder than they would have liked.

For three days they waited through screening sessions and physicals. When Hoa emerged from her first meeting with the doctors, shawl clutched around her sides, she glared at both of her children again and found a bench upon which she sat for the following eight hours straight. Something wrong was happening, she said. Leaving the homeland would bring bad karma.

Then toward the end of the third day, they were told through harried interpreters that they would be divided up in order to make processing on the US mainland easier. Some refugees would go to California, others to Arkansas. For Hieu's family, it was the latter, Fort Chaffee.

Because they were among the first arrivals, though, there was little food and fewer supplies at the Arkansas camp; the quarters, storage areas, medical facilities were still being prepared. In various stages of shock, they paced the grounds under the new sky, bewildered by the different angle of sunlight.

Five days later, volunteer agencies began sending people and supplies and soon food wasn't a problem, though the cooking was still suspect. Hoa had begun speaking again, cursing the decision to flee. She would have gladly been shot, she said, if it meant being able to die on ancestral soil. The very air of the new land threatened her, not to mention the language, the horrendous meals, the lodgings, and the soul-biting uncertainty of everything imaginable looming over it all.

After another round of physicals and interviews, a small Lutheran agency in Oregon offered to help settle the family, and within three more days another plane trip was upon them. For Hieu and Lang, the velocity of their lives began to catch up, making each sink further inside themselves, like Hoa had so deftly demonstrated over the previous years. It was a skill that both would hone throughout their lives, one that would shape their destinies.

In Portland, it was nearly a week before any of them managed laughter, Phat, Mai, Dat included. Only Phat had ever even heard of Portland. A colleague once told him that its climate was a little like that of Dalat. And indeed, the chilly, wet early May days framed the family's state well, bringing a tender quiet to the humbling Halsey Square apartment they all shared, the kids sleeping in the living room on inch-thick foam pads donated by the Lutheran agency, the adults on two thrift-store mattresses in the one bedroom.

Halsey Square, a low-income housing complex, had turned into a common first stop for First-Wave Vietnamese, along with some Laotians and Cambodians, a cluster of cracked worlds. It was a place that, years later, Hieu would find himself driving by occasionally, late at night, when the past had pulled him out of sleep, momentarily out of mind.

On the beach, rain still pattering his poncho, Hieu continued to stare at the waves, though now a less violent spectacle, Twin Rocks almost clear of clouds. He was chilled, he realized, and sore after having crouched in his hole for over an hour.

But something held him in place. The calming din of waves. Mist and cloud blurring the line between water and sky. The childlike desire to see clear across, all the way west and south to Vietnam.

And then a familiar thought: so little could be easily explained. How he would elevate his thinking, learn to cope better with the greyness of things, he still didn't know. Perhaps he'd look up Harlan Fullbrook, his dear old Portland State advisor, when he got back to town, see if the old man had any tips. He recalled Dr. Fullbrook saying something once about gathering up the world's toughest, best questions and using them as a pillow. Then there was Miriam Gilligan, his astronomy professor, how she had once boggled the auditorium-sized class by saying, "If we know from Doppler redshifts that the universe as we know it is expanding, what is it expanding *into?*" Questions lurking behind even the most impressive of answers.

He stood and shook out his poncho. To be alone and silent at times: crucial. Even better in front of a vastness. Full of a stillness felt too rarely, he turned and wove through the dunes, the sound of ocean dying.

Hallucination

For three days Nate inquired each morning and late evening about Mick Lassiter's return from the business trip, always receiving the same smiling, indefinite response from the pretty English concierge. But the time to rest and explore had actually suited him, despite his concern over some of the more bizarre guests.

The evening before, he'd been sitting alone at one of the open-air restaurant's bamboo tables, sipping a beer and sketching the giant sheer-faced rocks at either end of the beach, when a lanky thirtyish man wearing only mauve swimming trunks shuffled in and took a table next to his.

The stranger made eye contact with no one as he said just under a yell, "Big Daddy Mojo." No hello, no self-absorbed chuckle. Half of his beard and the opposite half of his mustache were shaved off, he smelled of fish, the little toe on the foot nearest Nate was missing, and soon he began chanting the sacred *Aum* mantra, eyes shut, while slightly rocking back and forth sideways. The others in the restaurant went on talking and eating, but the fish smell got thicker to Nate; he finished his beer, grabbed his journal and headed for the bonfire that was already high and hot.

Only a few steps onto the sand, though, one of the Thai waitresses, a woman of twenty he'd met just that morning, caught up and asked if he was all right. When he turned and saw her confident black eyes catching glints of firelight, he smiled.

"Please don' be alarm abou' him," the waitress said. "He is on the private fishing crew. He come in and do that two, three time a week after work."

She went on to explain that the chanter's reason for growing only half of his facial hair was that he considered it a symbol of his dual nature. Nate nodded, more than satisfied; but the woman saw fit to continue.

The missing toe, she said, was due to an acid freak-out the previous summer. On the beach right in front of the restaurant, only a few feet away in fact, the man had begun screaming *"Be gone,"* and eventually sliced off the little toe with his Swiss Army knife, then swallowed it, an act that was apparently over-the-top for even the more hard-core, "Whatever, man" guests. Why Mr. Lassiter allowed the poor soul to stay on continued to bewilder most everyone on staff; but while they were wary, folks just let him do his thing.

When the waitress finished, Nate found himself asking if she planned on attending the beach party. Maybe they could have a drink. It felt, he would write later, as though a tiny sexually frustrated terrorist had hijacked his judgment. Did it amount simply to a case of loneliness, the need for some more talk? Regardless, the woman grinned and replied no, she was having dinner with her boyfriend at a resort up-island. Another striking letdown, much like when he'd tried to flirt with a shapely American in tight cut-offs only an hour earlier. In the restaurant, when Nicolette said that she'd been a horticulture-psychology double major, he hadn't been able to resist asking if she was a plant therapist. But she didn't find that funny, she said twice, picking up her daiquiri and rejoining her friends.

Back in his bungalow after the beach party, at which he'd indulged in numerous swigs from shared jugs of moonshine, he studied the shadows in the grooves of mosquito netting and brooded, journal open, about why thoughts of Lang had come less frequently since his arrival on the island.

> —I haven't been sober that often. Like the days in Amsterdam.
> I suppose I can see the lure of all this, how a guy could set out and
> not come back. I don't know. Shit.

Later, between mini-naps, he reviewed his vow to himself that he would never cheat on a woman. Never had, never would.

One hand gripping the bedpost to steady the spins, he meandered back into thoughts of Sammy, how a place like Ko Lanta really could make the rest of the world seem forgettable. Then again, it was too easy to dive into some damn tropical fantasyland. Too cowardly, especially when links to the outside world still existed, even links of injured love.

Soothed by familiar conviction, self-righteous as part of him knew it was, Nate yanked the sheet up and rolled with the fluidity of a walrus onto his side, then passed out for good, fully clothed and shod.

———

At five-thirty in the morning, one of Lassiter's employees, an effeminate teenaged Thai with slicked-back hair, knocked and summoned him to a large teakwood house tucked up in the forest across the road from the restaurant. Nate hadn't noticed the trail leading up the hill, having spent all his time on the beach or in the restaurant.

Still fairly drunk, he followed the quiet sway-hipped boy up the trail, images from *Heart of Darkness* teasing at him, gnarl-limbed trees in the shadows making it seem like he was entering some nightmare world, or maybe the movie set of a nightmare world. The sound of waves soon muted and the air's scent changed from sea salt to moist foliage. When they approached the house's polished front steps, the boy said, "Sir, your sandals please," removed his own and placed them in the ruler-straight row off to one side of the door.

In the dining area, they found Lassiter on a floor pillow at the near end of a long, low table, a platter of scrambled eggs flecked with bits of ham heaped before him, three Thai boys sitting on either side. On one wall, a print of Hieronymus Bosch's *The Garden of Earthly Delights* hung next to a blue and white tapestry depicting two copulating tigers; on another, a steel sculpture—what appeared to Nate to be a semi-truck muffler—was mounted above a small marble fountain, two cherubs pissing into a fish's mouth. Lassiter, a pink-cheeked man every bit as large as Nate had envisioned, made no attempt to heave his muumuu-covered body up from his pillow; instead he laughed, his precisely clipped white-whiskered chins jiggling, then said, before anything else, how Nate looked much like Sam.

For a few beats Nate stared numbly at him. Throat tight. Then his eyes swept across the boys: each looked up with a gentle smile, the one who had led him to the house now seated midway down the table.

Lassiter motioned for him to sit and nodded at the boy to his immediate right to begin dishing the eggs. "Had I known you were coming, I'd have postponed my trip."

When everyone's plate was full, he asked when Nate had last heard from Sammy, but didn't wait long enough for a reply, distracted as he was by one of the boys having dropped the serving spoon. Eggs churning in his mouth like wet clothes in a dryer, he said that he hoped the room's decor didn't cause discomfort; he'd just remodeled and had doubts himself. At length, after downing his first serving and asking one of the boys to fetch more water, he explained that Sammy had worked for him as a cook, that "the loony bloke" left abruptly, without telling anyone, about five years ago now. He then mentioned that a woman named Jackie Yamada, his chief assistant, had been quite close to Sammy.

"We all knew him rather well, don't get me wrong," he said. "But Jackie and he were intimate."

Two of the boys began tittering and Lassiter reached under the table, leaned toward the nearest and whispered something.

"What was he like while he was here?" Nate said, still trying to get a handle on the situation. He hadn't touched his eggs.

Lassiter cleared his throat, a hawk of phlegm catching before a labored swallow. Three boys rose and started taking away the dishes, those remaining adopting various post-meal attitudes on their pillows. The rising light outside had begun to filter through the canopy surrounding the house, and Nate could hear birdsong.

"Your uncle had, let me see … certain gifts." The boys giggled again, some hiding their smiles behind their hands. "I guess I should be more explicit, though." Lassiter lowered his head, pressed a thumb to his lips. "Sam had a routine, you see. I encourage all my employees to fully express themselves, do what relaxes them and so forth, while maintaining a high work standard of course." Just before one of the boys cleared his plate, he ran an index finger over it to mop up some of the remaining egg juice, then slipped the finger into his mouth. "Your uncle liked to swim every morning to keep in shape—ten, maybe twelve long laps about forty meters off shore—then he'd stroll out of the water and lie on the beach, watch the sky brighten. Build up the poetry, you know.

"The boys laugh simply because your uncle is rather endowed. He has a sublime body in fact. I never witnessed the spectacle myself, mind you, but it was described many times, and I have a decent imagination. How else do you think I built this place?" Lassiter permitted himself a half-smile, then reined himself in when he caught Nate's blank stare.

"So the boys loved to watch him emerge from the sea, the water falling off his tight abdomen. To be even more frank—and please do excuse me—they'd sometimes spy on him with Jackie, also. Peek through the cracks in the bungalow walls, you know, get their cheap little thrill before coming back up here to make breakfast. It was all good fun though. They miss him. We all do." A hush fell, and Lassiter gazed over at the Bosch print. "Sam had such a *presence*."

Toward the end of the spiel, Nate had begun to waver. Circuit Blast, another of his travel terms, meaning complete mental overload. Like Circushead, but weightier. He managed to catch something about some kind of favor that Jackie Yamada would routinely perform for Sammy, but he didn't initially comprehend. Then Lassiter motioned to the boys that he wanted to stand. Time for his massage. When they had pushed him, pillow and all, a workable distance back from the table, the boys—two on each arm, two behind—hoisted him up and stood in a circle around him, all at least a foot shorter. Lassiter assured Nate that Jackie Yamada would fill him in on whatever he needed to know when she returned from a short business trip into Krabi, invited him to breakfast the following day, and began to waddle away.

"You know," Lassiter said, turning to face him again, his breathing strained. "I did wonder if I wouldn't meet you here someday. Sam did speak fondly of you. Not often, mind you, but fondly when the subject came up … I couldn't help but think he must have been a rather significant figure for you."

Still cross-legged at the table, Nate hesitated—a brief, intense eye contact—before giving a single nod. He focused on the tiger tapestry, and Lassiter and his boys disappeared.

That evening after dinner, he waited on the beach in front of the restaurant. A fisherman had cut off and swallowed one of his toes in the near vicinity, an obese expat was groping teenage boys just up the hill, travelers with filthy clothes and heavy eyelids abounded, and he was about to meet a woman who had regularly licked butter off his uncle's balls. The nightly bonfire already raging fifty yards and a world away, Nate watched the slow metamorphosis of storm clouds on the horizon, still visible against the blue-black sky, and listened to the chatter in French, German, and Thai behind him.

Close to an hour later, Jackie Yamada came up from behind and asked if he was the one who had been asking around about Sammy. She looked younger than he'd imagined, her face in the low light clear and expectant, only a few wrinkles about the eyes, delicate smile lines. Her long black hair fell forward over one shoulder of a close-fitting white pantsuit.

Back in the restaurant she thanked the young waitress for pointing Nate out and ordered a pitcher of canned beer. She observed his face as she listened to the story of his journey.

"He must be pretty important for you to come this far with so little to go on," she said. When Nate looked away and took a drink of Singha, she reached across the table and squeezed his hand. "I do understand, though."

The pitcher nearly dry by the time the sky had gone black, Jackie Yamada's initial suspicion dropped like a robe outside a shower. His steady eyes and quiet way relaxed her, she said. His sincerity was clear.

After downing two more glasses from the second pitcher, she leaned forward and let slip in a low voice that Lassiter had bought off the local authorities from the beginning, when drugs really began to flow onto Ko Lanta in the early nineties. A third of the workers made a little extra in his "dating service" ring.

"Your lobster, sir. The trimmings are waiting in bungalow fourteen," she said, one eyebrow raised.

The conversation tonight, the entire day for that matter, still seemed to Nate like a hallucination.

Jackie Yamada went on to admit that she and Sammy had been loaded during most of their two years together, that Sammy had "a number of unhealthy habits for a man so fit." She stayed on at the Sun God Bungalows because she couldn't deal with seeing her family back in Okayama; it had been twelve years since she'd talked to her parents. Though a part of her despised Lassiter for his excesses, she liked living on the edge, in a world far from repressed Japan. The appeal of leaving behind the money-mad life for warm sea breezes, afternoons of reading novels and making love. Odd jobs here and there to earn a simple living. Amazing how easily a person could reinvent herself. When Nate told her what it felt like to be on the other end, having only fears and memories to go on, she only gazed at him, her eyes void.

The restaurant had cleared out, most everyone else down at the bonfire. The sound of an off-tune acoustic guitar fell away behind the clank and clatter of pans and dishes in the kitchen.

"He liked to go up to Bangkok every few months," she said. "One of his war friends ran, maybe still runs, I don't know, this little budget hotel in a garish area right off Khao San Road. Sam might have gone up there, I never found out. Clean break, you know."

A rise of laughter from the beach came, and Nate said he needed some time to process the day. He hoped she understood.

"You try Bangkok," Jackie said, pushing out her chair. "I'm sorry I can't help more. It was called the Sawatdee Guesthouse, of course. A guy named Dennis. Best of luck."

Nate thanked her. Watched her walk away until the white pantsuit disappeared in the darkness. She reminded him a bit of Lang, he realized, the slim body, the directness and feistiness. But he couldn't imagine Lang living among people who'd run so far, so long. Couldn't imagine her trying so hard to forget family.

Out on the beach, a good distance beyond the bonfire, he lay back and checked out the sky. At first just listening to the waves, then considering possible courses of action. He recalled not receiving any news from Lang or Hieu back in Jakarta, the unique loneliness of the road. And here he was trying to face up to his life by jumping into the sedative cloud of Lassiter's fantasy.

Still, it was good to be out in the open, especially after the cities—an odd reflection given that he would most likely head up to Bangkok the next day. Follow the lead, what the hell.

He lay there awhile longer, the air traced with salt and smoke, the sand cool, and thought he wouldn't mind a hardheaded woman there with him, the smell of her hair as she leaned back into him making the world seem safe enough for honesty. He imagined Lang, her unreadable face, arms open at the beginning of an embrace. Everyone an endless puzzle.

He got up and trudged out beyond the fire's light toward his bungalow. It had to be a matter of trying not to pin everything down. Valuing things as they are. Letting go.

Portland Police Department   Case# 96-0081A2 - Sex Abuse I
Transcribed Tape - 12-30-96

Wallace: This is Detective Sergeant Don Wallace sitting with
Malisha Jones and her aunt and legal guardian, Cherise Logan.
This is, let's see, Monday, December 30th, 1996, and we're at 103
North Mallson, Apartment 31, Portland, Oregon. 9:35 a.m. Okay
(unintelligible) Ms. Jones and Ms. Logan, you're both aware that
this conversation is being tape recorded?

Jones and Logan (simult.): Yes.

Wallace: This is my third conversation with Malisha Jones.
The last interview took place here in the apartment as well.
The case number is 96-0081A2, Sex Abuse I. Both Ms. Jones and
Ms. Logan have already heard me repeat the specific charges
against Mr. Hieu Nguyen, a science teacher at Wilson Green High
School. So let's begin this morning by letting you both know
that some of these papers in front of me are transcripts from
my previous conversations with Ms. Jones and three of these are
transcripts from my discussions with Sasha Anderson. I'd like
to refer to a couple of things in them today. First of all, Ms.
Jones, I'd like for you to recount again what happened to you
on November fifth of this year in Mr. Nguyen's science class.
Focus in on exactly what happened when he came up behind you.

Jones: We been over all this already.

Wallace: Right. But as I said earlier, I need to be absolutely
clear on what happened.

Logan: She's just so tired of answering all this stuff. She
thinks you don't believe her. I personally think you're siding
with (unintelligible) or however you say his name.

Wallace: This is standard procedure for this kind of investigation, Ms. Logan. I have to be sure of every detail, like I explained a minute ago. Please understand. This will go quickly.

Jones: (unintelligible) I said all this before. (Pause) I was
trying to get Sasha's attention 'cause she looked so messed up. I
just wanted to smile at her or something, you know. Tell her I'd
talk to her after class. But then Nguyen came up behind me and
snapped my bra and rubbed my shoulders. When I turned around
to do my work, he whispered, "Good choice." About a minute after
that he said to put away our journals for dismissal.

Wallace: You say Mr. Nguyen snapped your bra, then rubbed

Portland Police Department   Case# 96-0081A2 - Sex Abuse I
Transcribed Tape - 12-30-96

your shoulders, in that order?

Jones: Yes. Man-

Wallace: Did his hands linger? Did he massage your shoulders?

Logan: This is getting ridiculous.

Wallace: I'm perfectly serious. Because I'm positive that the
other students sitting at Malisha's table would have noticed if
Mr. Nguyen was standing behind Malisha giving her a back rub
after reaching down and snapping her bra. Every one of those
students have said on record that they saw or heard nothing
unusual, only Mr. Nguyen saying "Good choice" when he walked
up behind Malisha, and Malisha turning around to resume her
work.

Logan: Good God.

Jones: It wasn't like that. Man, I said that before. Ain't you
listening? It was real quick. Nobody else saw it. They was all
working they little asses off.

Wallace: The transcripts from my first two interviews with you
state that Mr. Nguyen snapped your bra, then slapped you on
the upper part of the buttocks. The transcripts from all three
of my conversations with Ms. Anderson show that she heard that
version from you, that Nguyen slapped your buttocks. Today is
the first mention of him rubbing your shoulders.

Jones: Man, you just want to mess me up! I don't believe this!

Logan: Calm down. Malisha, (unintelligible). Having all these
interviews at her age, going over the same stuff like this, it's
too much. This whole thing has been too much.

Wallace: Certainly. It's been very hard on a lot of people. But
it's just that I'm concerned about this slight change of story.
Today's discussion coupled with some interviews I conducted just
before the winter break make me suspect something isn't right.
Is there something-

Jones: I can't believe this! You always thought we was lying!

Logan: Girl, calm yourself! Answer the damn questions so we
can be done with this!

Portland Police Bureau   Case# 96-0081A2 - Sex Abuse I

Transcribed Tape - 12-30-96

Jones: There ain't nothing I can say.

Wallace: Malisha, you know I'm being fair here. I don't need to remind you that this is a criminal investigation. Now I need to know something else. May we continue?

Logan: Give her a minute please. (Unintelligible) with the man.

Jones: All right. But I just want to say that I been messed up by all this. So if a detail gets mixed up, it's 'cause I'm sick of going over it.

Wallace: Malisha, yesterday I had taped conversations with three of your classmates who have been mentioned in earlier student and staff interviews. These individuals claim that you, along with Ms. Anderson, are fabricating these stories against Mr. Nguyen in order to get him fired. How do you respond to that?

Jones: Who said that?

Wallace: Confidential, I'm sorry.

Jones: Well that's a nasty-ass lie.

Logan: Malisha!

Jones: Well it is! Why would we go through all this if we was lying? You think this is fun or something?

Wallace: In separate testimonies, I've heard that you were the engineer of a plot to get Mr. Nguyen fired because he gave you an F last quarter, and because he's so strict, and that you and Sasha Anderson coordinated your stories before going to Mr. Winchill.

Jones: I do not need to listen to this. You just racist like all the other damn -

Logan: Could we take a break?

Wallace: Certainly. (Pause) Ms. Logan, please discuss once again with Malisha that this is a criminal investigation. I need full cooperation.

Logan: Yes, I understand that. Malisha? Get back out here!

The Right Thing

When everyone finally finished the steelhead and crab he'd brought from the coast, Hieu rose to fetch the envelope that had arrived a few hours earlier. The letter from Nate had brought a final comfort to his day, a perfectly timed gesture of goodwill, after the long, quiet drive over the wet highways during which he dreaded his reentry into the city. He'd pulled up in front of the house, beneath Bing, still preparing himself for the rush of family life that was about to hit. How quickly the seaside calm had faded. But the letter was waiting, the postmark reading *Surat Thani* in faint grey ink.

"I want all of you to hear it," he said, stepping back into the kitchen. Anh, Lang, and all three kids had stayed put, as he'd asked; they broke off their conversation about a girl at Vo's high school who'd recently had her epicanthic folds removed in order to, as she put it, have "a more American look."

Lang shifted in her chair, then pushed herself back from the table, crossed her legs and lowered her head. Anh and Hieu glanced at each other before Hieu began.

> Dear Nguyen Clan,
>
> Here in southern Thailand on a gorgeous island called Ko Lanta, sitting in shorts and sandals at an open-air restaurant table for one, sipping a beverage that for some reason requires a small floating umbrella. Let's see, we've got some palm trees, sunshine, creature-filled forests, and then there's me, missing all of you.
>
> Vo, Le Phuong, and Dat would love it here. There's plenty to do, like snorkeling and volleyball, but there aren't too many kids, come to think of it. Please give them my best. Remind Vo to stop listening to that madness he calls music. It'll bring on some nasty disorder, I know it.

Hieu looked up at Vo, who was shaking his cocked head, restraining a smile.

> I was sorry not to receive any letters from you back in Jakarta, so I'll expect something in Bangkok (please send to the American Express office). A bottle of Bailey's would work fine, thanks. I'm also sorry about this being my first letter.

Hieu glanced up again, this time at Lang's bowed head. She'd been quiet again over dinner.

> No, I haven't found my uncle, but have managed to be fortunate on some leads. It seems that he worked as a cook here at this resort for awhile, and he did apprentice as an artisan on Bali before that. A woman here tells me that he went up to Bangkok (she thinks), to some hotel one of his friends owned (or still owns, I hope). I'll keep you posted, as I sense that I'm getting closer.
>
> Anyway, I should probably get some sleep, as I'm sure you can tell. I'll call from Bangkok (or God knows where) in a week. I want to make sure the investigation is over, like it should have been before I left. Also, please let Lang know that I think about her often.
>
> Love,
> Nate

Hieu folded the letter and set it next to his plate flecked with strands of crab meat, and for a long string of moments no one spoke. Then Anh instructed the kids to clear the table and begin their studies; she would be upstairs to check on them shortly.

When Dat, the last to have a turn at the sink, finished rinsing his cup, Anh leaned toward Lang and said, "We want to hear what you're thinking."

Hieu nodded, though Lang didn't see as she was still concentrating on her plate.

"We're family," he said. "We—"

Lang's head shot up. "You're one to talk."

"We're not talking about me right now." His right hand raised just in front of him, palm out, Hieu glanced over at Anh again.

"So strange, you know?" Lang said. "It's all right if you close off and torture everyone with your anger, but when anyone else gets upset, they're not allowed to proceed in their own way."

Hieu took a deep breath, in through the nose, out through the mouth, and Anh, needing to go at least one night of the week without a blow-up, reached over and placed a hand on Lang's arm.

"Of course you have to deal with things your own way. We all do."

At that, Hieu snapped his chair back and walked rigidly out of the kitchen, his plate and mug left on the table. When his steps faded, Lang shifted to face Anh.

"Your husband frustrates me so much." Her insomnia-reddened eyes made Anh look away.

"Me, too. But I think he's trying harder."

"He's *always* tried hard. At everything. That's what makes him so frustrating. Nothing can come naturally."

Anh leaned back and tilted her mug for a last sip of cold tea. The house silent save for a creaking of upstairs movement.

"How do you feel about the letter?" she said. "It sounds like he misses you."

Lang sighed. "That's what you're supposed to write." She finished off her own tea. "I don't know what I feel right now."

"I understand."

"He sounded upbeat, though, didn't he? I mean, *positive.*"

Anh nodded twice, mindfully. "I think so."

"Like he knows he's doing the right thing."

"I think so, yes."

"I can't believe ... how angry that makes me."

The women gauged each other a few moments before Lang closed her eyes and bowed her head again as if beckoned into a prayer.

The Blaring City

Garish, to Nate, seemed too tame a word to describe Khao San Road.

A slam of signs. Men hawking bootleg tapes and CDs, key chains bearing the king's likeness, Hmong quilts. Smells of incense and weed, broiling liver kebabs in the heavy air. Throngs of young Westerners parading along the sidewalks. Under an Aeroflot sign in front of a ramshackle travel agency, he ogled the scene and felt much like he had a short while before when, in a desperate move to distract himself, he'd braved the traffic over to the Oriental Hotel.

On the hotel's rear patio overlooking the boat-choked river, he had ordered a dish of roasted almond ice cream and pulled his guidebook and journal from his pack, wishing he hadn't forgotten to bring his baseball cap, the sun feeling like it was about to ignite his hair.

—Four hundred babies born yearly in gridlocks here. Welcome!

When the ice cream came in a tall crystal dish, he set upon it, opened the guidebook and began scanning for other must-see attractions, marking up the central city map with little stars, exclamation points. Since it was Saturday, the fifteenth of February, and since he didn't know if he'd be in Bangkok another week more after learning of his uncle's absence, he figured he might as well subject himself to even bigger doses of Circuit Blast. The hell with it. Anything to ward off the thoughts of Sammy. The fear of forever coming up short.

That morning, coated with a layer of grime by the time he'd been delivered from the southern bus station by a stoic tuk-tuk driver, he had found Dennis Brown, Sammy's war buddy, hulked behind the Sawatdee Guesthouse's front desk, calculating room tabs. While a part of him hadn't trusted Jackie Yamada's tip, another part had imagined the guesthouse lobby scene quite accurately—backpackers making plans, posters advertising various day trips. But unlike the greeting he received in the fantasy, Dennis Brown only glanced up at him, no welcome at all. Bull-necked, with beefy wrists and a hard-edged face that Nate thought could probably give Monty pause, Dennis held the horseback ride photo up close and set down his pen. His eyes changed—a hardly percep-tible softening—before he said that yeah, Sam was an old friend who'd stopped in to help out for awhile, but he'd "picked up and cruised after six months, God knows where."

Suddenly not in the mood for further words, Nate asked for a single, strapped on his pack again and climbed to a tiny room with Formica walls so thin he could almost hear his neighbors dreaming. While he planned to speak with Dennis more later on, to be sure, he needed time to unwind from the long trip and the city's butt-kicking welcome. The racket, smog, and tension from the swerving tuk-tuk ride had ham-mered him into wanting nothing but the safety of bed.

However, the walls proved too aggravating. Noises from other budget travelers, late risers, soon filtered in: an argument between two English couples over whether to leave for Kathmandu or Kuala Lumpur ("I need to soak up the energy of the Himalaya *before* I deal with bloody KL, Andy," whined one woman), a Frenchman singing "You Make Me Feel Like A Natural Woman" surprisingly well, feet thumping up and down the narrow staircase.

Nate tossed his guidebook, journal, and a half wrapper of chocolate wafers into his day pack, locked his room even though it would take only a lethargic kick to crack open the balsawood door, and descended to the now-empty lobby. The front desk vacant, he consulted the torn-out city map he'd stuffed into a pocket of his khakis, put on his shades, and headed back out into the blaring city.

Next day, a thick fatigue draped over him, he sat alone at a sidewalk table in front of the Sawatdee and considered how the prospect of find-ing his uncle had kept him going despite the travel stress, confusion, and tempting detours. But now his hopes, as he put it in his journal, had sunk like a turd in a tub. He eavesdropped on conversations ranging from Calcutta's best restaurants to the limits of relativism, and soon added,

—"Advanced Denial," the new one-day seminar by master N. Davis, author of *Adventures in Neurosis* and *Vacations for the Insane.*

Definitely time to take stock. Reevaluate plans. He observed his surroundings, feeling weirdly outside himself. Across the garbage-strewn alley, a shaggy Westerner from a neighboring guesthouse squatted in front of a scabby-headed, caged Rhesus monkey, feeding it ashes from three ashtrays. Farther on, a legless beggar sat on a piece of cardboard next to an emaciated water buffalo. As he watched the beggar work, he let the sadness come again. Caught up in the sappy-ass notion that he was merely days away from a reunion, telling himself so often that he had to be getting close, he'd felt connected to Sammy. But now the slipping feeling was back and his body seemed to be following his mind downward. For a reason that completely confounded him, both his eyes had become bloodshot a few hours before, right around the time he developed an urge to piss every fifteen minutes, a burning sensation making matters worse. Had to be psychosomatic.

After lunch a short while ago, he'd found Dennis Brown at the front desk again, this time working a crossword puzzle. The dome of his large head tanned and freckled, the back sprouting enough thin hair for a ponytail, Dennis had taken one look at his eyes and said, "Whoa. You hung over or what, bud?" Since no one was waiting to check in, Dennis dog-eared his puzzle book, cleared his throat and forced a cough, looked around the lobby for a few seconds, then startled him by saying that a guy deserved to know about a missing loved one. Before he could respond, Dennis added that he and Sammy were in the same platoon, witnessed "things people just shouldn't see."

Dennis pointed to a row of folding chairs against one of the lobby walls and stepped around the counter.

"We each extended our tours," he said, taking a chair, "mostly because of the rush of it all."

Sam had been a sight in those days. One of the most ferocious soldiers, at least on the outside. Quick. Thorough. Always determined to get to a buddy who'd gone down, no matter how ugly the scene. Or, as one of the other perpetually wasted guys, Harold Weatherford, had put it from time to time: "Sam's a *crazy* mo-fo."

Nate's stinging eyes remained locked onto his uncle's friend. A tattoo on Dennis's closest forearm read *Wide Awake*, just the small words in faded grey through the curly brown hair, no accompanying design. The man seemed to fall easily into recounting his impressions of the war, as if he were asked regularly about them. Or perhaps he'd merely thought on his words after their surprise meeting yesterday.

Still without any prompting, Dennis mentioned that foot rot was a major problem, and that the villagers usually looked at them like they were from outer space. Then he jumped to a description of the smell when he first arrived at Tan Son Nhut: trash and shit burning along the edges of runways. He talked about the incredible heat and having to get used to exotic insects, then meandered into a couple of stories about how, "in a flash," the platoon would go from butt-scratching boredom to total chaos. "Sounds weird to some people, but I don't think we ever felt so goddamn alive."

Nate let the pause stand, absorbing the tail-end of the flurry. The traffic sounds, reggae music from the restaurant now gone to him.

"What about when he showed up here."

Someone shouted from the kitchen and Dennis excused himself. In his wake, Nate remained seated, gazing at the vacant front desk. He tried to picture his uncle behind it, greeting backpackers from all over, handing out keys, signing people in. He envisioned the photograph on Nolan's cafe wall back in Penelokan: Sammy next to old Nyoman, palming the big blue Foster's can.

After a time, Dennis returned and muttered something about needing to train new personnel way too often. Too much turnover with all the vagabonds he hired. He settled back into his chair and said, "When Sammy showed up, let's see …" He sighed. A woman wearing thick black eyeglasses burst from the kitchen doorway and said, "*This* one?" as she held up a black-and-white-striped apron, and Dennis nodded. When she'd gone, he glanced sidelong at Nate and folded his arms over his belly.

"What can I say? I was jazzed he came. You do not go through something like we did and just forget the bond." He turned his head again and waited for Nate to look over at him. "Though guys do try."

Sam had talked about his family all the time while they were in Vietnam, but never mentioned anyone back home during his time at the Sawatdee. All he ever said about it, on his first trip up to Bangkok while he still worked the job on Ko Lanta, was that his return to the States after the war had been "totally fucked."

When Nate remained silent, Dennis proceeded with random thoughts, still no sign of the previous day's reticence. "We took some R and R here on our first tour. Pretty outrageous scene then. Smack, cocaine, brawls. Just lettin' it all out. I mean, there was everything. These shows with girls gettin' wild ..."

A group of five backpackers, each person in baggy shorts and T-shirt, loomed in the doorway, checking out the looks of the place.

"But like I said, it was great to have him here." Dennis's voice had gone back to its deeper, flat tone. "People loved the guy. The old Davis charisma. Had the ladies around here goin' nuts."

Nate stood, legs weak. He wanted to hear more, he said, but was feeling strange physically. Off somehow. As he began to move away, though, he caught himself and turned around.

"Do you think he's crazy now?"

Dennis's expression didn't change. Eyes distant again after the flash of recounting old days. He looked off at the Sawatdee's entrance, the backpackers gone. "You know, man ... I only knew him after he'd already killed people."

Back in his room after settling his bill at the outdoor table, Nate stared into the mirror above the little sink. It was as if someone else was looking back, his demon counterpart. He had just returned from the toilet down the hallway, the burning still strong, when he noticed a twinge in his left ankle, on the inside of the joint, and another pain along the sides of the same foot's Achilles tendon. His right wrist, too, had begun to stiffen. He stood before the mirror, thinking again that he must've slept in an awkward position the night before, and that the bloodshot eyes were due simply to fatigue and the Bangkok air. Maybe his diet lacked some essential vitamins. Whatever it was, he would rest a few days. Come up with that new plan.

By the next morning, though, the wrist and ankle pains had worsened, and now his lower back hurt, around both sacroiliac joints. A fever and chills had arrived sometime in the night, also. At dawn, after trying and failing to walk, he pissed into an empty Gatorade bottle and resolved to wait until he heard someone stir and ask them to get Dennis.

To pass the time, he gazed at the pallid yellow shade drawn over the lone window, listened to the first distant whines of motorcycles and scooters, and wrote slowly in his journal, a loose grip on his pen.

　　　—How fast everything changes.

He turned onto his unscarred side and studied what he could see of the contents of his open backpack on the floor next to the bed: flattened brown sandals, laundry and sewing kits, his toiletries in a Ziplock bag. Then finally he heard someone—a skinny Hungarian named Béla it turned out—coming down the hall. He called out a hello, explained his predicament.

An hour and a half later, Dennis having already checked on him twice, on the second visit bringing some poached eggs and a pot of green tea, the door opened again and a woman carrying a grey leather bag stepped in, Dennis right behind her. It was a mark of a strong spirit, Nate would later think, that before inquiring about his illness or even introducing herself, she came directly to the side of the bed, took his hand and smiled. Nothing overdone, just a kind acknowledgment of the situation. Unlike the so-called experts who usually seemed to ignore the soul. At the time, however, the move mortified him, the room smelling, as Dennis had described a short while earlier, like an "egg-fart-sweat stink." She had calm eyes, a good smile. Thick dark hair.

Dennis introduced her as Dr. Mary Youngblood, a friend who worked at a US–sponsored women's clinic nearby, the only "medic" he'd ever really trusted. The doctor asked Nate to call her Mary, told Dennis she'd come find him after the exam, and began digging though her bag for a pen that worked. She explained that she and Dennis had met at the US Information Service library in Bangkok, that she'd been watching a news report on Vietnam War MIAs when Dennis sat down across the table, nodded a gruff hello and watched with her. She'd helped run a clinic off Siam Square two years now since moving from Santa Barbara, where she'd practiced at a hospital. Dennis occasionally called for help with ill Sawatdee employees.

When she was ready, Mary Youngblood sat at the foot of the bed and asked him to recount the sequence of symptoms.

Before he began, he looked at her a moment longer, then shifted his focus to the window. Odd, after her flurried initial set-up, that she suddenly didn't seem to be in any hurry, though Dennis would later mention how she ended up being late to a Red Cross meeting.

He wound up his macho version status report by asking what she thought.

Mary put the pen and pad back into her bag, then came to the head of the bed again. "That you're in quite a bit of pain."

During the exam, his sweat-dappled T-shirt hiked up his side and she asked about the scar.

"I teach high school. Former student decided to come after me a few months ago. At least I think it was a former student. Out in the parking lot after work." He pulled his shirt down, and she remained there looking at him. "Tried to go back right afterward, get back into things … But it didn't quite work out."

"Do you think you could tell me a little more about it?" she said, eyes still steady. "My younger brother's a schoolteacher, middle school. He absolutely loves it. Most days." She returned to the foot of the bed, tucked one leg under her.

Though he began haltingly, only the rough framework of events seeming at all worthy of reportage, Nate soon found himself elaborating on his return to Wilson Green, and how he hated leaving those kids halfway through the year like that, but the stabbing had pushed him toward the Asia journey. When after a good ten minutes the doctor remained seated—nodding, occasionally asking questions—he pressed on, giving into the surprising urge, telling a bit about Hieu's case, then Sammy, and even Nolan, Mick Lassiter, and Jackie Yamada. For nearly ten minutes more he talked. With a look-away grin, said that he must've been lonelier than he'd thought. Needed to get out more. Sounds from the hallway were clear to him now, a conversation in Swedish, someone running up the stairs.

"Important spot you're in, seems like." Mary rose and bent to open her bag again, then stopped and craned her head up, a few strands of hair falling over her face. "You know, I don't want this to seem like some tired come-on or something, but listening to just that part of your story ... You seem familiar. I'm not sure why."

She smiled and Nate didn't reply. He was conscious again of the room's smell, peeved that he hadn't asked Dennis for a candle or some incense sticks, at least an orange or something.

After taking a blood sample and doling out some fifteen-hundred-milligram ibuprofen pills, Mary admitted that she was unsure about what all the symptoms amounted to, that she'd never before encountered such a bizarre combination. She would check with some colleagues and bring the results of the blood test tomorrow. He should rest, try not to worry.

—⁓—

Alone that evening, in the light of the vanilla-scented candle that Dennis had brought, he propped himself up against the pillows. Though he'd wrapped his bandana around his wrist for a brace, his writing was still slow and faint.

> —The doctor here asked about the scar. It hit me how well I've been blocking things out. It still blows me away to think of the power of whatever has chained up that kid's mind. Hard to believe he was driven to such an act just because I flunked him and called his mom weekly about behavior. So what brought it all back to him a year later? Was he struggling with what he planned to do, or were his nerves cool?
>
> If I'm being honest, I don't know that I want to be a part of that world anymore. Too many people too comfortable with victimhood. Granted, there are many who try extremely hard in many ways, but I'm tired of putting out fires.
>
> I want to say fuck it, but then can't seem to do that. (Sweet easy

cynicism.) Then I ask, How do we come to let ourselves get hooked
on frustration?

Nate tossed the journal down into his pack and listened. Traffic in the
distance. Someone's heavy breathing from the room to his left. The ibuprofen was helping some, but the pain still bit hard and often, especially
in the left ankle. He tried to clear his mind before sleep, but Aaron's voice
kept cutting in.

Round one, you dumb-ass bitch.

No face. No discernible body type.

He'd been thinking about what he would order for take-out at El Loco
Burrito as he slipped his key into the lock. The darkness was thick that
night, only one other car—Clyde Jackson's white Volvo wagon at the
other end of the lot—visible in the gloom. A shower had just passed and
the air was cool, a super-fine mist still falling, clouds low. He heard no
footsteps or rustlings, no movement other than his key turning in the
lock, when it happened: the ripping between the two lowest ribs on his
right side.

Through the ringing of his mind, the words in his ear. *Fuck you, Davis.*

When the powerful arm let go, he could only turn and lean against his
truck door and hold his leaking side, the key chain pressed into the small
of his back. It had been done so quickly, the idea of giving chase absurd.

White shoes flashing across the field.

After emerging from beneath the first wave of shock, he still believed
unshakeably that the deep voice belonged to the boy with whom he'd
clashed so many times the year before over everything from missing
assignments to classroom vandalism to threats flung at most everyone,
including himself. A kid just brave and strong and troubled enough to
follow through.

But the police said they needed more to go on, Aaron's alibi was tight.
They'd gone to his house on Borthwick Street and found him playing
Nintendo with his three older brothers, wearing a pair of blue sport
sandals. They'd taken him in for further questioning and found his as-
tonished, supportive mother working swing at the Nike outlet store on
Martin Luther King Jr. Boulevard. Yet when the news reached Nate at

the hospital the next morning that there wasn't enough evidence to hold Aaron, it didn't change what he knew.

He untied the bandana from his wrist and blew out the candle. Wiped his face and neck, dropped the bandana into his pack.

Eyes closed, he pictured the Brightwood cabin. The surrounding trees and the old porch steps. But then it was the recollection of Mary touching his joints that distracted him. The slow-moving hands that knew how hard to press.

He pushed the thought away and called up an image of Lang, his companion half a world away who definitely deserved more tenderness. He would be a better man, learn to cherish what he had. Be more disciplined. Certainly there were people one occasionally met who did seem familiar—beyond sexual attraction, people who did explode time with their presence. It was simply a matter of understanding those meetings to be nothing more than novelty's sly enticements.

A Mysterious Ailment

44/99 Khao San 24
Soi Rambutri
Bangkok, THAILAND 10090

19 February 1997

Ms. Lang Nguyen
Hello Portland!
3400 N.W. Flanders
Portland, OR 97210

Dear Lang,

I didn't know if you followed through on getting a new apartment, so I thought I'd send this to the magazine. (What a lead! Hire me!) Anyway, I just tried to call you, then Hieu, but you're both out it seems. I apologize about not getting in touch sooner. A combination of our argument, my desire to dig into this trip, and a bout of illness.

Now and then I'll look at my watch and imagine you sleeping or writing, or maybe taking a bath. Lang, I've also been thinking that I should have been more tender right before I left. It was such an incredibly strange time. I want you to know that I'm sorry about being distant. I get that way to such an extent sometimes that I mistake the closed-off feeling for what I really feel.

But then being away has been good, even though I haven't found Sammy (and am now at a complete loss on that front). I guess we just come to certain points where we need to step back and try to make whatever form that takes reasonably healthy, you know? Do you believe this too? Or is my leaving still hard to understand? I'd love to hear what you're thinking these days.

Actually, I'm a bit shaky right now. It seems I've contracted a mysterious ailment that has brought arthritis to my right wrist, left ankle, right knee, and lower back. I've seen a doctor, had a blood test and everything, and we still don't know what it is. (She thinks it might be rheumatoid arthritis, but Jesus, I'm only thirty-eight.) I'm downing loads of ibuprofen and some prednisone. Don't mean to alarm, but I wanted you to know what's up. I had a serious urge to talk with you just now, so I hopped down to the lobby telephone and let your number ring about 400 times.

I'm sure you're kicking butt at *Hello Portland!* The editors see they've hired a tigress of a writer. I look forward to reading your latest stuff when I get back. As to when that happens, I'm not sure yet. So much depends on this ridiculous illness and on whether I can get any more tips about Sammy. I honestly don't know where else to look, though. I can't quite imagine him going back to Vietnam, but who knows?

How's Hieu? I trust the investigation is over by now. Has your mom finally come out of her room? How are Anh and the kids? Let me know what you're thinking, cat. I should be here a while more.

Love,

Nate

Armor

Lang returned from an upscale delicatessen on Twenty-Third Avenue with Tran Vu, a fellow reporter who'd been hired three weeks before her, and found Nate's letter on her desk next to a heavily edited story about a controversial new zoning ordinance. Before opening the letter, however, she forced herself to glance over her editor's comments and cross-outs, then looked out the window above her desk at the two dripping cedars just beyond the glass. Her cheeks and scalp felt warm.

Halfway through the letter a third time, she swiveled her chair and scanned the office for Tran, a steady-eyed man with soft hands and a calming smile four years younger than herself; after only two lunch dates, something was definitely happening, something that made her slip into daydreams too often. Tran nowhere in sight, she turned to face her disaster area desk again, letter still in hand. She needed to wait awhile before writing back.

It seemed that Nate was still interested, but over the course of the month he'd been gone, she had moved beyond rage and grief to a state she knew came too easily—the withdrawal that had always made living bearable during tough times. She admitted that she shared the ability with both her mother and brother, but while it irritated her whenever she saw it in either of them, she could usually tolerate it better in herself.

As a schoolgirl trapped in an overstimulating classroom, understanding only a little English, she'd quickly honed her ability to harden up, turn inward. Her first teacher, Mrs. McAllister, talked so fast compared to the English speakers on Phoenix Island and at Fort Chaffee; school exhausted Lang, the straining to translate alone. But it was during the lunchtime recesses, especially, that the feigned aloofness saved her from breaking down. When other students either ignored or jeered the handful of Southeast Asians sitting on the school's back steps, she learned to keep her face expressionless. But many of the words—dink, dog-eater, Chink, nip, gook—penetrated the armor, and she cried sometimes when she got back to the Halsey Square apartment, and even later when the family moved into a two-bedroom bungalow on Sixty-Third Avenue near Sandy Boulevard. Whenever she saw the same distant look on her family members' faces after they came in from the outside world, or when she heard the muffled crying, Lang knew exactly what was happening.

So in that way, she felt close to her relatives, even though it had become more and more difficult to get past the layers of defenses and have loose, open conversations. It seemed that, for everyone in the family, the more they wore their armor during the day, the harder it was to remove it in the evenings. Hieu and Dat experienced the same wariness, if not outright hostility, at their high school; Hoa and Aunt Mai picked it up on their trips to the grocery store; Uncle Phat encountered it in various subtle and not-so-subtle forms as he worked his janitorial and landscaping and, later on, real estate agent jobs.

Because the Nguyens were among the First Wave, the people of Portland, on the whole, had been cautious. Most people were trying to forget what had happened in that mysterious land they'd seen on TV; they certainly didn't need reminders. Some Portlanders, while far from cruel, just didn't know how to approach a person who looked so out of place, who probably couldn't speak clear English. The new type of foreignness had been a touch too foreign, Lang always suspected. Nevertheless, though she didn't blame people for keeping their distance, it had sometimes made living seem a bit too hard, too tough.

For Hieu, it was Wilson Green High School that eventually became the most difficult place in which to keep himself intact. On the commons his first day of duty in September of '84, a scrawny boy yelled, "Go back to China!" when Hieu asked him to pick up his littered lunch sack before going inside. His third month, a week before the Thanksgiving break, a girl mocked his choppy speech in front of his entire first period class, making him step into the hallway to steady his breathing before filling out a detention form. And there had been a number of other comments that first year as well, when his accent was still so heavy, when he was suffering the usual initiation pangs to boot. Conducting classes in a highly idiosyncratic second language had, in fact, brought him to the brink of quitting. While he'd specifically requested an inner city placement—all part of his plan to somehow atone for laying the pinless grenade and mine—he drove home most days cursing his idiocy. But he stuck with it, even after spewing stored-up emotion in front of Anh and young Vo a few times, and after developing an eye twitch that provided the more persistent, daring students with added ammunition.

For Lang, while she wasn't involved with difficult kids, the armor seemed to gain layers over the years, to the point where she often found it difficult to distinguish her facade from her innermost self. The incidents of blatant racism, while increasingly rare, could still be accessed at any time, the words and looks lurking along the edges of her mind. Occasionally it occurred to her that she might be projecting narrow-mindedness onto others to the extent that she received what she emanated, but it had always been easier to see the world in stark terms. When it seemed that most everyone else insisted on dwelling upon humanity's divisions, it was extremely hard not to play along.

Though she did have many acquaintances and a few friends of different races—people from Portland State, the journalism community, and Gerrard's Gym, where she worked out four days a week—there remained a certain distance in those relationships. Of course most everyone, she had come to admit by her late teens, wore some kind of armor, each with a distinctive individual or family crest across the chest; but it was a cold fact that some people lugged heavier gear. After debating herself about opening up more, she would invariably conclude that she'd been through too much to let down her guard with a person who didn't intimately understand the suffering she and her family had experienced.

Her feelings toward Nate, then, had always perplexed her to a degree. From the moment they met at Old Town Pizza for Vo's twelfth birthday, the strength of her attraction had always made her slightly uncomfortable. To be close with someone from such a different world, who didn't know what it was like to live through the horror of something like a bomb strike, had often of late seemed impossible to her, especially when Nate got so caught up in his intellectualizing, his searching. To set out on a journey to find someone who didn't want to be found still seemed so idiotic. The man clearly had no real idea about what it meant to lose something dear, even though he always claimed he did. Again she told herself that Nate was simply unable to endure the type of relationship she needed: one that made the world seem safer. Her conviction provided an odd kind of comfort.

She watched the rain dripping off the cedar limbs outside her window and latched onto the well-worn thought that Nate was still a boy. A boy trying to become a man in a most ungraceful way. She held his letter in her lap, though, reluctant to face the job of rewriting the zoning ordinance story that was due in just under two hours. But when Tran Vu came up from behind and whispered in Saigon Vietnamese that he'd had a terrific time at lunch, her body relaxed. Her mind cleared. It felt good to smile, she thought, as she slipped the letter into one of the piles on her desk.

Portland Police Department   Case# 96-0081A2

Transcribed Tape - 2-18-97

Wallace: This is Detective Sergeant Wallace with Sasha
Anderson. It's 9:05 a.m. on Tuesday February 18th, 1997. We're
in the interview room here at the Portland Public Safety
Facility, North Precinct. Ms. Anderson was excused from school
this morning as I felt it was necessary to conduct this interview here. In this room as well are Ms. Anderson's lawyer, Ms.
Talia Sherman, and Ms. Anderson's mother, Marguerite Anderson.
All right Sasha, uh, Ms. Anderson, are you aware that this
interview is being tape recorded?

Anderson: Yes.

Wallace: For the transcript, note that I'll refer to Sasha as
Ms. Anderson during our discussion. My questions will be for
Sasha Anderson only. The case number is 96-0081A2. This is my
fourth interview with Ms. Anderson, one of the two girls who
allege that they were touched in a sexual manner by their
science teacher, Mr. Hieu Nguyen, at Wilson Green High School
on November 5th, 1996. Over the course of the past month of
this investigation, a number of inconsistencies have come
up in my interviews with the victims and also certain witnesses. The purpose of today's discussion is to address those
inconsistencies.

Anderson: Seems like you made up your mind, sounds like.

Wallace: Ms. Anderson, please just clearly answer my questions
this morning. I realize we've gone over this information in detail before, but it's very important that you answer truthfully
and clearly. This is-

Anderson: A criminal investigation.

Wallace: Ms. Anderson, please don't interrupt me. (Pause) All
right, uh, so let's begin by recounting what happened immediately after Mr. Nguyen asked you into his office.

Anderson: (Unintelligible) I can't do this no more. I'm
sick of it. I'm so sick of this. Just shut that thing off.
(Unintelligible)

Wallace: Ms. Anderson, we need to get to the bottom of this now,
so all of us can stop being sick of talking about it.

Portland Police Department   Case # 96-0081A2

Transcribed Tape - 2-18-97

Anderson: Fuck this whole thing! We just wanted to get his ass fired, okay?

Wallace: Ms. Sherman (unintelligible) the record. All right. Ms. Anderson, now please explain what happened. We all want to get this over with. Try to help us understand.

Anderson: (Pause) We was pissed off 'cause he's so fucking mean. We both got Fs in his class even though we turned in most the work.

Wallace: So you made up the entire story then, both of you?

Anderson: Carson helped us. We thought he shouldn't be around kids. He's cruel. He just dumped...

Wallace: He just dumped what?

Anderson: Nothing. Man, fuck this.

Wallace: I need to know everything now.

Anderson: We gonna get arrested? Because we had a right to do what we did.

Sherman: Sasha.

Wallace: Ms. Anderson, please tell me why you and Malisha carried things this far. Do you realize what these accusations have done to Mr. Nguyen? Do you understand how many people have been involved with this invest-

Anderson: You know what? Fuck that man. He's a nasty fuckin' gook. I'm serious, fuck him. Fuck all this shit.

Part Three

—⁓—

Two Makes of Man

Gratitude is heaven itself.

—William Blake

A Secluded Stand of Spruces

After meeting with his baggy-eyed long-term sub the day Wallace called to report that the case was closed, Hieu sat rigidly on his stool at the front of his classroom and took in the lab counters, posters, and charts. Such a familiar, comforting space, and still, even after all that had happened, the sense that it could be magical. But at the same time, everything had changed.

He stood and walked around the room in a dreamy state much like the afternoon he'd been informed of the accusations. He could still detect the energy, the fierce daily struggles, as he circulated around the tables. In front of the photograph of the startled Vietnamese woman in the paddy he stopped and stared: the elephant grass, hamlet in the distance, the woman's annoyed, yet graceful expression. She had indeed been jolted out of her rhythm.

The intercom clicked on, followed by Winchill's voice: "Hieu, could you stop in on your way out please?"

When the room went silent again, he stepped over to Sasha's table, pulled out her stool and glanced at the open office door. The image of the room had tumbled through him so often during the twelve weeks he'd been out, the afternoon of the alleged touching turning over and over; he had dissected it countless times, probing for details he could have possibly overlooked in the buzz of teaching. His terse exchange with Sasha. How he'd followed her into the office and tapped her sternum with the very same index finger he had once run across her cheek.

His feet looped around her stool's legs, he pictured the spot to which he'd taken her in Washington Park the previous summer, and he allowed himself to dwell a moment on her body, an indulgence that could still alter the rhythm of his breathing. Her legs had pressed against the edges of the stool he was sitting on. He imagined her clearly, like he always could, then snapped up off the stool.

At the classroom doorway, he hit the lights and viewed the walls and tables, trying to steady himself with slow, deep breaths, looking back and forth between Sasha's and Malisha's seats as if the girls might suddenly appear by the sheer force of his furious will. How they had managed to keep their story together for three whole months, and the gall it took to lie again and again to a police officer, still amazed him. Why Sergeant Wallace had begun to reinterview so many people toward the end of January was even more perplexing, especially when it seemed that he was about to break the case open, at least according to Clyde and Desiree. But then America had almost always been like that; confusion seemed to be the norm.

When he pulled his door shut, the hallway's quiet jolted him. It seemed that no one else was around—no voices, no music drifting out of Mitch Vance's room, no distant clattering of Monty's keys or dustpan. On the way to the main office, he peeked into rooms and still couldn't find anyone, something he'd experienced only a few times during the early mornings when he had come in to prepare for a particularly complicated lab or to have some quiet time to grade tests, plan lessons. He knocked on Winchill's half-open door and was relieved to hear a reply.

"It is dead around here," he said.

"Most of them already took off probably." Winchill closed the thick classroom supplies catalog in front of him. "It's been one wild week, I tell you. Had another bomb threat. Some jerk taped something up that looked pretty darn good. Timepiece, the works. They left it in a stall, one of the second floor toilets."

The news slid off Hieu like water from an otter. So strange being back. Lonely. He dwelt again upon the sense he'd been left far behind in the mad race of days.

"The craziness goes on," he said, realizing that he had sat down in the same chair in which he'd absorbed the initial shock of the accusations. He recalled the tightness in his chest, Falsworth's and Bailey's averted eyes.

Winchill, fuller of face after the holidays, reached into a manila folder and pulled out three letters.

"I wanted to show you the copies of the expulsion forms," he said, handing them over. "The kids received these yesterday. What happens with the police we're still not sure, but they won't be back here. Carson's is there, too."

Hieu surveyed the documents, and after a time said, "I wonder how they will turn out."

One hand spread over his chin, Winchill searched Hieu's face.

"They deserve some hard consequences. That's part of why I asked you to stop in. Have you considered defamation of character suits? You'd win easy. These people need to understand how serious this was. It'd help them in the long run, I'm sure."

Hieu didn't take his eyes off Sasha's form.

"I ..." He examined the letters of her name—such a disparity between the indifferent black type that reduced her to a case and the memory of her saying "Treat me right" under the cover of fragrant boughs and a dimming summer sky. "I think they have probably learned enough already."

Winchill leaned forward, elbows on the desk, thumbs pushed under his chin.

"Just a thought, but please consider it. You went through too much. You deserve some compensation."

Hieu set the papers back onto the desk and stood. "Anything else? I am sorry to rush, but I need to get home. Today is my daughter's birthday."

"Is that right? Well, I do need to show you one other thing, but it's in the lounge. Just take a minute or two." Winchill pushed himself up, tucked the tip of his peanut brown tie into his matching slacks. "Found something I thought you'd like to see."

At the lounge door, he stopped and insisted that Hieu go in first, motioning like a butler of old movies—the bow, the sweeping, palm-up bid to enter—and as Hieu came through the threshold, the entire Wilson Green staff, including Uli Wegman, shouted "*Welcome Back!*"

Hieu blushed, eyelids fluttering. He struggled to take in the old faces, the balloons and signs, the tables packed with cookies, chips, and soft drinks. Terrell Martin turned up Bob Marley's "Satisfy My Soul" on a portable stereo, Desiree hurried over and engulfed Hieu in a long swaying hug, and the party began full force. Monty, toting a sign that read *Innocent!* in rainbow letters, swaggered up and gave a slap on the shoulder; Uli smiled and extended a greeting card; Clyde held out a piece of pudding cake, locking eyes with Uli for a moment before pulling Hieu into a one-armed embrace; and Winchill leaned in the doorway like a proud father, arms crossed, watching his relieved, overworked brood make merry. "You all deserve it," he said, no one hearing him. "You really do."

—⁓—

On his way home nearly an hour later, the recollections of his evenings with Sasha Anderson came flooding back. For some reason the investigation's resolution had brought more grief than relief.

Up to that point, he had been able to cope with what happened over the summer fairly well, and he'd convinced himself that Sasha was dealing with it too. But when Winchill handed him the expulsion papers, his attempt to forget about the trips to Washington Park had split open like a week-old wound. How they'd gone to the park twice, warm evenings when Sasha had worn thin sundresses. It was just that she'd been so irresistible, he told himself again. So expressive and assured. It was something, a freshness, he'd never before known.

As he drove through the back streets toward his family, he reviewed the line of thinking that had, since summer, allowed him to get at least some sleep most nights: Always struggling, needing to be so industrious, he had simply never lived out his early years. Even in the States, in high school, he'd been too shy and tormented by his still-warm memories of the war and escape to bother with indulging desires, the so-called darker impulses. Passions had to be suppressed in order to sustain the energy required for survival, let alone success, in the hard new land. Then at Portland State, with the pressure to keep his biology department and general university scholarships, he'd graduated in three years, dividing his time between study, family matters, and a part-time job in the Portland State library, only dating a couple of times, his final semester, the woman he would end up marrying a year later, a woman to whom he was only marginally attracted, but whom he respected and trusted and slowly came to love. Experimentation of most any normal kind had always seemed too indulgent. Too risky.

So when Sasha slipped him a note one morning the previous spring, he'd found himself rereading it for days afterward, wondering just how to respond, wrestling an astonishing urge. The note said up-front that she wanted to be with him, that she had never wanted a teacher before, but he was too tempting—his "deep" eyes, his strong body. He was strict and all, but still nice, and she always liked how he was fair with her, she respected that. She didn't care if he got angry about the note, didn't care if she got in trouble. She wanted him.

While he had tried to dismiss the words, he understood immediately that Sasha Anderson represented a rare, perhaps one-time chance. She *wanted* him. But she was, of course, only sixteen, a fact that allowed him roughly three hours' sleep each night for two weeks straight before he managed to summon the courage to reply.

Sixteen, but so experienced, Hieu kept thinking as he pulled over and parked his minivan under a sycamore, knowing he couldn't go home and face Le Phuong yet. Sixteen going on twenty-three. It was just that Sasha was so undeniably sexy: the confident eyes, provocative breasts, the full, glossy lips. Clear skin smelling of coconut lotion, her body fit, but not especially athletic, her movements had been so sure for her age. It seemed that many people still didn't realize (or were too scared to acknowledge) how sexually knowledgeable a sixteen-year-old could be. And they probably weren't aware that students could receive free counseling on birth control options at the school's health clinic.

He had decided to be noncommittal in his response—a folded note stapled to the back of a respiratory system assignment he passed back—to see if she was actually serious. The note read: *Am I understanding you correctly?* But when he received her reply two periods later, hand-delivered in the packed hallway right outside his room during passing time, he resigned to the draining lust. In an instant, after speeding through her words, he had decided.

> Mr. Nguyen,
>
> I think about you all the time, but especially at night. I want to touch you. I've never felt quite like this. I know this is crazy, but I can't get over it. You are just too sexy I guess.
>
> Yours,
> Sasha

The day school let out in mid-June, after enduring her glances for an entire, rackingly long month, he had written another note, following the same procedure as the one before. *Friday, June 20. 7 p.m. Middle of Pioneer Courthouse Square. Come alone.* On her way out the door, having read the message in class to his horror, Sasha caught his eye and nodded once. It had been too easy.

The warm, clear-skied evening of June 20, he waited in the coffee shop above Pioneer Square, scanning hard for her, trying to squelch his nerves over a cup of ice water and a chunk of biscotti. He'd calmly told Anh that he was going for a drive to have some time alone, that he would be home in a few hours. Lying had been so exciting, he recalled now, watching raindrops coat the windshield. But how he'd been able to go through with it still stunned him. It had been too simple to convince himself that he wasn't some depraved fiend, merely a human being with understandable-enough desires.

It had been surprisingly easy, as well, to approach Sasha after spotting her in a white sundress walking alone from the bus mall across the square. And while the drive through the crowded streets up to the park was awkward at first—he jabbered about how he didn't make it downtown often enough—everything ended up going smoothly, especially after Sasha loosened up by turning on the radio and changing the channel to a pop station, then rolling down her window and singing softly. Her boldness had made all the difference, he thought. She'd been irresistible, enough for most any man to lose his mind for awhile.

In the western section of the park, they found a secluded stand of spruces in an arboretum that he had discovered on one of his solo hikes a few months earlier. On a piece of soft ground, they laid out an old quilt he'd found at the bottom of a cardboard box in his basement, a thick green-and-white checkered spread. Then, from his wicker picnic basket, he pulled out a bottle of sparkling cider and two plastic cups, some black grapes, a mango, a box of crackers. Lines of low sunlight streamed into the grove, long shadows sprawling up a nearby wooded rise, ferns blanketing the slope.

There were no sounds outside their electric space apart from the occasional *pip-pip-pip* of a flycatcher, the nervous chitter of a swallow, and light gusts of balmy wind through the trees. Wordlessly, he peeled the mango with the Swiss Army knife Nate had given him for his thirty-sixth birthday four years earlier. The slippery fruit cupped in his hands, he motioned with his chin for Sasha to lean down and take a bite. She asked what kind of fruit it was, and when he didn't answer, she eased forward and bit off a piece. "Sweet," she said as he lifted his hands and ate into a chunk next to the tooth-scarred part. He still couldn't fully believe what he was doing, but the sensation spreading over his chest and groin couldn't be ignored.

It was after only a few more bites that Sasha leaned in and whispered that she was glad he liked her. She held that position, the front of her dress lowered to reveal her bare breasts, until he nodded, mouth open. He set the mango back into the basket and dropped the lid; Sasha sat up on her knees and stared into his eyes. It was as if he were in the midst of a most vivid fantasy, a gift that the spirits had, for some incredible reason, chosen to bestow. He brushed his index finger along her cheek, and when she licked her lips he let out a soft moan—a sound he had never before allowed himself to make—and from there knew it would be tough turning back. He sensed himself letting go, actually allowing himself to enjoy the gift of physical pleasure. He deserved this one thing, this one taste of freshness. Without any hesitation, Sasha kept looking into his eyes, as if waiting for a signal, and at length he reached up and brushed her cheek once more. He wished he was young again, in the forest surrounding his village; he wished that he and Sasha were the same age, they could ride each other under the sun-spotted trees into some kind of better future. But it was still perfect to break out of the dutiful mold, even if only for awhile. Fling off the soul-stifling yokes. For awhile, he could rise from himself. Soar.

But when she began to lean forward again and whispered that she was on the pill, plus had brought some condoms, he stopped her, mumbling he didn't want to move too fast. A gush of worries: someone discovering them, his possibly embarrassing overexcitement, pregnancy and disease, his having never used a condom. And then the barely noticeable but steadily pricking fear that his feeling of entitlement might not vanquish the shame.

Four evenings later, though, at the exact same spot under the 150-foot spruces, they again drank sparkling cider. For four days and nights he had wrestled himself. Daydreams. Nightmares. Nausea. That second evening, Sasha wore her other sundress, her pink one with small white polka dots, and she gasped when he ran his fingers along her collarbones. He still couldn't bring himself to kiss her, but the light touching along her face and neck was easy enough.

That second time, however, she had eventually begun to speak breathlessly, saying in an almost aching voice how much she wanted to do it with him and wanted him to protect her, how she wanted to be his secret lover. She asked him to treat her right. At that, she pulled away a bit and gauged his astonished expression. "Just treat me right," she said. "I haven't been with a guy who treated me right. I been with some, but they don't know how to do it good." And it was then, hearing the urgent, almost panic-laden words, that he had frozen, his decision rising before him like a startled cobra.

On the drive back to north Portland, he promised himself not to see her again, even though her coconut lotion wafting through the minivan was, to his amazement, making him hard. Just up the block from Sasha's house on North Phillips, he pulled over and switched off the engine and the headlights, then fled the torture of yet another pause by turning to her and saying, "You are very beautiful, you know."

"So when are we goin' up there again?" She reached for his thigh and he flinched. "What's *wrong?*"

"I think … this must stop." He couldn't look her in the eyes.

And so it went. Sasha asked him three times what exactly he meant, and when he didn't reply, flipped him off, her stiffened hand an inch from his lowered head. She called him a typical man, a pussy of a man, her voice raised by then. He wouldn't even kiss her because he probably didn't know *how* to kiss! She punched the horn twice, got out and slammed the door, still yelling. A few porch lights turned on and dogs barked and he kept his headlights off as he drove away.

At home he examined his eyes in the bathroom mirror, astounded that he'd given in to the spirits' honor-testing trick, convinced that he had shamed not only himself but his family, living and dead. For a long time he sat on the edge of the tub and promised himself never to let anyone know, no matter what. He could still hear Sasha saying that she wanted him, and his upper chest felt like it had been punched.

Later that night as he lay awake in bed, having risen completely out of desire's haze, it abruptly occurred to him that the girl would tell someone, that somehow the secret would come back and bite him. But then he could make himself crazy, worrying about Sasha calling and divulging everything to Anh, or even to one of the kids. Strict thought control was the only answer. He wouldn't be able to live otherwise. He listened to his wife breathing beside him, to the creaks and sighs of the old house. Harden up to the fear. Like always, the only way.

Beneath Bing's dripping limbs, he pulled up and spotted Le Phuong through the blurry front room window, watching for him. He needed to compose himself, redirect his thoughts, in order to be fully present for his daughter's tenth birthday, an event she'd been asking about for over a month. For each of his kids' birthdays, he had always planned some kind of celebration, be it going out on the town as a family or having a party at the house with school friends.

He climbed the steps, legs feeling shaky, and Le Phuong opened the front door.

"Where were you, Daddy?"

"Some things at school. Are you ready for your present yet?" Hieu smiled and held a manila folder packed with welcome back cards over his head, the rain still falling hard.

"Daddy." Le Phuong gave him a look. "We've been ready since five o'clock. It's already six."

Inside, he found Anh, Hoa, Dat, and Vo in the front room, wearing their best clothes like he had asked. Hoa and Vo were both frowning, Hoa looking a little too formal in her shiny lime green *ao dai*.

"I'm sorry," he said. "There was some more business about the investigation." Probably best not to mention the surprise party.

Again, the crash of worlds. Only moments before, he'd been thinking of Sasha Anderson, her face in the forest light. He gazed down at Hoa's steady black eyes, trying to reach her with his apology, and it occurred to him, as it often had the previous few months, that he might not be worthy of their patience.

"The concert begins at eight," he said. "The reservation at Hollander's was for six, but I'll call. We can be there in fifteen minutes. Phat and Mai are probably there already."

Le Phuong's eyes had widened.

"Concert?"

"Mozart and Schubert. DePreist conducts."

At the mention of the symphony, Vo mumbled something, Dat giggled, and Hoa's expression remained the same. While Le Phuong hugged him, Hieu glanced down at his frowning mother again, the high-collared *ao dai* bolstering her presence.

The eyes …

She detected something. She had finally glimpsed his heart, something too clear now. He was certain of it.

Gestures

It felt, at times, as if someone were running an X-Acto knife up and down his Achilles tendon. The wrist, too, still throbbed, swollen to the point where he couldn't make out any outlines of bone. But his back seemed to be getting a bit better, the steady rounds of prednisone and ibuprofen doing at least some good. While the fever and chills had mostly gone, he remained weak, sometimes delirious, thoughts stray and fantastic, on the verge of dismissing the entire experience as a vivid dream until the next slice of pain.

Dennis continued to bring up meals and sticks of incense, usually lingering a short while to tell more about Sammy or share the latest Sawatdee gossip, and Béla, the Hungarian schoolteacher who'd first heard his call for help, stopped in now and then between trips out into the city. But mostly Nate passed the hours by himself, thinking, trying to sleep, often just staring at the window or at the rowboat and ducks painting on the wall opposite him. Sounds of life nearly always filtering through the walls.

Lang. He admitted it: some of the intense attraction had worn off. Natural after several years. But then he still didn't quite trust himself. Maybe the slight loss of interest amounted mainly to outside stresses. The drain from old wounds. Too many unconscious forces at work probably, and besides, he did love her.

At length, he worked himself into the belief that finally, after four up-and-down years, he was beginning to grasp that she wanted to live a more predictable life, squeeze out uncertainty as much as possible. He didn't know if he could abide her inscrutable ways, but he would try again. Be more stable. More confident.

He then spent the following half hour listening to the newly arrived Australian couple next door having sex.

Unable to sleep that night, he lit a candle and pulled out his journal.

> —Remember this, how everything is stripped down.
> Lots of thoughts of Lang and people back home. I'd like to tell them I'm sorry about being such a shit, not looking past the petty annoyances more often to their best aspects.

But when Mary visited the next afternoon, the regret didn't seem quite so pressing. She found him half-asleep, absorbed in another foggy meditation, when she arrived with chicken noodle soup, two orange sodas, and the results of the latest blood test. Though this test, like the first, signaled only a reaction to fecal-borne bacteria, the pain's specific cause still undetermined, she said that a regionally known arthritis expert from India she'd met last year would be in Bangkok day after next for a conference at Chulalongkorn University and that she would find a way to bring him to the Sawatdee. (As she recalled, Dr. Lal had insisted that he owed her one because she'd helped drive him around town during his visit.) She apologized again for her confusion, but the arthritis sections of the books she'd consulted hadn't listed the collection of such disparate symptoms. Her colleagues were stumped, too. She was reluctant to prescribe treatment beyond the ibuprofen and prednisone.

"So you'll have to put up with me a little longer," she said.

They regarded each other for a few beats, then Mary smiled and opened the cans of orange. Outside the door, Béla was talking with a Canadian woman about places to stay in Chiang Mai. Nate took a well-disguised sniff to see if the room still smelled of incense, which it did faintly, and when Mary turned away to open the soup containers, he swished his fingers through his hair.

"Actually, I'm surprised you're going to all this trouble."

Mary continued arranging the lunch, slipping a plastic spoon into his soup.

"Well, maybe I'm one of these women with an over-developed sense of giving." She held out one of the sodas. "Or maybe I live close by, say only five blocks away, so this is no problem at all. Or … I could be doing it because Dennis is paying me handsomely. Guess you'll just have to live with the mystery."

She sat at the foot of the bed and began eating, her soda propped in the gap between his blanketed feet. She asked about his joints, and Nate gave a quick run-down, aware of how she looked cupping the soup, her face genuinely interested through the rising steam, lips slightly parted.

"And your head?" she asked. "How about your thoughts?" The question made him stir the soup. "Just wondering how you've been dealing when you're alone is all. The not knowing makes it harder, I'm sure."

Though the admission made him curious even as he spoke, he told how he'd been escaping into thoughts of Lang, how he wanted to get clear about whatever was keeping him from leaping into marriage. When Mary only nodded and kept spooning soup to her mouth, he pressed on, saying that he regularly seemed to find something to worry about regarding his girlfriend. Most everything else for that matter. Sad case.

"There's this Chinese saying." Mary paused for a drink. "It is the height of stupidity to look for the donkey you're already riding on."

But then shortly Nate noticed that she'd become quieter. Didn't look him in the eyes as much. At least it seemed so.

When they'd both finished eating, he asked why she chose to live and work in Bangkok. Time to hear some of her story. He'd babbled quite enough.

Mary lowered her head for a moment, then gave a half-smile, as if she'd come upon some calming thought. Divorced with one kid (a bright and bookish daughter, a senior on the Pepperdine basketball team), she'd sold her Santa Barbara house, sent most of her stuff up to her parents' place in Yreka, promised her daughter that nothing would change her motherly feelings and they would see each other at least three or four times a year, then set out with two duffel bags, a few references, and the address of the Siam Square clinic where she ended up being hired. She chose Bangkok because a colleague at the Santa Barbara hospital had lived here a decade earlier and enjoyed its pulse and convenience as the region's hub. She

wanted some adventure in her life, pure and simple. Wanted to use parts
of herself she didn't know existed, learn how to trust herself again in light
of the divorce. The color in her cheeks high, Mary concluded by saying
she'd about had enough of Bangkok, though; she was getting ready to
plan her return to the States. Needed to find a place she would "have a
hard time taking for granted." Somewhere not quite so far from family.

Nate watched her face, glanced now and then at her body as he listened. Fit thighs through the thin blue slacks. Smooth skin. The graceful gestures—a particularly fine way of tucking her hair behind an ear.
When she spoke of her daughter, he noticed, she set her spoon into the
container and leveled her eyes straight at him. She seemed to be someone
who realized that a moment needed to be treated with care. Probably
from being around so many sick people.

But then, he didn't know what she was about at all. It was too easy to
project depth onto someone who appeared intelligent and articulate.
Too risky.

That night, he tried to ignore thoughts of her. Browsed the *International Herald Tribune* with which Dennis had bundled up dinner, observing that it had been nice not reading any newspapers or watching
television the past few weeks, the ever-important twaddle. Life did seem
more elemental now. Slower. As uncertain as things were, maybe the
illness was actually aiding him. Strange consideration; helpful though.

The newspaper lowered to his lap, he closed his eyes and listened. For
a time he heard only traffic, then came murmuring voices from down
the hallway and a buzzing from someone's travel alarm. Like the clothes
dryer buzzer in the basement of the house on Lincoln Street. Sammy
running up the stairs, yelling his name. He was four, maybe five, playing
with his Hot Wheels in the front room when Sammy charged in, yanked
him up and dropped him into the big white hamper with all the warm
clothes. He flung Sammy's socks and boxer shorts all over the sofa and
carpet, and then his uncle, laughing a high maniacal laugh, threw a loud
Hawaiian shirt over his own head, picked up the hamper and gave a wild
spinning ride. The fresh laundry smell, the heat of the soft clothes. Pure
home. Things would turn out okay. Everything would be all right.

The X-Acto pain dug in and Nate gripped the blanket. Eyes wet. When the usual steady throb resumed, he dropped the newspaper onto his pack and settled himself enough to piss into the Gatorade bottle he kept under the bed. At length splayed his journal across his lap. Continued to breathe deeply, like Hieu had shown, and soon calmed to the point of being able to write.

　　—I think of Dennis and Mary bringing food and clean sheets, and of Béla stopping by. The simple gestures. Then I ask myself, How did I become a person who overlooks so damn much?

The Spirits Work That Way

Though the case was officially closed now, the tension in the house remained almost unbearable to Hieu, his mother glaring at him every chance she got, especially during supper with everyone gathered around the kitchen table. He had tried to confront Hoa in her spartan bedroom the day after Le Phuong's birthday, but she'd refused to speak, only shaking her head, intent on the small shrine dedicated to her husband: the one photograph that had ever been taken of the obstinate man enclosed in a pewter frame above two votive candles, a bowlful of sticky rice, a plate of sliced mango, and two incense sticks burning in an applesauce jar.

In the photo, Hieu's father stood in their village's central meeting area, holding a bamboo pole in one hand with two plucked ducks hanging from each end, his face grim, body lean under the short-sleeved shirt and rolled-up trousers. Still young, free of opium's headlock. For Hieu, the photograph amounted simply to proof that his father had indeed been tough, or at least expert at portraying tough. But for Hoa, it was a relic to be honored daily, part of her solitary worship. Every morning and evening, and oftentimes at random points during the day, she prayed for the soul of her husband as she prayed for the souls of her ancestors; though their spirits remained with the ancestral land, she believed that her prayers still counted for something.

Yet Hoa prayed for the living, too, especially her children and grandchildren. She devoutly sent Minh good thoughts, wherever he was, and she always asked that Hieu and Lang could find their ways in this life. The sessions brought simplicity and structure to her days in the midst of such a disturbing world; the bedroom shrine calmed her, helped her remain in contact with her visions and sorrows, especially with everything that had happened of late with her troubled younger son.

Hieu's fear that she understood whatever it was that had begun to surface within him was being fed by the day. It seemed to him that the old woman had always been able, sooner or later, to detect the contents of her children's hearts, a talent he hadn't inherited. When his mother locked herself in her bedroom the following afternoon, two days after Le Phuong's birthday, after he'd tried to corner her once again with questions about what exactly she was so upset over, he opted not to knock or talk through the door, as he had so often over the years. Instead he turned away, grappling words, needing to lash out. Anh would be the perfect target, certain to put up a good fight. But she was still at work. On the stairs, though, he came upon Vo, who was just getting home from school. They brushed against each other, Vo's backpack falling from his shoulder.

"Excuse me, turbo," the boy muttered.

At that, Hieu spun, leapt the three stairs that separated them and grabbed his son by the jacket collar.

"Let go-a me!" Vo's eyes were level with Hieu's mouth. "I didn't do nothing!" He tried to pull away, but Hieu picked him up by the front of the jacket and pushed him against the wall, jamming his head against one of Le Phuong's framed watercolors, a scene of a mother elephant and her calf walking through high golden grass.

"You will not talk to me that way."

"Let go!"

Hieu held Vo against the watercolor, searching the boy's pinched face, a part of him dazed over what was happening. He turned and saw Dat and Le Phuong at the bottom of the stairs, clutching their school packs, mouths agape, and it was then that Vo brought his knee up hard into his father's crotch. Having freed himself, Vo grabbed his pack and ran up to his bedroom, and from behind the locked door yelled, "Psycho!" When the shouting died out, the old house creaked and went still. Hoa remained in her room.

In his fetal tuck on the stairs, Hieu steadied his breathing. Unfurled himself and sat up. Le Phuong and Dat stood frozen, tears tracing lines down their faces. Silent, equally motionless, Hieu kept looking at them as he tried to slow the spinning world.

When at length he felt strong enough to rise, he gave a little nod before turning away and gingerly stepping up to Vo's door. He listened awhile to his son's crying.

"We will talk later," he said.

Vo screamed "Psycho!" again, and Hieu checked his impulse to pound the door. He returned to the top of the stairs. Dat and Le Phuong were still waiting, faces glistening.

"Sorry you saw that," he said, descending. Sweat droplets dappled his forehead and his eyelashes were moist. On the landing he reached out, and after a brief hesitation during which they glanced at each other, Le Phuong and Dat came forward and hid their faces in the sides of his soft sweater.

—*w*—

Next day, after a solo lunch of peanut butter toast and tea, Hieu reclined in his easy chair, lifted the inch-thick police report from the lamp table, and took in the house's quiet. The kids were at school, Anh at the district's central office leading another ESL seminar, Hoa over at the Vietnamese American Community Center helping out with preparations for an evening awards banquet.

Earlier that morning, having dropped off his still-silent mother at the center's front door, he had forced himself to drive back over to North Precinct in order to take Wallace up on his offer of a copy of the investigation's transcripts. The documents were, after all, open to the public. While he kept telling himself it would be best not to dwell upon everything that had happened, he couldn't seem to suppress his curiosity about the other testimonies in the case, namely Sasha Anderson's.

But as it turned out, the shock came not from anything Sasha told the sergeant; Hieu accepted that she had come close to pulling off her story. Nate's testimony, though, was something else altogether. Brow arched, he reread the interview transcript, unable to comprehend why his friend had seen fit to divulge the locker room conversation. No wonder the case had dragged on. The day of the ice storm, he recalled.

He ingested Nate's exact words yet again, shaking his head at various points, then dropped the report back onto the lamp table and observed the room. The photographs of Vietnam provided some solace, as did the lingering smell of *pho*. But more than ever he was caged. He needed to do something. He stood and began walking around. *Psycho! He's mean … pushes students way too hard … He mentioned something about girls here being sexy and curious.*

Hieu stopped in front of a photo next to one of the bookcases, a shot of a Saigon avenue, cyclos and scooters and bicycles tangled at an intersection. *Don't forget what they did to father … We usually couldn't tell who or where the enemy was. We just shot first, asked questions later.*

 He sat back down, picked up the report and flipped to Nate's testimony. From time to time he looked off blankly as he tried to hear his friend's voice telling Wallace everything. Calf muscles clenched, thumbnails pressing into the report. He needed to get away. Perhaps the coast would be good again, this time for a longer stay. Right foot tapping the floor now. Then he remembered his request to use the Brightwood cabin. While he knew Nate hadn't received his letter in Jakarta, the suspicion of purposeful neglect jabbed nonetheless. To confront the bastard would be so sweet. To heave their friendship into Nate's face—yes, that was what he wanted.

He slammed the report down and reached for the phone.

In the house on Lincoln Street, Acacia was heating some leftover chicken pot pie and watching the noontime newscast on the twelve-inch kitchen TV, a story about some Canada geese that had developed an affinity for an elderly southwest Portland woman's front yard. Grandpa Davis, still recovering from a bout of bronchitis, reclined on the sofa in the living room, watching the same newscast, just managing to hold down another coughing attack. He had almost launched himself into another fit a few minutes earlier by calling out to his daughter to ask when lunch would be ready.

When the phone rang, Acacia paused the microwave, turned down the television, and took a long drink of Dr. Pepper. Hearing Hieu's voice, she pulled out a chair from the nook table.

"Well hey there," she said. "It's been ages, you. You got my card in December?"

"Yes, thank you. The case is closed finally."

Acacia eyed the TV, a woman wearing impressive gold earrings mouthing something to the reporter. "Has Nate talked to you at all? Does he know?"

"He must not if he has not talked to you."

"You know, I'm a little worried 'bout that guy …" She trailed off, still staring at the television. "Haven't heard anything except for a postcard from Bali 'bout a week after he left."

Discussing Nate made Hieu want to yell.

"Ms. Davis, I am sorry to be abrupt, but I called to ask a favor."

"Oh hey, absolutely." Acacia ogled Will Thornton, her favorite weatherman. His shoulders and chest filled out his suit so nicely.

"I asked Nate recently if I could use your cabin possibly for a few days, to help get my head clear after everything … My family and I have always had such good times up there, and since I did not hear anything back from Nate, I wanted to ask you."

Acacia turned away from the TV and told Hieu to hang on while she started the microwave again. She looked out at the backyard laurel for a few moments, raindrops pelting the leaves, then reached back for the phone.

"Sorry 'bout that, I'm just heating up some lunch. You know, Hieu, I don't know if that'll work actually. During the winter it's all shut up and everything. There's a lot of snow up there right now."

"I can shovel, or chop wood. Things have been quite crazy lately, as I am sure you can imagine."

She heard her father call out, asking who it was.

"Hieu, I feel horrible 'bout this all of a sudden. But the more I think on it, I just can't, I'm sorry. Dad's always been real strict about letting it out. He wouldn't even let his own brother use it once. It's absolutely nothing against you. Please understand."

Hieu swallowed, the silence stretching.

"Yes," he said finally. Perhaps Nate really had been in contact with Acacia, for some sick reason told her about the locker room comments. "I was only curious. Thank you for considering it, Ms. Davis."

When Hieu hung up, Acacia held the receiver to her neck. She knew her reply had surprised him, but the decision was easy. No question. Then, from the front room, her father's second cry for lunch sent her scrambling back to the microwave. On the TV, the two male anchors were flirting with the big-smiling consumer alert reporter.

The more Hieu thought about it, the excuse Acacia fed him was further evidence of Nate's betrayal. She would never have denied such a request if she hadn't known about the locker room talk. Even Acacia, who had always been so kind, who'd invited Anh and him and the kids over for dinner a couple of times, then up to Brightwood for summer sleepovers—even she was against him now. *We just wanted to get his ass fired … He's mean … I just hate him so much.*

But then it was right for her to be suspicious. Completely right for things to unravel. The spirits worked that way. It was how the world was. Simple. Kill people, take a sixteen-year-old girl into the woods, deal with the aftereffects. The spirits were speaking, yes, letting him know that one by one, each aspect of life he held dear would slip away. *You're holding something in … Family is everything.*

In front of another one of Le Phuong's watercolors—a five-by-seven-inch scene of a lone Douglas fir on a steep incline, the rest of the hill razed and brown, the sky grey—he stopped cold. Only a few more years and Le Phuong would be in high school. He allowed himself to picture a middle-aged man spreading out a blanket for his daughter and he shuddered. Swept his hands over his face. A moan escaped him, and then he was weeping silently, forcing himself to focus on the watercolor, shapes and colors merging.

Hieu sat at the dining room table and laid his head onto his arms, and soon another memory cut into him, a hamlet scene: his father curled up on the sleeping mat; Hoa cooking in a corner of the hut, skillfully ignoring her husband's gripes; Lang bringing in another load of firewood; the pigs rooting around just outside the door; soup and smoke and sweat smells, then a whiff of duck barbecuing on the neighbor's spit. *Family is everything. Don't ever forget.*

A Fissuring

In the hot, dim room, sleep was haphazard, like the previous few nights, a drifting between pain-wracked consciousness and dreamworld wandering. Moments before, the spasms in his back having temporarily eased, Nate had been lost again on a fogged-in mountain trail, the narrow path through the woods visible only a couple of steps ahead. Unfamiliar terrain, yet the same undeniable urge to move onward. In the grey mist this time, however, he'd come upon Aaron Harrington leaning against a hemlock stump, sagging pants, oversize hockey jersey, cold stare and all. It was when Aaron said in his low voice, *Fuck you, Davis* that Nate opened his eyes and noticed his heartbeat in the afflicted wrist and ankle.

As though a kind of presence had entered the room, goose bumps raised on his arms. Suspended again in the compact space between pain and dream. It was wrong an hour before, he knew, to have taken threefold the amount of ibuprofen and prednisone Mary had prescribed, wrong to give in so completely like that. But he'd needed to escape.

As he broke into another sweat, it occurred to him that maybe the state he was now experiencing amounted to a long-needed fissuring of the ego, a glimpsing of something larger—an energy of which he was only an infinitesimal part. He still felt suspended, yet perfectly aware for a few beats, and when he reemerged into near-full consciousness, sensed only that he'd brushed against something he would probably later have a tough time grasping. A power normally too awesome to face was guiding him along, and his mind usually went on resisting in spite of its buried knowledge that the power would never go away. Beyond (yet at times hidden within) words, beyond most rational human interpretations of divinity, the energy filling the room lived on in its inexhaustible glory.

He was sure of it, though the only proof he had was the prickled skin on his arms, the shivers now flicking over his shoulders.

A couple of hours later, Mary arrived with two cups of fresh-squeezed orange juice and Dr. N.P.S. Lal, the arthritis specialist from New Delhi.

Dr. Lal, a towering, husky man with a hairy, severe face beneath a navy blue turban, surveyed the room with a slow turning of head. When a half-naked German couple began oinking, chasing each other, throwing bars of soap and wadded up hand towels out in the hallway, the doctor let out a soft sigh and closed the door. But soon after Mary's introduction he appeared to relax. Lowered his nicked-up bag to the floor and asked Nate to recount his symptoms dating back three weeks.

Nate looked at Mary and Dr. Lal for a few seconds before answering. The conjunctivitis, urethritis, spreading arthritis. The Achilles tendon. Dr. Lal then asked about any major stomach ailments the previous month, and Nate reported the shrimp kebabs in the Jakarta airport, the toilet runs in Kuala Lumpur.

"My friend," said Dr. Lal, a half-smile barely escaping his beard, "you have what is known as Reiter's Syndrome."

A somewhat rare condition, he added when Nate only gazed at him. Triggered by a food poisoning episode and a certain genetic marker known as HLA-B27 positive. At that point, he pulled a thick grey book from his bag and started flipping pages. Mary lowered the juices to the floor, sat at the foot of the bed and gently squeezed Nate's toes through the blanket. The oinking in the hallway had ceased.

"Here." Dr. Lal handed him the book.

And indeed, there it was. All of the symptoms listed in the *exact* order they had occurred. Speechless, Nate lowered the book to his lap.

Within a few minutes the turbaned giant had filled a syringe with cortisone and injected the ankle and wrist. Dr. Lal then prescribed a full series of shots when Nate returned home, which would be best to do as soon as possible; he would come back in two days' time to administer another round right before leaving for India. Efficient to the last, the doctor gathered his book and bag and said he was sorry to rush, but needed to be getting over to the university, where he was scheduled to give another lecture in an hour's time. He said good-bye, scanned the room once more, and made for the door. Mary handed Nate one of the juices and accompanied her consultant back down to the lobby.

The room quiet again, he eyed the Band-Aid on his wrist. So that was that. Incredible. He could still feel the cortisone advancing around the ankle: a bizarre sensation. He pictured Dr. Lal's face, the earnest eyes and the beard, and heard him saying, "You have what is known as Reiter's Syndrome." To have an illness named did make it a bit less frightening, but the advice to get back home still burned. He realized the degree to which, in spite of the uncertainty, he'd clung to his belief that he might not need to give up the search for Sammy; the period of illness, while significant, possibly transforming, would surely be only one leg of the journey.

From the corridor, morning noises soon drifted in. Holding the plastic cup in his hands, he told himself not to think about his uncle. Better to let go, somehow trust. Full of a conviction that made his gut relax, he lifted the cup's lid and took a sip of orange juice and was overcome by the taste. The wash of sweetness on his tongue, the ache of cold on his teeth. Never before, it seemed, had he been so conscious of a flavor. And right then Mary returned.

"Wow," she said. "I didn't know you could look that happy."

"Didn't know anything could ever taste so good."

She'd seen it quite a lot, she said, a reawakening of the senses. A paring away of worry, too.

"Still a little stressed, don't get me wrong." Nate took another drink. "That just snuck up on me."

Mary rested at the foot of the bed and drank at her juice awhile before bringing up Dr. Lal, how he had insisted the consultation be free of charge. He liked to do it that way now and then, he said, before getting into the taxi. Dennis had come out to see him off, too. Offered to pick up the bill.

Cup against his chest, Nate watched her talk. Her eyes and her mouth. When she stopped and asked if he was all right, he looked away, then faced her again and said, "I still don't know why you're doing all this ... But thank you."

The room was too quiet now. More hallway sounds.

He peered into his pack, sweeping glances at her profile. He needed to lighten things up, but she said, "So what's worrying you?"

The question made him conscious of his facial expression. Each possible sign of nerves, just how long to keep eye contact.

"Worrying me?"

Mary smiled.

"You just said you were stressed. I don't want you to worry about your treatment is all, I think you'll notice a difference pretty soon. He's considered one of the best in his field in this part of the—"

"It's not that. At least I don't think … I don't know."

"You okay?"

He was confusing himself, too. Circuit Blast. In the scramble for some centering subject, he pictured Lang. Lang drinking tea in her kitchen.

"Sorry," he said. "I'm a little out of it … Sort of worried about my girlfriend I guess. We haven't talked in awhile." Though it felt like the right thing to bring up Lang again, he noticed how hard it came. "Maybe you can tell me how a person knows when it's right?"

Mary took another drink. Shrugged. "Maybe when a feeling stays strong enough to make it so you don't have to keep asking that question." Her face flushed when Nate lowered his eyes. "But listen, I'm no expert in this field."

Nate tossed back the rest of his juice and mentioned how he sometimes had a challenging time understanding Lang, cultural differences seemed to get in the way, the baffling nuances. And like that, he regretted his words. Too much disclosure, not to mention the unmanly vacillation. Best now to shut up, yes, and so he asked Mary to share more of her thoughts. He'd love to hear a quick story before she left for work. Anything.

She gave him a long look, another smile. On the subject of tough relationships, she began by saying she had been married almost eighteen years to a real estate agent, a man eight years her elder named Stuart who ran beach volleyball clinics for teenyboppers on the side. She acknowledged early on that she'd married too young, but she loved the man and believed through most of her twenties and early thirties that they would weather the various stages of marriage, unlike so many of their friends.

Her family was of the collective mind that you wed for life, come what may. Out of the entire clan, only a second cousin was divorced, and that was because her husband had been caught on videotape (by a voyeur next-door neighbor) drunk off his ass and humping the sedated Newfoundland on the backyard deck one evening when he had the house to himself.

Nate's attention now riveted, Mary went on to say that her family—both parents, two brothers (her oldest sibling, Mitchell, died in Vietnam), and a few aunts and uncles—remained in the Yreka area, the majority involved in either the restaurant business or logging. Her mother and father owned a place called Mama's Kitchenette and another named Mama's Luncheonette, both in Yreka; her brother Ted dabbled in real estate when he wasn't flipping burgers (Mary met Stuart through Ted at a Sacramento convention in 1976); her younger brother, Lance, taught middle school P.E. and coached baseball; and the only other person she cared to bring up, her Uncle Maxwell, drove a log truck out of Fort Jones, "a tiny little town just southwest of Yreka." When she mentioned her uncle, she grinned, so Nate asked about him.

Uncle Maxwell, Mary resumed after checking her watch, used to take her for rides in his semi (nicknamed *The Mighty Brown Lemming* for some disconcerting reason), and would sometimes let her steer, even on the wet and winding highways. Occasionally told logging stories, too, that made her laugh and cry both.

One time, in the fall of '55, he'd been up in the Siskiyou Range helping clearcut fifty acres of 140-foot-tall incense cedar. The morning air cool, sunlight filtering through the remaining trees, Maxwell was walking alone on a steep slope re-marking one of the cut's boundaries when something made him stop. It wasn't exactly a howling. Wasn't a coyote-like yapping either. More of a wailing sound, like an extremely large old woman *keening*. (At that point, Mary cocked her head back and gave a low-volume approximation, like her uncle would have done, she explained.) Shivers wiggling over him "like spooked caterpillars," Maxwell dropped into a crouch; the sound came from what seemed like thirty yards uphill. Too close. He could see a few of the other guys through the brush and trees, standing out in the middle of the cut, frozen and facing the baffling sound. It was as if the creature was in mourning, as if it had finally realized it could do nothing to stop the invaders from carrying its home away on trucks.

Bigfoot, the crew decided only half-jokingly when it gathered at the base of the hill a few minutes later, when the keening stopped; no other animal any of them knew had ever sounded like *that*. In time, Maxwell set out up the slope again, "eyes big 'round as softballs," and it was then he first admitted there was a part of him that hated what he was doing.

Mary paused, tucking some loose strands of hair behind an ear.

Maxwell once said with a wink that he couldn't see the forest for the trees when it came to his profession, but had to keep filling the demand for wood, especially now that the Asian markets had really opened up. He needed to be true to who he'd been all these years. "What the heck else can I do?" he'd said the last time they saw each other, at Christmas three years before.

When Mary bit the lip of her cup before taking a final swig of juice, Nate raised his eyebrows.

"But what about the sound? What happened?"

She looked at him, holding back a grin at first, then giving in to it.

"Well," she said. "Not one of them ever heard it again. So I guess I'll end the story like Uncle Max always did …" She assumed a solemn expression and leaned forward, close enough so Nate could see faint caramel-colored freckles on the bridge of her nose that he hadn't noticed before. "What do *you* think it was?"

Later that morning, he wrote slowly.

—It's confidence that makes people most sexy. Her unpretentious swagger is infectious.

—On confidence: So many of us end up rattled. The rug gets pulled out and we never quite seem to recover balance. Even though Mary's dad sounds a bit like Grandpa Davis and her mom sounds slightly touched (on her days off the woman watches motocross races and Australian rules football as she alternates between jogging on her treadmill and downing Nutter Butters), they seem to have given Mary a steady sense of welcome during her childhood. They truly

wanted her, I'm guessing. How they showed it I'm not sure. I think of
so many Wilson Green kids, that "rug pulled out syndrome." Not that
Mary hasn't struggled at times, but I suspect her basic grounding, that
poise, came from the relatively stable Yreka world.

And later still, moments before Dennis brought up another noodle
soup lunch:

> —After telling one last detail about her divorce (Stuart, the prick,
> admitted to having a three-month affair with a college freshman from
> one of his volleyball camps), Mary changed the subject. "Nate, I think
> maybe your girlfriend might need more reassurance."

It's strange to admit there's a reason I met this woman, but more
often than not lately I find myself believing it. Glimpse of an over-
arching order? Unexplainable.

So Beautiful, So Sexy

In front of the Vietnamese American Community Center on Sandy Boulevard, Hoa stood under the big green awning clutching her purse, waiting for her son to pull up. A storm had begun to move in; with Arctic air swooping down, freezing rain had turned to snow in the twenty minutes she'd been waiting. Her mittened hands getting cold, she tried to contain her annoyance by being mindful of it.

Half an hour after he was supposed to be there, after she had gone back inside to call home, Hieu sped up in the minivan and tapped the horn. He slid to a halt, tires jamming into the curb.

"I'm very sorry," he said, running around to open the door. "I was preoccupied, then the weather slowed me."

Hoa got in, scowling, and pushed her long black coat up under her legs. She didn't speak until they pulled away.

"Now." She turned her head a few degrees in Hieu's direction, but refused to look at him. "You tell me what has happened with you."

Hieu, still riled from the police report and Acacia's answer about the cabin, slowed down and glanced over at his mother.

"What has happened? What do you mean?"

"Don't be stupid. You're playing too many games already."

The snow had begun blowing horizontally in spurts, the boulevard almost completely covered, and the traffic crept along. In Portland, it took about an eighth of an inch to set off city-wide disaster sirens.

Hieu signaled and pulled over in front of a Vietnamese grocery.

"I'm not playing games," he said. "Believe me."

"Something is troubling you, I see it plainly. Now what has happened? It's time to say it."

He tightened his grip on the lower part of the steering wheel.

"I just came through a very difficult situation. I'm exhausted, you know that. Please relax."

"No." She was looking at him now, squeezing the sides of her purse. "What? Why are you doing this?"

"I refuse to be lied to." She pointed a finger at him. "Your eyes remind me of your father's, hiding knowledge of bad things. For him it was evil he met in his dreams. For you, I don't know, but your eyes speak. So don't deceive me. The lies have infected everyone already."

Hieu wanted to shout. He wanted to flip on the radio and turn it up.

"I'm not like father that way. His eyes were clouded, mine aren't."

Thinking he'd effectively ended the conversation, he eased away from the curb. Hoa faced forward again and glared at the snowflakes spraying against the windshield.

"You're wrong," she said.

The minivan still running, Hieu helped his mother up the steps and into the house, and asked Dat to tell Anh that he would be home before dinner. Back on the sidewalk, under Bing's frosted limbs, he turned and looked up at the house, the brightly lit front room; a hard gust blew dozens of flakes against his face, but he stayed put, wanting it to be a more welcoming sight than it was. He wanted to feel it, that it was enough. But he needed to do something to relieve the swelling shame first. Something courageous. Such times called for stretching one's self, pushing past a comfort zone that had grown too large, come what may.

It took about fifteen minutes to negotiate the streets over to North Phillips, to Sasha's block. He had never seen her house up close, having dropped her off down the street both times after returning from Washington Park, but knew the address from the police report. In front of a home with five snowy-backed cement deer, several pinwheels, and two birdbaths in the yard, he parked and sat in the near-silence, the engine clicking fast. The street was dead except for two kids at the end of the block throwing snowballs at other parked cars, the trees snow-caked and still. It was a matter of honor, the only way. He got out and began baby-stepping along the sidewalk.

From the front, Sasha's house looked to be about the size of a large garage. Streaks of missing white paint with some darker color underneath, two accordioned soda cans poking out of the snow in the yard near the porch, and an old Ford Tempo with a disfigured back bumper gathering

flakes out front combined to confirm his presumptions. While the houses
on either side looked no more glamorous, they were almost twice the size
of Sasha's, each with a second story.

Hieu knocked on the screen door and forced himself to hold his
stance. There was yelling from inside, a thud against the door, a child
shouting "Momma!" He couldn't make out Sasha's voice. Then, with a
yank that made him back up and nearly slip off the top step, Marguerite
Anderson opened the door, holding a yellow terrycloth robe over her
large midriff. Her white socks had beige stains at the toes. Behind her,
two chubby-cheeked, wild-haired girls were peeking over the top of a
love seat strewn with magazines, two naked Barbie dolls, and a stringless
pink mini-ukulele.

"Hello, I am Hieu Nguyen from Wilson Green. Sasha is—"

"Why you here?" Marguerite held the screen open, the cold making
her eyes water. Her blotchy, fatigued face made Hieu think of windowless pubs.

"Very sorry to bother you, but I would like to speak with Sasha if she
is here."

Marguerite Anderson scrutinized his eyes and after a few long moments motioned with her head for him to enter.

"Sasha!" she yelled.

Hieu slipped off his shoes, left them on the porch, then stood just
inside the doorway, taking in the spectacle: more abused toys scattered
over the rust-colored carpet and motley furniture, the two girls giggling
behind the love seat, some crayon marks along the bottom four feet of
the yellow walls, a beanbag chair smashed up against the boarded-over
fireplace, floor plants in two of the corners. The room smelled of bathroom spray and cooked meat. When his eyes returned to Marguerite's,
she was watching him.

"You probably think you're above this." She gathered her robe around
her again.

"Oh, I have three children. I understand."

She began sliding Legos into a pile with her foot. "I don't know if you
do. You ain't from this neighborhood."

"No, but—"

Just as Hieu spoke, Sasha came through the doorway leading to the kitchen. She said something under her breath when she saw him, then a quiet fell.

"Hello," he said. Seeing her made his cheeks flush. He glimpsed the lines of her body, even through her grey sweatshirt and matching sweatpants, and then noticed also that she was wearing tennis shoes. Marguerite in her socks had thrown him; he'd thought it was a shoes-off household and now here he was in his socks looking like an even bigger fool. To say nothing of the inch of lost height. *Idiot.* He should have gone with his initial observation that there weren't any shoes on the porch or just inside the doorway. He blushed harder.

Marguerite looked over at Sasha and grunted something Hieu didn't catch; she picked up the two girls by their pudgy midsections, said, "Anything happens, you holler," and left the room.

He let the pause stand this time. Sasha really was so beautiful, so sexy. It was true: she looked older than most high school juniors.

When a door slammed at the back of the house, muting the girls' yammering, she stepped forward.

"What are you doin' here?"

"I wanted to—"

"You can get out right now." She swept past him and opened the door. "What the hell you thinking coming here?"

A tremor began to attack his hands.

"Sasha … I am sorry. But did you need to put any of us through it? Malisha made you?"

She shook her head, lower jaw extended, and Hieu sensed he was losing himself. This is what it had come to.

"Does your mother know?" he said.

"She know what? About the case? Hell yeah she knows, where you been?"

He heard the two girls screaming from the back room, then Marguerite's thundering: "Quiet down or I'll beat both your butts!"

"I mean does she know about last summer." His hands continued to shake, but he didn't care now if she saw.

"No … she doesn't."

"I am sorry all of this happened. I think—"

"Well fuck you then. I ain't sorry for what we did, what do you think about that? I'm just sorry you such a pussy." She made a smacking sound. "Man, I can't believe I was ever even into you. Come here and try to get all sweet. Get the fuck out!"

He stood there, possible responses rioting through him, as Sasha held the screen door open, another chill invading the room. He wanted to squeeze her shoulders. Touch her forearm. Anything to make her understand that he had never meant to hurt anyone. But he could do nothing of the kind. Before he even reached down for his shoes out on the porch, the door slammed, echoing against the neighboring houses and up the street. The snowball-throwing kids were gone.

Back in front of his own house, Hieu let the engine run to keep the heater pumping. The evening had brought even heavier snow, almost two inches more in the forty-five minutes since he'd dropped off his mother. The sky had sunk closer to the ground. A "free beef when you purchase new all-weather tires" commercial came over the radio; he turned it off and listened to the heater and the engine, unable to stop replaying the outburst.

Amazing that she hadn't revealed the affair during the investigation, considering how angry she obviously still was. Incredible, too, that Marguerite Anderson didn't know of her daughter's deeper motives regarding the harassment charges.

He peered up at the house, at the back of someone's head bobbing in the front room window, and tried to tap back into the confidence that Sasha would keep the secret. After all, he'd convinced himself the summer before. She had promised so solemnly that she would never tell, right after they entered the park the first time. She'd turned and looked him in the eyes and said, "This is our secret, no matter what." But while the threat of her pinning him with any more allegations (trumped-up or not) seemed slim, there was something else. His mother had seen through him. Perhaps everyone else had as well. To continue with such pressure would only invite more senseless arguments, more insomnia.

The head continued to bob in the front window. A numbness snaked through him, bringing on a feeling of suspension from his life. He examined the house's shadowed shape and was struck by how foreign it appeared, how utterly different from the hut in which he had grown up. Then there was the vibrating minivan in which he sat—a thing so unlike any other he'd known as a boy. Yet again, here was the confusion he hated most. How did he end up this way? How did all of it happen?

When two more heads began bouncing in the window, snagging his attention, he shut off the engine and climbed the steps. On the porch, he heard the music, a man yelling something or other, bass guitar thumping, drums pounding. He jingled his keys in the lock, but Vo, Dat, and Le Phuong didn't hear him come in. The three were dancing to a song so loud and so aggressive that he could only stand there a moment, especially with his daughter jumping and flailing her skinny arms, flashing a huge smile to match the boys'. It was Dat who finally wheeled around in a hard bounce of limbs, spotted his father, and stopped instantly. Vo rushed to turn off the stereo and the aftershocks of the song ricocheted through the room.

"We're celebrating the snow," Vo said, trying once again to make his voice deeper than it was. "No school tomorrow."

"Where's your mother?"

"Safeway with Grandma to stock up. The weather dude said six to eight inches." At the mention of more snow, Le Phuong and Dat grinned at each other.

Then Dat, whose hair was messed up more than usual, sweat trickling down his face and neck, surprised everyone by walking over to Hieu and reaching up with both hands.

"Want to do the Snow Dance, Dad? I can teach you easy."

A few seconds of silence followed. Hieu looked down at Dat, back up at Vo and Le Phuong: they were actually his children. They shared the house with him. They'd come from his union with Anh. When he thought of his wife, his hands left his sides and engulfed Dat's, and the kids' bodies loosened. Hieu smelled the room, the familiar scents of the six-person household, as he continued to look from child to child.

Astonishing that he had helped bring them into such a tough world. He gave Dat's hands a little shake and smiled down at him. Le Phuong and Vo shared a glance.

"You can dance, but please keep it low," Hieu said, letting go. Dat craned his neck and furrowed his brow. "Go ahead, it's okay. I'll just wait for your mother."

But the excitement had vaporized. Hieu left the room and Le Phuong explained to Dat that the dancing was over, at least for awhile. Something had happened and they needed to be quiet again. Vo ejected the cassette and ran upstairs.

In the kitchen, Hieu put on some water for tea. He sat and noticed his reflection on the window pane across the table.

So much for the Golden Mountain Dream.

He would make himself do it. Tell her.

The Pinch of Knowing

Nate downed more ibuprofen, then spread-eagled over the damp bedsheets and pictured his classroom. To help block out what Dennis had reported about Sammy, he would try to concentrate on teaching. The why of it.

His first year at Wilson Green, he'd been required to present a unit on ancient Mesopotamia, a subject he knew next to nothing about. The Sumerians, he studied right along with his rowdy freshman humanities class, had developed a fascinating system for dealing with student behavior problems. There was the teacher, of course, who delivered the lessons, and then there was the disciplinarian, who toted a three-foot switch. The two worked as a team to keep students challenged and focused—an effective team most likely, Nate speculated in front of the slightly uneasy class one hot September afternoon.

There had been other fantasies, as well, about how to best manage students. After he'd transformed into a thicker-skinned veteran, he would tell some classes, during lighter moments, about his idea for keeping a baboon or mandrill in a cage at the back of the room, how he would escort anyone who chose to misbehave to the cage and lock him or her inside. Still, after almost ten rollercoaster years at Wilson Green, he appreciated the Sumerian approach. There was an economical elegance about it. He would have a guy named Ozzy sitting on a stool by the door, then send him over to a foul-mouthed miscreant's desk to inflict a prescribed number of whacks. Ozzy would be perfectly stoic and unobtrusive, except when he got the chance to warm up his switch; the guy would go bananas then.

Yet the discipline issues hadn't completely defined the experience. There were the students who returned to Wilson Green as young adults saying how he'd changed their lives. Plus the notes and cards over the years. He kept one letter framed on his desk, though it was usually

obscured by a paper pile. It was from his third year, from a shy girl named
Tia Thurmon.

> Dear Mr. Davis,
>
> I wanted to write this to say thank you, I have learned so much
> from you, about life and even about myself. You have helped me to
> have confidence in myself, to try to reach my goals, and to enjoy
> life. You made a difference for me, Mr. Davis, and I think you are a
> teacher I will never forget. I hope I will see you again in the future.
>
> Sincerely, Tia

The challenge of teaching attracted him early on. Teaching in a tough
neighborhood seemed noble, especially by his mid-twenties. On his
Europe trips, on the buses crisscrossing the United States, he had told
himself he couldn't abide a soul-cramping occupation to fill his hours. He
wanted a robust life, even if it meant experiencing a few detours.

When he told friends and family, after he'd finished his MA and cer-
tification work in the summer of '85, that he'd finally become a teacher,
he invariably received a sympathetic smile, a hollow-sounding *great*, or
something along the lines of *wow*. But it never fazed him; he knew what
he was doing. To both Grandpa Davis and Acacia, though, his choice
of work was something to be proud of. When they returned from the
graduation ceremony to the house on Lincoln Street, Acacia asked him
to sit on the sofa in his handsome green cap and gown for a photo, she
was so happy. She lined up the shot and said with a crooked mouth that
she'd once thought about being a teacher, but had never been too good
with kids.

Nate waited for the camera to click, grin tightening, and withheld comment at first, the fact that he agreed with his mother's self-assessment
embarrassing him, then replied, "Thanks a lot."

"Oh, you know what I mean," Acacia said, still taking her time. "Things
just worked out different for me is all."

The bulb flashed and the party officially began, friends, relatives,
neighbors packed in, the champagne making most everyone sloppy
before long.

At length, on the sofa, behind a coffee table photo of Tripod (who
had died of a chocolate overdose nine years earlier, after getting into a

package of fudge under the Christmas tree), Acacia held Nate's diploma and sipped at her third glass of bubbly. Nate, trapped across the room by a sheep-eyed neighbor who was explaining which spark plug brands to avoid, glanced over at his mother and managed to break free.

"You're looking deep over here," he said, settling next to her. He noticed her arm, how a wattle of wrinkled skin sagged against her sundress.

Acacia set the diploma down on the coffee table.

"Oh, just thinking how fast it's all going. Drunk thought, don't mind me."

"There's more I'll bet."

She patted his knee, a hint of hesitation in the gesture. "Suppose I was thinking 'bout your dad a little, too."

At the mention of his father, Nate sat forward some.

"Hey," Acacia said. "I was only thinking 'bout how he would've made a great teacher someday is all. Like how you're going to be a great teacher. Now come on."

"Yeah. What a teacher he would've made."

Acacia jutted out her lower lip and scanned the room. "Let's not get into it tonight."

"I just wondered what was up. Sorry I don't want to hear about him, but I don't."

"Yep. Case closed."

Nate wanted to say more to his mother, but silence seemed the best course. They sat there and managed to pull it together, reshelving their feelings about the man who'd run away a spooked teen and never turned back.

Acacia had heard from her high school sweetheart only once, right before Nate's second birthday, a quick long distance call from an undivulged someplace to "see how the kid's doing." But there hadn't been much to talk about after she cussed him out for what he had done, the way he'd left especially, just vanishing one day after slipping a note into the crack at the bottom of her locker: *I'm really sorry, but I'm not ready to be a dad.*

Though she'd eventually come to understand how a seventeen-year-old could react to his girlfriend's pregnancy by running like hell (perhaps even to a relative in another state), Acacia had never come all that close to forgiving. What made it most difficult was the fact that she still, after so many years, felt late-night longings for her first (and pretty much only) love. As their son had grown older, also, she'd begun to see even clearer resemblances: the defined jawline, the shoulders that looked like they could bear more weight than they could. But while Nate looked vaguely like his father, he acted more like his uncle, the winsome surrogate who'd been there through the toughest years. It was Sammy, Acacia always knew, who had saved her—Sammy and her parents. Sammy who'd given so much of his time up until the day he, too, buckled and fled.

She turned to her son again and raised her glass.

"To the teacher," she said, her eyes welling.

Nate looked at her, a woman just sixteen years older, smiled and picked up his own glass. He was on a good path, he felt. He'd won his mother's and his grandfather's approval by getting a real job, by leaving behind the restless, wandering ways that made them so nervous.

Only when his actual teaching duty began in September did the fire in his gut start to flicker a bit. By the end of the first week at Wilson Green, the energizing sense of vocation began to transform into a creeping sense of dread. There soon came days when he would turn off all the lights after school, close the door, sit at one of the student desks in the middle of the room, and simply stare off. By the end of the month, he'd already quietly wept once in his dimmed room, cursing his decision to pursue such a calling, it was too much.

But he hung on. While most of the other teachers hadn't bothered to offer any real support, at times fueling the despair, it was Hieu and Desiree who'd saved him from becoming another early casualty.

The final school day that first month, Hieu knocked at his door, rousing him from another after-school funk, gave an understanding chuckle and invited him over for breakfast the next morning. Years later, Nate sometimes recalled how Hieu promised it would get easier, said that he'd gone through the same thing his first few months. It was Hieu who insisted upon sharing breakfast a couple days a week that first year. While Nate never forgot Desiree's well-timed supportive comments or the hilarious Far Side cards, it was Hieu and Anh and the steaming bowls of *pho* that had made things seem endurable.

The shade raised, window opened more, he hopped back to the bed and swallowed another round of prednisone. A couple—Scottish or Welsh?—down the corridor had been going at it for the past ten minutes, the woman unabashedly moaning, occasionally shrieking, "Go Troy!"

Tired of reviewing his career, he let the thoughts of Sammy come. Though the trip hadn't been a waste, far from it, what with meeting Mary and Dennis, he had, when it came down to it, failed to find his uncle. The burn: he could go through the rest of his days never knowing what else happened.

But then, while it was clear that Sammy didn't want to be found, it wasn't enough to just let that be the end of it. There was absolutely no excuse for letting certain things go.

Earlier that humid afternoon, Dennis had stopped in with some cups of lychee and ice chips, mostly to see how things were going, but soon plunged into another story about how Sam had dated a Vietnamese woman during his days at the Sawatdee. She'd been an itinerant front desk helper, too, a thirty-year-old displaced by the war. She'd refused to become a prostitute. Sam cared deeply for her. Asked her to come away with him even, someplace calmer, but she refused. He then offered to take her back to Vietnam; to that she hadn't replied. Right after that exchange he quit, explaining that the woman would be staying on and that he hoped to meet Dennis again sometime down the line.

To Dennis, it seemed a natural-enough good-bye, not much of a surprise considering what they'd gone through together. There was a detached aura that marked each of them, he admitted, an "aloof pessimism" that made the world easier to handle—a reaction they'd developed quickly and honed to perfection during their tours.

There was another story as well. One Nate should hear. Before he began, Dennis looked away, chewing a few ice chips. This is what happened: In early '69, the platoon had been out on patrol one evening not far from the Vam Co in the north of Long An Province when they'd come upon a fogged-in copse. Birds made their twilight calls, but other than that there were no sounds. Big red ants everywhere, tree trunks vibrating with them. The point man, Harold Weatherford that time, held up a fist, then moved on after a good long listen. Only a few steps more, though, and

Harold jerked backward and collapsed. Bouncing Betty. Guys fired into the forest like they couldn't take another *ounce* of anything, and when the shooting stopped, it was Sammy who went first to his fallen buddy. Sammy who picked up Harold's right hand and wrist twenty feet away, then went back and knelt down and said that everything would be all right.

"I remember him kneeling in that smoky light," Dennis said, shaking his head, "saying real soft, over and over, things would be cool. Without the least bit of irony in his voice, you know. Sam *believed* it, even though it was damn clear Harold was outta there. A couple of us were working on the guy's arm and stomach like fuckin' crazy, but Sam just held Harold's good hand, kept telling him not to worry. 'It'll be cool. Hang in there, man, we're all right.'" Dennis shook his head again and went silent.

The story made Nate's toes curl under the sheet. Yet Dennis still hadn't revealed any hints that might send him off in a specific direction. The tales only made things worse, brought back the pinch of knowing he might never get the chance to speak adult-to-adult with his uncle.

That evening, Mary listened while he tried, in more precise terms, to explain how much Sammy had meant to him. He told the story of Sammy dropping him into the warm clothes hamper—the smell of home, the feeling of safety. Playing Frisbee and croquet in the backyard. The horseback rides. No matter what, he had to at least find out what really happened.

Cross-legged at the foot of the bed, Mary remained silent. An American out in the hallway belted out a laugh, then shouted, "You chicks suck! Give 'em back!" before running elephant-footed toward the sound of laughter.

Nate only watched her face.

Two Makes of Man

—2 March 1997, Bangkok

Move ahead with plans to go home. Apparently the bad pains can return if the condition gets triggered by any more food poisoning. This morning Dr. Lal came by and reiterated that I should get back and find good treatment.

Again the guy impressed me. I think it's the combination of intensity and empathy. He's also gentle with the needle, and smiles only when he means it (at least it seems so). Mary and I talked about him after he left for the airport. His presence and his attention to detail.

So I need to settle on a return date myself. Mary says she'll help with the arrangements, but both she and Dr. Lal recommend more rest before the trip. When I'm fit enough to get around better, in a few days maybe, Mary and Dennis want to drive up to Ayuthaya, the old capital. (They keep saying I need to give Thailand another chance, and would both like to get out of town for a day besides.)

So, then. I'm relieved and uptight at the same time. Even though I don't have a clue about where I'd go if I could, I hate giving up like this. But then, who knows? This could be the first leg of a longer journey.

I just hope he's alive.

Later that morning he hopped down to the lobby with Dennis's help, phoned Lang and got a recording that said the line had been disconnected. He called Hieu and after many rings Anh picked up, her voice sounding either sad or tired, he couldn't tell from the bad connection.

After a few clipped answers about how things were going, Anh said she'd go get Hieu and the line went silent for almost a minute; when she finally returned, she reported in an even flatter tone that he couldn't come to the phone. Nate asked if something was the matter and she replied only that she hoped everything was going okay on the trip. Did the

investigation turn something up? he said. No … it wasn't that, the case
was closed. She sounded even shakier all of a sudden, so he didn't press,
instead opting to ask how Lang was; he was wondering about the disconnected number. But at the mention of her sister-in-law, Anh released high
dolphin-like cries into the receiver, eventually gathering herself enough
to say that he would have to speak with Lang when he returned, she
couldn't talk about anything more just then. Nate managed to tell her,
right before the click, that he'd be home in a week.

Behind him in the lobby, a group of backpackers had just checked out,
now huddled around a guidebook. Dennis preoccupied fifteen feet away
with one of the cooks, a leathery, baggy-eyed man Nate guessed was the
heroin addict Dennis had once mentioned. From the interior portion
of the restaurant came John Cleese's faint but unmistakable voice ("Are
you totally *de-ranged?"*), a re-showing of *A Fish Called Wanda* on the
big screen.

The pulsing in his joints. Heart racing. He gazed at the side of Dennis's
massive head, at the group of deliberating travelers, then dialed the house on
Lincoln Street and reached Acacia after four and a half rings (he'd pictured
his mother standing next to the kitchen telephone, waiting just long enough
to make it seem like she'd rushed in from some momentous activity).

After a brief report on the illness, on the trip in general, he asked if
there had been any word from Lang.

"Nothing," Acacia said, a trace of hurt in her tone. "Only Hieu. He
called a couple weeks ago 'bout using the cabin."

"Listen, I'm sorry to be abrupt, but I'm a little boogered out here. Was
everything all right when you talked to him?"

"Sounded like he's had a rough go of things lately, but no word on any
problems."

"So he went up to the cabin then?"

"I'm still doing some work on it. It's a mess right now."

He told her about his coming home, remembered to inquire about
Grandpa Davis, then asked if she could do a big favor and maybe drive
by Lang's place. Just make sure everything was all right. But his mother
only sighed. No doubt she was pissed about it being his first phone call,
but she also sounded as if it were something more.

Immediately after the good-bye, Nate dialed the Nguyens again and this time got Vo.

"Man, everything's all wacked out around here." The boy's voice just above a whisper. For a reason he still didn't get, his dad had been sleeping on a cot in the basement the past week. His parents were fighting bad, his grandmother freaking out every chance she got, sometimes yelling from the top of the basement steps. As for Lang, he didn't know what was going on, he hadn't seen her for a week or so.

Nate asked to speak with Hieu, and only a few seconds later Vo returned to say that his father had gone out.

During the speechless, arm-over-shoulder hop back upstairs, after Dennis had finished convincing the young junkie on staff to see Mary during her next visit, Nate considered the reaction in his chest when Anh started sobbing. How he'd thought there had been some kind of accident, Lang had been hurt. How he'd wanted, more than anything, to be home.

Back in bed, Dennis downstairs again, he thought of Hieu's refusal to come to the phone. And why had Anh so stubbornly resisted even hinting at what had happened? They knew each other better than that. Established a solid trust ages ago.

In his journal he wrote only,

—What the hell is going on?

When Mary arrived that evening with chicken kebabs and four cold cans of Singha, he brought up the phone calls.

"So the boy—Vo?—he didn't give any clues?" Mary said, handing over dinner.

"Sounded scared to be talking. But I didn't get the impression he understands it too well."

She took off her raincoat, hung it on the doorknob. A thunderstorm had begun to subside, the hiss of downpour softer from the cracked window.

"It could just be a little clash, Nate. Have you ever seen them—"

"I know. I hope so. But I've known them ten years, and this just ..."

Mary assumed her favorite spot at the foot of the bed and held out a beer. "Doctor's orders. You know, as far as your girlfriend's number goes, people do move. Phone company screws up, too."

"Yeah."

They drank in silence, listening to the rain, then Mary said: "I plan on making those plane reservations tomorrow morning. You'll be home soon, just try to relax tonight."

They focused on their food, occasionally looking at each other. Nate chased a mouthful with a swig of beer.

"I don't know … I guess I was still thinking about setting out again. Head for Vietnam maybe." Mary only began nodding slowly. "When I heard Anh's voice, though, I mean …" His words faded again without a reply. "I appreciate your input on this. I feel better already."

Mary lowered her kebab. "Come on."

"No, there's not much to say, you're right."

Her cheeks had flushed, but her face remained calm. "The only thing to say is you need to take care of yourself. You know you're not in shape for that kind of travel. So please don't take your worries out on me."

"And how would you know what I'm in shape for?"

He squeezed the beer can until it was shaped vaguely like an hourglass, avoiding her eyes.

"Jesus. Sorry …" He molded the can as close as he could back to its original form. "Been in this damn room too long." He glanced at her. "Forgive me?"

Though she concentrated a little too hard on her kebab for a time, Mary mentioned that she'd brought a surprise for dessert.

"Before we have it, though, I'd like to know something …" She set her dinner between Nate's sheet-covered feet and waited till he'd finished his beer. "Do you remember the middle of last week when I came by, your leg was shaking with that bad pain? You were all feverish?" She gauged his mild squint. "Do you recall at all how you asked me to lie down beside you? You said that when I'm here things seem better?"

Nate remained still, eyeing his legs now. His breathing shallower. "I think."

"Well it's all right. I get that sometimes. House calls especially. They feel overcome by something, want to reach out."

He assumed a professorial expression, forehead flexed.

"But I always keep a certain distance," Mary said. "Without hurting their feelings, you know? It just happens sometimes."

Nate nodded.

"But then you also told me how when I'm here you feel like you're really being yourself. You're seeing your life through your own eyes, you said."

"Yeah."

"Please ... look at me."

When he lifted his head, his frown dissolved: a face that still sometimes made him forget where he was.

"Even if you were delusional, I guess I just wanted you to know that that was one of the best things anyone's ever said to me. You can see through your own eyes. I loved that. I think you win best pain-induced confession."

Nate made himself smile. He didn't say that it was true, all of it, and that he'd been crestfallen when she hadn't obliged and laid down next to him, let him hold her awhile. He thought he heard Béla in the hallway, back from his trip to Chiang Mai, and told himself again that Lang would be waiting for him in her new apartment, it would be a new beginning when he returned. It was as if, he would write a few weeks later, a multiple personality disorder had occasionally seized him those days in Bangkok, as if two makes of man had chosen his medicated mind as the ideal battleground.

For dessert, Mary pulled two cocoa milks from the sack on the floor beside her and said she'd remembered how he had raved about the drink toward the end of the same feverish X-Acto pain ramble the week before, he'd been so parched. Gave not-so-subtle hints for the greater part of an hour.

Since he had obviously done his share of jabbering, he said, it was her turn again. So what were her plans? She still hadn't opened up that much in the two weeks they'd known each other. His smile dropped away, however, when she began by saying that she was just beginning to come into herself. Like that, they were back on the level he'd wanted to avoid; but he kept looking straight at her, the tiny chocolate smudges at the corners of her mouth.

After being someone she wasn't and not having the courage to admit it for most of her adult life (the dinner parties packed with expert opinion on national politics, the real estate sales club banquets, countless meals in front of the big-screen as Stuart flipped between CNN and VH-1), she felt she was only now coming to know the power of shaping her thoughts, of diving into activities she honestly *wanted* to do. A blind acceptance of the forces that kept her convinced that she deserved her half-lived life had had her completely bamboozled. The divorce and leaving for Bangkok were the springboard events: the first times since childhood she'd leapt for something so unknown. They were leaps for what she knew deep down to be her path, and it was "like layers of mildewed covers being slung off." At least at first. Scary as hell, yes, but perfect. Most of her family back in California—including Jess, her daughter, and even Uncle Maxwell—still thought she'd gone too far in coming all the way to Bangkok, but she tried not to let it get to her. It was, she continued, a "determined celebration" of the unknown that had made her life feel right again; while she would never stop paying the bills and trying to be a solid mom, she wanted to "give instinct the wheel" more often. At least living felt like an adventure again, you know?

When Mary stopped, Nate hesitated, then looked away. Raised his cocoa bottle like he was toasting something and tilted back a drink. The chocolate at the corners of her mouth made him think of playgrounds, backyard picnics in a town like Yreka. A little girl in pigtails riding around on her banana-seat bike with playing cards in the spokes and a basket tied to the handlebars with a Raggedy Ann doll and a half-eaten Ding Dong inside. Neighborhood scene: gangs of musky kids dashing through sprinklers, riding bikes over elderly folks' lawns. Mary must've been a mischievous little bugger, especially when she got a sugar high. Then he looped back to something she'd just said.

"I'm curious, when you mentioned giving instinct the wheel ..."

She only smiled again and said he already knew what she meant. She was sure of it.

—⁓—

On the ride to and from Ayuthaya, in Dennis's old Corolla, Nate kept saying how good it felt to get out, to the point where, re-entering the

outskirts of Bangkok, Dennis swung his head around and with a charm-
ing (yet arresting) mock glare said, "We believe you."

To Nate's initial disapproval, Mary had arranged for a wheelchair that
fit snugly into the Toyota's trunk; she and Dennis took turns pushing,
weaving around Ayuthaya's crumbling temples, Buddha statues, and
hordes of sightseers, occasionally offering up tour guide tidbits on the
drama of centuries.

At one point, when she walked on ahead to "take in the ghosts a minute," Dennis stopped the chair at pathway's edge, bent down closer to
Nate, wiped a dense constellation of sweat beads from his forehead and
said that he'd asked Mary to come by the Sawatdee often at first, as a favor,
because he'd been worried about the sharp pains and all the other weird
symptoms, but that she had soon taken to the visits.

Dennis stretched up again when Mary turned around to rejoin them.
"Just wanted you to know so you didn't think she was really some loon.
Should've said something earlier probably." When she was within forty
feet of them, Dennis grinned at her. "I tell you though, man, they don't
come much better. Integrity and soul on knockout legs."

That evening after dinner, Mary lounged cross-legged at the foot of
the bed, reading *A Prayer For Owen Meany* in Spanish. Nate alternated
between thinking about his homeward flight less than thirty-six hours
away, trying to ignore the nettling vagueness over Lang and Hieu, jotting the occasional impression of what had gone on during the previous
couple of weeks in the Sawatdee room, and looking up in front of him:
tan bare feet tucked into folds of long black skirt, hair unclipped, falling
over blouse, a can of Singha propped in lap just below the novel.

    —I think of the Sammy–Jackie Yamada–Dennis Brown connec-
    tion that allowed me to meet this person and don't look kindly upon
    the thought of good-bye.

But two mornings later, in front of the Sawatdee as Dennis snapped
their photograph with each of their cameras, the farewell was upon them.
Though only just past dawn, a few sidewalk tables were already full of
travelers awaiting early buses or trains, plus some hardened all-nighters
sucking on cigarettes, sipping Nescafe. The ash-fed monkey across the

street glowered at the waiting taxi, its black fingers clutching the wire cage, framing its haunted face. The driver, a young Thai with the sinewy arms and obscure expression of a kick boxer, waited as Nate tossed his pack into the backseat and returned to the sidewalk. Off behind the taxi, an elderly grocer bent low to sweep his store's entryway with a bundle of twigs.

In the same long-sleeved maroon tee and blue jeans she'd worn the evening before, Mary waited next to Dennis, who could only meet Nate's eyes for a second or two at a time before looking over at the tables of breakfasting travelers or back into the dark lobby.

"All set then?" Mary said, no one else appearing ready to wind things up. When Nate pressed his lips together and nodded, his eyes not leaving hers, she pulled out a business card from a back pocket and explained that last year she'd taken a short trip to Calcutta with some friends and actually met Mother Teresa (one friend knew one of the young nuns working as a Missionary of Charity at the Mother House). They'd gone to an evening prayer service and come upon Mother Teresa getting her photo taken with a group of Japanese priests, passing out something in between shots. Set on finding a way to meet her, they managed to slip away from the nun who'd let them in, and then, sure enough, the beaming old woman hobbled up to them when she finished with the priests.

"God bless you," Mother Teresa said, holding Mary's hand.

At length the famous nun lifted a card from her sari and held it out. It read: *The fruit of SILENCE is Prayer. The fruit of PRAYER is Faith. The fruit of FAITH is Love. The fruit of LOVE is Service. The fruit of SERVICE is Peace.*

After handing cards with the same message to the other visitors gathered around, Mother Teresa had waved, then disappeared into a crowd of blue-and-white-habited nuns and left the room. As Mary read the gift again, though, she noticed there was another one stuck to the back. She'd kept both, wondering when the right person and moment might come along.

"And here I am," Dennis said. "You're wonderful, you know that?" He leaned toward her and lowered his voice. "This won't hurt his feelings, though?"

Mary gave Nate the card, then wrapped an arm around Dennis's waist and gave it a few pats. "Our good-bye's still a ways off. I'll get something better for you. Burger King certificates."

Still failing to form words, Nate pulled her into an embrace and after nearly a minute heard one of the nearby travelers say, "Go for it, brother."

Finally in the taxi, he reached out the window for another arm wrestling grip handshake with Dennis, and Dennis gathered himself and said, "You know you've done it right if it hurts to say good-bye."

Then, without further ceremony, he was off, turning to watch them shrinking out the back window, waving, heading back into the Sawatdee. When the driver turned on the stereo, an atrocious cover of "Have You Ever Seen the Rain," he faced forward and opened a side pouch on his backpack and tucked the Mother Teresa card into his journal, the same page as the paper-clipped horseback ride snapshot.

There would be no cinematic last-second change of plans. No demands for the driver to turn around. But he also understood that something had happened in the spot he was pulling away from that made Dennis's final words sting like a fresh-cleaned wound.

On the plane, he propped his ankle on some bunched-up blankets, rewrapped the Ace bandage around his wrist, closed his eyes and immediately started replaying the evening before. The delicious vegetable curry that Mary had brought. The six beers and the chocolate bar they'd shared. And then how she curled up next to him and spooned for awhile, her back against his chest, his arm wrapped around her. Talking more about Portland and Yreka. Listening to the traffic sounds, each other's breathing. Mary saying right before she left, "I wish you the best with Lang, Nate. Even though you must make her crazy sometimes, she's a lucky woman." She kissed his hand, below the Ace bandage, then went to the room Dennis had arranged for her down the hall. She wanted to be sure to make the early good-bye.

Still, as much as the moments had pierced him, he worked himself back into thoughts of Lang. Then recalled her disconnected number, the fact that she hadn't once written. But he pressed on, rock-willed.

—Pockets of sanctuaried time make connection easier. Remember this. Believe in the reaction in your chest when Anh broke down over the phone.

As he put pen to paper, however, another thought wouldn't let go: it was like some mad custodian, maybe Monty, was sweeping away the instincts he most needed to follow. Then again, as much as Mary had stirred him, there was the strangely pleasing pain of certain sacrifices. Choose your love, love your choice.

So often it had been this way in his life, the back-and-forth. The not-quite-trusting what he thought or felt. As if by admitting either he'd just be setting himself up for heartbreak. Every time.

In Los Angeles, at a restaurant in the domestic terminal, he waited for his flight to Portland, journal open next to a half-eaten Danish pastry. He'd been taking his pills, but Mary had been right about the probability of stiffening up during the haul over the Pacific. Even the sacroiliac joints felt like they were swelling again.

Soon he watched a group of slack-faced teens go by.

—I wonder what Aaron is up to. I try to put myself in his shoes. Memories. The flashy clothes and hallway bravado. But there's a bright kid under all the bad-ass homeboy shit. Why not just accept that and get on with things? He's larger than life now. I see that.

Still have no desire to see Wilson Green again. Maybe the stabbing really was the final omen pointing me away from teaching. I've probably been blind to a lot of signs. But I do miss looking kids in the eyes. Trying to listen. They're people, not projects. Fuck it.

Questions of the day: How to find more of a balance? How to make TIME for Lang, work, reading, exercise, friends, and maybe even a kid someday?

Refuse to let days and weeks blur.

Circushead over the previous twelve hours, cruising high over the ocean: Nolan on Bali, Mick Lassiter and Jackie Yamada, Mary and Dennis. Lang, Hieu, Sammy.

So often, as ever, Sammy.

The thoughts went on slam-dancing, soon to the point where he couldn't settle on one subject for more than a few beats, and it made his eyes dart. He proceeded toward his connecting gate, dealing well enough with a sudden sweaty dizziness.

Part Four

—⁓—

An Opening Into the World

*For they are the moments when something new
has entered into us, something unknown;
our feelings grow mute in shy perplexity,
everything in us withdraws, a stillness comes,
and the new, which no one knows,
stands in the midst of it and is silent.*

—Rainer Maria Rilke

Ping-Pong

In the basement, on an aluminum frame cot next to some boxes of old dinnerware, Hieu twirled his racquetball racket, having sat up when he heard the doorbell ring and someone's quick footsteps heading toward the front of the house. The basement was cold except for the space right around the furnace, the cot placed just beyond the ring of heat. As odd as he knew it was, he had told himself that he didn't deserve any warmth; he preferred to feel chilled, the discomfort bringing on a curious satisfaction.

He'd chosen the cot over a motel because he needed to remain near his family, despite the fact that no one in the house would speak to him beyond the most necessary remarks. Even Hoa had finally quit her daily sermons from atop the basement stairs, and Le Phuong, normally the most diplomatic member of the household, seemed bewildered and distant too. While he understood that his actions with Sasha Anderson were inexcusable, he still held to the hope that by sleeping in the basement, enduring the insult of being beneath the house, he might earn back a measure of respect. After all, he had shown at least some courage in admitting his sin to Anh; perhaps she would slowly come to forgive him, then the others might follow, if he could hold on and prove how much he wanted to make things work out.

He sat hunched on the cot, the fatigue from a week of tortured sleep toying with him, and strained to hear the muffled exchange above. Then came the footsteps toward the kitchen, one pair lagging unevenly behind the other. He could make out Anh's voice, but the other one, a male's, escaped him. It wasn't until the steps crossed the kitchen and the basement door opened and Anh said "Please go down" that he realized with a widening of the eyes who it was.

At the top of the stairs, Nate called out a hello, gripped the flimsy railing and began his descent. His movements were especially measured, the left ankle, right knee, and right wrist still tender from another round of cortisone shots a few hours earlier.

From the airport, he had dialed Lang's disconnected number again, then taken a cab, adrenalin-whacked, straight to Providence Medical Center and waited ninety minutes before receiving treatment from one of Portland's foremost arthritis experts, a hook-nosed grouch with tooth-pick wrists named Dr. Murphy Wright-Wickham. Quick to respond to Nate's report of Reiter's Syndrome by taking both blood and urine sam-ples, the doctor ordered a rush on the lab work and within the next hour injected the joints. Another hurricane-speed consultation: the solemn expert instructed plenty of rest and another visit one week later, then scurried out, clipboard pressed to his chest. But despite being treated like a specimen, Nate had been relieved to the point of drowsiness; to get a reconfirmation, have the sickness named aloud again, made his gut relax.

At his apartment, a cool grey evening settling in, he realized after a cursing search that he'd lost his key. He made his way around to the manager's basement pad and got no answer, dropped his bag under the picnic table in the backyard, then hobbled up to the corner market's phone booth a block away and tried the one number he'd always hoped he could rely on in such a situation.

Forty-five minutes later, Acacia pulled up with Grandpa Davis in her '83 Plymouth Horizon, his spare key stuck upright into a pile of brownies on a paper plate. The greeting card envelope taped to the plate reading *Welcome Home, Kid.*

But it was a brief, tepid reunion out on the apartment house's front lawn, Grandpa soon complaining about standing in the mist. They went inside for some tea and munched a brownie each as Nate fielded ques-tions about the flight and the arthritis, exhaustion creeping over him. After only fifteen minutes, he cut off the discussion as politely as he could, promised to come by the following day, and saw them off after giving each another one-armed hug. He hadn't wanted to hurry things, he assured them, but felt like he was about to pass out.

Seconds before he fell into a luscious sofa nap in the cold, quiet apart-ment, though, the worries about Lang and Hieu had dug in again, thoughts strong enough to make him sit up. He called the Nguyen's and got Anh. Her voice sounding stronger, she apologized for the last time they'd spoken, it had been a rough day, then asked about the flight. In the next breath after his report, Nate inquired about Lang, why her number was disconnected;

but again Anh refused to discuss her sister-in-law; he should definitely come over and talk to Hieu about Lang, the situation being "complicated." She also mentioned that there had been "a kind of crisis," that Hieu had sequestered himself in the basement, things were "somewhat tense." Regardless, it would be good for him to come by.

When he asked why Hieu had refused to speak during the last phone call, Anh paused for a moment.

"Just come over when you feel rested," she said. "We've missed you."

On his way to the Nguyen's after a hot shower, a dozen stale Nilla Wafers, and a cup and a half of the Javanese coffee he'd brought back, Nate replayed the conversation, guessing that Hoa probably wasn't included in the "missed you" comment. He wondered again how he'd be able to penetrate the old woman's armor, get her to see that he meant Lang (and Vietnamese traditions) no harm. But it would be worth it to keep trying.

Driving felt foreign, and painful with having to press the clutch. By the time he pulled up beneath Bing, the ankle was throbbing again, not quite the X-Acto knife pain, but closer than in over a week. He turned off the truck and eyed the neighborhood, the trimmed lawns and shrubs.

Easing down into the basement, grabbing the railing, he could feel the cortisone in his ankle. A low squeaking when he walked, cartilage and bone rubbing.

"Got any more light down here? I'm about to bite it, man." Every other step made him flinch. When no reply came, he said, "Well kiss my ass then, daddy-o."

Hieu came to the bottom of the steps, still holding his racquetball racket. Though the light was dim from the one bare sixty-watt bulb above the cot, he could see that Nate had lost at least ten or fifteen pounds—the sunken cheeks, baggier than usual pants.

"This is as light as it gets down here," he said, no trace of good humor. They stood five feet apart now.

"I'd hug you, man, but you look like hell." Nate glanced over at the cot, then at the stacks of cardboard boxes and coiled garden hoses, wicker baskets spewing snow boots and tennis ball cans and fishing rods, a gaudy cloth wall hanging depicting rusty leaves fluttering over a barn and silo scene. His eyes returned to Hieu's. "Nice digs."

Hieu only stared at him, his own face thinner than the last time they'd seen each other. When Nate didn't look away, he stopped twirling the racket. "So why are you here?"

The question made Nate smile.

"I'm selling desk calendars."

"Please," Hieu said in the same subdued tone. "Tell me why you are here."

Nate held onto the end of the railing, waited for Hieu's slow-expanding grin. Then he swallowed.

"Why am I here?"

"I want to know why you are here. How you can come into my house and act like everything is okay."

Nate squinted, then ran a finger and thumb along the bridge of his nose. "I'm missing something. I just got back."

"Please do not play."

"What? What the hell you doing?"

"The sergeant. You act like nothing has happened." Knuckles whitening, Hieu squeezed the racket. He saw the confusion on Nate's face and his voice raised. "I saw the police report. I saw what you told him. It was all there. Very clear."

"Jesus …" Dizzy again, Nate looked away. The blur of miles. "Look, I don't know why I said any of that. I didn't tell you because …" He sank down and sat on the steps. "I have no idea what made me say that."

Hieu began drumming the racket into a wide-open palm, then lowered it to his side, walked away and settled back onto the cot. The sound of someone in the kitchen seemed to ease the tension a notch, reassuring back-and-forth footsteps. Head hung, he leaned forward and rested his elbows on his knees. "It came at a very bad time."

Nate focused on the cement wall before him and listened to the clatter of dishes above, wondering who it was.

"As you well know, I can be a master idiot," he said, getting up. The pain now back to droning numbness, he took a few steps toward the cot and stopped. "I don't know what else to say. I want you to forgive me. I guess maybe I got freaked out with the tape recorder and everything. And maybe … Look, part of it was I doubted you." At that, Hieu's head raised. "I thought you might have given into it, I didn't know."

Hieu set the racket onto the cot and rose. "Excuse me?"

"Oh come on … I guess I thought there was a chance you were guilty. Maybe the girls were telling the truth, I didn't know. But then I was in a bad head right before I left. Christ's sake, man, take it eas—"

Hieu covered the steps separating them like a wildcat, slapped his hands against Nate's collar and grabbed two fistfuls of Gore-Tex.

"You are a bastard." He pulled the jacket upward, making Nate cock his head. For an instant, he thought of Vo and the knee to the groin. "Get out of my home." He shoved Nate backward and turned to the cot, not seeing that Nate had stumbled hard onto a tangle of garden hose and rolled his ankle.

Wide-eyed, pale, Nate took two hops forward and flung himself onto Hieu's back, throwing both of them onto, then over the cot to the concrete floor. Not until they were fighting did he fully realize what had happened.

In no time, Hieu spun himself on top and jammed a knee into Nate's abdomen.

"Get out of my home."

Muscles under Nate's right eye twitched, veins at his temples bulging. *"Your* home? Banished to the fucking *basement?"*

Hieu slapped him across the face and immediately pushed himself off, and right then Anh came to the top of the stairs.

"What was that?" she said, her head poked through the doorway. "Was that Nate?"

Hieu took a quick deep breath and walked over to where he could see her. "I dropped a box to clear a place for him to sit."

Anh retreated, refusing to carry on a conversation.

As her footsteps faded, Nate propped himself on his elbows, the heat of the slap still prickling. He looked over at Hieu, the man leaning against the wall at the base of the stairs, chin tucked to chest like a scolded kid.

"Feel better?" he said, pushing awkwardly against the cot's frame to stand.

Hieu stepped forward, kicked his racket out of the way, rearranged the cot and sat back down. He motioned for Nate to join him. "Please," he said, avoiding Nate's eyes. "Please."

"She is living with one of her colleagues. Two weeks now. Vietnamese guy." Hieu sat on the floor cupping a mug of Darjeeling in both hands, looking up at Nate, who reclined on the cot, ankle propped on a rolled-up beach blanket. "She has not come over very often."

When Nate didn't reply, only kept staring at the pipes crisscrossing the ceiling, Hieu took another sip and readjusted himself.

"Things have been even more crazy since you left. I could have used some matches at the club." He knew that he was talking in order to avoid the silence, but like so often lately, he couldn't seem to control his thoughts; it was as if something possessed him at times. "The kids will not speak to me now, even though they are not certain what exactly is going on." There was an especially puzzling feel to his mind the past week, like he'd been asleep a long time and the spin cycle of moments had gone on altering the world in its subtle way, life leaving him for lost. With almost animal panic, he was pushing against an even tougher new existence. "Something did happen, Nate. Last summer."

Nate looked over, and Hieu pretended to examine the intricacies of the furnace.

"You were right. I could not resist."

"What?" Nate sat up, turned and leaned over the edge of the cot.

Hieu set his mug onto the floor.

"I took Sasha to Washington Park. Two times." He glanced up, to see that the words had completely registered. "I cannot believe it myself sometimes." He rose and reached into one of the wicker baskets, pulled out a flat orange tennis ball and began bouncing it hard, gradually moving toward the stairs. "It was only twice, then I stopped it. We did not have sex, or kiss even, or anything like that, but ..."

"Holy shit, Nguyen."

"You can imagine how Anh took it. Then my mother. She began screaming that I was damaged and the spirits were destroying me. She went to her room pulling her hair." Hieu bounced the tennis ball again. "The kids avoid me now. They walk out of any room I enter. So I thought it would be best if I came down here."

"Jesus, I'm ... I don't know ..."

"I am losing everything, Nate. I was not going to tell you because I hated you anyway." Their eyes met and Hieu forced a smile. "It is kind of like how you told Wallace things you regretted. All of this has made me wonder how I could be so stupid. I do not know if I trust myself anymore."

Hieu stopped the bouncing, tossed the ball up once, caught it and hurled it across the basement, hitting the front of the washing machine with a clang that jolted them both.

In the dying reverberation, Nate pushed himself up and began limping toward Hieu, who had taken up his position against the wall at the base of the stairs. It was one of those extraordinary moments when a man sets out into a crucial response without any firm idea about what he'll say only because he's too embarrassed or shaken or frightened to stall any longer. Nate wanted to erupt. But there was too much to unleash, too much happening. Other thoughts. Lang. Home. Everything.

When they were two feet apart, he raised his head. An excruciatingly long look. Hieu, fighting down the ready explanations, strained to compose an adequate good-bye, though surely no words would do.

Then, in a move that ripped through at least some of the shame, Nate said, "Human after all."

At the kitchen table, Hieu gave up his usual seat, insisting with pronounced formality that Nate take it. Anh was in the living room reading *Tam Cam* to Le Phuong and Dat again, Hoa meditating in her bedroom, and Vo was out cruising malls with some friends, an activity he'd begun to favor more and more lately. Since there was a guest in the house, Hieu considered it safe to briefly emerge from his underworld.

"Man, I'm buzzing," Nate said. "But I want to hear more. Don't hold anything back." He'd slipped into the state where a peculiar serenity takes over and allows one to continue ingesting, even seek out, more and more details in spite of overwhelming news. As for Hieu's admission about Sasha Anderson, it seemed that the only way to deal with the shock was to let it sink in further.

Hieu gave a nod and listened to Anh's animated mean, stepfather-like voice.

"Well, after you left, you know, Lang became very quiet. Like I said, she stopped calling, did not come over too much. Then it was a few weeks ago she told Anh that she was dating a Vietnamese guy from work." Hieu took another drink of tea, letting the words settle. A relief to be talking about something besides Sasha. "Nate ... I think she could not get over you leaving. She said something once about you making up your mind too easily. I heard this from Anh, of course. When we were still speaking."

"She moved in with the prick?"

"I know. Her lease was up, she took a leap. Talk to her. She still cares for you, is what Anh said. But I know that she took your leaving as a sign."

"I was open about everything. I thought she was just steaming for awhile." Nate ran a hand down his face. "You have her new number?"

"Anh has it." Under the better light, Hieu saw just how lean his friend's face was. "I am sorry about you getting this right after coming home. And about downstairs, too."

The conversation dropped into a pocket of silence, the sort that was oddly comfortable.

"So what about you?" Nate didn't bother to disguise the note of bitterness. "You'll just live the rest of your life down there?"

It was like a game of Ping-Pong, issues knocked back and forth.

"I do not know what will happen, if they will ever trust me again. But I feel better for some reason. I think it was good to slap you down there."

Nate puffed out his cheeks and flipped him off, exhaled and rose.

They shook hands, a quick, light grip, and Hieu made his way toward the basement door. "Go sleep. You look worse than I do, you know."

Nate pulled on his coat, went out and gave Le Phuong and Dat a left-handed high-five each, hugged Anh when she stood, and explained that he was about to collapse. After promising Dat that he would have more time for a horseback ride another day soon and telling Le Phuong he wanted to hear some cello next visit, he set a hand on Anh's shoulder and said, "Hang in there."

Out on the front walkway, when the door closed behind him, he stopped and drew large breaths of the misty air and looked at Bing's silhouette against the dark grey sky. He felt like throwing up. Slow and easy, teeth clenched, he moved down the steps, thinking only of his bed.

An Opening Into the World

At two the next afternoon, Nate got up to calm his yowling bladder, then went back to sleep for another six hours.

Despite a thick desire to doze through until morning, he eventually heaved himself out of bed again, showered and shaved, and fixed a can of tomato bisque that had been in the cupboard for two years. In the middle of dinner, he set down the oversize wooden spoon from London's West End with *Piss Off, I'm a Bachelor* engraved on the back, reached for the phone and took a long pull on his beer.

Only two rings gone and a man with a nearly accentless voice answered, "Good evening, this is Tran."

Nate pictured a silk-robed dandy.

"May I speak with Lang please?"

"May I ask who's calling?"

Mind suddenly cramping, he came close to snarling something along the lines of Genghis Dengalenghis from MasterCard. "Nate Davis," he said. "An old friend."

There was silence on the other end; he couldn't tell if the pompous fop was still there. He thought he heard whispering, then Tran picked up again.

"I'm sorry, but she can't come to the phone at the moment. May I take—"

"It's an emergency actually."

"Emergency?" Tran sounded unimpressed.

"Her mother," Nate said before he could stop himself. "It's very serious."

Another short lull and Lang picked up, a heavy-breathed hello.

"Your mother's fine," he said. "Listen. I love you and I want you to meet me in an hour at O'Riley's." Then he hung up.

Hearing her voice made him a little queasy. But times like these called for a bold approach, a strutting, doubts-be-damned resolve. He paced a series of laps around the apartment, plugged in the stereo and turned up some Chopin, then hit the bathroom for a prolonged flossing and brushing session, the likes of which he hadn't subjected himself to since high school. The music filled the chilly space, the delicacy of the opening notes making his cheeks tingle. He had no idea if she would show, but he'd make his stand. Get to her no matter what it took, tell her what he'd come to realize. Had she not received his letters, by chance?

His neck dabbed with *Chief,* the same cologne he'd worn since his Portland State days, he consulted the mirror on the back of the bathroom door: black cable knit sweater, relaxed fit blue jeans, low-top hikers, his face looking slightly better after some sleep. It would have to do. No time for second-guessing. If only Mary could see him: digging into something with such passion.

O'Riley's, a spacious Pearl District pub dating back eighty-one years, was a rare establishment in that it had not only evolved gracefully, its humble character consistently kept intact, but catered to a variety of people: blue-haired English lit majors dissecting William Gaddis novels, the peppy J. Crew crowd, the occasional disgruntled-looking couple wearing Birkenstocks with grey and red hiking socks, small groups of old men watching muted ESPN, and then the steady Wranglers-and-work-shirts folks who usually occupied the stools and tables around the dartboard area.

Nate found a table for four, ordered a rum and Coke and a smoked salmon quesadilla from a glum, pallid waitress, and began to wait, scanning the pub every thirty seconds or so, an impulse he tried not to mind giving in to. He alternated between simmering over the fact that Lang wouldn't show and trusting that she would if he could just maintain some patience, and soon the battle wore him out. After downing two more drinks, he ordered another quesadilla and some onion rings and distracted himself by watching one of the more raucous dart matches across the room. Tom Petty's "You Got Lucky" played in the background.

Nearly an hour later, absently stirring a Bloody Mary, he eyed his half-eaten bowl of nutmeg-sprinkled custard. His appetite was about as strange as his life, he'd quipped to the pale waitress, who responded by looking down at him as if he'd uttered something in Bengali. Committed now to brooding, having long since ignored his embarrassment over sitting alone in a crowded bar, he failed to notice Lang standing right next to him.

"You're looking happy," she said.

He pushed back his chair, scrambling for one of the suave openings he'd rehearsed.

"It's all right, don't get up." Lang took off her black pea coat.

She looked trimmer. Her green cashmere sweater tucked into black jeans. Hair a bit shorter. She seemed even more attractive now.

Nate scooted his chair in, still speechless, mind squalling.

"Bold phone call," she said as she sat down.

"Your man was impressed then?"

The waitress appeared with a menu and Lang declined. A cheer erupted from the dartboard area and she glanced over at two enormous guys in tight-armed T-shirts who were playing.

"So how are you, Nate?"

When she turned to look at him, he saw that her eyes were clear, calm.

"A little drunk actually. But I needed to see you tonight. I just got back."

She watched the darts players again, and Nate leaned forward.

"You need to hear me out," he said. The firmness would impress upon her how much he had indeed changed, how the journey had transformed him into a more confident, stable man.

"Let's not start this with you telling me what I need to do, okay?"

He smiled. Back into the game already. "Listen … After what I realized on the trip, it killed me when I heard. I can't tell you how much I thought about you."

Lang lowered her eyes and didn't reply.

"I understand I'm a selfish nutcase." He had to keep going. Time to let go. "And I know the way I left pissed you off beyond measure. But I honestly thought the time apart would be good. Plenty of couples go a lot longer without seeing each other … All right, I've said this before. But I thought when it came down to it you understood." When he finished, he barely remembered what he'd just said; now his head felt like a sand-filled shoe.

Finally she looked up.

"But here's the catch. I didn't understand. You wanted me to, but I didn't. I still don't. We were trying to work on a *relationship,* my brother was in the middle of something very serious, and all you could think about was chasing your pitiful uncle." Jaw flexing, Lang paused. "I guess I just saw, finally, that you're unable to commit. I don't know if it's in your blood to make that kind of jump."

Nate raised his chin to the ceiling before settling his eyes on her again.

"You're just scared," he said. "You can't bear the thought of living with the possibility your companion might need to be away from you for a little while. I mean, what's so hard about that, really? You—"

"What's hard is you're *gone.* Just … outta here. You're all of a sudden out of my life, you're uncertain about your own life, you're doing something guys in their *twenties* do, Nate. I'm *thirty-six.* This isn't college. I need something more sure than you, and …" Her eyes were wet now. "I think I finally have it."

Nate concentrated on the bowl of custard. More cheering from the dartboard area.

"I'm sorry," she said, resting her forearms on the table. "But things feel good right now. We live in a comfortable house and I know Tran's happy to be with me. He's content, you know? We just clicked. Like it was meant to be." She made herself keep looking at the side of his face. "I guess you going off just showed we weren't right together after all."

Nate leaned forward to rest an arm on the table, too, and nicked the straw that had been precariously propped in his Bloody Mary; the straw flipped from the glass, flicking red droplets in a tight spray that stopped half an inch before the arms of Lang's sweater.

"It did the opposite for me." He tried to focus, conscious of the drama his drunkenness was enhancing. When she raised her head again, the sight of tears made him swallow. "I do love you. There were these moments in Bangkok, I don't know … All I felt up against just vanished at times, and I thought about you. Thought about home. I understood how self-absorbed I'd become."

"But you don't get it. You're *still* self-absorbed. You can't see I've made a decision. I've chosen to be with someone I can trust."

The declaration standing soldier-like in the compact quiet of their table, it occurred to him that she might actually be resolute.

"This is too … This happened too fast."

"It did?" Lang wiped some strands of hair from her face and gave a pained smile when the waitress brought her a glass of water. "Nate, you're the one who voiced doubts over the past year, it wasn't me. I'd have married you two years ago if you'd asked."

It was dreamlike by then.

"Do you still love me?" he said. How bald, almost crude, the question sounded.

She let the words float for awhile.

"I tried to take a larger view. But it came too hard. You just snapped a bond."

A peculiar heaviness spreading through his limbs like he'd been slipped a sedative, he could think of nothing else to say. Couldn't find an opening into the world he'd chosen. At least not now. He nodded once and stood, set some bills on the table next to the ejected straw, bent down and kissed her high on the cheek. He lifted his coat from the rack nearby and walked away. The sounds and various faces lost on him, he didn't turn to see if she was watching.

———

Next evening, Nate lay in bed, as he had all day, dissecting the events since his return. He listened to the rain on the bedroom windows, to a couple of squirrels calling to each other, their clackings through the winds of the latest storm. Pillow folded under his head, he let himself imagine Mary sitting at the foot of the bed, reading, drinking a Singha. It really was only a matter of hours earlier that he'd held her. Bangkok seemed so distant. Memories of the Sawatdee fading already, episodes getting dreamier. It was like a part of his mind was shutting down, the miles working their amnesic spell. Where had the insights gone? To come to one or two realizations about how to live, only to have them slip away:

how to make sense of that? To be broken down again just after you'd built up more passion for living than you'd known since you were a kid: what did it mean? The questions made him tired, so he rolled over and flipped on his alarm radio, a station playing some Duke Ellington. He recalled an Ellington interview he'd once heard someplace where the reporter asked where inspiration came from. Ellington chuckled and said, "All I need is a deadline."

When the song ended, he made another bathroom trip and, en route, latched onto a temporarily comforting notion that maybe great music was all there was in the world that ultimately made any kind of deeply satisfying sense, that answers to all of the best questions were hidden somewhere in the crescendos and improvised solos, in the guiding beats and most gorgeous arrangements. The thought embarrassed him, but he liked it anyway.

He wandered out of the bathroom and into the kitchen and spotted the blinking red light on his answering machine. He had turned down the telephone's volume the night before when he finally returned from the O'Riley's debacle. Prior to coming back to the apartment, he'd cruised the downtown streets, surveying the late night denizens, familiar office buildings, restaurants. At the corner of Broadway and Morrison he'd come upon a dozen teenagers sitting on the steps of the closed coffee shop, huddled close, each face so hardened. Rugs pulled out, everywhere. When the light changed, he stayed put, just watching, until one of the huskier boys barked something he didn't catch and gave him the finger.

At Fourth and Stark, he observed another group of kids—a larger, rougher-looking bunch—lugging bedrolls over their shoulders, some holding bottles of what appeared to be Night Train. There were ten in all, each wearing black, one boy with a dense series of silver hoops along both eyebrows, a big wooden stick tied to his pack.

Soon, though, he had tired of driving around. Took the Burnside Bridge back to the east side and made his way through the heinous corridor of fast-food joints on Weidler over to Fifteenth Avenue. It was one-thirty when he got in, but the shock over what had happened at O'Riley's still caromed through him. He threw his keys onto the kitchen counter, checked the messageless answering machine, turned down the telephone, stripped off his smoky clothes, then fell into bed to begin his muddled review of exactly where he'd gone wrong.

The machine took only a couple of seconds to rewind. Nate flipped up the volume and braced for what he hoped would be Lang's voice.

"This is Hieu. Please pick up." Monotone. The machine's hiss. "It is a few minutes after four, Nate. I just returned from the police station. I need to talk."

Page 1   Case# 97-0011A13

Portland Police Department
Portland, Oregon
Special Report

Report Type: SPECIAL Case Status: Pending Classification: Crime

Incident Type: STATUTORY RAPE Subject of Report: INTERVIEW OF VICTIM

Report Date: 3-8-97

Location: Portland Public Safety Facility

      2236 N. Hargrove Street, Port., OR   97203

Name: DET. SGT. DON WALLACE DOB: Sex: Race:

Address: PORTLAND POLICE DEPT. Phone#: 823-2120

Employment: Position: Phone#:

Subject: NGUYEN, HIEU TRAN DOB: 08-08-55 Sex: M   Race: A

Address: 2959 N.E. LOFTON CT. PORT., OR 97212 Phone#: 269-8894

DETAILS:

MENTIONED:

Hieu T. NGUYEN, suspect, see above. Wilson Green High School teacher.

Sasha ANDERSON, victim, DOB: 02-20-80, 300 N. Phillips, Port., OR 97201. Junior at Wilson Green High School.

Marguerite ANDERSON, mother of victim, DOB: 11-2-64. (same address)

Malisha JONES, mentioned, DOB: 03-02-80, 103 N. Mallson Apt. #31, Port., OR   97201. Junior at Wilson Green High School. Lives with aunt, Cherise LOGAN.

Sgt. Don Wallace / 7181   Approved_____

Portland Police Department
Portland, Oregon
Special Report

ACTION TAKEN:

This morning at 10:45, Sasha ANDERSON and her mother,
Marguerite ANDERSON, arrived here at the precinct office and
waited for me to return from another assignment, refusing to
be questioned by any other officer. At 11:20 in the interview
room, Sasha (I'll refer to her by first name and to her mother
as Ms. ANDERSON) said that she wanted to tell me the real reason why she and her friend, Malisha JONES, had accused their
Wilson Green High School science teacher, Mr. Hieu NGUYEN, of
sex abuse (case #96-0081A2). After receiving an affirmative
nod from her mother, Sasha said that she and Mr. NGUYEN had
engaged in sexual intercourse twice during the summer of 1996,
and that she and JONES were trying to get back at him.

Sasha said that the sex was initiated by NGUYEN, and that she
had complied because she was frightened. Also, NGUYEN had recently come over to the ANDERSON house and attempted to fondle
her. Ms. ANDERSON then said that she had walked into the front
room and witnessed NGUYEN "grabbing and pinching at Sasha's
breasts and butt, trying to get him some." She demanded that he
leave. According to Ms. ANDERSON, NGUYEN did leave promptly,
but only after saying that she was a "fat bitch." I asked Ms.
ANDERSON if she had known about any sexual relationship
between her daughter and NGUYEN in the summer of 1996 and she
said no. I then asked Sasha why she hadn't reported the incidents last summer and she replied, "Mr. NGUYEN said he'd hurt
me if I told anybody. I was scared, I didn't know what to do.
I told Malisha (JONES), though, and we figured out how to get
him. She was pissed, too. Malisha understood what I was going
through. That's why we lied about him doing that stuff in class.
We just thought it would be a better way."

Trust

Saturday the eighth of March, noontime, Sergeant Wallace phoned and asked Hieu to come over to North Precinct for a quick questioning. Something regarding Sasha Anderson had surfaced.

Hieu said he would be right over, hung up in slow motion, and leaned against the kitchen counter. It was as if he'd just been spun on one of those octopus-like carnival rides that Dat was fond of.

The house was still quiet, as it had been for over a week. Only a few businesslike exchanges had transpired between Anh and himself, the latest over an electricity bill that appeared to have been miscalculated by the company. The kids, too, were maintaining their distance, Le Phuong and Dat having further altered their personalities to conform to the new standard of even heavier tension, Vo spending nearly all his free time out with friends now.

Phone calls from smoky-voiced boys Vo had never before hung around had begun to worry Anh, though she didn't bring them up with Hieu. Even her concern for her eldest son wasn't enough to break through the bitterness over what her husband had confessed. The only other person with whom she felt remotely comfortable discussing the matter was her sister-in-law, but there was too much aloofness just now, Lang losing herself as she was in her new love, skillfully blocking out the pains in her other life.

In fact, loneliness had begun to chew at Anh, the hours of interior monologue over what to do about Hieu making her physically ill. Headaches and back pains attacked more often now, sometimes lingering two or three days. Though divorce remained taboo in the Vietnamese community, this was America; surely the matter's outcome was somewhat relative to place. Then, of course, there were the kids. She knew the crisis had hurt them, but it wasn't clear (at least with Dat and Le Phuong) what form the damage had taken. They didn't know the specifics, but clearly understood that their father had done something awful.

In the dark, tucked safely into the queen bed she'd picked out so many years before when a great adventure was just beginning, Anh mulled it all over nightly, especially the indescribable emptiness over having lost faith in her husband. It usually took three or four hours to slip into sleep. She had certainly never thought it would come to this.

From the beginning, their university days, she had trusted him. Something about Hieu's intense presence and his inspiring story of survival made her feel more connected to the new world; all that he had been through and how passionately he wanted to succeed made her confident. While her family had emigrated in 1979 through the Orderly Departure Program, and while she'd known some English before arriving, the transition was still devastating at times. With eyes that could soothe, then instantly excite, Hieu had convinced her that life would be full and rich no matter what, if only they worked hard and never gave up.

After the wedding, and after Vo was born nine months later, her love had deepened, adequately filling some of the space left by their meager sex life. The sex had always been all right, but slightly perfunctory, Hieu performing well enough, then rolling over after a few kind words, a final caress or pat, and a good-night. Over the years, she'd grown adept at convincing herself that she didn't need any after-sex touching anyway, that Hieu made up for his lack of tenderness with such a noble character. She'd always told herself that it was just his way, that he had been so profoundly shaped by all he'd endured. But now, with the confession, she suspected what his distance had really meant all along.

Hieu had indeed divulged his sin. Told all about Sasha's notes, the first meeting in Pioneer Square, the picnics in Washington Park, and even about how close he and the girl had come to kissing. Or going even further, he didn't know. He had tried to cleanse himself, not bothering to think that she would replay each detail in her alone hours, when everyone else had finally drifted into sleep.

Hieu returned from the interview with Sergeant Wallace and found Le Phuong sitting alone in the living room, reading a biography of

Beethoven. The perplexing disparity: Sasha in her coarse little universe; Le Phuong growing up amid books, music, and tradition, with parents encouraging exposure to the soul of things. When he saw his daughter as he came through the front door—her frightened eyes when she raised her head—he acknowledged again that he hadn't been as sorry for something he'd done since watching the black soldier blow apart.

"I need to speak with you a moment," he said, easing down beside her on the sofa. Le Phuong concentrated on her book again. "Please don't be afraid."

She faced him, and Hieu dared to reach out and put his arm around her. But he didn't know where to begin and for a time they sat there rigidly. Then Le Phuong scooted over and leaned into him. The clean smell of her hair made him close his eyes. To simply hold your child: it was shattering sometimes.

"It's all right," he said. "Everything will be okay." He needed to comfort her. Be a good father. He couldn't say that daddy might be going away, that sins were coming back to haunt him worse than he ever thought possible. "I'm just dealing with a mistake I made."

Le Phuong pulled away and began searching his eyes, so Hieu squeezed her shoulder and rose. "Please don't worry," he said. And then he could only turn and leave the room.

Back in the basement, on his cot, he lay analyzing the Wallace meeting, waiting for Nate to return his call. Though he was far from certain he could rely on Nate anymore, there was simply no one else with whom he felt comfortable discussing such matters. He knew he needed to get away, sort out his head before Monday morning's follow-up interview, and he wanted somebody with him. For a reason he hesitated to dig into, he didn't quite trust himself out in the world alone.

At the North Precinct, in the fifteen-by-fifteen interview room, Sergeant Wallace had explained the latest charge in a tone that suggested he thought Sasha Anderson was probably lying once again. Clearly, after the toilsome investigation that had ended only three weeks ago, the man was tired of the whole mess.

After reporting that Sasha and her mother had come in earlier that day with the new charges, Wallace sipped at his Dallas Cowboys mug of black coffee, remarked about how much rain they'd been having as he rearranged some papers, then turned on the tape recorder and began asking, in a mildly irritated voice, the standard: How do you respond to the charges? Have you ever had sexual relations with a minor? After two minutes of hearing Hieu deny everything, Wallace rubbed his eyes and said that it was all he needed at the moment, that he had to get more papers in order, finish some work on another case besides, and that Hieu would need to return at nine sharp Monday for a more in-depth discussion.

When Wallace shut off the recorder, Hieu commented on how Sasha seemed so bent on revenge. How could a schoolgirl get away with such things anyway? Wallace replied that because Marguerite Anderson had come forward, too, the charges would have to be investigated. But of course the previous case's outcome would be considered, absolutely.

Hands under his head on the cot, Hieu pictured the sergeant drinking coffee, shuffling papers, and his chest started to feel tight. He definitely needed to see Nate. He'd so missed being able to unload some of the stresses, either through their pretzels-and-beer sessions or whacking a racquetball. In spite of what Nate had told Wallace, Hieu needed the one person who had so often, without even knowing it, helped him feel more at ease, more at home.

Under the crisscrossing basement pipes, outside the range of the furnace's heat, he closed his eyes and listened as far out as he could hear: the gurgling refrigerator directly above, a few low creaks, and then a vehicle going too fast down the street in front of the house.

The spirits still seemed convinced that he should pay. Hope, he was almost certain now, was the greatest sin of all.

Treat 'Em Right

"Got your message, what's up?"

"I need to get together, Nate."

"Actually, I told my mother I'd come over for dinner. Fill them in about the trip and all."

"It is about Sasha."

"What's up?"

"I would rather talk face-to-face."

"I guess I could reschedule if it's—"

"No. What about tomorrow? We could drive out of town. I need to get away."

"All right …"

"I will pick you up at seven?"

"Okay. But can you tell me what it is?"

"See you in the morning."

—〜〜—

Nate peered at his eyes in the mirror as he shaved and cut himself on the corner of the mouth. As odd as the conversation had been, he kept trying to put it on hold, again resolving to respect Hieu's mysterious, occasionally abrupt style. Hieu had always shown a certain dramatic flair, a brashness from time to time that balanced his usually staid demeanor. There was the day when Vo got into a fistfight over at Slateman Middle School his sixth grade year and Hieu received the call at Wilson Green during an assembly for Black History Month. After taking the call in the main office, Hieu barged back into the auditorium with a clattering of doors, distracting the dancers and musicians onstage, snatched up his clipboard from the chair next to one of his gaping students, and jogged out the nearest exit. It was Nate's third year at Wilson Green; he and Hieu had just begun playing racquetball on Thursdays. He'd been struck by Hieu's vehemence, the utter disregard for the proceedings. As he splashed more water onto his bloody nicks, he considered the cryptic phone call once more. The eerie, drained voice. Whatever it was couldn't be as bad as Hieu made it sound.

On his way over to the house on Lincoln Street, he thought about where they would go in the morning, no question. He still had a key to the cabin—a copy he'd made without telling anyone—hung on a mug hook in a cupboard back in the apartment. Despite the touchy situation with Hieu, it would be great to see the old place again. Walk beside the Salmon River, through the damp woods, maybe even up Wildcat Mountain—depending on how the ankle felt—to take in the view from the clearcut. He would clean things up, prune back a few shrubs, talk with Hieu about whatever the latest crisis was. An insight or two about Lang might even enter into him. To his amusement, the same old excitement began building.

Up until his early twenties, the family had taken at least one weekend a month in Brightwood: hiking, skiing, fishing, or simply going up for a night of cards or Balderdash to get away from the city. Especially as a little kid, he'd always looked forward to the one-hour trip east up Burnside Street, then US 26 through Sandy, even though the cabin had no television; the fact that Grandpa, Grandma, Acacia, and Sammy were all resourceful made things fun. Whether it was Grandpa showing him how to tend various shrubs, Grandma leading walks to identify flowers and insects and trees, Acacia occasionally teaching a new card game, or Sammy racing him to the fishing hole to stalk steelhead, he normally had plenty to do. While everything had changed when Sammy left, a certain thrill gone, the trips continued on, the cabin still a steadying retreat.

When Grandma Davis died in October of '75, it had been Grandpa's suggestion to take a few days up at the cabin—just Acacia, Nate, and himself—to get away from the house on Lincoln Street. It had happened so quickly: with Grandpa at his spot at the kitchen table, flipping through the funnies, holding up his end of the small talk as usual, his wife of thirty-three years had fallen onto the linoleum mid-sentence, a half-opened can of green beans sitting on the counter next to an empty pot. She had died in the car, only a mile or so from Providence Hospital. Grandpa reached over for the third time to find a pulse, then pulled up under the branches of an oak and held her close. He later told Acacia that they had sat like that for quite a long time; he'd leaned his wife against himself, put an arm around her, and listened to cars and trucks speeding by, the world's response to an old couple sharing a long overdue pause.

The doorbell rang, two sharp blasts. Nate's ring. Acacia wiped her hands on a frayed dish towel that had been in the house since well before her mother's death, then unlocked the front door. In the background, Grandpa struggled to get up from the sofa by pressing on his new black cane.

"Bordeaux," Nate said, handing his mother the bottle, watching his grandfather's trembling effort.

Acacia looked over at her father and lowered her voice. "Believe it or not, he kept asking what time you were coming. Getting sentimental on me."

In the living room, Nate shook his grandfather's hand and noticed that the old man's grip was nowhere near as strong these days. The pale, withered paw engulfed by his own brought on a bolt of sorrow. His body seemed to be shrinking as well; you could no longer consider him stalwart.

"How do? No need to get up."

Grandpa finally eased his grip. "Like I have a choice most days." He dropped back onto the sofa, bloodshot eyes watering. "So, you feeling more talkative today? Or you fixing to fall asleep again, make us feel 'bout as exciting as two table lamps?"

"Sorry about that, I was spent. Major jet lag."

"I'm just messin' with you. Heck, a flight like that they'd have to have the coffin ready for me at the gate."

Nate sat at the other end of the sofa and took a quick whiff of the room: the mustiness of steady inactivity.

"The flight attendants were great. Brought pillows—"

"How's that arthritis anyway?"

The interruptions never failed to jar, but Nate flowed along. "A little better. Still feel the wrist and ankle some, but better."

Grandpa turned on the television and immediately began changing the channels.

"So … you find anything over there?"

"You're talking about Asia?"

"Yes I'm talking about Asia, you peanut head." The old man resumed flipping channels. Since three months earlier his daughter had finally given in to his desire for cable, he'd grown fond of the new remote control, often pressing numbers as though it were a video game. When his grandson didn't reply, he picked a station—Nickelodeon, a kids' documentary on beavers. "Well? Anything *happen* over there?"

Nate eyed his grandfather's face a few seconds before replying: the thick eyebrows like poisonous white caterpillars, the coin-thin upper lip, pink-rimmed eyes.

"I didn't find him, if that's what you mean. You'd have heard by now, don't you think?"

"Well, good lord, we hardly heard anything, so I don't know …" Grandpa turned back to the TV, a scene of a beaver gnawing a fallen limb filling the screen. "Like Sam that way I suppose."

"Come on now Gramps." There was a flash of orange at the far left edge of Nate's field of vision; Acacia stood in the entryway, again wiping her hands.

"Nate? You think you could open that bottle for me? Sorry to interrupt you guys." Then when they reached the kitchen, she said, "Please don't get him riled up. Doctor Lombardo says an argument could pretty much do him in."

"Please. He's been arguing for—"

"Nate." Acacia held a hand out in front of her. "Just don't let him get to you tonight." She continued to wipe her dry hands, weaving the old towel between her fingers, while Nate pretended to check out the makings for chicken pot pie on the counter. "We were a little worried is all. I knew you were probably okay and everything … Anyway, I think for him, you going just brought it all … Just don't get into it with him, please."

From how his mother worked the towel and avoided his eyes, he saw that the trip had been harder on them than he'd ever considered. But then if he was guilty once again of failing to anticipate the impact of his journey, so be it. Couldn't seem to please anyone anyway.

"I guess I assumed you understood my reasons," he said.

Acacia went to the stove and stood over the large pot of boiling chicken; she turned off the burner and gave the smaller pots of corn and green beans a few stirs.

"Hey, I had no problem with it at first." She picked up the towel again, gripped the ends and yanked outward. "But then you didn't let us know what the hell was happening. There was awhile there when Dad was convinced you'd found him already, two of you were off living it up somewhere. I don't know, India or someplace. Nate, you gotta understand what this guy's mind can do these days. I think he was surprised by how much your trip affected him."

"But it was you, too."

Acacia peeked back into the chicken pot, spooned out a piece of floating skin. "Well sure. For Christ's sake, what do you think? I'm a mom."

Nate went over and sat at the nook table and scanned the kitchen. So many meals, holidays, birthdays, all of Grandma's cakes and brownies and oatmeal cookies coming out of the oven. There were still marks on the door to the basement, showing his boyhood heights, the last dated 4-22-78. He had just returned from his first Europe journey and Grandpa, in a rare jolly mood from the champagne, insisted that he stand at the door. Five-feet-nine inches. At five-six, Grandpa had reached up, made the quick pen slash, then clutched Nate's hand. "Giant!" he'd bellowed.

The kitchen quiet now, Nate gazed at the basement door. Respect the old man's style, just let things be. Clearly the best way.

"It was probably selfish of me," he said. "Should've gotten in touch sooner."

Acacia covered the pot of chicken and came over to the table, gripping the towel.

"Look. It happens. And then we figure out we need to take care of people. Just don't be one of these people who realize it after they've already shut everyone out. I still pray every day that your uncle, God bless him, will learn that one simple thing."

At the mention of Sammy, Nate took in the rest of the kitchen, at least what he could see around his mother: the yellow linoleum floor, the aphid-green refrigerator with about thirty faded Far Side comics stuck to it with various novelty magnets, the wooden spice rack Grandpa made when he was a boy back in Willard, Ohio.

Acacia stood still.

"Listen to me a sec," she said. Her face composed into the overly dramatic glower that had rarely failed to make him wince during his teenage years. "I've learned something from taking care of that geezer in there. We take care of the people we love, Nate. Treat 'em right. Please understand that. Don't go and be like Sammy."

Nate stood and grabbed the unopened wine from the counter. Turned back and faced his mother.

"It never changes, you're always on him. I'm sure the guy has plenty of decent reasons why it's a complete bitch to reach out and we have no real clue what those reasons are."

Grandpa called out, *"We eatin' or what?"*

Acacia said, "Be ready in a few!" Then she stepped closer.

"Stop romanticizing him. It's getting *extremely* old. His choice how he deals with things. He ain't just a victim."

"You know what?" Nate hesitated, and then walked out of the kitchen, Acacia right behind him. He grabbed his coat from the chair by the front door and leaned into the living room.

"Gramps, I'm heading out. Sorry to miss dinner."

Acacia stepped around in front of him.

"Do not leave this house."

"I'm sorry I didn't call or write more, Gramps. Had my head up my ass, I guess."

Grandpa frowned at them. On the TV, four jowly men in dark suits were sitting around a table trying to prove each other wrong.

"Nate, do not leave this house," Acacia said through clenched teeth.

"Still feeling that jet lag, you know. Can't seem to carry on a conversation I'm so knackered. I'll talk to you soon, though, Gramps. You take it easy." He ignored his mother's glare. Turned away, reached for the doorknob, glanced back and said in a softer tone, "Enjoy that chicken pie" before handing her the bottle again and stepping outside.

Acacia stood on the threshold, squeezing the towel in one fist.

"You know, you're every bit the goddamn stubborn shit as Sam. Every *bit*. Makes for a real great life, kid."

His back to her, fumbling to get his coat zipper unstuck, he said goodnight in the calmest voice he could muster.

The Most Wonderful Sight

At ten minutes before seven, Hieu knocked on Nate's back door, his minivan humming in the driveway. A compact storm had passed shortly before dawn, ground and air moist, winter mingling with spring.

"Morning," Hieu said, more statement than greeting.

Nate tucked a thermos under an arm, brushed past him and headed for the driveway. Still edgy from the clash with his mother the evening before and then another near-sleepless night during which thoughts of Lang, Hieu, Sammy, and Aaron Harrington had worked him over.

"What is it?" Hieu pulled the door closed.

"Let's just hit the road."

When they set off down Fifteenth Avenue, Nate unscrewed the thermos and poured a lid- and cupful of the last bit of Javanese, fresh and black.

"Here's to a couple-a messed up cats," he said.

Hieu reached over for the cup, pushed in a CCR cassette with the other hand, and steered with his blue-jeaned knees.

"To Brightwood," Nate toasted.

"Brightwood."

They raised their coffees to the tight opening licks of "Bad Moon Rising" and it struck Hieu again how good it felt to be putting some distance between himself and a world that seemed to have his number.

On US 26, half a mile past Sandy, after a spell of twenty wordless minutes during which they listened to the CCR and took in familiar sights of fog-dappled berry fields and nurseries, Nate rolled down the window and stuck his head out. A startling cold. Another nursery flashed past, then Shorty's Corner store and cafe before he pulled himself back in.

"All right," he said. "So lay it on me. What's up?"

Hieu, shaken from his dull-eyed road lull, turned down the music and gathered himself.

"Sasha and her mother went back to Sergeant Wallace. There is a new charge, statutory rape. I need to go back in tomorrow for a full interrogation, lawyer and everything."

Nate turned away and looked out at the blur of trees. He was aware of his stomach now, the same old constriction.

"How did Wallace react?"

"He seems skeptical." Hieu paused again, noticing the lingering taste of coffee, how it blended sourly with the toothpaste. "I spent most of yesterday in the basement, trying to see some kind of reason for all of this. I think the spirits are trying to break me. Maybe I am supposed to become a better person, or something poetic like that. Then I think, No, I am only paying for a very bad decision. When I think about what to do, though, I get stuck. It is like something has me in its hands. Squeezing." He glanced over at Nate for the first time since he'd begun. The words had poured out. His face was hot, as if something had suddenly infected him.

"Nasty situation, man." Nate was ashamed of his thoughts, how a part of him believed it all served Hieu right. Maybe with everything else going on he hadn't stepped back far or long enough to absorb the severity of what his friend had actually done. "So tell me again, just so I'm clear. What the *hell* were you thinking anyway?"

"About?"

"What do you mean *about*? Sasha! Taking her up to goddamn Washington Park. For God's sake, Nguyen."

Hieu turned to face him a moment and the scowl made Nate look back out over the road.

"I do not need this today. I told you what happened. I cannot be more up-front with you."

"Look, I get what happened. I just can't believe it."

"I screwed up, I understand very well. I do not need anyone to beat that into me. I just—"

It was the first time Nate had ever heard his friend's voice break, or at least that's what he thought he heard. Hieu reached down and turned the music back up and resumed glaring at the traffic. Cars with skis and snowboards in roof racks sped past. They were coming down Cherryville Hill now, doing sixty-five or so, yet the teenagers in the cars seemed to be using the decline as a ski jump, tearing past the minivan like it was a mail buggy.

"Ding-a-lings," Nate said. As angry as he was, he didn't quite trust himself; maybe part of it amounted to being strung out over Lang and Acacia. It had happened too many times before, his lashing out from fatigue, pent-up fears. "Can you imagine 'em on the slopes?"

"Nate, I just want to get away. I am not looking for magical answers or sermons. I only wanted to talk and get away. Thank you for coming up."

Nate looked over at him, the stoic profile. In light of everything that was happening, all the forces in the mix, probably best to rein in the indignation for the time being.

"I've been wanting to get up here myself, man. It's been a long time." He noticed again that he tended to add "man" to the end of sentences when he was nervous, something Lang had pointed out more than once.

"When were you up last?"

"Let's see ... I didn't come up last summer because my mother was doing some remodeling, something about painting everything, replacing floorboards. Says she's still not done. I asked in the fall how things were coming, she said I couldn't see it before it's finished. Wants it to look just right before anyone goes up, I guess. So ... Probably last April was the last time. That's when I had this made." He pulled the key from a leg pocket of his cargo pants, and the *Brightwood, Jct. 1/4 mile* sign came into view. "There was a day I almost came up, though, the week of the stabbing. Decided to drive up the Gorge instead. Spur-of-the-moment." It was definitely right to keep steering the conversation away from Sasha Anderson. Calm things.

Right before the Salmon River Bridge, they pulled off the highway down the forty-yard paved road, then the pothole-strewn lane that cut through the woods to the cabin. There were only a handful of mailboxes at the turnoff, only a few families hardy (or crazy) enough to live in a rainforest on the western slope of a Pacific Northwest mountain range. Lingering fog hung in the understory. Mosses padded trunks and limbs. Trillium, ferns, and myrtle lined the narrow lane. Hieu slowed to a crawl, his eyes flitting over the scene: a landscape he'd so often daydreamed of, the previous four months intensely. A fantastic green-shrouded place, the thought of which usually settled him some.

They passed the occasional driveway leading to other cabins, then the junction with the old road for the riverside properties. A quarter-mile in from the highway, someone's German shepherd burst from the woods and began barking at the minivan's back bumper, trotting after it twenty yards before giving up.

And then the cabin came into view, a sight that made Nate crack a smile. Built of alder and oak, stained to a dark hue, roof moss-caked, the one-room retreat was small and cozy, the most recent woodstove installed by Grandpa in the summer of 1961, immediately after he bought the place. It had been owned for forty-eight years prior by the man who built it, a flinty, shaggy-haired fellow named Harrison Webster whose grandfather had come west from St. Louis in 1851 in search of adventure and decent soil and ended up—after finding the most majestic, frightening, seemingly endless stand of trees he'd ever seen—becoming a logger.

When Grandpa Davis bought the place, Webster said he hated to let it go, but was just plain sick of living in the rainforest. The long grey days where you could hardly tell the sun was up were too much for a single man. Because his wife had passed on the year before, he'd had enough of the mountain lifestyle and was moving into Gresham, just east of Portland, to a brand-new retirement community. Grandpa Davis still liked to joke about Harrison Webster, how the old guy had ever managed to fit in with a bunch of city geezers after so many years up in the rustic cabin.

As they pulled up to it, driving through the front yard's two-foot-high bluegrass, Nate was a kid again, ready for a trip to the river with Sammy or a walk through the woods with Grandma. When the engine stopped, he stepped out into the grass and drew a deep breath. Remnants of the clash with Hieu seemed to fade as he smelled the river in the distance, a scent that loosed still more memories.

"What do you say we head up the hill, catch the view before we go in?" he said. Then absently, "I should mow this before we leave."

"Let me piss first." Hieu trudged across the yard, toward the cluster of cedars. Even though there was an outhouse in back, he remembered how both Nate and Grandpa Davis had once relieved themselves under the trees on the semi-secluded south side of the cabin, when the women and kids had been picking up supplies over at the Brightwood Country Store across the highway. It did make a man feel more virile to urinate in the wild, the dauntless penis hung out in the elements.

"Watch the trillium," Nate said from the porch. He sat on the damp steps, a hand on one of the smooth posts, and looked out at the yard. Hadn't Acacia been up recently? She normally wouldn't let the grass get so long. Then he swiveled and eyed the old milk can that Grandpa had painted royal blue one summer. The paint was badly chipped now, but the can had stayed in its place all these years, standing guard beside the door. So often, he and his Grandma had lined up cones they'd collected on their walks in a proud display just next to it.

Hieu came around the corner. The color in his cheeks had risen.

"You do not want to go inside first?" he said.

Nate stood with a grunt, his ankle tight. "Let's head up Wildcat."

When they'd gone a few yards up the lane that rose behind the cabin, he added, "We have hiked up here together, haven't we?"

"The first time I came. Anh and the kids were not here."

"It was raining like crazy, that's right."

"The river was very high," Hieu said. Walking through the forest felt perfect. A beautiful thing how the woods could soothe a person so fast.

Ferns and buttercup lined the pebble and packed-mud lane, Douglas fir boughs cutting between the stands of smaller cedars. The dogwood flowers weren't quite ready, the air a touch too cool, but there was still a sweet combined fragrance of the trees, the soil, and the river on a light southwesterly. While most of the ancient firs had been cut by families like the Websters, and later by a dozen timber companies, the younger ones were still high and thick, the canopy keeping summer temperatures comfortable. In the heart of spring, rhododendrons bloomed in patches of soft sunlight. Downy woodpeckers, hummingbirds, and the occasional eagle sheltered on the trees, and evening grosbeaks chattered as they vied for food on the forest floor. The sounds of the birds and the lushness of the land when he first visited Brightwood five years before had pulled Hieu down the tunnels of his past, making him walk off alone to let the old images have their way.

At the trailhead, he stopped to tie his boot and recalled his first trip up Wildcat Mountain, how the sight of the clearcut made him feel cold.

He shut his eyes for a moment and breathed in, the smell of chimney smoke from a nearby cabin blending with a tinge of earthy dampness on another gust.

"Your ankle can handle this?" he said.

"We'll see. I want that view."

"I have probably said this before, but you were lucky to have this when you were growing up."

"You have said that before."

Hieu broke a smile. "It is true. You do not realize how lucky you are."

Nate turned away and began the climb, embarrassed by the comment, as he was whenever Hieu uttered it. On one level he agreed—he was lucky, very—but usually it remained a detached sort of thought. Like he was still scared to admit that life could actually be good at times.

"I've been thinking about teaching," he said, turning his head so Hieu could hear. Though the pace was slow, he acknowledged just how out of shape he was. "About going back, you know."

Hieu's breathing was even, stride firm. He didn't feel like talking anymore just then, preferring instead to take in the stillness, but picked up the conversation.

"You are thinking of quitting?"

Nate stopped. "You don't sound too surprised."

"I have been thinking the same thing for myself."

"Jesus …" Whether it was fatigue or astonishment or the fear that he might have to gulp his athletic pride if he allowed his joints to cool any longer, Nate could think of nothing else to say. He resumed the heavy-legged push.

But as they climbed on, the canopy thinning, a rhythm set in, their footsteps almost synchronized. Breaths cutting through the silence. The soil underfoot grew harder, the air colder, and eventually the wide-open space cleared by Raker and Sons Forest Products eight years earlier came into view and they stopped. To be walking through a stand of Doug fir and western hemlock, animals waiting for the lumbering humans to pass along, then to glimpse the gnarl of a clearcut, even after eight years, never failed to jar either of them. In a sixty-acre swath, all of the trees had been removed in a matter of days, an action that had gone largely unprotested by residents at the base of the hill.

The stark line between woods and wasteland again put Hieu in mind of Tay Ninh Province. As when Nate had first brought him up here, he stood frozen amid the stumps, picturing his village.

"You said the company replanted this?"

"They passed out fliers that said they did, but the rains were heavy that spring. Washed most the saplings away. I don't know how many they actually planted, though." Nate took off his raincoat and tied it around his waist, wiped his face with his sweatshirt sleeves.

In the throat-tightening quiet that followed, they moved farther into the cut, through ankle-deep mud and tangles of trailing blackberry to a large, level fir stump, got up onto it and looked out over the forest and the highway in the distance below. On the hills all around, large parcels had been sawed, a dusting of snow clearly outlining some. The greying sky was immense after the dim forest, the brightness bringing out deep browns in the dead wood surrounding them. Here and there, ten-foot high firs popped up between stumps.

While the clearcut depressed Nate, he'd usually felt compelled to take it in. Some native tribes had once burned hundreds of acres up around Rhododendron and Zigzag to grow their huckleberries; but the destruction, in the end, didn't come close to matching the thou-shalt-conquer dimensions wreaked by a handful of industrial logging companies, especially up in the national forest.

Full of the normal observations, he failed to notice that Hieu had already hopped off the stump and started back toward the trail.

"Oy!" he called. "What's up?"

Hieu, now thirty yards away, turned and said just under a shout, "I am going to the river."

Seeing the cut again, Hieu understood instantly that it was time for another walk by himself, no matter how brusque it came across. He would likely be just as irritable afterward, but he needed to be alone. It wasn't, it turned out, a time to be talking to anyone.

Nate, jolted once more (but telling himself he shouldn't be), didn't say anything else. It was a strange time, period. No other way to see it. Give the man some space. But then again, how far should a friend go in bringing up what he feels is the cause of another's discomfort? Was it really better to refrain from pointing out such things, not dig too deep? Or were you being shallow, even cowardly, by not broaching a subject that needed to be discussed? With Hieu, he believed that the abruptness amounted, undoubtedly, to something endured in Vietnam. He had tried to bring it up a few times, but Hieu always caught on, interrupting that he understood perfectly well why he was the way he was and that he didn't need to be psychoanalyzed by his best friend. "We are dealt our hand and we deal with it" was the usual response.

Having filled himself on the view, Nate stepped carefully off the stump into the mud. Let bygones be bygones. Hieu was just being Hieu.

At the cut's edge, he pictured what the hill looked like before the harvest, when Sammy had taken him on hikes, and remembered how sometimes he'd ridden his uncle's back on the journey down, winding through the trees. It had changed so quickly, the hill. Like things changed after Sammy left.

Back on the road to the cabin, the ankle pain pounding again, he gimped along, a sword fern at the base of a rhododendron catching his eye, raindrops clinging along the fronds. A hummingbird drank from a red sugar water dispenser that hung from another old cabin's porch. Wind swayed the cedars on either side of the road and new leaves on the vine maples fluttered, fragile as newborn birds. Nate absorbed details and soon spotted the cabin through the trees, the most wonderful sight. He pulled the key from his side pocket and took another deep breath. Build a fire, eat a sandwich, a few potato chips. Look over the old things. Perfect.

Before opening the door, though, he peeked through the window and saw that someone had recently been inside. Local kids maybe. One of the twin beds along the back wall was unmade, some dishes piled in the sink, a pair of flannel-lined blue jeans hung over one of the chairs, and a book lay open, face-down, on the old velour love seat that Grandma had bought in Sandy at an estate sale. It appeared that whoever had broken in wasn't there, so he pushed the door open and stepped inside. On the stove, a pot of tapewormish egg noodles in cold water, a pot of white sauce with tuna fish caked to the sides. A loaf of wheat bread sat unwrapped and half-eaten on the counter, and at least a dozen empty cans of creamed corn and Beanee Weenee were stacked in the plastic wash basin next to the crumb-covered toaster. From under the unmade bed, a green duffel bag jutted out, sprouting grimy socks and underpants, a bong with a rainbow sticker pasted across it that read *Mai Pen Rai* next to the bag.

Nate walked over to the love seat and saw that the book was a wrinkled paperback of *The Brothers Karamazov* opened to the middle. There was no bookmark, but on the lamp table, propped against the empty planter shaped like a piglet that Grandma had brought up when they first furnished the cabin, he saw the photograph and a surge of heat spread up his chest. It was himself, riding on Sammy's back, wearing his black-and-red cowboy hat and a pair of cut-offs; Sammy's teeth were bared, long brown hair tied back. Nate lowered himself to the love seat and stared at the photo. Glanced at the duffel bag. The dish-piled sink. He turned the picture over and read the neat cursive: *With my buddy, 1962.*

Battle

He couldn't seem to stand.

Lightheaded, he surveyed the cabin. On the wall opposite him, the small oil painting of a Bavarian cottage that Grandma had copied out of a travel magazine still hung next to a photograph of Harrison Webster and his wife Aida standing on the cabin's porch in 1948—his expression amused, hers severe. The door in the picture was open slightly, like the door now, the cool air gradually dissipating the mustiness. Nate noticed the wood floor, the muddy boot streaks, dust and crumpled pieces of newspaper in the corners. He raised the photo of Sammy and himself and scrutinized it again; it was one he couldn't remember having seen, though there had been a number taken of the wild horseback rides.

It was as if he'd fallen into a trance, the numbness that kept him seated didn't seem to be letting up. A soft, steady ringing in his ears. Where his uncle was at the moment was anyone's guess, but judging from the state of the cabin, it was someplace mucky. All over the table and counter, he saw now, were dark smudged fingerprints.

He gazed at the photograph, his breath still coming in shallow bursts, and didn't hear any footsteps or see anyone step into the room at first. Then the door clicked shut.

A man lowered two tin pails onto the floor next to the table in the center of the room and said, "What are you doing?" Nate wasn't sure who it was; the bearded face made it too hard to tell. "Who are you?" The voice was sharper. The stranger approached, and it wasn't until he was within three feet of the love seat that Nate managed to swallow.

"I'm Nate Davis. This is …"

When the words came out, his hands began to quake. It was Sammy. He could see the eyes more clearly now, though the years had altered most everything else. In quick glimpses, he saw that his uncle was much too thin, cheekbones and eye sockets too prominent. The dirty jeans, work boots, and checkered flannel shirt looked gawky. Long grey-brown hair pulled back. Sammy unclenched his fists and stood still.

When Nate got up and raised his head again, he found that he was looking directly into his uncle's eyes. They were the same height.

"Nate Davis," he said.

They stood there a few moments, studying each other, before Sammy gave a faint nod and turned away, picked up his pails and dropped them onto the kitchen counter. He set a cereal bowl half-full of milk into the sink, tilted one of the pails until black soil with maroon and pink worms wiggling through it spilled out, then reached for the other pail, stopped himself and lowered his head. The pause seemed like a full minute to Nate.

"Acacia promised not to give anyone the key."

As though the memory had come seeping from his bones, Nate now recognized the timbre of the voice. He fixed on Sammy's back, the shoulder blades through the thin flannel. His hands still trembled, but he wasn't as dizzy.

"I had a copy made. She doesn't know … But the door was unlocked anyway."

Sammy let out a chuckle, still facing the sink. "Crafty." He turned around and folded his arms.

Nate saw him swallow, the lump of his Adam's apple just visible through the heavy whiskers below the fuller beard. "I wouldn't have bothered if she hadn't started acting so uptight about people coming up."

"She was helping me out." Sammy rubbed his face, smearing soil over his nose and cheeks. He motioned Nate to the table.

Nate eyed the heap of squirming worms on the counter, gave a nod and pulled out a chair. It felt like a ball of yarn had lodged in his throat.

"So, what's the deal with the worms?"

Sammy went over and sat down across the table. He hung an arm over the back of his chair and his face relaxed. It seemed now as if he might've been expecting such a situation.

"I gather 'em for the store. Fishing bait. The guy gives me a couple cans of food for every Styrofoam cup I show up with."

Another hush fell, Sammy looking straight across the table. It occurred to Nate just how unlike the meeting was from his imaginings of the lithe Thai girl rubbing oil on his uncle's feet, that is except for the part about being asked who he was.

"You keep a mean house," he said. There was too much to talk about. When Sammy raised his eyebrows and gave a half-smile, Nate saw the wrinkles that had settled in around the eyes. He thought of the Sun God Bungalows. Dennis's story about the Bouncing Betty.

"What can I say?" Sammy glanced around. "This is just for awhile … Though now it looks like it might be a shorter gig than I thought." Eyes drilling ahead again, he smiled full-on. Yellowed teeth. "But then I guess it sort of depends on how you react to all this." He leaned forward and set his elbows onto the table, fingers interlocked. "Sis said you went off searching for me."

Nate couldn't tell whether the tone was condescending.

"Look at this place, man."

Sammy chuckled, inspecting the room again. "Oh, I don't know. I kind of like it like this. Suits my lifestyle."

"And that is …"

Sammy arched his eyebrows again and grinned.

"My lifestyle?" He cocked his head once on each side, stretching his neck. "These days, a little worm hunting, some reading, walking in the woods. Being by myself. Your regular Waldenesque experience." He stared at Nate for a few more beats. "And what about your lifestyle? How the *hell* are you bud? My God."

Nate pushed his chair back and turned for the door, expecting Sammy to say something else. When nothing came, he gripped the knob, said, "Look at all this, man," and went out onto the porch.

On the boot-worn top step, he sat and pressed his hands together to quell the shivers. More clouds had begun to move in, dulling the shades of green. He heard his uncle get up and shuffle through the cabin, doing lord knows what. Then Sammy appeared in the doorway.

"You care for some breakfast? I haven't eaten yet. It's just cornflakes."

"I'm heading out when my friend gets back." He needed to ask more questions, get ahold of himself, but he only sat there.

"Your friend," Sammy said, another smile slowly expanding. *"Ladyfriend?"*

"Hieu Nguyen. A colleague. He's down at the river."

When he heard the name, Sammy walked out onto the porch, then down a few steps below Nate. He stood motionless and looked at his nephew's face in the natural light.

"Vietnamese friend," he said.

Nate raised his eyes. "What does that mean?"

"Means it's good to have friends with different backgrounds."

Sammy turned and lowered himself with a sigh onto the bottom step. Wind shook the hemlocks across the lane for a time, and then there was only the far-off sound of the river.

"Pretty wild, huh? Meeting like this …" When Nate didn't reply, he shook his head. "Yeah, I know. I didn't imagine it quite like this either."

Nate watched his uncle—the greying hair tied with a blue rubber band, the soil-splotched shirt—and remained quiet. Eyes wet.

"Be as pissed as you need to be. Don't know what else to say."

Another gust brought the river smell and Nate pictured the old fishing hole, and before he could check himself said, "So what happened anyway? What … happened with you?"

Sammy held his position on the bottom step and let the words fully evaporate. The clouds, tinged with blue-black now, had dipped further to the earth, the air vaguely metallic.

"Jesus … I bee-lined to Indonesia, then got a few jobs in Thailand. But I hear you already know that." The wind picked up even more, swaying the bluegrass, and Hieu's minivan creaked. "After Bangkok, I went back over to Vietnam a couple years, traveled around. Lived in this little place called Trang Bang. Then about a year or so ago I realized I had enough money to fly home, so I did. Don't really know why, just time I guess. Felt right for some reason."

The breeze made the goose bumps rise on Nate's forearms.

"I stayed with a friend down in Ashland for awhile, took tickets at the Shakespeare theater. Then one day I get up and think I better call your mom finally." Sammy stood, turned around and rested a boot on the bottom step. "But she's got this crazy-ass caller I.D. thing I'd never heard of. Finds out where I am, shows up the next afternoon."

Nate rose and stepped to the end of the porch.

"Hey, don't be mad at her," Sammy said. "She took one look at me and knew you wouldn't dig it at all."

"I can't believe you've been up here. She had no damn ri—"

"Hey bud. She's not the one responsible for me being up here. I asked her to keep things quiet. Promised I'd come down and see people again after awhile. She did me a huge favor."

Nate focused on the minivan's windshield, dim reflections of limbs.

"So you were planning to, what? Get high, re-read the Russians till things seemed groovy enough?"

Sammy began climbing the porch steps, and Nate moved back toward the door with a startling thought: crack the prick across the face. *Do it.*

But then he saw his uncle's eyes up close. Perhaps it had been honed in Vietnam, or maybe through dealing with the likes of Mick Lassiter over the years; regardless, Sammy had mastered the nuances of a chilling glower. There would be no such battle, at least at the moment. Nate got out of the way.

He heard Sammy pouring the cornflakes, sitting down at the table. The first drops of rain had begun to fall and a thunderclap sounded over Huckleberry Mountain to the southeast. Nate looked down at his Grandpa's old blue milk can, back out at the multiplying streaks of rain, and then as if he had been shoved by invisible hands, leapt off the steps, landed hard on his right foot, and set out hobbling through the grass. He didn't know what to do, what to think, so he headed for the river.

The Confluence

After leaving Nate up on the stump, Hieu had hiked fast, dwelling on how flimsy his good spirits had been, how the usual dread simply waited for the best moment to spread through him again like ink through water.

As he approached the Salmon River, hearing the rapids at the confluence with Boulder Creek, he pictured the clearcut again, how the spectacle so eerily matched his memories. Then, on the trail of those images, it was the young black soldier, how the man's legs had ripped from his torso. The closer he came to the river, the forest summoned scenes rapid-fire: Minh sending him off with the motivational speech, Hoa and Lang drifting away on the raft, the horse snake sliding over his campsite a day from Saigon. His father's blue-glazed eyes.

Hieu stood on the bank next to the confluence, all other sounds drowned by the rapids. Upriver, clouds had begun to swoop down into the narrow valley, water merging with sky on the near horizon. Boulder Creek roared, the runoff heavier than usual for early spring. A hermit thrush darted low across the river and up into an old lichen-barked alder on the opposite shore. It was one of his favorite spots. A place where he could take stock, get perspective, feel welcome. Like the Pacific beaches in that way, but more special. He'd come upon it during his first visit to Brightwood five years before, on another solo hike, when he had never heard of Sasha Anderson. Some answers that would renew him might flow down the river right before his eyes. He needed it to be that easy, this once.

After enduring the nights on the basement cot, then hearing of Sasha's new charge, which he would have to answer to in detail, and then seeing his friend preoccupied again with his own problems, Hieu wanted relief in a way that he had never suspected could feel so intense. It made his mouth go dry. He watched the blur of white and grey in front of him, mesmerized, and let himself slip into thinking what it would be like to feel the cold all around, then inside him. What it would be like to be swept away, pulled into a swirling world where only a humbling wildness could direct his fate. A stunning notion. He would have to answer to no one. He could drown the VC days, silence whatever it was that had made him into something so horrible. The water would take care of everything. It would be easy. And then the familiar collection of words arrived, as if signaling what he should do. *I just hate him so much … He's mean … We just wanted to get his ass fired.*

Toes flexing, he looked down at the rocks at his feet—some moss-covered, others bald and shiny grey—turned slowly and glanced back at the wall of flora. Prickly currant and salmonberry rose behind him on the bank. It was all so beautiful. It would be easy, yes, to slip in and taste the cold. Feel it on his teeth.

You're holding something in.

But as he stared again at the confluence, the sound pervading everything, he heard another voice. Le Phuong's.

I love you, Daddy. What's wrong with you?

Arms spread, legs quaking, Hieu turned and dropped onto his knees on the rocks, guttural cries jerking through him, insignificant against the din. For an instant, he was outside himself, hovering a few feet out over the river, aware of his smallness against the backdrop of trees and pounding water. And then the perception was gone and all he felt were his banged knees, the pain snapping him back to what he had nearly done. The sobs went on, dying away in the thunder of sky and river. Nothing could happen, he understood so completely at that moment, that could make him leave his children fatherless in such a hard, tough world.

Nothing.

Knowledge of Something Unutterable

By the time Nate appeared, Hieu had calmed himself to the point of being able to speak, though he still breathed unevenly. Wind kicked water up onto his boots and jeans, and the rain had already coated his hair and face.

"I am fine," he said. "I was doing some thinking." From his spot on the rocks, he looked up and saw that Nate seemed shaken, too—the tense mouth, fidgety wet hands—and asked what had happened.

"Man, I can't quite believe I'm saying this ... My uncle's back at the cabin."

Water dripping off his chin, Hieu unfolded himself, knees still throbbing, and stood. "Sammy?"

Nate nodded and resumed the hike back up the bank.

Gingerly at first, Hieu followed, mildly relieved to be walking away from the magic spot.

"What is he like?" he said. Time more relentless than usual; already he was on to something new, forcing himself to put his own world on hold.

Nate turned his head a little and kept walking. "He looks like hell, but I suppose he's nice enough."

"What happened?"

"I'll tell you on the way back. Let's just get out of here. I don't want to get into anything more with him right now."

Hieu remained silent the rest of the way over the rocks, Boulder Creek beside them hurtling toward the river. After what he'd just experienced, he imagined that leaving wouldn't be so easy.

The sky opened further, puddles in the old lane's potholes churning. When the cabin came into view through the bars of cold rain, they saw that a light was on. Chimney smoke melded with cloud.

Of course they would go inside, Nate acknowledged; there was no way he could just leave. But what exactly he expected from Sammy he still didn't know. Indonesia and Thailand hadn't really helped clarify it, and seeing the man after almost thirty years certainly hadn't either. Yet he didn't need to figure it out right now; it might be enough simply to hear more about his meandering journey. It was a matter of staying calm.

"I'll just introduce you real quick before we head out," he said as they entered the front yard. "Tell me what you think."

The tall grass soaking the few remaining dry spots on his jeans, Hieu pushed the minivan keys back into a pocket and followed. He had by then gone back to dissecting the moments beside the river; while he sympathized with Nate's position, he couldn't help replaying Le Phuong's words.

On the porch steps, they thumped the mud from their boots, avoiding a banana slug that was sliming its way toward the milk can. They stopped to listen. Faint piano, Chopin, and footsteps. The door opened and the music poured outside from a small black cassette player that Sammy had set on the table.

"Weather never messes around up here." Sammy smiled his yellow-toothed smile. He had wetted and combed his hair and changed out of his work clothes into a pair of clean blue jeans, a grey sweater, and moccasins fringed with tiny red beads.

Nate followed Hieu through the threshold and saw that the table had been wiped down, the counter cleared of worms and soil. Floor swept, bong stashed, dishes rinsed. Only a trace of the former mustiness lingered in the coffee-scented air.

"So this is your friend." Sammy closed the door, turned the music down to a barely audible tinkling, and extended a scrubbed hand. "I'm Sam. Welcome."

Hieu smiled, recovering himself, and shook. "Hieu Nguyen, hello."

"Coffee?"

Before replying, Hieu glanced at Nate, who was still taking in the transformed room. "Thank you, yes."

The duffel bag had been shoved under the bed. The silver worm pails side-by-side next to the door, beside the old straw broom. Nate eased down onto the love seat.

"Nate?" Sammy said, holding out a mug for Hieu.

"No thanks."

"Peanut butter sandwich? I made up—"

"No thanks."

A silence fell during which Hieu sat at the end of the table nearest the door and began sipping his coffee. Sammy pulled out the chair at the opposite end. The plate of sandwiches remained on the counter.

Outside, a jay's cry rifled through the steady patter of rain.

"So how long have you been up here?" Hieu said.

Sammy reached over for the cassette player and stopped the music. "Little under a year now."

"Really? Where before this?"

Hieu showed no signs of nerves: the boldness baffled Nate. What was prompting it? With strangers, he'd always been so reticent.

Sammy sat cupping his mug in both hands, then pushed his chair back and crossed his legs at the knee.

"Oh, all over the place," he said, glancing over at Nate. "Most recently Vietnam." He took a drink and began jiggling his dangling foot. "What about you? When did you come over? Just curious."

Hieu remained placid. Maybe after what had just happened beside the river, he thought, conversation came easier. Maybe human contact was what he needed most.

"Right before the fall," he said.

Sammy's fingers began drumming the sides of his mug. "Suppose Nate's told you I was over there."

"He mentioned it, yes."

Hieu saw that Nate had folded his arms and lowered his eyes, and it was then, observing a shape of such discomfort, that something clicked. The mask of calm ripped away, like that. The black soldier. The blast of leaves. He'd met other American veterans and had allowed himself no internal response; but for some reason now it was different. He had never expected to meet Nate's long-gone uncle, let alone sit and discuss Vietnam. And of course he'd never envisioned things coming to such a point beside the river. So quickly, the singular understanding that had filled him after hearing Le Phuong's voice over the rapids was being obliterated. He looked from Nate back to Sammy and saw that the uncle who'd become the stuff of legend was staring at him.

"Did you fight by chance?" Sammy said, watching Hieu's eyes.

Hieu took what he thought was a well-concealed deep breath through his nose. "I did, yes."

At that, Nate cleared his throat and leaned forward. "I was thinking, it must get a bit boring up here after all your adventures." He felt entitled to the jab.

Sammy kept his head perfectly still, facing Hieu, but his eyes moved.

"I don't believe in boredom."

"It's just strange that—"

"My turn to interrupt, Nate. I'd like to visit with Hieu a minute more, if that's cool." Sammy smiled again and focused on the man across the table who sipped at his coffee too frequently now. A gust slapped rain against the north window and carried a dog's single bark in the distance. "Listen, I'm sorry … I just always get kind of uptight when I think of how shitty so many of the ARVNs were. We'd never seen so many cowards …" He couldn't seem to help laying it out. "Which company were you in?" Unbelievably rude, he knew, yet he gave in once again to the notion that such feelings were occasionally beyond control; at certain times, it was still as though he were split down the middle like a fire log, as though he were watching part of himself burn from a slight distance.

As for Hieu, he'd never been accused of being a cowardly member of the ARVN, let alone challenged so openly about anything save for Uli Wegman's barbs about science department matters. At Portland State, his second year, there had been a pretentious wang in a political science class who'd made a sour remark about the shaky partnership between the US and the ARVN while looking his way, but never anything so blatant. Confident he'd think of something, but afraid that the something might set Sammy off, he opted for another drink of coffee. His face flushing as the quiet stretched. And then he let out the first thing he locked onto.

"To be honest," he said, "I have blocked it out. I cannot even remember which company."

Nate's head shot up. He had heard Hieu mention fighting only once, after one of Anh's dinner parties. They'd been out on the front parking strip beneath Bing, Hieu having walked him down to his truck after a

couple snifters of brandy. A warm July night. They had just finished talking about Vietnam again, Anh recounting the pulse of wartime Saigon.
Out on the parking strip, Hieu mentioned how it had felt good at first
to enter the crazed city after spending such grueling weeks in the forest
stalking other men. Immediately after the comment fell out, though, he
had reached up for one of Bing's limbs and shaken it to distract with
something odd. But Nate hadn't pressed, despite his buzz.

"You don't remember your company?" he said. While he didn't want
to put Hieu on the spot further, he succumbed to the urge to get to the
bottom of a few things. Considering the extraordinary circumstances he
was in the midst of, everything seemed open to scrutiny. He wanted to
know more about what it had been like, beyond what the documentaries
and books could give him. Then he realized he hadn't taken in Sammy's
response yet, and shifted his eyes. Elbows on the table, his uncle held his
hands prayer-like up over his mouth.

"It is impossible to speak of sometimes," Hieu said. "I am sure you
understand what I mean, Sam."

Sammy continued to rub his upper lip and the sides of his mouth and
gazed at Hieu like he was deciphering a secret code. The pauses longer
now. The rain shower passed, the only sounds in the cabin the hum of
the small refrigerator and the rustling of his pant leg as he continued to
jiggle his foot. At length he stood and began stepping around the table
toward his nephew's friend.

Right hand clenching into a fist, Nate bent forward on the love seat. Just
as he shifted his weight to the balls of his feet, though, Sammy dropped
into a crouch beside Hieu's chair.

Sammy raised his head and said, "It is hard to speak of. I do understand, yeah."

Nate settled back again, eyeing the contour of the form his uncle and
Hieu together created; he suspected that he was in a state bordering on
shock, yet he needed to stay put, flow along, see where it would all lead.
Nevertheless, as he watched Hieu's face he was acutely sorry for having
subjected him to such an ordeal.

Shoulder blades back against the chair, Hieu sat with his head up, concentrating on his breathing, avoiding Sammy's eyes.

Still crouched, Sammy wanted to stay in control, too. Tried to keep his breathing even. He examined the side of Hieu's face.

"But you know what?" he said. "Why don't we try and talk about it anyway." He smiled then, a smile Nate didn't remember. "It's just that, you know, I can't help but wonder if it was you who ran off when we needed you most. I think it just might've been. I actually think I recognize you. Really."

Nate sat frozen.

Then, like nothing at all up to that point had fazed him, Hieu looked down at Sammy and replied, "And it was you who said, 'We shoot first, ask questions later'? I think I remember you, too. Yes."

Sammy reached up and pressed a hand on the table next to Hieu's hand.

"You know what?" he said, still smiling. "It *was* me. Absolutely. You got me, Hieu. You really got me."

When Hieu said nothing more, only faced forward again, Sammy rose and placed his hands on the back of Hieu's chair. "Man, was I overjoyed when we finally caught on to what was goin' on over there. You're absolutely right, it was me."

Hieu kept his eyes ahead, no response.

"Third planet from one of billions of stars in this little galaxy alone," Sammy went on. "Little bombs and tanks, little guns—"

Hieu pushed his chair back against Sammy's legs and stood just in front of Nate.

"Please," he said. "What is this? Keep it simple … This was one country in a line of many invaders. Very simple. Arrogant men failed to see the complexity. Everything black and white to them."

The rush of words made him blink fast; all his life, he'd spoken only with family about such matters, rarely at that. Sweat ran down his spine and settled in the waistband of his underwear.

Nate expected to see Sammy's glower again, but his uncle only nodded slowly, took another long look at Hieu and said, "Ahh … All right, I see," then went over to the sink, turned on the faucet and held his hands under the stream.

Lightheaded again, Nate rose. He needed to speak. Get out before anything more happened. But then Sammy said something else—a response that lit up his memory of the man he had once wanted to fashion his life after.

Fresh-scoured hands still under the tap, Sammy said, "I didn't mean to let loose on you, Hieu." As though he had slipped into a less angry self like a clean pair of shoes.

Hieu reached over, pushed his chair back in.

Sammy shut off the faucet, wiped his hands on his jeans, turned and leaned against the counter. A trucker's horn from the highway, then stillness.

"It may be simple. Probably is. But I've still spent a hell of a long time trying to figure it out, and I'll bet you have too ... What kind of answer ever satisfies, though, you know? It's like pinning down a dream."

Hieu didn't respond.

Sammy, searching for a reaction, stepped up to the table again. "We're just hangin' tough, right?"

Some other kind of conciliatory gesture was called for, Hieu thought. But no one made a move. After a quick nod, he said he would meet Nate outside, needed to be getting back soon. He thanked Sammy for the coffee, their eyes meeting again only for an instant, and went out onto the porch.

When the cabin was silent once more, Sammy ran his hands over his face in a long downward sweep.

"Nate, I'm sorry."

Nate only stood there.

"You must be thinking, What now?"

"Don't know what I'm thinking."

Before Nate knew what was happening, Sammy cupped his hands behind his neck, dropped his arms back to his sides, and came closer. An arm's length away.

"Have this picture with me wherever I go ..." From a back pocket, he pulled the photograph that Nate had seen on the love seat. "Man, you loved those rides."

All of a sudden, Nate wanted to reach forward. Instead he said, "Guess I am wondering what happens. How long you planning on staying up here?"

Sammy sighed and glanced down at the chair Hieu had occupied.

"Don't know. A little longer I think. Maybe come back to town in a month or so, find a job someplace. Get back into things nice and slow."

Nate heard the minivan start up, Hieu turning on the heater most likely.

"Where you planning on living?" Every word that came out still sounded wrong.

"Oh, probably just crash with some old friends at first, if they even remember me."

"I'm sure they will."

Another quiet.

"Listen," Sammy said. "I need you to remember something. And I'm being straight-up here." He made sure Nate was looking at him before he continued. "Some guys dive into themselves and can't climb back out even when they feel ready, you know? It would've been a mess if I'd stayed around after I came back that first time. Total fuckin' mess. But I'm sorry. You didn't deserve any of that crap at all."

Nate stood there, watching his uncle's eyes.

"I just want you to know it had nothing to do with you, Nate. Always had nothing but good thoughts for you."

Nate hesitated, gauging Sammy's expression. He turned away and rapped his knuckles on the back of the chair in which Hieu had sweated just moments before, then stopped and looked back at his uncle. Extend a hand, a part of him said. Reach. Say *something*. But when he searched for the words that could possibly give form to the jumble of questions still swirling through him, nothing came. He tried to smile and his mouth didn't move. The look in Sammy's eyes: knowledge of something unutterable.

From the porch, cold air in his nostrils, he spotted Hieu inside the minivan: one hand spread wide over his face, shoulders twitching with each muted sob. The engine was still running and only a few raindrops fell. Unable to settle on which direction, ahead or behind, offered the clearest image of brokenness, Nate tilted his face to the grey Brightwood sky.

Part Five

—◄◄◄—

Voices

A man needs a touch of madness,
otherwise he will never be free.

—Zorba

Distance

In one of the North Precinct's interview rooms the following morning, Hieu watched Sergeant Wallace press the cassette recorder's play button. Beside him, his lawyer, Blake Saylor, scribbled something onto a pad of yellow paper, the portly man's charcoal suit lending an even more severe air to the proceedings.

Wallace, who had in so many words reiterated his skepticism of the latest charge right before pressing play, again explained Sasha's claim that Hieu had fondled her during his visit two weeks earlier. Mrs. Anderson, also, apparently witnessed him pinching her daughter's breasts and buttocks.

"First of all, I need to get clear on why you went over to the house."

"To apologize." Hieu realized that he shouldn't have worn a wool sweater, his armpits and back already moist.

"Apologize?"

"That might be the wrong word. I just wanted to tell her that I was sorry about how things had worked out. I do care about my students' lives."

Hieu heard Blake Saylor jotting another note.

"But go over to her house?" Wallace said.

"Not wise, I understand, but I was at a very stressed point."

"I'm still confused. You wanted to say you felt sorry for one of the girls who had, only a short time before, tried to pin you with a charge of sex abuse?"

"It sounds strange, I know. But I felt sorry for her."

A few responses past him now, it was time to make the final decision about admitting the trips to Washington Park. He had already convinced himself that there wasn't any evidence of the picnics, and he knew Sasha's word was already suspect in Wallace's eyes. But then there was the truth. From the Brightwood confrontation, the sting of lying still lingered.

The afternoon before, both the riverside experience and the clash with Sammy firing through him, he had gone back down to his cot and committed to thinking hard. The house had been empty, Anh having taken Hoa, Le Phuong, and Dat to a matinee of *Babe* at the Hollywood Theater on Sandy Boulevard. In the cool, dim basement, he wrestled the issue of admitting his sin to Wallace. What would it accomplish? Anh and Hoa already knew what had happened and that fact alone had brought nearly unbearable despair; why make things harder? Yet it *was* all his fault, regardless of Sasha's advances; he would simply deal with the consequences. The spirits would teach him the best way they saw fit.

But after deflecting another of Wallace's questions, he saw that a final decision wasn't, in fact, showing itself.

"I'm curious why Sasha's mother would back such a charge," Wallace said.

Hieu strained to focus. It felt like a part of him was sitting off to the side of the table, watching his own mannerisms, then the sergeant's, for any tell-tale signs.

"I do not understand why. She loves her daughter. Allies, you know."

Wallace looked over at Blake Saylor, then met Hieu's eyes again.

"Sasha, as you know, lied to me on record almost three months. You think all this amounts to is her failing to learn a lesson? About telling the truth?"

"Maybe. She is a very tough girl." He was too aware of how he might be coming across and his eyes began to itch. "I am not sure why she or her mother would come forward with all of this, but it is nonsense. I only went over to visit for a minute, to wish her well. I had no physical contact with her, like I have said already."

Wallace sat forward, focused on the middle distance.

"Now … I have one more question about your house call, Mr. Nguyen, and it's basically the same one I just asked. I want to hear your answer again, make sure I'm clear." In the midst of another pause, Wallace's eyes rose again. "Why would this mother and daughter want to come after you? You believe this amounts to Sasha being embarrassed over the outcome of the other case?"

It was time. Wallace already knew something more—the man wouldn't keep pressing if he didn't. Maybe Sasha had indeed brought out something new, some kind of proof of their picnics? Let it come, he thought. It wanted out, the simple admission that, yes, he had taken a sixteen-year-old girl to Washington Park. While they hadn't had sex, yes, he had wanted her. He'd wanted her badly. But then in another flash, he pictured Anh, her face when he spewed the details. How she had finally doubled over crying.

"Like I said before, these people have many problems." He felt the muscles around his mouth relax some. "I do not know why they would come after me with such a charge. You have already said that they did not even call the police after I went over. You have expressed doubt about their versions of events, how their stories do not quite fit. I do think it was because Sasha was embarrassed about the outcome of the Wilson Green case, yes. She lost face."

He had spoken fast, letting impulse lift him. Like up at the cabin during Sammy's rant, it was as if a part of him long locked away had barged in, gun raised, and demanded control.

High on lying's buzz, he added, "Did anything else come up?" And immediately clasped his hands under the table.

Wallace studied his eyes. "Like?"

The question bounced in Hieu's mind; he tried to cover himself with a raised brow.

"I am just wondering if we have covered everything. Or are there other things we need to discuss?"

Another silence.

He held his face in the expectant pose. It would come out any second, the admission erupting from his core. When he shifted his weight he felt his undershirt wet against his lower back. The room seemed to vibrate, the edges of his field of vision jittering. The sergeant would pull it from him, a matter of moments.

But Wallace sat back. Rolled his pen between a thumb and index finger.

"I've laid out my concern about your visit to the Andersons, Mr. Nguyen." He set his pen onto the table. "But of course we need to bring up what Sasha reported about last summer. As you already know, she said that with the classroom allegations she was trying to get back at you for quote 'dumping' her after the two of you had engaged in sexual intercourse. She said you drove her up to Washington Park on two separate occasions. Please repeat your initial statement on that."

For the first time since the beginning of the interview, Hieu glanced at Blake Saylor, who remained focused upon the yellow pad before him. A heaviness spread over his chest, the same feeling as in Winchill's office with Falsworth and Bailey sitting on either side. The spirits had arrived. It was a matter of honor now. He must own up, somehow start fresh. He heard Minh's voice, the usual: *Family is everything.* And then there was only the weight on his chest. He made no effort to hide his daze.

"I am still … shocked about that."

"Shocked." Wallace's eyes didn't blink.

Minh's voice came again, and Hieu's breaths began to even out, the heaviness dissipating some. *Family is everything. Now go.*

"Like I told you before … I cannot believe she would go on the offensive like that." The sentence sounded warped to him. The still-odd shapes of English words.

"So to be absolutely clear, you're completely denying her claim?"

Hieu turned to Blake Saylor, who was now watching him with a slightly open mouth.

"Of course I am denying it. Like I said before, it is ridiculous." He looked directly into Wallace's eyes. "I have never taken a student anywhere in my car. She did not notify the police last summer, there was no medical examination, like you said. It is horrible to be accused of such a thing. A nightmare."

It was clear, when Wallace's posture relaxed and his frown faded, his face resuming its usual nonplused look, that the man was to-the-bone tired of the case, perhaps his job.

Hieu watched the sergeant jot something onto a page stapled to the inside front cover of a manila folder, stick the folder back into its green file, and shut off the recorder.

"That should be everything," Wallace said. "I'll be in touch if anything else comes up. But this really should be all."

A warm wave spreading over him, Hieu stood and numbly smoothed out the front of his sweater. Wallace and Blake Saylor exchanged what to him were a few jumbled words, and then Wallace got up and stretched a hand across the table.

"Mr. Nguyen, I'm sorry you had to go through this again." He picked up the file. "Just too many inconsistencies between their versions of events during your visit. You'd think this time the girl could get her story straight." Wallace opened the door and led the way down the hall out to the front counter.

Blake Saylor right behind him, Hieu carried himself as calmly as he could, saying hellos to some of the other officers he'd seen on earlier visits, and admitted to himself that he had expected, in the end, to tell what actually happened. But was it really all over? Wallace seemed almost too burnt-out to trust.

When he stepped out of the precinct, however, and smelled the moist spring air, he thought that, all things considered, he'd probably done the right thing. There had always been something empowering about leaning away from honesty when the situation demanded it.

———

At home the few weeks following the Brightwood trip, in the soft hours when everyone else had gone to bed, Hieu and Anh gradually began talking again, increasingly long sessions in the living room. He told her about what had happened beside the Salmon River, and then inside the cabin. Made himself share the impact of both experiences, how he had heard their daughter's voice so clearly over the rapids, how half an hour later Nate's uncle had almost drawn his longest-held secret completely out of him.

Then one night in late June, face in shadow, he haltingly asked his wife if he could sleep beside her. He wanted to fold up the cot, re-emerge into the life of the house. Her eyes locked onto the silk pillow in her lap, Anh hesitated nearly two minutes. She consented finally, though would end up refusing her husband's touch for another six and a half months.

The first two weeks after putting away the cot, Anh breathing quietly next to him, Hieu continued to replay the events of his life. He wanted to make sure he appreciated more. Noticed things. Though the world was no less confusing, something had changed. When he played with Dat and Le Phuong, or helped them with their schoolwork, he came to see how his attention was more focused. There was less distance now.

And with his mother, too, when she finally began speaking to him again toward the middle of summer, he sensed that they might be able to mend, given time and great patience, at least part of their relationship; they might even come to a kind of better understanding. Hoa was clearly in no mood for any more forays into anything that could distract the family from the sacred everyday things. There had been enough mistakes.

But as far as Vo was concerned, everyone—Le Phuong and Dat included—knew something needed to be done. At the first family meeting after Hieu came back upstairs, Hoa demanded that her grandson be home-schooled, an option Anh and Hieu found themselves seriously considering, especially in light of a recent shoplifting incident at the Multnomah Mall MusicWorld. It seemed that ever since the stairway episode, where he had kneed his father between the legs, Vo had seen fit to dive even further into his rebellion, getting suspended twice for fighting, flipping everyone around the house all the attitude he could. He refused to speak Vietnamese, even with Hoa (who demanded it, as always), ignored Anh's discipline, and distanced himself from both Le Phuong and Dat. With his psycho father in the basement, acting even weirder than usual, he naturally figured he could do nothing worse.

Hieu had long since recognized the path his eldest son was choosing, but the line between allowing your kid to expand his world and letting him fumble his future was so often indistinct. Though he'd always been confident that Vo would end up making the right decisions, it was clear now that a change needed to happen, the kid had even bigger issues than they'd believed. Anh had also filled him in about the growing number of phone calls from rude boys.

At the second family meeting during which Anh again took the lead in laying everything out for inspection, Hieu offering only the occasional back-up comment, Hoa grew especially agitated. Her grandson's aggressive disregard for tradition making her bottom jaw tremble, she refused to speak directly to the object of the meeting, preferring to use the third person.

"Thinks he knows everything," she said. "So proud of himself."

Anh, ever the mediator, kept trying to open Vo up.

"Can you tell us how you're feeling right now?"

"Bored."

"Don't you see we're trying to help?"

"Don't care." Vo slouched and looked off into the spaces between each person. Dat and Le Phuong remained quiet as usual.

It wasn't until the third meeting in as many nights that Hieu bent forward from his place at one end of the sofa, his wife's approach still not convincing him. He had surely earned back at least some of his right to take a stand.

"Again we've dropped everything to come together out of our concern for you only to watch you act like a punk," he said. "We're your family and we will not let you disregard us. We deserve respect."

"*You?*"

"Excuse me?" Hieu thought of how quickly he could fly from the sofa and snatch the boy by the front of the shirt. Something about Vo's eyes, however, made him sit still.

"Man, you go and freak out whenever you want, go around scaring everybody around here, and you expect me to *respect* you?" The question made Le Phuong and Dat look to the floor. Hoa squinted at Anh, then at Hieu. "You can go do whatever bad things you do, but I can't even hang with my friends? What's up with that? I'm almost seventeen!"

Hieu watched his son slump back. It would take longer than he had first thought. He shared a look with Anh, and right then, in a moment that made him shudder undetectably, he slipped into a belief: he would find some way to show Vo, no matter how long it took, what it meant to live in the greyness of being both Vietnamese and American. It would be his new mission. His immense challenge. Then he caught Le Phuong's and Dat's eyes and nodded as if to say, *Don't worry. Everything will be okay.*

When he turned next to his mother, she was looking straight at him with what he thought was the faintest hint of a smile. Clearly, it was his duty to be a better man.

Work

The third day into fall quarter, Nate acknowledged that he'd somehow managed to forget about the students with attention spans of caffeinated hummingbirds. The boggling myriad of ways in which kids try to needle. Still, overall, it felt right being back at Wilson Green.

Friday night of that first week, he opened a bottle of local beer, piled a few handfuls of potato chips into a cereal bowl, put on some John Coltrane, kicked back on the sofa and zoned out on the front room's various objects. When the chips were gone, he dug out his beat-up journal from a pile of books and teaching journals on the floor beside him and reread a few random entries. There was one from early July where he'd written of his conviction about returning to Wilson Green; he had just let Winchill know of his decision even though thoughts of Aaron Harrington continued to haunt. After three overnight trips to the coast during June alone, to Desiree's family's cabin down at Manzanita, he realized that he was beginning to tire of the time off, that when it came down to it he just plain missed the on-fire moments of giving himself over to what he considered something significant. Demented as it was.

He tilted back a few more swigs and found another summer entry that said it best:

—We need good work to keep a good rhythm.

Pleased with his observation, yet wary of diminishing it with what would probably turn into a typical rant if he picked up his pen and added to it, he set the journal aside and commenced an attack on the rest of his beer. At length, the jazz helping loosen him, he fell to thinking more about school: a scrawny freckle-faced sophomore with wolverine eyes named Jerry Vincent Jr. who had, the first day back, refused to open his binder and write a personal bio paragraph; the dour, stringy girl with black lipstick, one Jamie Tolman, he'd sent to Max Walker's office with a referral the third day for calling someone a "butt-ugly faggot," how when he told the girl to step into the hallway she shouted, "This ain't fair! You didn't hear what he called me! I'll get you fired for this!"

While the latter incident had peeved, his outward reaction still intrigued him. With the rest of his second period freshmen spooked to silence, he'd ambled to the front of the room, pulled out his wallet, leaned against his desk and removed the Mother Teresa card, then read the message aloud. When he finished, a Ritalin-filled boy in the front row asked, *"Mutha who?"* so he took a couple of minutes to explain how the industrious nun had kept on in the face of setbacks. It was the second time in a week he found himself consulting the card, the first being seven mornings earlier when he'd pulled into the parking lot on the first teacher planning day.

He'd fully expected the attack to begin replaying as soon as he saw the lot; when it did, he just sat in his idling truck and gazed out over the soccer field, sprinklers shooshing. And it was then that thoughts of Mary came: the scene of her standing with Dennis in front of the Sawatdee in her T-shirt and jeans, the story about Mother Teresa, the card and the embrace. The memory of that morning six months earlier having subdued the panic, he opened his truck door, breathed the sweet, watered-grass air, reached for his wallet and looked at the photograph of Mary and him, the one Dennis had taken the morning of the good-bye. The Mother Teresa card remained tucked in the plastic slot right across from it.

That first planning day, he had come upon Monty in the staff lounge; the burly albino dropped a gigantic box of construction paper he'd been carrying toward the supply room, jogged over, gave a grinning high-five and said, "Nate-o's in the house, watch out now!" Then in the hallway outside his classroom, he'd hugged Desiree and made plans to work with both her and Clyde Jackson on an outdoor education grant. He felt wanted. Welcome. It was worth the madness. Somehow.

For the most part, everyone on staff seemed upbeat. Ready to move forward from the previous year's trials. Winchill, however, was another matter. By the end of the second day back, the main vein of gossip concerned Chilly's sullen demeanor, the fifteen or so pounds he'd put on over the summer, and the flourishing garden of unclipped grey hairs sprouting from his nostrils. Perhaps the drama of Hieu's case had snuffed the last bit of fire in him, people said. Maybe something at home. The poor man had been so bombarded by behavior problems over the past decade, that had to be part of it. Apparently a raging mother had charged into the main office in early August and chewed him out at high volume for being racist because he refused to reinstate her son after a bowie-knife-brought-to-school incident two months before. Chilly had let the woman vent, asked if she wanted to step into his office to talk it over further, then stood patiently next to the head secretary's desk as the harpy called him a "fat-ass heartless mother-fucker" and stormed out.

But the situation with Winchill was ultimately just another in an on-going series of crises that would be faced with overall steadiness and a certain sleeves-rolled-up faith that, at least to Nate, made the place oddly irresistible. Life could be worked out. Grappled with. Despite all the narrow-minded state and district rhetoric about drastically upping standards and test scores regardless of family conditions, there was still room for some messiness at Wilson Green, for the real complexity of things. A person could struggle, fail, push onward. Even heal.

For him, the opportunity for some kind of healing had arrived, he wanted to believe, in the form of Obadell Hollis, a freshman who'd recently moved up from Orange County. The first day of school, first period, Obadell sauntered into the room just after the tardy bell with a black bandana on his head, oversize carpenter jeans sagging, plopped down in the middle of the back row and said, "You Mista Davis?" No binder or pencil with him, no loose sheets of notebook paper. When Nate didn't reply because he was talking with another student at the front of the room about locker assignments, Obadell repeated the question louder, adding "Yo!" at the beginning, and the buzzing class hushed.

Nate assured the student with whom he'd been speaking that everything would soon be all right concerning lockers, not to worry, then picked up his attendance sheet and began stepping up the center aisle.

"Yo?" he said.

"You Mista Davis?"

"See me outside a sec." He looked straight into the boy's eyes, battling memory. How things with Aaron Harrington had started off like this.

"Man, what I do?"

"Let's talk in the hall."

"Man." Obadell jerked up out of his seat and headed for the door, saying something under his breath that made a sleepy-faced girl in another back-row seat widen her eyes.

Nate told the kid he would be with him in a minute, returned to the front of the room to introduce himself and to give instructions on note-taking for the personal bio mini-lesson, and as he spoke, noticed a tinge in his scarred side, pain he hadn't felt for a few months. The hallway exchange nearly upon him might offer up a chance to alter his life story—an opportunity to turn a phantom back into a human being in need of attention, discipline, some forgiveness here and there. He wouldn't play the savior; there would be none of that. He'd only do his best to make the kid feel welcome. Safe. The boy might even, down the line a ways, come to trust him.

When he stepped into the hallway, he found Obadell sitting against a locker near the big pewter garbage can, head hung.

"So …" Nate knelt and waited for the kid to look up at him, but Obadell wouldn't make eye contact.

"Man, I didn't do nothin' in there. You crazy."

Nate set his attendance sheet and pen onto the floor.

"Let's start over," he said, feeling as though he was about to choke. He extended a hand. "I'm Mr. Davis."

Obadell shot a series of glances between the floor and Nate's fingers.

"Ain't you gonna send me to the office, get this done with?"

"I'm just introducing myself." Nate kept holding out his hand. "So, here's your choice. You shake and we go back in there and start the day right, or you take a time-out in the health teacher's room and write me a letter about what I should know about you, what life was like where you used to live. You choose."

The boy made a smacking sound and looked off down the empty hallway. "Man, I *hate* writing." He smacked again, then shook Nate's hand—a quick, soft grip.

Nate stood and opened the door.

"Good to meet you, Obadell. After you."

Obadell shook his head, walked back into the classroom.

The recollection of the brief conversation made him pick at the label of his empty bottle, the front room suddenly too quiet. He got up to start the Coltrane again, and then headed for the kitchen, where he prepared three tofu wieners on a slice of toast and another bowlful of chips. Popped another beer and returned to the sofa.

Something about the way John Coltrane had played the tenor sax—the searching, wailing sound—made him aware again of his own desire to find that rare balance between discipline and bold, freewheeling exploration. A controlled yet daring style. He seemed to look constantly for it in others. Strangely enough, it was Hieu of late who appeared to be modeling the elusive equilibrium, opening up some, letting his rarely seen looser side out more often. Of course the man already had the discipline part down pat, but there was a new lightness about him.

Two days earlier, Nate had stepped out into the hallway during his afternoon planning period and heard Hieu through the half-open door just across. Drawn again by the power of a natural, he'd gone over to one side of the doorway, only a few students in view. It was a lab on photosynthesis, note-taking time before an experiment. Hieu's voice sounded so crisp, animated, his speech pattern so different from when he was one-on-one. The man was *on,* making it clear exactly what he expected, going over the lab's time frame. Then the clatter of stools started up, kids jumping to it.

And the guy had actually been joking around with people at lunch and during meetings. At a staff briefing just the morning before, as Winchill was expounding upon the virtues of switching to a different bell schedule, Hieu had turned around to Clyde Jackson and said, "It is too early for a beer?" Monty, who'd been cleaning out one of the microwave ovens right behind Clyde, replied a little too loudly, "Not by my watch, bro," at which point Chilly stopped speaking and put his head down a moment.

Lately, too, it was a bit more comfortable one-on-one, Hieu acting less guarded during the post-racquetball talks, even before the beers arrived. Though there were definitely days when the lingering distance between them seemed to confirm that grown men were meant to go it all alone, upper lips stiff, Nate made a point of looking to his friend's best aspects; despite his concern over what had happened with Sasha Anderson, he tried to stay focused on the present, such as when Hieu often brought up Anh and Hoa and the kids. Hieu had even begun seeking advice on Vo, his biggest current concern, as the boy had been caught shoplifting again, a CD by some band called Poop. Vo had also gone missing in the night a couple of times the past few weeks. It wasn't just a matter of the kid going through a stage, Hieu worried; Vo's disillusionment had deepened since springtime and, of course, rival Asian gangs occasionally recruited in the neighborhood.

Still, for the most part, there seemed to be an air of genuine gratitude about Hieu—a quality Nate hated to admit he felt slightly jealous of. Whenever the man spoke of family life, Nate never failed to note his own loneliness, how he would most likely return from the North Side Racquet Club to his empty apartment, make a quick dinner for one, turn on the TV to hear other human voices. But there was more that fueled the envy, namely Lang's decision to stick with Tran Vu. To say nothing of how things had turned out with Sammy.

After three phone calls and another earnest letter sent to *Hello Portland!* magazine, he had finally met Lang again for a drink one wet mid-May evening. They'd sat at a window table, reflected traffic lights on the pavement outside, and he hadn't wasted much time making his case once more. But while she'd been polite, intent, and had even (he thought) thrown some sexy glances his way during the spiel, she ended up crisply reiterating her needs. Her decision about Tran Vu. Nate only gazed at his fork, the shadow of a ceiling fan swishing over the silver.

On some blurry, distant, sickeningly noble level, he believed that maybe it was for the best, such a bold decision had probably been good for her. Empowering and all. But he remained depressed most of the summer nevertheless, the trips to Manzanita arranged mostly for brooding. When he said good-bye to her in front of the restaurant that rainy May night, he'd wanted to give in to the connection he still sensed; Lang was undeniably more attractive now. But her eyes revealed no doubt. Again he'd wanted her to see his changes, that he could be solid in a relationship, and yet it also struck him how much he hated feeling like he'd checked his virility in the damn coat room.

On the walk to his truck, his key poking between two of his fisted fingers, he'd succumbed to a vision of the Sawatdee Guesthouse, the thin-walled room with Mary sitting before him, and the timing of it made him stop for a few beats and look off at nothing in particular. Just the lights on the grey street.

Incredible how many things, over a lifetime, a person could let slip away.

In his front room, the Coltrane still playing, he picked up his journal again after fetching one more beer. Slow footsteps above paced back and forth, the sound accentuating the Friday-night lonesomeness. The worn journal open on his lap, pen in hand, he closed his eyes to locate a beginning image or phrase that might capture the longing that the music brought on, and after a time settled on this:

—When Mom handed me the letter, I knew he'd gone.

Voices

In the cabin at the start of winter break, alone, just before dawn, Nate pulled on some clothes, then ran the tap and took a swig of frigid water. He looked over at the carving, which was still atop the toaster where Sammy had left it, with the strip of masking tape across the bottom that said *For Nate.* Then he sat down at the table in the quiet and once again opened the letter that his mother had given him last spring, the letter he kept tucked in the back of his journal.

March 13, '97

Dear Nate,

There's nothing too profound that I can say about why I'm leaving, but let me try to explain. First off, it upsets me, too. Why is it that some of us belong in a no-man's land? My theory is this: I wouldn't be any good to anyone if I tried to settle down. I really wouldn't. I'd do something dumb and fuck things up even more, I have a feeling. Your mom seems to understand this, but I don't expect you to.

It was a supernatural force that reunited us, Nate. So GREAT to see you again. My old buddy. I've thought about you so much over the years. I always hoped you were living a strong life and that you'd grown up better able than me to handle things. After seeing you again, I think you're more than strong enough.

I don't have much else to say except that you need to find some like-minded people you can love, if you haven't already. It's the only thing that has ever really kept me from killing myself (but it's also what has kept me scared of being in one place too long). Fucked up indeed, my friend, but it's who I've turned out to be.

I love you and miss you, and I'm doing the best thing for

everybody. Don't search for me any more. I'll only keep leaving.
My destiny I guess. You, too, need only be true to yours.

Onward,

Sam

Nate sat for several silent minutes in the cabin's low light.

In a letter to Mary two months ago, he had tried to explain how, at first, he didn't know what to feel about Sammy, but then the strange, fluid mix of anger and pity was the emotion that stepped forward.

Where did the guy go? What better place?

He wrote also about what had happened with Hieu in Brightwood, and about Lang's decision, and then his own decision to return to Wilson Green. He told her how he remembered the times at the Sawatdee, all those talks they'd had. Told her how much he missed her. How often he thought of her. And though he hadn't heard back—didn't even know if she received the letter—it had felt good to cast a line anyway. Though they hadn't corresponded much, it helped to know that she was out there in the world of billions of people, one of the few who knew his story, who believed in who he was and who he wanted to become. As he believed in her.

On the way to the trailhead, he stuffed his hands in his front pockets. A quick trip up the hill to check the view one more time, then a coffee and toasted bagel before heading back to town for some last-minute holiday shopping. He picked up the pace, trying to loosen the ankle, and the clinging sleepiness began to fall away. Fog hung in the Douglas firs and the hemlocks, the shorter cedars standing out against the grey, and only a few lights were on in the other cabins, smoke slithering up into the trees from just one chimney. Soon, all he could hear were his own footsteps and breathing. It was the quiet, he thought, that made the air feel colder than it probably was.

At the trailhead, he stopped for a moment. Already nine months since the climb with Hieu on the day that had shaken them both so hard. As he started up the incline, scenes of that morning flickered: Hieu walking alone, weaving through the stumps back to the trail; Sammy dumping the worm pails; Hieu beside the river looking so spent, almost humbled; the near-wordless drive back to town. His ankle beginning to hurt, as it did from time to time, especially in the mornings, he hiked faster, pressing through the pain. He needed to get to the clearcut. See the sky. The only desire that now filled him was to break past the mind, quit the slideshow. Sweat soon coated his chest and drops fell from the tip of his nose.

At the halfway point, he bent over, panting; the ankle was almost numb, the pain wearing itself out. He realized, also, that he was standing just beneath a cloud, the trees thirty feet ahead cut off by a slow-meta-morphosing mist. The urge to shout suddenly struck, but he held back, instead stepping forward again. As hard as he tried to concentrate on his breathing, images still came: holding the old photo of Sammy giving the horseback ride, then a random shot of Aaron Harrington exploding out the classroom door, referral in hand. Nate sensed something in front of him; he raised his head and stopped once more. The cloud was growing thicker, the trail only a few feet away completely shrouded.

Aaron's exit still hanging in his mind, he focused on the obscure line where trail met cloud. Sweat streaming off his face, down his neck, he leaned into the hill and listened. Behind him, he thought he heard birds, maybe gray jays—a few low *chucks,* then stillness again. The smell of de-caying wood and the forest loam came on a light breeze. Such a climb so soon after sleep made his senses dance, yet the memory of Aaron lingered.

Removed from school, only a day into winter break, it struck him how he'd been able to go back to Wilson Green in late August with a certain confidence. *We move on,* he recalled thinking. But now, pressing into the trail, he could taste the old dread. Teacher caught out in the open. Sitting duck. Referrals, parent phone calls, suspensions, revenge. It was moments like these, ambushed, that he'd felt like running, always.

He looked back down the trail, then up again into the cloud. Another gust blew across the hill and cooled his face.

Make a move.

Breaths shooting out, eyes flitting.

Get warm, go back to the city, leave this shit behind.

Then another voice within himself when he gaped back into the grey:

Hey, don't stop.

"Hey," he said as if someone was right next to him. The word sounded frail in the cloud.

It was Sammy who'd always said to relax whenever they'd set out into the woods. They were Sammy's words. So often he'd been spooked by the forest and his uncle was always gentle about it, yet still urged him on.

He could see only a few feet in any direction now, the cloud creeping further down the slope. There were no more words, no sounds other than his breaths and the occasional rush of wind.

And then, like a ghost had slipped from the mist, Aaron's voice. *Fuck you, Davis.*

Nate stepped into the hill. White shoes bouncing into the darkness of the soccer field, Clyde coming out the staff lounge door after another long day.

From familiar dead limbs and rocks, he knew he was near the summit. He moved slower, trying not to trip, and eventually found himself talking.

"I'm yours, man ..."

The slope began to curve out and soon came the line in the mist where trees stopped and stumps began. Dark clumps everywhere. Amused by the imaginary conversation, he kept at it, watching his steps in the frozen ruts.

"Do what you need to do, bud. We're both scared as hell, but go ahead and see it another way."

He climbed up onto a low, wide fir stump and tried to make out forms in the grey. The cloud snaked through his legs, the cut-off tree beneath nearly invisible.

As fast as the old scenes had fallen on him, he now sensed a calm. The fear of being alone on the mountain faded, the bizarre words for Aaron Harrington hushed. The cloud hovered all around him, his breathing and the wind again the only sounds, and now there came only one voice.

Like the tree that had once grown from the deep-down roots below, his arms spread a bit, like limbs, he stood and listened. It was Sammy, carrying him on his shoulders through the wilderness, saying with such certainty, *It'll be all right, Nate. It'll be all right.*

The Grey, Green World

In the middle of the neighborhood streets on a cold, wet Sunday morning at the end of winter break, Hieu jogged in his dark sweatpants and hoodie, though he kept the hood down, letting the rain soak his hair and face, fine droplets on his eyebrows. This was the new weekend morning routine. This was the need. Late morning, alone, in the streets on the asphalt, never the sidewalks.

As usual whenever he ran, his pace neither fast nor slow, he took in the sights, smells, and sounds, flecks of memory sometimes alighting on him. A few weeks earlier, a large pack of cyclists had put him in mind of a Saigon intersection. Once in the fall, a recycling truck had dumped its load of glass into another compartment as he was passing by, and the sound made him flinch hard, as he had over loud sounds since he was a child.

Today, the grey light and the rain reminded him of the coast down at Twin Rocks. There were days in Portland where he swore he detected a hint of sea air.

He ran long, as always. After a few miles, it was normally easier to let go of the mind some, just notice his surroundings, like now. Slow church bells, a few blocks away, that sound that for some reason never failed to make him feel calmer. The old houses. Old trees. And as he jogged down the middle of Cleveland Avenue this morning, here were two women in what looked to be their mid-twenties, running together toward him, and when they went by, one of them gave a smile and a quick wave. He held up a hand and tried not to turn his head, but several paces onward he did look, briefly. They were pretty, both of them, and fit. Strong and alive.

He ran slightly longer today, up and down the neighborhood streets, breathing the wet air, and eventually tired himself out. That sweet soreness in the legs. Face flushed. He stood in front of his house beneath the monkey tree, and after stretching his hamstrings, paused there for a few moments, glancing around. The house. The minivan. Anh's car gone. The street was quiet apart from the rain patter and the distant traffic. He took some deep breaths, his heartbeat slowing.

Inside, the lingering smell of *pho* mixed with Hoa's steaming mug of jasmine tea. She was sitting in front of the TV by herself, her mug cupped in her hands, one of the blankets up over her legs. She was watching a nature program that appeared to involve deep-sea fishing, and she didn't look away from it when he passed through the room. From upstairs, the sound of Le Phuong's cello.

In the kitchen he found Dat at the pine table writing a story for school tomorrow, the boy all set up with his paper and pencil, his crayons. Hieu tore off some paper towels and wiped his face and neck, took off his hoodie and sat down next to his son.

"How is it coming?" he said.

"How do you spell cheetah?"

Hieu spelled the word and watched Dat write it. The kitchen was still, backed by the cello and TV sounds. Dat's scratchings. Sweaty-faced again, Hieu remained seated, his body tingling, and glanced to the wall at Le Phuong's finger-painting of the monkey bridge over a river in Vietnam. At the photo of the teenage girl leaning against a bicycle in front of a jam-packed Saigon food stall. Then he caught their reflection, his and Dat's, in the window to his left. This aging man, at a pinewood table with a young boy, the boy's mouth forming English words. Dat reached for the cashews on the dish at the middle of the table and took one; he kept it in his mouth without chewing as he went on writing slowly.

"How do you spell savannah?"

"Hmm." Hieu did his best with the word, and when he was done, Vo walked into the kitchen and opened the fridge.

In his white socks and black jeans and sweatshirt, his hair gelled back, Vo stood there and stared for a good minute, holding the door open, tapping it with two fingers. Hieu stole glances at him; it seemed that the boy was aware of them over in the nook, that he was daring his father to say something about holding the fridge door open. Finally, Vo took out the jug of OJ and poured himself a glass, and without looking over at them, padded back out of the kitchen.

Hieu heard the front door. Anh's keys clinked into the ceramic bowl on the table at the bottom of the stairs, and then she stepped into the kitchen with two paper grocery bags. Hieu rose from the table.

"More in the car?" he said in Vietnamese.

"This is all," she said in English.

Before leaving the table, he looked down at Dat's work and placed a hand on the boy's upper back. Dat went on writing, still sucking on the cashew.

To the sounds of cello and a fishing program, without speaking more words, Hieu went over and began helping his wife put away the groceries. Rice, penne, cilantro, red peppers. At one point, they came together at the sink—Anh washing an apple, Hieu drinking a glass of water—and their shoulders touched, briefly. They paused and stood there side by side at the sink, and for a few beats they gazed out the window that overlooked the backyard shrubs and lawn, at the grey, green world outside.

At the reflection of them together, here in this house, after everything.

His Own Eyes

Rain hadn't completely stopped for three days. There were lulls, spells during which a near-freezing mist fell from a slightly lighter sky, but wave after wave of stormclouds still charged in from the west. The soccer field was a series of muddy ponds, the widest of them at the goalmouths, the commons asphalt usually peppered with expanding rings.

Nate sat at his desk in the quiet of after school, a three-inch stack of short stories and his planning book in front of him, and looked toward the grey light at the streaming windows, the blur of the world. The sound of the wind and rain against the panes made his shoulder muscles loosen. The room was still too hot, Monty having somehow broken a control mechanism down in the boiler room just before classes had resumed three days ago; Nate still didn't understand why the school was baking, nor did any of the other teachers he had talked to. But most of the kids didn't seem to mind, a number of them saying it was better than being cold.

A few minutes earlier, he had turned off all but one classroom light, left the door wide open, unbuttoned his denim shirt and untucked his Glacier National Park tee, and stood a moment by his desk surveying the poster of Mia Hamm chasing down a soccer ball: the concentration on her glistening face, the lines of muscle in her legs. Looking up at her seemed to make him sweatier, though, so he'd gone over and opened a window. But then the wind kept blowing rain against the building, his pant legs and the floor around him soon dotted wet. He'd turned away to tackle the next day's plans and the stack of stories.

From a bottom drawer of his desk, he pulled out his new *Fresh Ideas* notebook, a blue binder packed with teaching suggestions he'd received at a downtown Hilton winter break workshop entitled "Keeping the Fire Alive," part of a National Humanities Council conference.

While he didn't intend to throw out his most successful units, he'd come to decide that he needed to challenge himself; though he had lessons for every day of a typical school year already written out, he needed some new ones. With all of the soul-draining pressure to boost test scores, he wanted to make sure he didn't lose his desire, a funkier style, the ability to connect with TV- and computer-stoned kids by orchestrating lively, relevant activities. He'd never cared much for conferences, but the workshop title and the drawing of bright orange flames on the brochure cover caught him.

When he began to leaf through the notebook, however, he stopped and looked to the windows again. Thoughts still darting from the day. He shut his eyes and pictured the parking lot and soccer field, then focused upon his new technique for getting perspective, a suggestion of Desiree's. His breathing slow and easy after a minute or so, he lifted himself away, up over Wilson Green, saw a few Frisbees on the roof and began soaring out over the neighborhood: the North Side Racquet Club up on Fowler Avenue, then Hieu's house, Bing's crown listing. He turned south and came upon the downtown skyline, the tops of the bank towers lost in clouds, flew up through the storm and into the cold blue, the summit of Mount Rainier to the north sticking out above the grey. And then higher still until the clouds broke in the distance and the land spread out in a slow arc. Up into blackness, storm systems swirling the planet, the moon catching light from the closest star ...

Nate opened his eyes onto the grey blur. Reached down and pulled open the top right drawer and lifted out the masking taped wad of toilet paper he'd tucked at the back. He cleared the pile of stories and the *Fresh Ideas* notebook from the area right in front of him, then began to unwrap the mummified wooden figurine that Sammy had left on top of the cabin's toaster. It was the little man on his knees, hands raised to the sky, head cocked back, mouth wide open. Nate set it on his desk. There had been no note, just the carving atop the toaster, in between the slots, facing the door. He'd spotted it when he walked in, set his bag onto the spotless table and lowered himself to the love seat. Stared at the kneeling man nearly ten minutes before examining it up close, the intricacies impressive: tiny slits at the corners of the eyes, the teeth, the muscle-streaked forearms reaching up from rolled sleeves. Waves in the shoulder-length hair.

He studied the figurine again, now framed by the paper stacks spread over his desk of ten and a half years, and fell to thinking about how Sammy, too, seemed afraid of happiness. How could such an absurd fear overtake a person anyway? What pain could be avoided by learning to see the world through your own eyes? He brooded on the latter question, still fixed in his belief that he would need to live with it awhile more.

Then Hieu appeared in the doorway.

"Come on in," Nate said, rewrapping the carving. "Just sitting here drooling a minute."

Hieu stepped into the room a few feet.

"Actually, I am leaving to go pick up Vo. Taking him over to the club for his first game of racquetball. He will crush me probably."

Nate finished replacing the masking tape around the tissue and set the bundle back into the drawer.

"We still on for Thursday?"

"Of course," Hieu said. He feigned a wipe at his forehead. "Your room is a lot hotter than mine, you know."

"That right? The rest of you scrubs paying Monty off? Some little racket I don't know about?"

Hieu bounced his eyebrows twice, raised a hand and walked out. In the hallway, Desiree was passing by; there was laughter, an exchange Nate couldn't catch. Then she leaned her head in, multicolored bead necklace and dream-catcher earrings dangling.

"My goodness, it *is* roasting in here. Too bad you're not in on the action, sweetie."

She laughed again and ducked back into the hallway.

Nate's smile lingered as he pulled the *Fresh Ideas* notebook toward him. He flipped to the middle, to a lesson on ancient Mesopotamia that involved dividing the class into Sumerian, Babylonian, Akkadian, Phoenician, and Hebrew families and videotaping skits about daily life. Only a paragraph into it, though, he glanced up at the windows yet again, concentration shot.

He scanned the classroom: the vacant chairs, the cobweb-streaked intercom screen above the doorway, the computer station next to his desk. He turned to take in the wall behind him and instantly his eyes settled on one of Michelangelo's *Unfinished Prisoners,* a print he'd bought at the

Galleria dell' Accademia on his first big journey. He stood and closed the notebook without marking his place and sat up on his desk, feet propped on his chair. It was a side view of a block of Michelangelo's beloved Carrara marble: an ox-strong man battling to break free, his left arm pushing against the weight above, left shoulder and both legs flexed, rough-chiseled eyes hinting at the knowledge of his predicament. Against the black backdrop, with lighting that accentuated the contours, the man seemed almost ready to emerge, on the verge of cracking through with a strong-beating heart.

Eyes closed again, the image of the prisoner gradually fading, Nate listened out as far as he could hear and after awhile drifted to floating from himself, this time up and away toward Brightwood. Over the town of Sandy and the highway's bend at Shorty's Corner, the nurseries and berry farms, the pitch of Cherryville Hill and the shadow of Alder Creek to the stump-strewn clearing on Wildcat Mountain. Past the confluence of the Salmon River and Boulder Creek, then around to the cabin, rain cascading down the mossy roof onto soaked ground. He held to the picture and remembered Hieu saying something once about how spirits stay with the ancestral land. Maybe his own spirit would one day find its way to Brightwood and Sammy would be waiting along with Grandpa, Grandma, and Acacia. Harrison and Aida Webster and mysterious others might be there, too.

Behind him, he heard keys jingling, footsteps getting faster and louder, and then Monty charged into the room.

"Nate-o."

By the time he got down and stood beside his chair, Monty was already upon him, looming over the other side of the desk.

"Listen, bro. Had to let you know there's a fine-ass lookin' woman coming your way. She was in the office asking for your room, says you're old friends. Just wanted to tell you in case you looked like shit, which you do."

Nate frowned up at him.

"What did she look—"

He saw her come through the doorway, to the right of Monty's shoulder, green umbrella in one hand.

Mary stopped and gave Monty a squinting smile as he race-walked past her, the *Visit Reno* key chain clattering. When Nate remained speechless, she stepped toward him down the center aisle, lowered her eyes briefly, then came around the desk.

"I got your letter finally … Bangkok, Yreka, San Francisco …" She set her umbrella onto the chair. "I miss you, too."

Nate, heart in throat, had already offered up a silent prayer of sorts. It had just come. *Thank you.* Mary's eyes telling everything he needed to know at the moment, he uttered the only other word that came clear.

"Welcome."

And in the silence that followed, something happened almost effortlessly, as if to prove that living with uncertainty did have a greatest secret. Without any other voice in his head to sway him from what he wanted of the world, without a voice to make everything seem unsafe, Nate opened his arms and leapt.

Acknowledgments

For their generous support and encouragement over the years, I would like to thank Helen VanBelle, Joan Saalfeld, Betty Barker, John and Denise Tuggle, Frances Davis, Andrew Pham, John Morrison, Ron and Cindi Pomeroy, Larry Colton, Peter Sears, David Kelly, Lien Nguyen, Bob Ogle, Heather Mingst, Chris Roberts, Brad Robertson, Literary Arts, and especially my wife Brooke Tuggle, whose belief never wavered.

Many thanks to Amelia Atlas, and also to my editors at Oregon State University Press, Tom Booth and Micki Reaman.

Of the books, articles, and documentaries on Vietnam that I consulted, I'm particularly indebted to the following: *Remembering Heaven's Face* by John Balaban, *A Vietcong Memoir* by Truong Nhu Tang, *Everything We Had* by Al Santoli, *Vietnam: Why We Fought* by Dorothy and Thomas Hoobler, *The Land I Lost* by Huynh Quang Nhuong, *Goodbye, Vietnam* by Gloria Whelan, and "Vietnam: A Televison History, America Takes Charge 1965-1967" on *American Experience* (PBS).

The opening epigraph from Pablo Neruda is a canto from his poem *Aún,* which appears in William O'Daly's translation as *Still Another Day* from Copper Canyon Press.